Spirit
of
the Rebellion

by

Debbie Peterson

Spirit of the Rebellion

Cover Art by *Tamra Westberry*

The Wild Rose Press
PO Box 708
Adams Basin, NY 14410-0708
Visit us at www.thewildrosepress.com

Publishing History
First Faery Rose Edition, 2012
Print ISBN 978-1-61217-024-4

Published in the United States of America

**He approached her with caution,
as if not wanting to frighten her further.**

Then, in a gentle but quiet voice said, "Shaelynn, are you all right? Did he hurt you?"

The questions filled her mind with all the horror of Perry's attack. Once again, she could feel his vile hands on her body. The mere image of that man's face, his breath, his intentions, sickened her. If not for Tristan, he would surely have—

The thought evaporated as the captain fused his gaze to hers. He winced visibly and stiffened. The moment Tristan believed his presence produced her outward show of loathing, he disappeared.

"No! Tristan, please, wait!" she called in a futile attempt to prevent his departure. Turning quickly toward the door, she grasped the handle. The knob did not budge. She frantically yanked the keys out of her pocket and searched for the one that would unlock the door. Her wet hands shook with the effort, and it took forever to find the right key. When at last she found it, she thrust it into the lock and turned the handle. The door swung open, and she slammed it behind her as she bounded up the stairs.

"Tristan," she panted, as she reached the top floor. "Please, you misunderstood!"

She fell against his door in her hurried attempt to reach it. Then, after grasping the knob, she turned it, knowing it wouldn't open, even before she made the attempt.

"You've got to let me in, you have to let me explain, please," she begged through the barrier that separated them. "I swear on everything dear to me, I'm not moving from this spot until you do. Do you hear me? I'm not leaving!"

Dedication

David, my love, this one is for you.
Thank you so much for all of your encouragement,
support, and assistance throughout the many hours
I spent laboring over my keyboard.
No wonder that all of my heroes
come from a little bit of you.

Chapter 1

In an instant of time, all sound suddenly ceased. The hooting of owls, the chirp of crickets, and croaking of frogs, all disappeared into otherworldly nothingness. Even the sound of the wind vanished despite the tumultuous swaying of the trees. An eerie silence accompanied Shae as each hesitant step moved her closer to the old abandoned church in the distance. The full harvest moon, veiled by wispy gray clouds, served as the only light to guide her path. A menacing mist gathered and swirled all around her, coming not from above, but from the ground below her feet.

A long cloak the color of dying embers hid her face in shadows. Yet, the need to disappear altogether overtook all sense of logic. She grasped the generous folds of cloth and enveloped herself deeper within them. The garment offered her a semblance of shelter and protection. But protection from what, she couldn't say. The beating of her heart accelerated as she advanced up the broken steps and faced the weather-beaten door covered with gaping cracks and jagged splinters. She could hear ominous voices, deep and guttural, coming from the other side. Terror over the very prospect of entering the structure alone consumed her. Yet, she could not escape what lay beyond the entrance. She *had* to go in.

Fear such as she never experienced before held her bound. Her hands trembled as they pressed against the door and inched it slightly ajar. The wooden portal creaked and groaned underneath the

1

pressure of her fingertips. From the small opening, she could see a rustic fireplace, charred by decades of smoke, at the back of the chapel. Inside the stone firebox, flames roared and belched in agitated fury as if the thing had a life of its own. Despite her reluctance, she squeezed through the doorway and into the room. She held her breath and crept forward. In an effort to conceal herself, she kept her back against the wall. Her eyes glued themselves to the ground as she stepped through the accumulation of dust and debris on the floor. All the while, she remained in the darkest possible corners.

A sudden ear-splitting shriek drew her gaze upward. Her eyes widened as she clamped her hands over her mouth, smothering the scream that demanded release. She wanted to look away, but a mysterious force compelled her to watch as the scene unfolded before her.

Near the podium stood Fenrir, the wolf son of Loki, more terrible, large, and vicious than what she ever imagined. Evil emanated from his very being. Fire spewed forth from his eyes and nostrils. Somehow, he escaped the tethers of the slim magic chain that held him bound throughout all the ages of this earth, and with a thirst for vengeance, he set his eyes on Odin.

The two Norse gods engaged in a fearsome, brutal battle, neither of them giving any quarter. They seemed evenly matched in strength and stamina as they tore at each other with relentless fury. The room thundered and quaked with their wrath while they fought. Shattered pieces of the pulpit and pews flew in all directions at once. Neither of them noticed the mounting destruction.

In rising ferocity, Odin took hold of the wolf and slammed him onto the floor. Fenrir groaned and writhed in agony. Then, seizing upon his only recourse, the wolf opened his mighty jaws, and using the remainder of his strength, lunged toward his opponent. With one vicious snap, he swallowed Odin whole.

Shae's eyes darted around the confines of the room. Vidar should burst into the room any moment now. The mighty warrior would come in and avenge Odin. He would stride forward and step on the wolf's bottom jaw. Then with his bare hands, he would seize his upper jaw, and tear the beast asunder. She waited, hidden in the shadows as Fenrir threw back his head and laughed wickedly over his triumph. The wolf stumbled to his feet. Vidar still did not come.

Only then did she notice the woman standing on the opposite side of the room. The hem of her blue silk dress swept against the floor, hiding all but the toes of her small black boots. She wore a silver necklace on which hung a small, intricate replica of Thor's hammer. The piece interrupted the flow of tiny white buttons and lace lining her bodice. Her pale blonde hair, pulled back in a tidy bun at the nape of her neck, starkly contrasted her deep blue eyes. Those eyes now claimed Shae's attention. They begged her to step forward and help. The woman deeply loved Odin and could not bear to see all the goodness in him devoured by this evil, which still lived.

Her sorrow compelled Shae to do something. Shae took a deep breath. As she stepped forward in Vidar's place, Fenrir caught sight of her. His fiery eyes became angry slits as he lumbered across the room. With each step he took, she could feel the floorboards shake beneath his feet. All the while, the wolf growled and hissed his hatred and contempt. She should take hold of his jaws and rip him open. By so doing, she could right the wrong and bring a measure of justice back to the world. But she didn't know if she possessed the courage or the strength to

3

battle the wolf. With no more than four feet between them, Fenrir crouched down and then in one fluid motion, he lunged toward her. His jaws opened wide as if to consume her in the inferno raging deep inside him. She screamed in utter horror as she braced for his attack.

With a start, Shae sat upright in bed gasping for breath. The awful image of the wolf remained vivid in her mind. She took a deep, ragged breath and held it. After several seconds, she slowly released it in an effort to banish the terrifying vision and still the rapid beating of her heart.

Her eyelids fluttered open. In a moment of confusion, she looked about the unfamiliar room with its nondescript furnishings and blend of drab colors. Oh yes, that was right; she remembered now. Her cozy little flat in Norway now belonged to her recent past. This overnight stay in a Tennessee hotel room began a fresh chapter in her life. One she desperately needed right now. Why then, did it have to begin with her recurring nightmare?

Twice before in less than two weeks time she endured this same dream, and the tale just didn't make any sense. In the first place, in the mythological story, Fenrir and Odin would fight the battle of Ragnarok inside the realms of Valhalla, not in a small country church. An unknown woman from the middle of the nineteenth century wouldn't be there to witness the event, nor would she implore Shae's aid in dispatching Fenrir of all the impossible things.

She leaned back against the pillows, and rested her arm against her forehead as she considered the meaning of the horrific dream. Surely, the nightmare must stem from her inner turmoil. Working on her doctorate degree in Ancient History, with its emphasis on the Norse cultural and mythology consumed a great deal of her time. The museum in Oslo demanded a large portion of her time and energy as well.

Certainly, not least of all, the inexcusable way Simon Hollander ended their engagement continued to wreak havoc on her soul. With all the commotion going on in her life, why wouldn't her subconscious mind conjure terrifying things while she slept?

She glanced at the clock on the nightstand. The alarm would sound off in about twenty minutes. Definitely not enough time to fall into restful sleep, though. So she turned off the buzzer, slid out of bed, and made her way toward the shower. Just before she stepped all the way inside, her cell phone rang. She sighed. For a moment, she debated on whether or not to answer. Then deciding it might be important, she slipped into her robe and hurried toward the nightstand. Of course, she arrived too late. Nonetheless, she picked up the phone from the table to identify the caller.

The missed call came from Norman Lamont, the representative of the Tennessee National Trust. The man assigned to "take very good care of her" while she carried out this new work assignment here in the States. A smile touched her lips as she thumbed the redial key and waited for him to answer.

"Good morning, Miss Montgomery," he sang into the phone.

"Good morning, Mr. Lamont, and please, just call me Shae," she said. "Are we still on for this morning?"

"That we are," he replied. "I am just calling to say that you will have no need to call a taxi. By now there is an older model jeep parked just outside your hotel room. The old Wrangler is black in color, and you will find the keys underneath the passenger floor mat. The vehicle doesn't look like much, but I assure you it runs quite well. Please feel free to use it during your stay."

"Well, thank you, that's very kind of you."

She heard him chuckle. "Balderdash! I'm just doing what they pay me to do. Now then, let me give you directions to my office. Don't worry, you won't get lost. I'm not that hard to find."

One hour later, she parked in front of the red brick building he described. She took hold of her bag and exited the jeep. Just as she approached the entrance, an older gentleman with white curly hair and mischievous blue eyes, opened the office door. He wore an immaculate blue suit and a friendly smile. She did not feel the least bit surprised when he introduced himself as Norman Lamont.

"I'm pleased to finally meet you in person." He took her hand in both of his, gave it a gentle squeeze and a pat for good measure. "I've heard so many things about you. All of them good, I might add."

Shae returned his smile, and as he escorted her into his office she said, "Thank you. You're very sweet. Everyone has been so kind and it has really made this transition much easier than I expected."

"Oh, it's our pleasure, believe me. We are all so very grateful you consented to leave your work in Norway for a time and help us out. Now then, we have just a few things to discuss before we leave." He waved a hand toward the chair across from his desk. "Please sit down, and make yourself comfortable. Would you like some kind of refreshment before we begin?"

"No thank you," she said. "I've just had breakfast, so I'm fine."

Once they both sat down he picked up the file atop his otherwise uncluttered desk. "This file is for you," he said. "The folder contains all of the phone numbers and addresses you might need during your stay. Feel free to call on any one of us, any time you feel the need. I have also prepared a number of maps that will assist you in getting around the area. These maps also include historic structures you might want to visit during your stay. Once you get into the file, you'll find I've included brief histories regarding the same. Todd Andersen tells me you enjoy that sort of thing?"

"Yes, I do!" Excitement coursed through her. "Historic places, buildings, and old ruins are a passion of mine."

"Then I'm sure you'll enjoy what our area has to offer. I hope I didn't leave anything out. If I did, just give me a call," he said.

"Thank you very much," she found herself saying yet again.

He slid the file toward her. "We've arranged for you to reside and work at Starling Plantation. This beautiful old mansion is in a rural community not far from here, and we feel it will serve your needs very well. At least, we're hoping you won't have any trouble during your stay."

"Why do you say that?" She raised a brow, leaned toward him, and gave him an impish smile. "Does the plumbing leak?"

"No, not at all. It's just that—" He peeked over his glasses and let out a sigh as if resigned to his distasteful task. "Do you believe in ghosts, Miss Montgomery?"

The unexpected question took her by surprise, though she tried not to show it. "Please, just call me Shae. Miss Montgomery makes me feel as ancient as the ruins I explore. To answer your question, yes, I do believe in ghosts. But not until I experienced meeting one myself. Does that surprise you?"

Norman merely shook his head and cleared his throat. He looked hesitant and unsure of how to phrase his next comment.

"You can go ahead and say it. I promise I won't run out the door."

"All right then, here comes the hard part." He

shrugged his shoulders as he clasped his hands in front of him. "I'm afraid we must express our sincerest regret in advance for your lodgings. However, there simply isn't any other place for you to go on our meager budget. Starling is far from empty, Shae. By all accounts, there are several spirits residing there. A known fact among the local residents is that the entities will not endure the presence of the living. Many people have made every effort to coexist with them over the decades, but none of them managed to stay very long. Finally, the last owner of the property deeded the entire estate to the National Trust back in the year 1979, and we have looked after it ever since."

She mulled his comments over for a handful of moments, and said, "I see."

"I want you to know that shortly after you agreed to come, I went out there during the renovations of the house and grounds. I informed our otherworldly occupants as to your impending arrival, or at least I made the attempt. We are hoping, since I told them you are not staying indefinitely, they will leave you in peace while you do your work. If not, perhaps another solution will present itself."

She gave him a reassuring nod. "Please don't give it another thought. I'm sure with a bit of time and patience we can get along."

Shae had no doubt she could get along with the spirits of Starling Plantation. After all, with a bit of perseverance, she and the spirit of her fierce Viking chieftain finally came to terms. After her tumultuous beginning with him, the ghosts of Starling should be a piece of cake.

Norman let out a sigh of relief and stood to his feet. "If you are ready, I'll escort you to Starling and give you the grand tour of the property. The others are going to meet up with us out there sometime this morning and bring the rest of your supplies."

During the drive to Starling Plantation, Shae reflected upon her unexpected move back to the States. Her mentor, Professor Todd Andersen, remained unaware of the underlying reason she finally accepted his offer. Not that this new assignment wouldn't be interesting as well as rewarding. He just didn't need to know how badly she needed to escape her current surroundings. No one needed to know. Her reasons shouldn't matter to him anyway, and the decision thrilled him no end.

Once she said yes, he magically produced her plane ticket, sent a host of movers to pack up and ship her belongings, and hustled her off to the airport before she could scream "uncle." Or at least it felt like it. In all likelihood, the flurry of activity took place because he didn't want her to change her mind.

Not that she would have. She did not want to endure what she would surely have to endure, once Simon returned from England. Simon. No need to dwell on that issue and she banished it from her mind. Right now, she just didn't have the time or the inclination to think about that. Instead, she focused on her immediate future.

Before long, they made the turn off from the main highway and traveled down a charming country lane. Majestic moss-covered oak trees, standing proudly for at least a century or two, lined each side of the road. Wildflowers in every shape and color grew everywhere in abundance. She found the rural setting beautiful, and she could see just a smattering of homes as well as other old structures along the way.

Her anticipation grew as Norman slowed his car and then turned left into the long, winding driveway of Starling Plantation. The property enchanted her at first glance. The full two-story brick home had either a third floor bedroom above the second story, or a large attic with two dormers. She couldn't tell which from where she sat, but she would find out soon enough.

Her gaze dropped to the small arched veranda at the center of the second story. The balcony held four white pillars spaced evenly underneath it. They formed a cozy little porch around the large entryway doors below. An antique porch swing sat off to the right. Beautiful gingerbread moldings adorned the gables, accenting the sloping rooflines. Two massive willow trees graced each side of the walkway, and she couldn't begin to count the other trees, flowers, and shrubbery that accented this historic home. She could hardly wait to see the inside of it. Shae eased the jeep to a halt, set the emergency brake after shifting into first gear, and turned off the engine. She took a moment to put her maps inside the glove box. They wouldn't do her any good inside the house. As she glanced in the side view mirror, she caught sight of a black Jetta, followed by a large, faded red work truck, coasting into the driveway. Norman had already exited his vehicle and ambled toward her as she stepped out onto the gravel driveway.

"I believe the first of your documents as well as your office supplies have made their timely arrival," Norman said, pointing toward the truck. "Come on then, I will introduce you to the other team players for our project."

A couple of casually dressed men got out of the Jetta and meandered toward them. As they met in the middle, the driver gave her a friendly smile and extended a hand toward her. Shae returned his smile and took the hand he offered.

"Hello there," he said. "I'm assuming you are Miss Montgomery, our highly anticipated translator, come all the way from Norway?"

"That I am," she replied.

He turned slightly toward his companion and rested a hand atop his shoulder. "I'm Reuben Wallace, and this is Ian Burns, keeper of the documents. I feel I must warn you it's a job he takes very seriously."

"Well, how do you do, Reuben Wallace and Ian Burns? I am pleased to finally make your acquaintances." Shae shifted her bag from her hand onto her shoulder as she accepted Ian's outstretched hand. In a conversation with Todd Andersen, he told her that Reuben conceived and overlooked the entire project here in the States, while Todd acted as his Norwegian counterpart.

"Please, you must call me Shae," she added.

"Anything else makes her feel ancient," Norman said as he gave her a wink. "Well, I see you have the filing cabinets as promised. We have a place already laid out for them. So if you will have your men follow me inside, the office is the first room to the right of the foyer as we enter. Shae, as soon as we get your office set up properly, I'll give you the grand tour I promised before I leave. Is that satisfactory?"

"That's fine by me." Shae turned her attention toward the red work truck. Two men, mismatched in height and size, struggled to unload the first of three steel filing cabinets from the back of the pickup bed. In the moments that followed, she had an overwhelming someone-is-watching-me feeling. Yet, as she glanced at each of the men, she found them all busy at their various tasks. Her gaze wandered slowly over the grounds, looking for the source. All at once, she could feel the sensation coming from the house itself. She gazed upward, finding herself drawn to the second story windows. Most specifically, she could feel someone's penetrating gaze from the largest window in the center.

Chapter 2

The Civil War captain sneered as he gazed out the center second-story music room window. Three vehicles descended upon Starling as if they had every right to do so. Six people exited those vehicles in a flurry of activity. He glowered as the man driving the second car made his way toward Norman Lamont, accompanied by his male passenger who swaggered close behind. More than likely, he now gazed upon their temporary "guest," the man the caretaker spoke so highly of during his previous visit.

The man looked as if had reached his late thirties, had a medium build, and probably stood about five feet ten inches or so. He looked soft. Therefore, it wouldn't take a whole lot of effort to oust him from the property. Experience taught him that his type frightened easily enough, and he almost looked forward to the exercise. After all, it had been a while since they last had the pleasure.

His gaze shot past his target and fell upon the female standing next to Norman. Perhaps she came to assist the caretaker in some way, or better yet, boost the man's courage. Of course, right now he could only see her backside. He couldn't complain about that particular view, though. The woman possessed captivating tresses that hung almost to her waist.

Her long spiral curls reminded him of the stories his mother used to spin of the beautiful Valkyrie maidens, choosers of the slain. Their hair, she said, came from spinning together all the colors of a golden sunrise, their beauty a gift of the gods. Odin charged the women with choosing the bravest of men killed in battle. They would bring the soldiers safely to Valhalla where the soldiers would eternally serve the pagan god within his vast army. According to his mother, the doomed men didn't seem to mind the escort.

As the group hovered around the large red truck, his Valkyrie woman stood off to the side apart from the others. Her gaze wandered slowly over the grounds. He willed her to face forward so he could get a better look. A few moments later, she complied. For a few precious seconds, she looked up and locked her gaze with his. If he still lived and breathed, she would have knocked the air clean out of him. By far, she was the loveliest woman he ever laid eyes on, a true Valkyrie in every sense of his boyhood imagination. However, somehow and in some way, she also seemed very familiar to him. Yet, for the life of him, he couldn't figure out why. Obviously, they had never met. He met his death at least a century before she entered mortality. Did she remind him of someone else perhaps?

Amy peered around his shoulder and looked down at the group herself. "Which one do you suppose it is?"

Her question abruptly ended his private musings. He turned toward her and shrugged. "I can't say for sure, but I'm assuming the man wearing the blue-striped shirt. The one with the look of self-importance on his face."

Amy concurred with a nod. "I suppose you might be right at that. But it makes one wonder why so many people needed to accompany him here today."

"In all likelihood they believe there is safety in numbers, Miss Amy," Beauregard replied in his slow southern drawl, as he, too, joined them at the window. "Notice how they all seem to cluster down there."

"Well, I for one am happy about whatever cause prompted the renovations of this house. The plantation has needed a bit of sprucing up for goodness knows how long. Now because of his assignment, it's finally done," she said. "We won't have to worry about the place falling down around our heads."

"Amen to that," Horace replied. "There is, after all, only so much a body can do without a bit of assistance."

From his seat at the game table, young Timothy placed a hand over his belly and roared with laughter. "'So much a body can do'! Pray tell, Mr. Worthington, when did you last possess a body that could do anything but shuffle?"

"Careful, son," Chauncey warned. "A comment like that might get your ears boxed by the old man yet. Ha! I've captured your knight, what are you going to do about that?"

"Simply take your queen with my bishop, and I'm not afraid of Mr. Worthington. Oh, and by the way, checkmate." Timothy rested his chin atop his hands and looked pointedly at the chessboard.

"It most certainly is not 'checkmate' you snot-nosed whippersnapper. It's a, it's— Aww, dang it." Chauncey heaved a sigh and shook his head in annoyance.

Timothy laughed and leaned toward his companion. "Want me to set 'em up again? I'll let you go first this time. I promise I won't take so much as a single pawn during my first couple of moves if it makes you feel better."

"You can set them up if you wish, but I'm going to have to nurse my wounded pride for awhile before I'm ready to play with you again." Chauncey moved away from the table, and ambled over to the least crowded window. He dropped his gaze to the scene below. "You're right, Captain. The man does have a look of self-importance about himself. I wonder what it is he's supposed to do that's so all-fired important?"

"I don't know, but I think I'm going to go down there and see if I can find out." Without issuing an invitation or waiting for a reply, the captain vanished from the music room. He appeared standing next to the tree closest to his Valkyrie woman. He had wondered over the color of her eyes and found no disappointment as he gazed into the jade-green depths. He found her even more striking up close—

****

"Hey guys," Shae called out just before the group of men disappeared through the front doors with the first filing cabinet in tow. "If you don't mind, I think I'll take a look around the grounds while you bring everything in. I think it might help if I stay out of your way, and I'd like to get my bearings."

Norman smiled and waved her on. "Go ahead, and have fun exploring. There is a small pond and a lovely gazebo around the back that might interest you. They are both original to the house. We'll see you back inside when you're ready to come in."

"All right and thank you," Shae replied as she strolled toward the back of the property.

Lush, green foliage, and flowers in every variety dominated the grounds. The pond Norman spoke of sat in the center, with four pathways extending in each direction. An angel statuette rose up from the middle, and water poured from the gold-trimmed pitcher she held in her right hand. She approached the pond and sat down on the rounded ledge. Water as clear as crystal invited her to scoop the cool sparkling liquid, and let it trickle back down through her fingers.

Her gaze wandered over the immense property

while her hand continued to toy with the water. Off to the right, she spied the gazebo. Yet, just as she stood with every intention of getting a closer look, a sudden heaviness permeated the air around her. The sensation made her slightly dizzy, and she found it a bit difficult to catch her breath. A shiver passed through her body. She equated the familiar feeling with the close proximity of her Viking chieftain. The ghost or ghosts of Starling must be near.

"Hello?" She wrapped her arms around her waist and looked all around her. "Is someone here? You can talk to me if you'd like. I don't bite," she said, trying her best to sound friendly.

No answer. Apparently, these spirits did not wish to speak to a mere mortal. At least, not yet. Not wanting to appear ruffled or afraid, she sauntered toward the house. She stopped every so often to admire and inhale the rich fragrance of the flowers along the path. Ian arrived at the front door about the same time she did, carrying the first of the archival boxes.

He shifted the large box into the crook of his arm so he could hand her a set of keys. "These are the keys to the filing cabinets. The cabinets are heavy duty and fireproof. You can set your files up any way you wish, of course. But please keep everything you are not working on locked up inside the cabinets at all times. I'm sure I don't have to tell someone with your reputation that these documents are fragile and irreplaceable."

Shae flashed him a smile as they entered her office together. "No, you don't. I'll take very good care of them, Ian. I promise. Truly, you don't have to worry."

"If I thought for one minute I needed to worry, I wouldn't give you the documents or the keys," he replied, giving her a wink.

Ian set the box down on the table, and then

turned toward the men who hauled in the cabinets. He gestured toward them with a wave of his hand.

"Shae, I would like to introduce you to George Burwell, and the hulking brute standing next to him is Perry Adler. They are the only two people, besides Reuben and me, authorized to pick up or deliver anything concerning this project. Unless, of course, I personally tell you otherwise. This precaution will ensure the safety and protection of the documents. Unfortunately, the press made a rather big deal about their discovery as well as their worth. Now, the possibility of theft has to be a consideration, I'm afraid."

Before she could open her mouth to respond, a cold blast of icy wind rushed past her. An instant later, a door slammed violently somewhere above them. All conversation stopped over the unmistakable, reverberating sound it made. Everyone held their breath as the sudden even pacing of heavy booted footsteps atop a creaky wooden floor became increasingly louder. The small group exchanged glances but said nothing. Shae looked over at Norman who simply shrugged an *I told you so.*

Moments later, Reuben and his company left the premises. Lacking the courage to meet her gaze, the man simply handed her his card, and told her if she needed anything else or had any further questions, she could give him a call. She stood at the door and followed their departure as Reuben and his men drove off without a backward glance.

"I think I would call that 'beating a hasty retreat.'" Shae raised a mischievous brow as the last of the taillights disappeared around the curve. All the while, she tried her best to ignore the sound of the footsteps.

"Yes, well—" Norman cleared his throat in an exaggerated manner. He looked up toward the ceiling and said, "Let's get on with your tour, so that I, too, can beat a hasty retreat out of the door. I will, however, wish you all the best after I am gone."

Shae laughed as they began their tour with the rooms on the ground floor. Rich tones emanating from the chimes of a floor clock beckoned her into the drawing room. The Simon Willard clock sat to the right of the handsomely carved mahogany fireplace mantel. A matching desk sat to the left. Above the fireplace hung a portrait of a little girl. The artist depicted her gathering a large bouquet in a field of lavender wildflowers. She wore a frilly white dress and matching lacy bonnet, both trimmed in pink ribbons. Hurricane lamps with frosted glass adorned the tables next to the rose-colored settee and chair. A Persian rug with a floral motif containing hues of pink and blue lay between them. The tea table in front of the settee held a delicate blue-and-white porcelain tea set. Ruffled white curtains framed the large, square-paned windows.

"I have to tell you, this room looks as if it came straight out of an antebellum magazine." Shae turned, and gestured toward the portrait. "Did the little girl in the painting live here or is she just—"

"Yes, actually. Her name is Louisa Starling, youngest daughter of Ferdinand and Leatha Starling, the original owners who built this house in the year 1799," Norman replied.

"What a wonderful piece of history. Tell me, are all of the antique pieces original to the house, or were they gathered from other places and transported here?" Her gaze continued to travel around the room, absorbing every delightful detail.

"Most of them are original to the house, yes," Norman said. "Since this home served as a hospital during the Civil War, the soldiers left it pretty much intact. The armies from both sides respected it for the function it served and simply left it alone. Other homes in this area were not so lucky, though."

Startled over the revelation, she wheeled around and met his gaze. "This house served as a hospital? Really?"

"Yes indeed, and it continued in that role long after the war ended. People feared contagious diseases back then and feared this home crawled with them, you see. So at the time, no one wanted to live here. Tuberculosis, known in that era as consumption, as you might already know, ran rampant in these parts. So did the cases of typhoid and yellow fever, malaria, and various other diseases. People died at an alarming rate.

"There are many who feel some of the spirits inhabiting this house are the patients who died during that particular time period. Years later the home sold to the first of many owners because, as I told you earlier, no one could stay here very long. Then finally, after the last resident deeded Starling to the National Trust, the organization opened it up as a museum of sorts. We gave tours with guides in period clothing and whatnot as a last ditch effort to maintain the funds necessary to run this house as well as a few of our other properties. Alas, the spirits wouldn't even allow us to do that. Pretty soon it attained a fearsome reputation, and so we closed the doors."

"Just exactly how many spirits are supposed to inhabit this house anyway?" Shae glanced toward the ceiling and followed the path of the footsteps with her eyes.

"That's a very good question, and we really don't know the answer. We've had a few psychics visit the home from time to time. The number of spirits they see varies with the psychic. However, I should think no more than eight. We needn't dwell on that, though. Come on, I'll show you the kitchen."

She followed as he led the way. As they entered

the room, he explained that although retaining its original look by the clever use of antique wood and stone, they had updated and modernized all the appliances. He showed her the location of the pantry, which they filled with everything she could need or want for several weeks to come. The tour continued as he took her from the kitchen, and then out to the mudroom where they kept the laundry facilities. Then finally, he escorted her to her bedroom. At once, she fell in love with the large four-poster canopy bed, with its rose-colored gossamer curtains tied to each of the large round posts. An elegant handmade quilt covered the mattress.

Before she could try out the softness of the topmost feather mattress, Norman drew her attention away from the bed and over to the spacious connecting bathroom. He said at one time, the bathroom served as the nursery for the Starling family. Shae allowed herself a brief moment to envision the babies the families rocked to sleep within its walls. The vision made her smile.

"We thought you would rather remain on the first floor for convenience sake, and well"—Norman shrugged—"most of the uh, *activity* is upstairs. Do you—would you like me to show you the rest of the house, or would you prefer to just get settled in and explore it on your own at a later time?"

Shae almost laughed outright at the look of horror on Norman's face as he asked the question. She could see he wanted nothing to do with the upstairs portion of the house. Especially since the sound of the footsteps had not in any way diminished.

"You know, I think I can handle things from here, and it's been a long day for both of us. So if you don't mind, I'll just go ahead and let you beat that hasty retreat."

"Oh, bless you, Shae. You are an absolute

angel." Norman produced an ear-to-ear grin. "As expected from all reports, I find you are a lovely and charming woman. I know we'll get along just fine. All of your suitcases as well as the boxes shipped from Norway should already be in your bedroom.

"Feel free to move things around a bit or add your own possessions to make Starling your home while you are here. There are several pieces of furniture and miscellaneous items in the basement, should you want to use any of those in the place of the ones we have out. Oh, and there is just one more thing I should tell you."

"Yes?" She raised a brow in question.

"The third floor attic room is locked, and it is better to keep it that way." His gaze bore into hers as he emphasized his words. "If you decide to replace some of the furniture with something else, please don't try to store the unwanted pieces up there. Use one of the bedrooms or the basement instead."

"All right, I'll remember that." Shae followed Norman out to the foyer and accepted his extended hand. "Thank you so much for everything. I appreciate all of your help and personal attention today. Your hospitality has made this move much easier than what I anticipated."

"My pleasure," he said as he dipped a hand into his pocket and withdrew a set of keys. "Now, these are the keys to all of the doors of Starling, as well as the other structures on the property. Feel free to explore them at your leisure. Some of them are quite lovely."

"Again, I need to thank you. You are very kind," she said as she accepted the keys.

"Think nothing of it and Shae—" He leaned a little closer and locked his gaze with hers. "Don't hesitate to call me if you should feel the need, no matter the day or the time, are we agreed on that?"

"Of course, but please don't worry about me."

She withdrew her hand to give him a reassuring pat on the back. "I'm going to be fine, really, I am."

Shae laughed after she made the comment; Norman beat a hasty retreat out to his car, as promised. After closing the door, she stepped into her office and locked away the documents Reuben abandoned on the table. Once she took care of the boxes, she made her way into her bedroom to unpack her things and settle in.

She opened the large empty wardrobe in search of her suitcases and then looked for them on either side of the bed. No luggage. She walked inside the bathroom and found it empty. Odd, she did see Perry lugging her suitcases inside the house, didn't she? As she recalled he struggled to bring them inside all at once, in fact. Norman confirmed that before leaving as well. After checking the hallway, she went into the drawing room, then to the kitchen, and even the foyer. Out of sheer desperation, she opened the entryway doors thinking that perhaps Perry didn't bring them all the way inside after all.

As she glanced outside and past the porch, she caught sight of her suitcases and all of their contents strewn chaotically across the front lawn. As she fought to still her rising anger over the petty display, she marched down the porch steps and out to the lawn. She cast her gaze all about, uncertain as to where to begin the daunting task. After a deep breath, she made her way toward the willow tree.

"Welcome to Starling, Shae," she muttered under her breath.

Chapter 3

The captain could hear Amy's unnecessary toe-tapping outside his door. He could feel her rising fury without the annoying sound, and it only served to fuel his own anger. He shook his head and closed his eyes. For whatever reason, he just assumed Norman Lamont referred to a man when he made his previous visit. The very idea of this particular woman living underneath his roof sent him reeling. He wasn't about to let her stay, although he couldn't pinpoint the exact reason for the resolve.

Despite his wishes, the other residents seemed completely at ease with this unexpected development. The notion of having another female about the premises filled Amy with obvious anticipation. Chauncey and Beau grinned stupidly in her direction once they understood the situation, and even Timothy seemed happy about the turn of events. No. He couldn't have her here. She needed to leave, and the sooner the better for all concerned. He couldn't conceive of any reason for the residents of Starling to attach themselves to someone, who even if allowed to stay, wouldn't be here very long.

"Don't you dare ignore me, Captain," Amy seethed. "How could you? Just how could you do such a hateful thing to that lovely girl?"

At once, he came through the door in an irritated huff. "I don't want her here."

She glared up at him. "I don't understand what the big deal is. They have settled her downstairs. She is only going to be with us for a very short while, and you don't even have to interact with her if you don't want to. You know, you can be such a bully at times. Why, you should see that poor little thing down there, picking up the things you scattered all over the place. You ought to be ashamed of yourself, sir." She placed her hands on her hips and stamped her foot in a fit of temper.

He sighed as she disappeared without waiting for the reply he didn't have. For he *did* see the girl, and he did feel terrible about his actions. Really he did. But he just couldn't deal with her being here. Didn't anybody understand that? He didn't know if he possessed the strength to stay away from her, and therein lay the problem.

****

After dragging all her suitcases in from outside, Shae spent the next few hours unpacking all of her things. Her empty stomach growled and gnawed in complaint throughout the entire process. However, once she put the last article of clothing away inside the bureau drawer, she recalled Norman mentioning several dinner entrées inside the freezer.

As she entered the kitchen, she could smell the strong scent of lilacs. She looked around expecting to find a bouquet of them somewhere nearby. However, she didn't find one. Perhaps a potpourri bowl sat amongst the canisters on the countertops. Shrugging it off, she pulled a country-fried steak dinner out of the freezer and popped it into the microwave. She leaned against the counter, and waited for the meal to cook. The steak, smothered in country gravy with mashed potatoes, smelled delicious.

As she sat at the large oak table and ate her dinner, she pondered over the ghosts of Starling. Aulric, her ancient Viking friend, made her life very difficult at first. He didn't want anyone touching his ship, even to preserve it. The vessel served as his tomb and as he told her often enough, he held very fond memories of the many places the ship had taken him. He didn't want it trifled with. Therefore, it took them quite awhile to reach an understanding and become friends.

However, during that particular experience she faced just one spirit, not a whole houseful. That meant she would need to make peace with each entity residing here. The task could take some time, depending on the number of ghosts and the temperament of each one. She only hoped that in the meantime, they wouldn't interfere with her work and the schedule she needed to keep.

She got up from the table and cleaned up the remnants of her dinner before she ventured out of the kitchen. An eerie silence had settled upon the house. The only discernable sound she could hear came from the soft tapping of her own footsteps as they echoed on the hardwood floors. That unnerving silence made her aware the pacing of the spiritual entity upstairs had ceased.

She stepped through the hallway and into the drawing room. The rhythmic ticks of the stately clock greeted her as she approached the piece for a better look. For several moments, she followed the swaying of the brass pendulum. Followed that is, until all of a sudden, the pendulum ceased to swing. The heavy brass arm impossibly positioned itself all the way to the right of the glass case, defying gravity. The clock grew silent and the lights from the wall sconces dimmed of their own accord. Any hint of moisture fled her mouth, and she found it difficult to swallow past the knot in her throat.

Nonetheless, she refused to show the spirit or spirits her fear. She continued her thorough unhurried inspection of the room. The small porcelain pieces, she picked up and examined. Her fingers swept over the softness of the furniture fabrics. She even took a moment to gaze out the window and appreciate the nighttime view. All the while, her thoughts centered on the ghostly inhabitants of this house. Once she turned away from the window, the clock resumed its normal function and the lights returned to their customary brightness. Did it surprise them that she didn't scream and go running from the house after their display? Better yet, would her actions make a difference on how they perceived her?

She tugged on her bottom lip as she glanced upward at the ceiling. Perhaps she shouldn't put off the inevitable. Should she try to engage the pacing spirit first? After taking a deep breath, she made her way out of the drawing room and over to the staircase. Yet, even as she approached the first step, she paused. She wondered if she should attempt to offer her friendship so soon, considering the welcome she received earlier.

No matter. The task needed doing. Shae ignored the thumping of her heart, took hold of the hand-carved banister, and ascended the stairs. As she stepped onto the landing, she could smell the rich scent of lilacs once again. The pleasant odor wafted off to the left. She decided to follow it.

The scent led her to a set of white double doors on the left side of the hallway. She gave them a gentle knock before she dropped her hand on the knob, turned the brass antique handle, and opened the door. After peeking inside and finding nothing out of the ordinary, she entered the room. She explored along the wall for the light switch and once she found it, she flipped it upward. An exquisite crystal chandelier, hanging center of the ceiling, filled the room with light.

As her eyes swept over the room, her gaze settled on a small table holding an impressive chess set off to the left. Two wooden chairs sat on opposite sides of the game board. She strolled over for a better look. The elegant red and ivory pieces were carved in the distinctive barleycorn style and placed in such a manner that it looked as if a game were in progress. An overstuffed, comfortable looking sofa and two matching chairs sat opposite the game table. She could see plenty of room for a TV in front of the furniture if she decided to put one in this room. If nothing else, a television would serve to add a bit of noise to the otherwise silent house. Perhaps she ought to consider a stereo as well.

She turned her attention to an intricately carved music stand, which stood in front of the tall center window. The stand held either a fife or pennywhistle on its shelf. Curiosity getting the better of her, she stepped over and picked the instrument up. She began tracing the smooth wooden tube with her fingertips. One played the piece from the side instead of the front, and that made it a fife. She returned it to the shelf and made her way to the piano.

The magnificent mahogany baby grand took up most of the space on the right side of the room. She brushed against the ivory keys with a backward stroke of her hand. Her lips curved into a smile. Notwithstanding the spiritual activity at Starling, and the ghosts' distaste for the living, someone dutifully kept the piano in tune. She eased herself down on the bench and placed her hands on the keyboard. Even though she hadn't touched a piano in quite awhile, she couldn't resist her first opportunity to play a baby grand.

She tried to recall something she could play without benefit of sheet music. After thinking for a moment, she began to play Mozart's *Concerto No 21 in C Major*, her father's favorite. Her fingers remembered each note to perfection. While playing the song, the first inkling of unseen company filtered into the room. The slight chill and heaviness in the air told her that at least one spirit stood in her presence, and in all likelihood, several spirits surrounded the piano. Her heart hammered wildly in her chest. She took a deep gulping breath, put something she hoped resembled a smile on her face, and stood up from the bench. Her gaze swept across the room in its entirety before she walked into the center of the room.

"Good evening." She peered all around her, not knowing exactly where the spirits stood. Nothing like speaking to an empty wall. Nevertheless, she filled her lungs with a bit of needed air and said, "If you don't mind, I would like to introduce myself to everyone. Perhaps I could tell you a little bit about me and why I'm here."

No one responded to her friendly overture. Shae knew very well that spirits could speak audibly if they chose to do so. In fact, they could appear as solid as any person still living *if* they wanted to. Or at least, Aulric could.

"My name is Shae Lynn Montgomery. I am the daughter of Bret and Amanda Montgomery, and I have three siblings. My twin sisters, Jennifer and Candice, are two years older than I am. The baby of our family is Nicole and she just turned twenty-four. We were all born and raised in the state of Washington. Just in case you don't know where that is, it's on the northwest coast along the Pacific. The last several years I have studied and worked in Norway, though."

Rambling on about nothing, to what appeared a room devoid of people, made her feel a little silly. But since she could still feel their presence, she persevered.

"My love for the Norse culture fueled my desire to seek a degree in the ancient history of that particular civilization and its mythology. Along the way, I became fluent in both the Norwegian and Danish languages. This in turn, led me here.

"You see, someone discovered some old military records, journals, and letters inside a home very near this one. I believe they found them in an old trunk, hidden away in an attic. Anyway, they found the bulk of these records written in the Norwegian language, and most all of them deal with the Wisconsin Fifteenth Regiment. This Regiment gained the reputation of fighting valiantly during the Civil War on behalf of the Union army. They played a big part in some of the major battles that took place in both Georgia and here in Tennessee. I'm told most of the men in this unit were either Norwegian or Danish by birth or heritage."

Shae stopped short as she heard the sound of a loud reverberating thump coming from the bottom of the door as if someone had kicked it. Once again, her heart accelerated as she waited for something or someone to come through the door or wall. But nothing more manifested itself. She furrowed her brow as she wondered if what she said provoked or offended the spirits in some way.

Not knowing what else to do, she continued her narrative. "Coincidentally, the uh, commander of the Wisconsin Fifteenth is a great-grandfather to one of my professors in Norway. I should probably mention the people of Norway are just as proud of this man, Hans Christian Heg, as are the people here in the United States. After the discovery of the documents, the men in charge of the National Military Park in Chickamauga, Georgia decided to create a new display featuring Heg and his Wisconsin Fifteenth Regiment.

"Once my professor got wind of this display, he wanted to create a similar exhibit at a museum in Lierbyen, Norway. And so, the project grew. The men got together and discussed the various needs of each exhibit. At that meeting, they decided to have all the records written in the Norwegian language translated into English. Records originally written in English concerning the regiment need translation into Norwegian, and perhaps even Danish for the museum in Norway. They have asked me to do this work, and I have accepted. The office they have assembled downstairs is where I will do the translation of all these documents."

While she spoke, Shae suddenly felt the intense cold she associated with anger or sorrow. She hadn't given it a thought before this moment, but perhaps Civil War soldiers stood in this room with her now. Some of them might have met their death at the battle of Chickamauga or Chattanooga, either Union or Confederate. The park rested just a little way across the border. Of their own volition, her eyes traveled toward the music room entrance, drawn there by an unseen force.

****

The captain vaulted upright from the door he leaned against, as she revealed her full purpose. He folded his arms against his chest, firmed his jaw, and shook his head in response to her words. Any weakening to his resolve he might have felt earlier instantly evaporated. The woman needed to leave this house, and if he had anything to say about it, she would leave right now.

Shaelynn Montgomery knit her brow and fixed her gaze upon him. She looked confused and uncertain. Did she feel his disapproval? He could only hope she did and that the feeling would be enough to make her voluntarily leave this house.

"Look, I should only be here for a year or so. I can promise you, I do not intend to take over your home. So, while I am here, I am hoping we can be friends," she said.

The captain sighed inwardly as he looked into each hopeful face of his companions. They wanted the girl to stay, and therefore, would do everything in their power to make that happen. Yet, it stunned him when she spoke of her purpose here. He served with the valiant men of the Wisconsin Fifteenth she so casually mentioned. Most of the men who served in that regiment, he knew personally, especially those under his command.

The last thing he expected or wanted to hear was that someone hired her to translate records from his division. That endeavor would lead her to read, perhaps even translate, what history recorded about him. He knew he could not bear the loathing that would surely fill those expressive green eyes once she did.

Frustration overwhelmed him. The anger over his impossible situation consumed him all over again. He made a step toward her.

"Wait a minute, Captain. Just wait," Amy begged as she suddenly blocked his path, halting his progress. "Give this some thought before you do anything rash."

He said nothing in return as he simply moved around her and continued his path across the room. Once he stood just in front of the girl, he came to an abrupt halt. Though difficult to appear brutish, he leaned down toward her face and growled out, "You are not wanted or welcome in this house. Leave now, before you regret coming here at all."

In response to his dire warning, Shaelynn wrapped her arms around her waist. Her eyes flashed with anger instead of fright, and she lifted her chin a notch in defiance. She placed her focus in the direction of his voice.

"I'm truly sorry you feel that way. Really, I am," she said between clenched teeth. "But unfortunately for you, I'm not going anywhere, and you are just going to have to find a way to deal with that. Now, you'll have to excuse me. It's been a very long day. I'm exhausted, and I'm going to *my* bed downstairs, in *my* bedroom."

Without waiting for a reply, she stomped out of the room. She took one final look over her shoulder before she slammed the door as hard as she could, and in a fit of pique hollered back through the door, "Goodnight! I'll see you all in the morning!"

He listened to her footsteps descending the stairs before he turned around. He looked into the eyes of his companions before he settled his gaze on Amy. She placed her hands on her hips and glared.

"I don't want to hear it, Amy!" the captain thundered as he looked at her recriminating expression. "You know I can't let her stay. Not now. Not after what she just said. We both know that."

"She might be able to help you," Amy retorted. "Why don't you stop being so bull-headed, and just give her a chance?"

"A chance to do what?" he shot back. "Look at me like everyone else did? Judge me without having all of the facts?"

"What if she doesn't?" She tilted her chin a notch as she presented the argument.

The captain sighed despairingly and closed his eyes. "What if she does?" he whispered. Without waiting for a reply, he retreated to his room to save further argument.

Chapter 4

By the time she entered her bedroom, Shae had regained control over her temper. She raised a hand to her brow, gently massaged her forehead, and blew out a sigh. The evening had not gone quite the way she hoped it would. Then again, she supposed the situation could have been worse.

The ringing of her cell phone silenced her thoughts, and she hurried to answer it. She activated the answer button as she lifted the phone to her ear and said, "Hello, Shae Montgomery speaking."

"Shae! It's Todd Andersen."

"Oh, hello, Professor." She glanced down at the clock and made a quick calculation. The man should still be asleep for heaven's sake. "Are you all right? I mean, it's just so early there—"

"No. Everything is fine," he cut in. "I just happened to arise early this morning and thought I would see how you were doing before you went to bed."

"Everything is good. I met everyone I needed to meet and I have already settled into my home here in Tennessee. Did you know they planned on letting me stay at Starling Plantation?"

"Yes, Reuben mentioned something along those lines. I knew you'd be pleased," he replied. "Tell me, have you had the chance to look over the documents yet?"

The question made her smile. Of all he might want to know, Todd Andersen would be most intrigued with the documents she came to translate.

"I have them in my possession, but I haven't taken them out of the boxes yet. I'm going to start work on that come morning."

"Of course. Such is expected. After all, it is just your first full day in Tennessee," he said. Despite his words, she could detect just a bit of disappointment in his tone.

"Don't worry, I'll call you the minute I have them spread out on my worktable," she replied.

"You better." Todd hesitated for a moment and then cleared his throat. "Um, Shae—"

"Yes?"

"Simon flew in today," he said, leaving a deliberate pause.

Shae felt her heart sink somewhere into the pit of her stomach. She did not want to discuss Simon with him or anyone else. Yet, she could tell by the professor's tone, Simon wasted no time in discussing their situation with him.

"Please, Professor," Shae began. "I don't really want to talk about Simon. Everything he needs to know, I said in the letter I left him. Can we just leave it at that?"

"Of course. I'm sorry, Shae. I didn't mean to pry, it's just that—"

"I know, you have the best of intentions and I appreciate your concern," she interrupted. "But everything is fine. Really, it is."

"All right then." He changed his tone to one of cheerful anticipation. "Please call me the minute you see the condition of those documents. Most especially, let me know if you find any records written by my famous grandfather."

Shae laughed. "Don't worry, you know I will. Good-bye, Professor. Tell everyone I said hi."

She released a sigh as she ended the call and placed her phone atop the table. Right now, she needed nothing more than a hot shower and a good night's sleep, because all of a sudden, an overwhelming weariness overtook her.

Despite the relaxing shower and her exhaustion, Shae found it difficult to sleep once she got into bed. She tossed and turned, and then tossed some more as myriad thoughts whirled chaotically inside her head. Each one willfully omitted Simon Hollander and instead, centered on the ghosts of Starling. Just what made her think she could win the spirits over so easily? Norman Lamont gave her full disclosure and fair warning. Didn't he tell her the spirits of Starling didn't tolerate the presence of mortals about the place? What part of that didn't she understand? And how in the world did she manage to tangle herself up inside her covers, anyway? She kicked her legs loose of the blankets as she sought a solution to her dilemma, which inevitably, stirred memories of her first ghostly experience.

In the beginning, Aulric treated her far worse. At least no one threw dangerous objects at her today as Aulric had during their first meeting. These spirits only threw her things *out*. Perhaps that meant she could eventually win the battle. Especially once they concluded, that no matter what they did, they couldn't force her to leave. She could be stubborn too.

The faint sounds of a fife ebbed into her mind then, thus halting all further consideration on the matter. She tossed back the covers and left her bedroom to find the source of the music. The mournful tune didn't come from upstairs, as she first believed. In fact, out here in the hallway she could barely hear it. She walked back into her bedroom, stood still for a moment, and listened again. Her gaze wandered toward the French doors, which led to the garden patio outside. The music originated somewhere out there. Not bothering with shoes or even a pair of slippers, she opened both doors and followed the haunting melody toward the gazebo. As she turned in the direction of the sound, a faint glow appeared near the railing. As she drew closer, the dim glow evolved into the solid figure of a young boy.

Once she approached him, he took the fife away from his mouth and gave her a timid smile. Shae returned it in kind. He looked no more than ten or eleven years of age, fair of hair and complexion. He appeared wearing a Confederate gray shirt with matching trousers and suspenders, all showing at least a couple seasons of wear. How did one so young come to be in this place? What reasons did he harbor for remaining earthbound? Her heart went out to him in the instant.

"Well, hello there! What is the name of that lovely song you just played?" Shae eased herself into a seated position next to him on the railing and placed her folded hands in her lap.

He scrunched his shoulders together as he toyed with his fife. "I'm not real sure. My mama always called it 'Hush-a-bye.' She used to sing it to me when I was a little boy."

Didn't he know? He was still just a little boy who needed an endless supply of hugs and lullabies from his mother. She cleared away the lump forming in her throat. "My name is Shae Lynn Montgomery. What's yours?"

"Timothy Laurens," he replied, as he looked her over with curiosity. "And I don't mind if you want to stay around for awhile."

"Really? Are you the only one around here who doesn't mind if I stay?" she asked. She hoped by asking the question, she would learn exactly how many spirits lived here and how many of them opposed her presence.

Timothy merely shrugged and once again began playing his fife. She overstepped her bounds with the question. At least he didn't choose to disappear because of it. She listened attentively as he continued to play, and after he finished several more of his enchanting songs, she tried again.

"You know, I have really enjoyed listening to you play your fife. You do it so well, I find myself hoping you will play it for me often." She smiled as he nodded his consent. "Do you mind if I ask how you came to be at this house? You don't need to answer if you don't want to, though."

He sat still for a moment as he considered her request, and then said, "Me and Pa signed up with the Thirteenth Tennessee Regiment in June of '63. They made me a fife 'cause I could play a tune all right, and they made Pa an ordinary foot soldier. Seemed like we marched all over the place durin' the months that followed. I remember it bein' hot and sticky. Then one day I got sick. I'm not real sure just when it started. I just recall this most awful feelin' inside my belly, and it lasted for the longest time. Then one day, I made a turn for the worse, and it didn't seem they could do anythin' for me in camp anymore. That's the day my Pa, and some of the other soldiers, took me here. Pa carried me most of the way, his self."

Timothy paused for a moment, and then said, "Pa stayed right by my bed the whole time. He kept tellin' me that I needed to get better, but not long after that, I guess I died. Miss Amy took care of me all the while, and after she joined us, she told me I breathed my last about the middle of December. I remember feeling scared at first—the moment I left my body behind—but Captain stood right by my side to help me through it. He made it so I didn't feel scared anymore. But then again, I guess I can always count on him to look after me like that. He's a pretty good fellow, you know.

"Anyway, Pa took it real hard—my dyin', that is. He cried, and just kept sayin' that my mama didn't get the chance to say goodbye. Pa didn't know how she was gonna be able to handle that. And I told him, over and over again, that I would wait right here for him to fetch her so she could."

Shae found it difficult to hide her tears as he related his sad little story. But at least he fixed his gaze on something in front of him, rather than on her, as he told it. She dabbed her eyes and sniffed as she lifted a hand to the corner of her eye. Did he still wait for his mother to arrive so they could have their farewell?

Aulric told her once, that a spirit never considered the passing of time. They didn't need to sleep or eat, and they never took much notice of the setting or rising of the sun. At least he didn't. In fact, Aulric seemed truly astonished to discover his death occurred over eight centuries earlier.

"Thank you for sharing your story with me." The words, though sincerely spoken, were inadequate. She wished she could take him in her arms and hold him. Maybe even sing that lullaby he used to hear from his mother.

He simply nodded in return. After looking into his eyes and wishing somehow to banish away the sadness, Shae sought for a change of subject.

"So, tell me, does anyone around here play with that lovely chess set upstairs?" she asked.

At once Timothy's smile returned. "We all do on occasion, except I play the game most of all. I always win though. Every once in a while, I will let the others win a game just so they will keep on playin' with me," he whispered secretively.

Shae smiled inwardly over the trusted revelation. "Well then, perhaps you'll allow me to play a game or two with you sometime soon? I think I would really like that."

His eyes lit up over the prospect. "Oh, I will. We'll have loads of fun, Miss Shaelynn. Wait and see."

"I'm sure we will. You must promise me one thing, though," she said as she gave him a sideways glance.

"Anythin'," he vowed, as he crossed his heart.

"You can't intentionally let me win, not even once," she said. "I need to earn all of my wins on my own merit. Are we agreed?"

Timothy threw back his head and giggled. "You got yourself a deal on that one, Miss Shaelynn."

With a bit of reluctance, Shae stood then, smothered a yawn, and said, "I am very pleased to meet you, Timothy Laurens. I think we're going to be great friends. Unlike you though, I need to get a little sleep before morning comes. I have to start my work then and need to feel rested. Do you mind?"

"Nope, that'll be fine," he replied. "I'll see you tomorrow."

Shae could feel his eyes watching her as she returned to her bedroom. She made some progress tonight, at least enough progress to quiet her mind. After climbing into bed, she switched off the light. She drew the soft eider down quilt up to her chin and quite easily fell into blissful sleep.

She awoke early the next morning, feeling surprisingly refreshed. Hunger drew her into the kitchen in search of breakfast. She opened each cupboard door in succession in order to familiarize herself with the contents of each one. Nothing mysterious there. She found the cupboards holding the dishes over the dishwasher and the food cupboards near to the stove. Simple genius.

As she came across a box of blueberry muffin mix, she resolved to bake them. That way she could have something to nibble on throughout the week without having to stop and fix herself a meal. She selected milk and eggs from the refrigerator, retrieved a mixing bowl from the cupboard, and got out the mixer. Yet, her thoughts were far from the simple task. They centered on her conversation with Timothy the night before.

He mentioned two other names while relating his story, *Miss Amy* and *Captain*. He spoke fondly of each one, and more importantly, he spoke of them in the present tense. That meant they were still here. The captain preceded him in death, and Amy died some time after. Perhaps Timothy could convince them both to be on her side, and that would give her at least three allies in this house.

Just after she placed the muffins inside the oven, the doorbell rang. She put the potholder down and hurried out of the kitchen to answer it. As she opened the door, George and Perry greeted her with an apologetic smile.

"Good morning! I didn't expect to see either of you again so soon," she said as she looked from one face to the other. "What can I do for you?"

George bobbed his head in greeting. "Well, it seems that Reuben, uh, forgot to bring in the scanner and the rest of your office supplies before we left yesterday. We put all of the electronic equipment in his trunk. So, out of sight, out of mind, I suppose. Anyway, we have them in the truck now, but we wanted to make sure you were awake before we loaded everything up on the dolly and barged in on you."

"Oh, I see." Shae bit back the laugh threatening to surface. In all likelihood, "forgetting" had nothing to do with it. "Do you need some help?"

"No, we can handle the task just fine. Just give us a minute, and we'll be right back with the rest of your stuff," he said as he turned toward his vehicle. In short order, they loaded the hand truck well beyond its intended capacity.

Shae laughed inwardly over the sight they made. George, who stood only about five and a half feet tall, kept peeking around from side to side in an ongoing effort to keep himself on course. Perry, at about six feet, still needed to stand on tiptoes so he could hold the top box in place and keep the cargo from tumbling over.

While they maneuvered toward the house, George's shoulders suddenly slumped forward while his chest caved backward. He then let out a yelp of surprise. Perry pitched sideways, then forward and tumbled end over end. The hand truck and boxes went flying hither and yon. Both men ended all tangled up in the mix. Shae rushed out of the door to give assistance.

"Are you all right?" She drew in a breath as she stooped down beside them.

George attempted to shrug off the accident. As he rose to his feet and brushed himself off, he said, "Yes, just a little embarrassed is all. I guess I must have lost my footing under the weight. Come on, Perry. Let's try this again."

"Well here, let me help," Shae set about retrieving the scattered folders. George didn't lose his footing at all. Someone *shoved* him, and he could have been seriously hurt because of it. The whole thing made her furious. On top of that, the poor man looked terrified.

"You know what? Let's just stack this stuff on the porch. I'm not ready for you to bring it into my office right now anyway, and I'll just retrieve it later when I am," she said.

Both men looked at her with a mixture of relief and gratitude. In just a few minutes time, they had everything stacked on the porch, jumped inside their truck, and drove away. Shae waited outside until the vehicle disappeared down the lane before she stormed back inside the house. She made it as far as the foyer before she unleashed her temper on the offending spirit responsible for the mayhem.

"Look, whoever you are! If you want to take your infuriating wrath out on someone, then take it out on me. Those men have *nothing* to do with my decision to stay here, nor should you punish them for doing their job. They can't change my mind or alter the course of the coming year no matter what you do. Do you hear me? And just to make it *perfectly* clear to everyone inside this house, I'm *not* leaving until I finish the job I agreed to do. There is *nothing* anyone can do that will make me change my mind. I'm staying put and that's the end of that! And just so you know, I am *not* afraid of you or anything you can do to me personally. So if it's a battle you want over territory, then I'll be happy to accommodate you."

The now familiar slamming of a door somewhere upstairs sounded in response to her tirade. She shook her head in frustration. At that moment, the strong smell of blueberry muffins wafted out of the kitchen and permeated all around her. A gasp escaped her lips as she suddenly remembered she had them in the oven. She ran into the kitchen to rescue them from burning. The muffins, baked to perfection and arranged neatly in a basket, sat on top of the stove. She blew out a sigh of relief. Without thinking she simply said, "Thank you."

"Oh, you're welcome, dear. What with all the fuss going on this morning, I knew you would forget you had them baking."

Startled over the unexpected voice, Shae whirled toward the point of origin. A very attractive middle-aged woman, wearing a long blue dress and a white three-quarter length bib apron, stood near the table. She had her hands clasped in front of her. Streaks of gleaming silver weaved beautifully through her chestnut hair. Her light brown eyes appeared soft and pleasant looking. The smell of lilacs surrounded her being. If Shae had to hazard a guess, she would say the woman belonged to the nineteenth century.

"Why don't you sit down now, and have some breakfast before you get started with your day." The ghostly woman smiled sweetly as she "transported" the muffins to the table.

Shae smiled her thanks as she sat down, took one out of the basket, and sunk her teeth into it. The muffin all but melted in her mouth. "I wished I could offer you one. They're pretty good, if I do say so myself."

The spirit laughed. "That's quite all right, Miss Shaelynn. My name is Amy Stoddard, and I am very pleased you're here. I think we'll get along just fine. You know, it's been awhile since I've had another female to chat with, and I must confess it is something I have missed."

"Well, thank you. That makes two of you who don't mind if I stay around for awhile," she said as she chewed another bite and swallowed it down. "I met Timothy last night, but then I'm sure you must already know that. He also said he didn't have a problem if I remained. Unlike someone else around the premises," she muttered under her breath.

Amy merely shook her head as if the situation warranted no further thought and smiled. "Don't you worry about the captain. Your opinion of him will change in time, I daresay. It's just that—well, he has his reasons for behaving the way he does. Don't judge him too harshly, dear. Right now he's just not too keen on mortals."

Aha! The *captain* didn't want her here. So much for Timothy running interference.

"Could you tell me why that is? Perhaps I can help change his mind," Shae said as she rose from the table to get herself a glass of orange juice.

A long, drawn out silence greeted the inquiry, she whirled away from the refrigerator, intending on making a quick apology. However, Amy conveniently disappeared from the kitchen. The spirits in this house minded no one's business but their own. One needed to respect them for that.

After cleaning up the kitchen, she dried her hands and headed for the porch. Despite what she said to George, she really needed to set up the office before she could begin her work. Just as she entered the foyer, she spied the supplies George and Perry delivered already inside the house. The neatly stacked boxes stood against the wall, just outside her office doors.

Once again and to no one in particular, she said, "Thank you for the help. I really appreciate it."

"That's quite all right, mum. Is there anything else I can do for you?"

Shae smiled broadly. In fact, she almost laughed out loud. The man who suddenly appeared in front of her reminded her in every way of Alfred the butler on the *Batman* series, right down to the rigid stance and subtle bob of his head. "No, I think I can manage from here."

"Would you like some assistance in bringing your supplies into the room, perhaps?" he asked.

"No, really, I can do it myself. I need to do a bit of rearranging before I bring this stuff in, so—" She allowed her shrug to fill in the rest of her sentence.

"Should you find it otherwise, Miss Montgomery, please don't hesitate to ask me. My name is Horace Worthington, and I am at your service should you need me. All you need do is call." Once again, he bobbed his head and disappeared.

Just as Horace vanished, the sound of a deep, exasperated sigh filled the foyer.

Chapter 5

The captain kept his presence concealed from Shae as she spent the better part of the day getting her office organized and her files set up. Once she seemed satisfied with the outcome, she took one of the boxes out the cabinet and set it atop the large table. Sheer curiosity moved him to peer over her shoulder as she began going through and separating the contents by language, type, subject, and date. The large stack of war records on the table dealt with the men, places, and battles of which he possessed intimate knowledge. But thankfully, he didn't see his name on any of them. At least, not yet.

He leaned back against the wall and crossed his arms against his chest as he considered the puzzle Shaelynn Montgomery presented. He had never come across a woman quite like her. She possessed a strong will and fearless nature. That made her dangerously alluring.

Curiously, a part of him actually wanted her to stay, though he would never confess that to his companions. Part of him wanted to know this infuriating woman and find out why she seemed so familiar to him. Most unsettling, he found himself drawn to her with no will or desire to counter the attraction.

Nonetheless, the part of him that used pure intellect and self-preservation demanded her immediate removal from this house. Regardless of his wishes, she remained stubbornly uncooperative in spite of all his efforts thus far. He shook his head with exasperation, gazed heavenward, and cursed

45

the fates that placed her here. Timothy entered the room just in time to hear his outburst.

"She's really nice, Captain," he said, coming at once to her defense. "I think it would be kind of nice to have her around for a spell."

He gazed down into Timothy's pleading eyes and smiled at the boy. "You think so, huh?"

Timothy toyed with his fingers as he nodded. "Yes, sir, I do. She even said she would play chess with me. Please, Captain—please don't make her go away."

The captain sighed deeply and closed his eyes. "Timothy, you know why I can't promise you that."

"But if you just explain it to her," he cajoled, "maybe she could help you, just like Miss Amy said. Won't you at least think it over before you do anything else that might make her leave this house?"

"All right. I'll *think* about it." The captain ruffled Timothy's hair and shot one last look at Shaelynn. Just before he disappeared, Timothy sidled up next to her, his eyes filled with obvious curiosity over her actions. His inquisitiveness made him smile.

"What are you doin'?"

A squeaky sounding "*Ahh*" shot past Shae's lips and her hand flew to her heart the moment she heard the unexpected voice.

"I'm sorry. I didn't mean to scare you," Timothy murmured as he cast a brief glance downward.

"It's okay, you, uh, didn't really scare me. I was just a bit startled, that's all." She smiled in an effort to reassure him as she placed the journal entry face down in the scanner and closed the lid. "And to answer your question, I'm scanning this document."

"Oh." He knit his brows in obvious confusion.

Shae grinned as she activated the scan. "That means this machine will make an exact copy of it for me. It's kind of like creating a photograph. Once I make it, I'll use the copy when I do the translation. That way, I won't have to handle and possibly damage the original one while I do my work."

"Is that why you're wearin' those funny-looking gloves?" he asked.

"Yep. The natural oil from my hands can damage documents that are as old and fragile as these are. So in order to protect them, I wear these linen gloves."

"Are you gonna do that with all of them?" he asked.

"Yes, all of them," she replied.

"All of them tonight?" he further pressed.

Shae shook her head slightly and let out a bit of a laugh. "No, I'm afraid it's going to take me some time to get them all done, probably several weeks. Why do you ask?"

Timothy dropped his gaze to the floor and shrugged. "I thought maybe we could play chess before you need to go to sleep again tonight."

A quick glance at her watch told Shae her workday ended long ago. She didn't even stop for lunch, and her stomach lamented that fact. Glancing back at Timothy, she said, "Tell you what, let me finish scanning the rest of the documents in this one little pile right here, get a quick bite to eat, and then I'll meet you upstairs, all right?"

His eyes grew wide with delight. "You got yourself a deal on that, Miss Shaelynn. I'll get everythin' set up right now so we're ready to play as soon as you get there." Without waiting for a reply, he disappeared.

Shae stared after him for just a moment before resuming her work. After finishing the first set of documents in the first box, she placed them in marked folders and locked them safely away. Then she tidied the office before turning off the lights. She hurried into the kitchen, and made herself a peanut butter and jelly sandwich. After taking a glass out of the cupboard, she went over to the fridge. She poured herself some apple juice before bringing her meager fare over to the table.

"You need to eat more than just that, dear," Amy scolded as she materialized in the chair opposite hers. "Why, it's no wonder you're no bigger than a mite."

Shae jumped a bit over the sudden appearance of the woman. She wondered just how long it would take to get used to the abrupt comings and goings of her ghostly companions. After swallowing the bite in her mouth, she shook her head and said, "Oh, you don't need to worry about that. My mother can tell you, when it comes to food, I can eat like a field hand. It's just that tonight, I have a very special date with a handsome young man. So it calls for something quick and easy."

Amy smiled and nodded. "He is patiently waiting for you, I know. Nevertheless, I am sure he wouldn't mind if you got yourself something a little more substantial to eat."

"I'm sure he wouldn't," Shae agreed. "He's a very sweet boy. You know, he told me about his death when we talked, and I just find it so hard to believe anyone would allow a child to get anywhere near combat. He should have been at home, coddled by his mother, not tromping through the mud and being subjected to disease and all the horrors of the battlefield."

"I know," Amy replied with a far away look in her eyes. "But you must understand there were many more just like him. Due to the nature of the war, it became a common sight to see young boys used as drummers and fifes. No one meant for them to participate in the actual battles, yet so many of them did."

"Timothy said he got sick, and that his father

48

carried him here. He said you were a nurse here at the time and you took care of him." Shae wanted nothing more than to take her hand as sorrow suddenly filled Amy's eyes over her comment.

"Indeed I did." She glanced over at Shae and gave her a sorrowful smile. "As I remember, we had a houseful of wounded soldiers to care for when he arrived. Yet, it didn't take any time at all for him to steal our hearts. He so patiently bore all of our administrations and without a single complaint. We tried everything we could think of to save him. Perhaps if he had arrived sooner we might've had a chance, but alas—"

"I'm sure you tried your best," Shae replied. "No one could or would have expected more of you than that." After drinking the last of her juice, she stood up from the table, rinsed her glass, and put it inside the dishwasher. As she dried her hands, she smiled at her companion. "Well, let's not keep our young man waiting, shall we?"

Timothy grinned from ear-to-ear the instant Shae opened the music room door. "Do you want to be red or white this time?" he asked as she walked over and stood next to him at the table.

The anticipation shining in his eyes spoke volumes. He would give her no quarter. She nibbled on her bottom lip to hide away her smile.

"Unless you have a preference, I would like you to go first. So, I'll be red." After his nod of consent, she took her place at the table. The boy moved a pawn forward. She followed suit with one of her own.

During the first half of their game, Shae assessed the skill level of her young opponent. She found he possessed an impressive ability. However, she reminded herself, he'd been practicing for well over a century, which definitely gave him the advantage over her. With that in mind, she began playing the game in earnest. About twenty minutes later, she moved her rook forward, captured his queen, and said, "Checkmate."

Timothy dropped his mouth in shocked surprise. His gaze fell to the board, and then lifted to meet her eyes once more. She scrunched down a little bit in her chair, shrugged, and gave him her most guilty smile. "Sorry."

At that moment, a very handsome Union soldier burst through the wall. He strode straight through the piano, came to a halt in front of the table, and studied the chessboard. The spirit had dark brown hair, dark brown eyes, and wore a neatly trimmed mustache, which touched the end of his jaw. In guessing, she would say they were close to the same age. At least, before he died, anyway.

He glanced at Timothy before he turned his gaze toward her. She couldn't help staring back. He opened his mouth as if to say something, but anything he might have said became lost by the sudden appearance of another ghost. This one bounded in through the closed double doors, startling her even further. She sat straight up in her chair as he approached.

This time her gaze swept over a slightly built Confederate soldier, probably somewhere around nineteen or twenty years of age at the time of his death. The young man had light sandy brown hair and dancing hazel eyes, full of mischief. He raised a taunting brow at Timothy and grinned before sharing the same smile with her. The whole scene unfolded in less than a minute.

"Oh! Well, hello," Shae managed to say between gulps of air. Her wide-eyed gaze flitted back and forth between the two men who now stood very close to where she sat. She took a deep breath in order to still the rapid beating of her heart.

"I'm sorry, Miss Shaelynn, you must forgive my ill manners." The Confederate soldier backed up a step and bowed slightly, with one hand outstretched. "Allow me to introduce myself. My name is Beauregard Thomson, and my elderly, overeager, uncivilized, tongue-tied companion here is Chauncey Dillon."

The Union soldier named Chauncey swatted playfully at the Confederate. "We didn't mean to burst in on you quite like this, Miss Shaelynn. You see, we intended to introduce ourselves one at a time so as not to overwhelm you with our presence all at once. Nevertheless, we just couldn't believe you were the one to say 'checkmate' to our young friend here. We didn't expect it, meaning no insult to your skill, of course."

Just how many spirits lived in this house, anyway? Shae wondered over the accuracy of the psychics. She still needed to meet the captain, obviously, for neither of these men wore the bars of a captain on his uniform. One could also assume that the captain wouldn't bother to comment on their chess game either. Unless of course, he wanted to send the pieces flying across the room or out the window.

"That's all right. I'm very happy you both—um, popped in. Is there anyone else I need to meet? Because if there is, we might just as well get it over with now," she said. Despite her playful manner, she hoped she could finally know the exact number of spirits residing in this house. She readied herself for the revelation. Their gazes dropped somewhat, and they appeared a bit nervous over her blithe comment. Understanding dawned on her then. Oh yes, the captain. His presence remained elusive.

Chauncey flashed her a bit of smile, shot a brief glance at Beau, and said, "No, it's ah, there's only the six of us dwelling here at present, and I believe you are aware of each of us now."

"Well, that's good to know." Feeling a little

awkward over the seemingly forbidden subject of the captain, she looked down and began placing the chess pieces back onto the board. "Let's get on with the next game, shall we?"

They played several more games as the evening wore on, and as luck would have it, she never lost. The look of determination on Timothy's face each time she said "checkmate" made her smile. Without realizing it at the time, she succeeded in giving him a new goal as he faithfully awaited his mother's arrival. She could feel his determination to win grow stronger each time he set up the chessboard, a thing he could do with both precision and speed. She shook her head over the ability.

The incredible skills spirits possessed continued to amaze her. She would never guess they could do the things they did without benefit of a physical body. How did they move things? How did they speak so clearly and with inflection and tone? How could they move their bodies as if they still lived and breathed when their spirits contained no weight or physical mass?

The most puzzling thing came in their ability to convey emotion. Their expression of feelings didn't just come from the expression on their faces. One could also feel their emotions as well.

She asked Aulric how he managed such feats. His answer took him a while to formulate, since he never stopped to consider it before. However, he told her that spiritual entities accomplished such tasks by using the ever-present forces that continually surround all of us. Then he said that one needed to combine those forces, using a great deal of patience and practice.

Later that night as she crawled into bed, her thoughts once again centered on the captain. Just who was he? What made him so angry and hostile toward the living? The other spirits thought highly of him. Timothy adored him, and he spoke affectionately of the way the man helped him through his death. Someone who did something like that couldn't be all that bad, could he? Amy even hinted he had just cause for treating the living the way he did. She just wished however unlikely, someone would come forward and explain his reasoning to her. Perhaps she could help him overcome his loathing. She found herself wishing she could just talk to the man face to face, and wondered how long it would take to get the opportunity.

The restless thoughts kept her awake far longer than she desired. In desperation for sleep, she slid out of bed and made her way outside. Perhaps a bit of fresh air might sweep away the clutter in her mind. Shae strolled along the path leading to the pond. The water splashing down from the fountain twinkled underneath the myriad celestial bodies in the evening sky. She sat down on the ledge, gazed down at the shimmering refection, and ran her hand through the water. She closed her eyes and took a deep breath. Before she could release it, she could suddenly feel the captain's presence.

At least, she thought the presence belonged to the captain. The intense cold that pervaded her surroundings made her shiver, and the darkness of night made the feeling even more ominous. She would not allow him to see her fear.

"Captain," she whispered as she glanced all around her. "Are you here?"

She waited for what seemed an eternity for a response. He did not answer. Even so, she could still feel his presence. "I have not come to this house to intrude upon your privacy or cause you any degree of pain or concern. Surely there is no harm in our coexisting under the same roof for a short time while I do my work, is there?"

Again, she waited, and again received no

response. She rubbed her arms to ward off the cold and sought for a way to reach this spirit. "Why can't you just show yourself? Talk to me. You might just find out I'm not such a bad person after all."

The chill dissipated somewhat and in the instant, she could feel the spirit waver in indecision. Her mind raced for something to say to press her advantage. "Perhaps I could even help you resolve the feelings of anger you have over the way you met your death, if that's what—"

Shae stopped short. The rage returned, and it returned with an intensity she'd not experienced until now. She gasped for breath. The water surging from the fountain froze solid the instant she uttered the poorly chosen words, as did the water in the pool.

The freakish sight made her shudder. She said the wrong thing. The knowledge filled her with instant regret and more than a little bit of fear. Yet, she found it much too late to apologize. For in the mere blink of an eye, the presence of the captain disappeared.

Chapter 6

"When are you going to stop all this foolishness?" asked Amy, and none too kindly at that.

"What?" The captain turned away from the music room window and with one eyebrow raised in question, met her gaze.

"Don't 'what' me, sir." Amy put her hands on her hips, furrowed her brow, and leaned even closer. "You know very well what I'm talking about. During these past several weeks, Shaelynn has made every effort to appease you, and you've yet to say so much as one civil word to her. You refuse to join in any of our conversations, even when you're in the room.

"She has gone out of her way to make our lives a little more pleasant. Just look at that huge television and that movie player—thingamajig. You've enjoyed your fair share of the movies she has supplied us with, and you can't tell me you haven't enjoyed watching them during the wee hours of the morning. She has even supplied additional board games to break up the monotony for Timothy. You have seen for yourself the pleasure those games have given him. She didn't do any of those things for herself. I guarantee it. She did them for us. Yet, never once have you offered so much as a 'thank you' in return."

"I didn't ask her to do any of those things for me or anyone else in this house." The captain crossed his arms and scowled. He didn't need Amy's stern lecture to remind him of his actions. Guilt washed over him each time Shaelynn extended a hand in friendship and he repelled the offer. And each time,

55

the task became ever more difficult to perform. One of these days, without question, he would lose—

"You didn't have to ask her. She does them because she has a good heart, and is a kind and caring woman. Surely, you must know this by now. She is offering you her friendship, and each time you refuse it."

"And how long do you think she'll remain my friend once she finds the official account of the events leading to my death? Do you think she will still want to remain all friendly and cozy with me then?" he shot back.

At once Amy's face softened, as did her voice. "Explain it to her, Captain. Explain it to her *before* she reads it, and this time, without the unnecessary displays of anger. I think you just might find she's a very understanding woman, if you just give her the chance."

"I don't know, Amy," he said. "What possible good could it do anyway?"

"You might be surprised. Would you at least *think* about it?" She disappeared from the room, without waiting around for his reply. Not that he had one to offer.

He blew out a sigh. Amy wanted him to think about it. Would it surprise her to know how little he did anything else? What would she think if she knew he thought of Shaelynn in ways a spirit had no business thinking about a mortal woman? The display to which she referred had nothing to do with anger and everything to do with mounting frustration. At that moment, an overwhelming need for solitude consumed him. He left Starling then and headed toward the place he could find it.

****

The chime of the doorbell sounded just as Shae secured the lid on the third box of documents, now completely scanned. She set them aside with a sense of satisfaction. Only one box remained, untouched. She glanced out the window and caught sight of the delivery van just as it backed up and then turned toward the main road. Once the vehicle disappeared down the drive, the front door opened and then after a brief moment, it closed again. Seconds later, Horace entered her office carrying a large padded envelope.

"For you, Miss Shaelynn," he said.

"Thanks, Horace. Whatever would I do without you?" she asked, flashing him a smile.

"With any amount of luck, you won't have to find out," he replied in his usual stoic manner. Then with a bob of his head, he disappeared.

Her eyes lit up in anticipation as she glanced down at the return address. Her mother told her to be on the lookout for this package. The wonderful woman had sent some updated family photos, and now at last, she held them in her hands.

Once she had the pictures out of the package, she spread them out atop the desk and drank them all in. The faces smiling back at her made her realize just how much she missed them. Her mounting desire to display them in the drawing room today, rather than wait for her next shopping trip, compelled her to look for suitable frames in the basement. Surely, she could find some antique picture frames down there. Moments later, she descended the darkened stairway for the first time. Just as she entered through the small doorway, a lightbulb with a long thick cord popped into view. She extended a hand upward and with a bit of trepidation, gave the frayed cord a tug. Despite the dimness of the bulb, she could see a treasure trove of antiques collecting dust.

The baby carriage in the center of the room captured her immediate attention, and she made her way toward it. She wanted a closer look and found the elegant craftsmanship of the old-style buggy amazing. A hand-carved wooden cradle sat next to it. She gave the cradle a gentle shove and gazed at it for a moment as it rocked back and forth. Did the little bed once belong to Louisa Starling? The thought made her smile. Once it eased to a halt, her gaze meandered around the room. Various tables, chairs, bureaus, and beds crowded the limited space. The chaos led her to believe those assigned to store the items, did so in fearful haste. Did the captain chase them about the house as they sought to fulfill their duties? She wouldn't put it past him.

A large bureau with a small oblong mirror attached to the top, sat in the far corner. She picked her way through the furniture in order to reach it. Once she stood in front of the piece, she opened each of the drawers. The strong scent of cedar wood filled the air as she did so. Bonnets, shawls, and baby clothes sat neatly folded inside the topmost drawers. An assortment of beautiful handmade quilts and blankets rested inside the bottom two. She found the items interesting, but they were not what she sought.

Shae turned around and looked for the most likely place one would store unused frames. A sideboard sat to the right of the bureau. Perhaps she might find something there. After careful inspection, she found the cabinets filled with a mismatched variety of crockery and little else. She let loose a sigh of disappointment.

Finally, she spied an old maple secretary with a double arched cupboard atop the desk table, and three drawers underneath. She made her way over to the piece and opened the elegant doors. The top shelves were empty, but as she tugged on the single drawer just below the second ledge, she could see a mixture of old photographs in almost every shape and size. Some of them were in a terrible state of decay. She shook her head over the neglect as she began going through them, one at a time.

Photographs from the very first daguerreotypes through the technology of the early twentieth century had accumulated inside this drawer. Some of the unnatural, rigid poses of the subjects gave her a laugh. The drawer contained pictures of infants, children, families, and couples. Mixed in the stack, she also found pictures of the dead. Lifeless bodies laid out on beds, propped up in chairs, and a few, inside their rough-sawn coffins. A gruesome custom at best. She shuddered and slid them off to the side. And then, just before she returned the entire stack to the drawer, one photo in particular seized her attention. The picture portrayed a Civil War captain, many years past his prime.

She picked it up for closer inspection. The stern face in the black-and-white photograph stared back at her. Streaks of gray weaved through the length of his long beard, just as it did through what little hair nature left him. She did not detect even a trace of warmth in his light-colored eyes. In a quest to find his identity, she turned the picture over. To her disappointment, she found nothing written on the back. She turned it around once more, and studied the austere face of the Union captain.

The longer she stared, the more convinced she became that the harsh face belonged to the captain haunting Starling. Surely, the man must have lived here at one time. The notion that he would not want to leave his home after his death made perfect sense. He most assuredly would not want outsiders invading it, either. The only question remaining, was why? Amy said he had just cause for treating the living the way he did.

What thing, real or imagined, made him feel that way? The man served on the side of the North, even though Tennessee was a Confederate state. Did his neighbors abhor him or make his life miserable because of that choice? Would they have somehow been responsible for his death? Of course, the most important question remained: could she ever break through the wall of his mistrust and find out?

****

Later that afternoon, the captain returned to Starling from his quiet place in the forest. He stood just outside the drawing room and took a moment to observe their gathering. Chauncey and Beau rose from their seats to stand behind Shaelynn. They all smiled down at a new set of portraits, which now graced the top shelves of the desk. Their various comments told him they looked at photographs of Shaelynn's family. He remained just at the entrance to listen in on their conversation.

"Do you mind if I ask you a personal question in return?" asked Chauncey as he gave Shaelynn a sideways glance.

Shaelynn asked him a *personal* question?

She turned to face Chauncey and gave him a smile. He had to quash the feeling of jealousy that smile prompted.

"You want to know about my single status as well," she stated, clearly amused.

"Yes, well—you asked us about ours, and it's just that I should think— What I mean to say is, well, I couldn't help wondering why such a lovely woman wouldn't have someone who—" Chauncey stopped and shrugged, not daring to go any further. He didn't blame him there.

"Well, it's like in all the fairy tales," she answered, giving him an impish smile. "You know, with evil witches casting their wicked spells upon the virtuous, fairy godmothers breaking them with good spells of their own. That sort of thing."

"Excuse me? I don't think I quite understand what you mean by that." Chauncey shook his head and knit his brow as he awaited her explanation. The captain found himself waiting as well.

"Sorry. It's just a little theory my sister Nicki and I have concocted. Of course, you must understand I've had more practice with the theory, than what she has. She is, after all, just twenty-four. But you see it's like this. The princess has to kiss the toad to get the prince. Unfortunately for us, all of our toads have been—well, just plain old toads." She laughed as she gazed into their still-confused faces.

Timothy chose that moment to interrupt them. The boy spared him nothing more than a sideways glance as he made his way to Shaelynn's side. He looked a little perplexed as he took in each of their expressions, but he simply said, "I thought you said we could watch the next *Lord of the Rings* movie today."

"Yes, I did. And I know you've patiently waited for me this whole week." She looked down at her watch, and then gave Timothy a conspiratorial smile. "You know what? I think we just might have time to finish them both, if we hurry. I'll race you upstairs!"

At that moment, she turned and ran as fast as she could toward the stairway, chasing the sound of Timothy's laughter. The captain stepped to the side before she ran straight through him.

He waited until they gathered upstairs before he made his way over to the desk. Shaelynn had arranged photographs of her parents, her twin sisters with their families, and one of her younger sister on the tiered shelves.

He gazed in depth at each of the portraits. He found all of the Montgomery women very lovely. But none of them even came close to matching Shaelynn in beauty. And her comment about the toads somehow pleased him, though he really couldn't say why it should. What possible difference could such a statement make to him, anyway?

Nevertheless, he spent the rest of the day pondering Amy's advice. If he reached out to Shaelynn, would she accept his offer of friendship? Better yet, would she believe him if he confided in her, despite what she might read later? A glimmer of hope took root inside his soul, but fear of disappointment kept it from sprouting. He closed his eyes and conjured a sigh. For the first time since his death, time had become his enemy. He needed to make a decision very soon, before the opportunity to choose escaped him altogether.

Chapter 7

The menacing black mist swirled ever higher, gathering upward around her body as Fenrir ambled toward her. His maniacal laughter sent terrified shivers through her body. Shae looked over at the woman in the light-blue dress. She witnessed her despair as she fell to her knees. Her trembling hands covered her face as she wept bitterly over the loss of Odin. Somehow, she had to help her.

Shae needed to act quickly if she wanted to take hold of Fenrir's jaws before he consumed her. Yet, before she could proceed with her plans, Fenrir took hold of his hated magic chain and seized her with it. At once, he began wrapping the tethers around her body. She struggled against the shackles with all of the might and strength she possessed. Shae found that no matter how hard she tried, she simply couldn't budge. The effort left her feeling weak and defeated. She cried out in the darkness of her dank prison.

****

Hearing her whimpers, the captain hurried through the French doors of Shaelynn's bedroom. On three different occasions now, he had heard these same pitiful cries. The first time he heard them, he wandered through the garden seeking solitude in the stillness of the night. Perhaps because of the stillness, he was aware of her restless sleep. Then without warning, she cried out in breathless anguish, and the cries cut deep into his soul.

The instant she cried out in terror, he rushed through the door and to the side of her bed. Just as before, she tossed her head from side to side as if seeking escape from something infinitely horrible. But this time, tears coursed down her cheeks, and she muttered something difficult for him to understand. He sat down on the edge of her bed, and drew close to her lips in an effort to make sense of her words.

"Nei! Du kan ikke gjøre dette... Du kan ikke gjøre dette, nei..." she murmured piteously.

The captain knit his brow in confusion. She spoke Norwegian. *No. You cannot do this,* she repeatedly cried. What terror held her bound as she slept, and what did it have to do with his culture? Just as before, he covered her hand with his own, giving her a measure of his strength and comfort.

"Let it go, Shaelynn. Wherever you are right now, you don't have to stay. You have the power to turn away and leave it behind. All you have to do is walk toward the sound of my voice," he whispered with a tenderness he had never shown her during her waking hours.

He waited as she stirred in response to his words. Her body grew less rigid, and her breathing slowed to a more even pace. That meant she followed his voice away from the horror of her dreams.

"I'm here and I won't leave you, you're safe now. Come with me and together we'll find a place of peace and contentment." He brushed her tangled hair away from her face. "Can you see it? We're almost there."

Shaelynn took a deep breath, and let go of her panic. She smiled then, in her sleep. He stared down in fascination as a small dimple appeared at the corner of her mouth. How could he have missed such a delightful feature? How, indeed. He'd never once given her cause to smile in his presence. Perhaps he ought to rectify that.

His hand traveled of its own accord to her cheek,

and he lightly brushed against her flawless skin with the back of his fingers. At once, he shook off the weakness and backed away from the bed. He would not permit himself to grow attached to this beautiful woman, no matter how much he might desire otherwise.

"I wish things could have been different between us, Shaelynn Montgomery, truly I do," he whispered. After one last lingering gaze, he turned away and left her room.

"Is she all right, Captain?" asked Amy as she met him there in the hallway near Shaelynn's bedroom door.

"She appears to be resting quietly, at least for now," he replied. "I don't suppose she has ever shared these nightmares with you and told you what they are about?"

Amy shook her head. "No, she hasn't, and I don't think it wise to ask her about them, either. I'm sure if she wanted us to know, she would tell us."

"Well, if she's going to confide in anyone, I'm sure the person will be you," he replied.

"Why would you go and say something like that?" Amy raised a brow as she awaited his reply.

"Because you are and always have been a woman who genuinely cares about people. You are kind, nurturing, and have a way of drawing such things out of a person without them even realizing it. Look what you got out of me." He tossed her a grin and a wink that bespoke his affection. "That's probably why you're still here. Somehow you feel it's your God-given duty to look after each of us who have chosen to remain behind."

Amy feigned indifference over his observations. "What lies beyond the light isn't going anywhere, and you needn't worry. I'll get there soon enough. Besides, look who's talking to whom about caring. For someone who wants the girl gone so badly, you sure come to her rescue often enough."

The captain muttered a reply and disappeared into his attic room without saying another word. All the while, he could hear the sounds of Amy's soft laughter.

****

Shae awakened early, to the now familiar sound of the captain's restless pacing on the floor above her. At least, she believed the footsteps belonged to the captain. Several nights ago, she gathered the courage to follow the sound. The steps led her to the third floor stairway. She looked up then and spied the door that Norman Lamont advised her not to touch. If not for the unbearable cold, which suddenly enveloped her body, she might have walked up the last set of steps. She would have knocked on his door and had it out with the spirit, face to face.

Did he endlessly pace in an ongoing effort to drive her out of the house, or did it stem from a deeper, more personal matter? The question needed answering, but she didn't have the time to ponder it today. Everyone counted on her to keep to the schedule to avoid any delay of the exhibit's grand opening. With a sigh of resignation, she climbed out of bed and dressed for the day, choosing her favorite blue jeans and an old college baseball jersey.

The morning sped by, and as she placed the last of the copied documents on the table, she stepped back and gazed at her handiwork in satisfaction. After locking the originals inside the cabinets, she picked up the phone and placed a call to Reuben. He answered right away.

"Hey Reuben, this is Shae." She picked up her pen and pad, and began scribbling a series of clouds in the corner of the page. "I wanted to let you know I'm finished with the digital scans of the first set of documents you gave me, and I am ready for the next."

"I'm impressed," he replied. "Well, let me take a look at my calendar here. Hmm. Let's see, my schedule is rather full for the rest of this week and the first of next. George and Perry are out of town on an errand until next week as well. So—"

"There's no hurry," Shae cut in. "I can start the translations with the copies I've already made easily enough, and you can deliver the next set of documents at your leisure."

"That's fine. Let's tentatively schedule the exchange for next Thursday, then. Probably early to late afternoon, if that's convenient for you," he said.

"No problem," she replied. "I'll be here." Just as she hung up the phone, Amy appeared in the doorway.

"Shaelynn, you missed your breakfast, dear. I am not about to let you miss your lunch as well," she scolded. "Those papers can wait. Now come along with me, and let's find you something to eat before you faint dead away."

Turning toward the sound of Amy's amused laughter over her choice of words, Shae grinned. She tossed her pen on the desk and stood up. "I suppose you're right. I am kind of hungry," she said as she followed her into the kitchen.

"I thought you might be." Amy smiled and gestured toward the table.

A bowl of fruit and a ham sandwich awaited her. Shae shook her head as she sat down and scooted her chair toward the table. "You are a marvel, Amy, do you know that? I can't begin to tell you how much I appreciate everything you do for me."

"Well, I'm happy you think so," she said as she sat in the chair just opposite her. "It's nice to be appreciated."

While Shae ate the lunch Amy prepared, she toyed with the idea of asking about the Union captain in the photograph. Yet, she didn't quite know how to tactfully broach the subject or get the answers to the questions she sought. She chewed on her lip in indecision and then finally said, "Amy, when did you come here? In the capacity of a nurse, I mean."

"Well, let's see." Amy looked heavenward as if trying to recall. "I think in February or early March of 1863. Why do you ask?"

"Curiosity, I suppose," she said as she picked up her glass of water and took a sip. "Did any members of the Starling family live here at that time?"

"Oh, no." Amy shook her head. "That's why the army surgeons chose this house in the first place. You see, the Starlings didn't want to be in the middle of a war zone. The danger did exist for the army to burn the house to the ground. So many homes around these parts were, you know. Anyway, Mr. Starling packed up his family and moved them north to wait it out. If memory serves, Mrs. Starling had family in Ohio—a brother, I think."

"Ohio," Shae repeated. "Did the Starlings fight on the side of the Union or the Confederacy then?"

"Like most families, they had kin who fought on both sides of the war," Amy replied. "More often than not, brother fought against brother, father against son. It all came down to ideology, and at the time, each person followed the tenets of his own conscious. Sometimes those ideologies tore families apart."

"Did the opposing views cause a rift in the Starling family?" she asked.

Amy shrugged as she clasped her hands together. "I don't really know. Information passed by way of gossip, mostly. I tried not to listen to such things."

"Well, did any of the family members ever come back after the war to claim their house?" she pressed.

"Jerome Starling, one of the sons, made a very brief visit," Amy said. "He came to assess the house and check for damage. When he found the house intact, he put it up for sale on behalf of the family. No one wanted to buy the property at that time, though. No one would even come close to this place unless sickness demanded it. So Jerome said he would let it serve as a hospital."

"I think Norman Lamont mentioned something like that." Shae wiped the corners of her mouth with her napkin. "Did any of the neighbors harbor any ill will toward the Starling family?"

"None that I was aware of," Amy said. "From all reports, they were a decent enough family."

The conversation drifted away from the Starlings as Shae finished up her lunch. Amy continued to reminisce about a variety of things as Amy helped tidy the kitchen and then followed Shae down the hall toward the office. The last of her narrative fell by the wayside as an icy blast of air catapulted straight through her body. Shae sucked in a breath and rubbed her arms against the sudden chill. Her brows lifted as she sought an explanation to the incident but just as she reached her office doors, confusion gave way to anger.

Her mouth dropped as her gaze darted about the scattered mess inside the room. Every document she labored over this morning lay in fragmented ruins atop the table, desk, and floor. Her furious gaze shot past Amy and with grim determination, focused on the stairway.

Amy extended a hand outward. "Shaelynn, please, you must understand that—"

"Of all the mean-spirited, hateful— Ooh! I have just about had it with the underhanded cowardice of that bad-tempered, cantankerous old man!" In her anger, Shae turned and stomped out of the office. Yet, just before she reached the stairway, Amy appeared in front of her, blocking her path. The woman never before looked so fierce. She didn't care.

"Get out of my way, Amy," she said between clenched teeth.

"The captain may be many things, Miss Montgomery," she hissed back. "But a coward certainly isn't one of them. You have the right to be angry after what he did to your office, but take great care in what you say to him. If you should think to heap your vile accusations upon him, you will find you are no longer welcome in this house—by any of us."

One by one, the other spirits of Starling appeared on the stairway as Amy said her piece. Shae looked into each of their stern faces. They all mirrored Amy's feelings, especially Timothy. Nevertheless, she met their stares with stark defiance. She made her way past them and went up the stairs, determined to have her say.

By the time she reached the captain's third floor room, she'd managed to calm down just enough to keep her temper under tight control. She hammered on his door, not really expecting an answer and not receiving one.

She folded her arms against her chest and rocked back on her heels. "It suddenly occurred to me, *Captain*, that in your own unique way, you just welcomed me into this house. Finally! And I couldn't be *happier* about that. After all, several weeks' worth of work just went into the garbage can. I can only assume that means having me around for a year, is simply not long enough to please you. Now we can extend my stay by at least that long while I start the laborious process over. Should you decide you want me here even longer than that, you needn't have a tantrum and destroy my things. Just let me know, and I will see what I can work out with Norman. I am sure he would be *delighted* to let me stay here for as long as I wish to stay." She huffed out an exasperated breath.

Without waiting for a response, she stomped down the stairway, into the foyer and out the door, making sure she slammed it just as hard as she could. She needed to get away from Starling and think. Once she stood in front of the carriage house, she opened the massive doors and entered while fumbling around inside her pocket for the keys to the jeep. She plopped into the seat, turned the engine over, and slammed the gearshift into reverse. After turning around, she dropped into first gear. She sent the jeep skidding down the driveway and onto the main road, leaving a trail of dust behind her.

Minutes later, she found herself driving aimlessly through the peaceful little community. The faster and farther she drove, the better she felt. At least, the intensity of her anger subsided, somewhat. After exhaling a very deep sigh, she allowed her thoughts to center on the captain. Other than the first few instances right after her arrival, he ignored her presence altogether. He kept to himself during the social gatherings she had with the other spirits and chose not to interfere. In fact, the doddering old war-horse never once threatened or personally harmed her in any way. So, what set him off today and why attack her documents, of all the irrational things?

Although his display upset her, it truly wasn't that big of a deal. She saved all of the scanned images to her computer, and she could reprint them easily enough. The task wouldn't take that much time. But *he* didn't know that.

In the midst of her thoughts, she caught sight of an impressive-looking belfry, rising above the trees in the distance. Something about that spire compelled her to take a closer look. She searched for a road that would take her to it, but couldn't find one. In exasperation, she pulled over to the side and opened the glove compartment. She extracted the handful of maps Norman gave her. Several minutes into her search, she found the one she sought.

If she read the map correctly, the belfry belonged to the Adaria First Presbyterian Church, built in 1832. Norman's notes stated that due to a tragedy, which transpired inside the edifice, the parishioners abandoned the structure in the year 1863. That piqued her interest even more. However, the map didn't indicate so much as a dirt road that would actually take her there.

As she relentlessly continued her quest, she drove down the street nearest the church. She spied a path that looked as if it might possibly lead to the building. Once she parked the jeep alongside the road just above the trail, she got out of the vehicle, and followed it.

About five minutes later, her heart dropped a beat and then thumped wildly in her chest as if she'd run a marathon. An irrational fear followed. A moment later, understanding dawned. Every tree, every shrub, every turn, told her that she followed the path of her nightmare. If she had any sense at all, she would turn around and go back the way she came.

But something beyond her ability to control, drew her ever nearer. Just up ahead she could see the path veering off to the right. When she made that turn she would see the side of the church. She held her breath as she approached the curve, forged ahead, and made the turn. The building loomed before her, just as she expected it would. And it looked almost as creepy in the daylight as it did in the moonlight of her dreams. Almost.

Three arched, dark, and foreboding windows aligned the center of the building. The middle window yawned larger, broader, and taller than the other two. The belfry followed the same arched design on all four sides and towered over the roofline. She could see the chimney rising up the back of the church. If someone asked, she could describe in detail, what the fireplace looked like inside.

"Hello there."

Shae gasped in fright as she turned toward the unexpected greeting. The voice belonged to a tall, thin elderly man who despite a pleasant smile, gazed at her with obvious curiosity. He shifted his weight, using his cane for support.

"Oh, uh—hello," she stammered in reply.

"I'm sorry. I didn't mean to startle you, miss, missus, or is it just plain miz?" He raised a friendly brow in question.

Shae waved a hand in dismissal while placing the other over her heart. "That's quite all right, it's just that I didn't expect to see anyone, I—" She shook her head then as if to clear it. She extended her right hand toward him. "My name is Shae Montgomery. You don't have to worry about the 'miz' thing. I never use it."

"I thought so. You are the brave young lady staying at the Starling. My name is Isaac Henry, and I am pleased to make your acquaintance." He took her hand in his and warmly shook it.

"And I am pleased to make yours, Mr. Henry," she replied, returning his friendly smile. "Do you live around here?"

"Oh, like you, we don't stand much on formality in these parts. So it's just Isaac, if you please. And to answer your question, yes I do." He pointed southeast of the church and said, "I'm not all that hard to find. My home is about a quarter mile in that direction. Should you ever find you need me, you'll find my door is always open."

"Thank you, that's very kind. Who knows, I just might have to take you up on that offer some time. So tell me, Isaac, do you come this way often?" she asked as her eyes darted toward the church and then back to him.

He chuckled softly, more as if to himself than sharing his laughter with her. "Ah. I take it you have already discovered the tragic tale of this place."

Shae shrugged as she tucked her hands into her pockets. "No, not really. Only that 'a tragedy of sorts' took place here, and the parishioners abandoned it shortly thereafter."

"I suppose that could sum it up." His gaze swept over the church, taking in every detail of the deteriorating structure.

From the man's demeanor, she could tell he had full knowledge of the church's history. To understand her recurring nightmare, she needed to know that history. She asked, "Would you mind sharing the details of it with me? I would really like to hear the story."

"Well, the 'tragedy' took place after the battle of Chickamauga in October of the year 1863. Those in charge of the Union army tried to have the story quashed, or so they say. In fact relatively few people had possession of all the details," he began.

"Anyway, I don't know how well you know the history of the battle which took place there, but the Southern Army triumphed over the North. The defeat resulted in over sixteen thousand Union casualties alone. That loss occurred in part, because someone informed Major General William Rosecrans that he had a gap in his line. Upon hearing the news, he began moving some of his units to close the supposed gap. In so doing, he actually created a hole that the Confederates, under Lieutenant General James Longstreet, promptly—perhaps even knowingly—used to their benefit. They successfully drove one-third of the Union army, including Rosecrans himself, off the field that day. Subsequently, the Union commanders launched an investigation to find the source of the false information delivered to Rosecrans.

"They gave a man by the name of Major Nils Adlundsen, charge over this investigation. The official report says that during the investigation he came to realize the traitorous information came from none other than his best friend, Captain Tristan Jordahl. According to the major, Captain Jordahl provided the Confederates with sensitive information and the like for well over a year. Also according to Adlundsen's sources, the South paid Jordahl quite handsomely for the betrayal to his country, or so it would seem."

"Oh, I think that's terrible," Shae hissed. The names of the two men were definitely Norwegian. Could they be part of the Wisconsin Fifteenth? Truly, she hoped not.

"Indeed," Isaac agreed. "The story goes on to say that because of their lifelong friendship, Nils thought to bring Captain Jordahl to this church and have him quietly arrested. Nils did not want to apprehend the captain in full view of his men. However, according to the report, once the two of them were inside the chapel, Jordahl resisted his arrest. Subsequently, a fierce fight broke out between the major and the captain. During the ensuing scuffle, they struck mortal blows. One of them died right here at this church. They sent the other man to Starling where he died a few days later.

"Of course, shortly thereafter, when the preacher tried to assemble his congregation for a normal Sunday sermon, it became obvious the entity or entities were not at rest. There are those who would tell you they have personally witnessed horrible sights and sounds coming from inside this chapel. And still do, to this very day. Many of the locals can attest to that fact.

"Over the years following the incident, the preachers and ministers tried everything they could think of to clear this place of the evil that invaded it. Yet, no amount of preaching, prayers, or even the sacred chants from a respected Indian shaman could exorcize the spirit or spirits that claimed this place. So, they simply abandoned the church and left it to time and the elements. What you see now is all that's left of that little known piece of history."

Shae only half-heard the last part of Isaac's story. The fact that one of the officers engaged in a life and death struggle here at this church and then met his death at Starling Plantation consumed her attention. Only one question remained unanswered, and nothing else mattered but the reply.

"Do you know which man they brought to Starling?" she whispered as she lifted a hand to her throat.

The intensity of Isaac's gaze made her most uncomfortable. "I can only go by what I have been told. However, you must also understand that while I heard this story in my youth, I heard it from the mouth of my own grandfather. He told me the story once, but he was very specific in the details he gave me. My grandfather said on that fateful morning, they transported Captain Tristan Jordahl to the plantation hospital."

Chapter 8

A thousand questions swirled around inside Shae's head. Could the captain residing at Starling possibly be the infamous Tristan Jordahl and not a member of the Starling family as she first supposed? Did he haunt the plantation because he betrayed his country and killed his best friend? If so, then why did all of the other spirits, including a Union soldier, like him so well? Wouldn't they abhor him, not defend him, if he were in fact Captain Jordahl?

Would her recurring nightmare have something to do with these two men and that terrible event? She could see definite similarities between the two stories. One didn't have to stretch the imagination to see Major Adlundsen in the role of Odin and the traitorous Captain Jordahl as Fenrir.

But wait. That didn't make any sense either. Isaac said the church itself housed the evil entity, and her dream confirmed as much. If the entity haunting this church was in fact Tristan Jordahl, then he wouldn't roam around at Starling. He would reside here at the church, wouldn't he? Perhaps the captain living at the plantation wasn't the man in the photograph, after all.

Still, she couldn't shake the nagging doubt deep inside with reason alone. Something just didn't feel right about this whole situation. She needed more answers and determination compelled her to find them.

"Shae, are you all right?" Isaac placed a gentle hand on her shoulder. His gaze, filled with kindness, probed into hers.

"Yes, I'm fine, really, I am," she murmured.

"How are you...getting along at Starling?" He raised a brow in question.

Shae managed a shaky laugh and dipped her head. "Actually, I am doing quite well, considering. A lot better than what I first expected, anyway."

Isaac nodded as he brushed a hand against his mouth. "Well, from the look on your face, I thought somewhere along the way, you might have encountered one of the men in the story I just told you."

"For a moment, I thought maybe I had. But logic would say that since Captain Jordahl died at Starling, his ghost should dwell there, and not here where the evil resides." She rubbed her arms against the icy chill that suddenly enveloped her and for a brief moment, she allowed her gaze to wander toward the church.

Isaac smiled then. He made her feel like the star pupil sent to the head of the class for her astute observations.

His gaze penetrated. "Puzzling, isn't it?"

While she mulled the unexpected comment over in her mind, Isaac glanced at his watch and then abruptly excused himself. He cited an appointment he needed to keep. Once Isaac disappeared into the thick foliage, Shae turned toward the church and took a halting half-step forward. Suddenly, a stale, smothering heaviness permeated the air around her. A putrid stench followed. Her heart hammered a slow even beat as she gazed at the all-too-familiar door, which looked identical to the one in her nightmare.

Evil did dwell inside that church. She could feel it all the way out here. Nevertheless, somewhere deep down inside she possessed an overwhelming need to enter the building and explore it. At the same time, stark terror over the thought of doing such an insane thing prevented her from carrying out that need. Self-preservation kicked in, and she inched her way backward. She turned toward the path and the safety of her jeep.

Once inside her vehicle, Shae sat behind the wheel in indecision. She needed some answers. Beyond measure, it shocked her to discover the very church haunting her dreams actually existed. And, the edifice existed right here in Tennessee of all the unexpected places. Then to learn what transpired between Adlundsen and Jordahl, which in many ways paralleled the tale of Odin and Fenrir, stretched the limits of her imagination. What did their story have to do with her, anyway? She held no power to alter past events. Despite the conviction, she placed a call to Norman Lamont. Perhaps he could shed some light on this mess. He answered his phone right away. She could hear the apprehension in his tone.

"Hello, Shae. Are you all right?"

"Yes, I'm fine, really. I'm sorry. I didn't mean for this call to alarm you. I just need, well—I want to ask you, is there a record of the deaths that occurred at Starling while it served as a hospital?" The lengthy silence on the other end of the phone gave her pause. "Norman, are you still there?"

"Yes, I'm sorry. To answer your question, there is such a record. The book is a journal of sorts, if I recall properly. However, I am not sure how complete it is. A great deal of time has passed since I last studied it. Nevertheless, I could make a copy of the pages that do exist and bring them out to you sometime next week. Would that be satisfactory?"

"Actually, if it's not too much trouble, could you just fax them to me as soon as you can? I really need them right now, and I'm sure faxing the ledger would be much easier than having you drive all the way out here," she replied.

"You are right, of course. I'll try to get them out to you sometime today or early tomorrow, then." A moment passed. Norman cleared his throat and said, "Shae, I hope this request doesn't mean you are encountering problems too difficult to endure."

"Not at all," she replied in an even tone meant to nullify his fears. "I'm simply hoping the record will provide me with a bit of understanding, that's all."

"You would tell me, wouldn't you, if things get too...unpleasant, shall we say?" he asked.

"I would, but you needn't worry. Everything is fine, really."

After ending her conversation with Norman, Shae turned the jeep toward the military park in Chickamauga. For whatever reason, she just needed to see the place and feel it for herself. By the time she arrived, very few visitors remained at the park. She didn't mind. Having the battlefield empty of tourists gave her the opportunity to explore the trails and see the monuments with nothing more than her own thoughts for company.

As she traversed the grassy, wooded battlefields, now peaceful and serene, she tried to imagine the thousands of men who fought and died here during that terrible struggle in September of 1863.

She pondered the blunder made by Rosecrans that cost a Union victory and wondered how many men died because of misinformation. Misinformation supplied by Captain Tristan Jordahl, a greedy man who betrayed his country in order to line his pockets. Did the men under his command ever suspect him of that betrayal? Did they respect him? Were they loyal and quick to respond to his every command, regardless of the danger he put them in? How many deaths could one lay directly at his feet?

Shivering against a sudden cold breeze that enveloped her, Shae looked around her environment. The sun had already dipped below the horizon.

Along with the setting, the serene, peaceful feeling that kept her company evaporated. In place of the calm, an ethereal shroud of mist sprang up, looming over the battlefield. Having no desire to encounter the ghosts of the past, she turned toward the parking lot.

During the drive to Starling, the unanswered questions plagued her mind. Yet, each one of them returned to the same one. Were the captain who resided at Starling and Tristan Jordahl one in the same? Would or could a ghost actually haunt two places? If so, then why didn't she feel the same evil she just experienced at the church at Starling? For nothing more than peace of mind, she needed to find the answer.

By the time she arrived home, darkness prevailed. None of the ghosts turned the lights on inside the house as they usually did in her absence. She opened the door with a bit of trepidation and turned the foyer lights on herself. An unfamiliar silence greeted her as she stepped all the way inside. The door to her office stood open, just as she'd left it. The shredded documents still lay scattered about the office. At least for the time being, Starling's residents left her to her own devices.

Shae sighed as she entered the office and turned on the lights. After picking up the garbage can, she knelt down on the floor and began going through the remnants. She would need to find pieces of the document headings to know which ones needed reprinting.

Piece by piece she scoured through the scraps of paper, placing the torn headings on the table and throwing the rest of them away. The laborious, painstaking process moved along at a snail's pace.

But then as she drew near to the end of her task, the tattered remains of the name *Jordahl* suddenly appeared in her hand. Her heart hammered inside her chest, a thing it did with increasing frequency. She had no idea which document the fragment originated from, but that information would present itself soon enough.

****

The captain worried over Shaelynn's lengthy absence. He expected her to return shortly after she left the premises, if for nothing more than to pack her belongings and secure her precious papers. But she didn't return. He spent the greater portion of the day pacing inside his room and gazing out the window for the familiar sight of the jeep, turning into the driveway.

The other residents of Starling left him in peace while he waited. Not even Amy came to berate him for his earlier actions, although he fully expected it. Perhaps they, too, now understood that Shaelynn needed to leave. But the prospect of that event left him feeling even more miserable. True, part of him wanted her gone.

Yet part of him wanted, even needed her to stay. Part of him actually hoped that if she learned what history recorded about him, she wouldn't form an instant judgment. He even found himself hoping she would listen to his side of the story before forming an opinion. He hoped Amy was right.

Once again, he turned his gaze to the window. But this time, the headlights of her jeep captured his attention. Tristan waited at the window until she arrived at the door. He heard the jangling of the keys and the turning of the knob before she stepped through the doorway.

She turned on the light inside her office and walked toward her table. He listened for several minutes, as she rustled through the shreds of torn paper on the floor. Why would she do that? Curiosity finally got the better of him, and he made his way downstairs and entered her office.

He found her standing in front of her worktable, engrossed in her work. Tattered pieces from the documents lay atop the table as she sorted through the fragments.

A loud beeping noise startled her, and she jerked her head toward the sound of its origin. Papers spewed out one of the machines in rapid succession. She stared at the thing as if confused. Yet, an instant later, that confusion seemed to give way to clarity. She hurried toward it.

After taking the stack of papers from out of the catch tray, she made her way over to her desk. She sat down, scooted forward, and focused her attention on the first of the pages. Bewilderment compelled him to sidle around to the back of the chair. He leaned over her shoulder to look at what she held in her hands. She had received some kind of medical log, which detailed the injured soldiers here at Starling. He read the journal entries along with her.

The first recorded item, dated June seventh, in the year 1862, mentioned Chattanooga. On that day, the ambulance wagons transported fifteen men to Starling from off the battlefield, accompanied by the field surgeon who needed more than a small tent to tend the wounded. According to the records their injuries were from minor to severe, but none of them life threatening. However, the following day a private by the name of Edmond Revel became the first recorded fatality at the plantation.

While reading the subsequent pages of the journal, he noted that Amy began her nursing duties at Starling on the fourth day of March, in the year 1863. In fact, she personally began making most of the notations beside each patient's name, taking great care as she did so. The names of other soldiers followed. He recognized many of them as friends and comrades.

September 19, of 1863, Beauregard Thomson

arrived at the Plantation, suffering from the gaping chest wound he received at the battle of Chickamauga. One of the doctors noted they could do nothing but make his final moments as comfortable as possible. Beau lingered two hours before death claimed him

Page after page of documented casualties followed. They were all valiant men, who gave their lives for and in behalf of their country. Finally, they arrived at the recorded entries for October 23, 1863. His name almost shouted at him from the middle of the page as if awaiting discovery. Tristan fastened his gaze on the notes that accompanied his entry. He didn't have many. Multiple wounds covered his body, many of them defensive in nature, the record stated. His doctor worked feverishly to save him and dear, sweet Amy, tended him around the clock. Yet, despite their best efforts, he died three days later. Yes, indeed, he could testify to all that.

The sound of Shaelynn's deep sigh ended his silent musing. He fixed his gaze to her troubled features and wondered where her thoughts had taken her.

"But that doesn't necessarily mean you are the only one," she murmured aloud as she leaned back in her chair and placed the pages on her lap.

The only one? What did she mean by that comment? He didn't have time to wonder long. For a scant moment later, she took hold of her pages, leaned forward, straightened the large stack atop her desk, and continued reading.

Another breath escaped her lips as they passed over the name of Chauncey Dillon. The record stated that he died in November of 1863. A few pages later, her fingers gently traced over the entry recording Timothy's death in December of that same year. She closed her eyes and shook her head ever so slightly. Several minutes later they happened upon the name of Amy Grimes Stoddard, this time listed as a patient. According to the journal, she contracted typhoid from the patients she so tenderly ministered to and died from the disease herself the last day of January in the year 1868.

At last, she turned the final page over on the desk. Her expression grew thoughtful as she turned her gaze to the torn fragments she had gathered. Then, with a look of grim determination, she pushed away from the desk, rose from her chair, and retrieved those fragments. She plopped them atop her desk and turned to her computer.

"All right," she said as she separated the remnants, "let's see what we have here."

The hum of the printer gained his attention and his bafflement steadily increased as several pages dropped into the tray. She gathered them up and began reading. One page in particular seemed to grab her attention more so than the others did, for she dropped all but the one, and with two hands, lifted the page closer to her face. He peered over her shoulder and read the missive for himself.

Hdqtrs. Fourth Military Dist.
Dept. Tennessee, Georgia
October 19, 1863

To Colonel Moore:

Colonel: Your letters of yesterday have been received and the warrant has been approved. Enclosed, I hand you an order addressed to Major Nils Adlundsen, directing him to report at these headquarters with a small number of his company and the prisoner, after his arrest, with the least practicable delay.

The brigadier-general commanding directs that you call Captain Jordahl and his company out in line, read the order of arrest to him in their presence and hearing, and ask him whether he will obey it without condition. If he refuses or hesitates, arrest him at once and send him here under heavy guard; use force, if necessary, and be prepared for any emergency.

W. A. Goudson,

Assistant Adjutant-General

Tristan scowled as he read the order for his arrest. The letter made him wonder what lies Adlundsen fabricated for Colonel Moore that would necessitate the need for a "heavy guard." Would they have used those lies to keep him silent?

He caught sight of Shaelynn's trembling hand as she finished reading the message given to Colonel Moore over a century earlier.

"If he had only followed the order as given, he need not have died in such a cruel manner," she whispered. Then just as she picked up one of the fragments to toss it away, she gave it a second look. She placed the fragment beneath his name on the letter she had just read and gasped. "The handwriting is different."

She stared straight ahead for a moment and turned at once to her computer with a look of sudden resolve. Comprehension dawned. She already knew.

Somehow, somewhere she learned the story of his death, the circumstances surrounding it, and connected it to him. Unquestionably, she now looked for the document matching the fragment. Above all, he did not want her reading that damning report. At least, not if he could help it. Not yet. Not until he had a chance to explain it to her first. He just needed a moment.

Despite his wishes, Shaelynn selected the next batch of documents and sent them to the printer. He hastened to interfere with its function. The machine responded with grinding sounds, clicks, and whirrs. The first of the papers rolled out smeared and unreadable. She turned toward the printer, brows furrowed.

Then, before she could assess the problem, he caused blank paper to spew out of the printer. He sent the sheets hurtling across the room in every possible direction. She gaped at the torrent in total dismay.

He whirled around to face her. Before he could form the words for his defense, she rose from her seat, stomped to the center of the room and spun around.

"Stop it!" she demanded angrily. "Just stop it. Exactly what are you trying to accomplish with all of this? Is this your pathetic way of trying to erase your contemptible deeds from history? Do you think I don't know who you are and what you did?"

At that moment in her tirade, the room grew increasingly colder. Shae could feel the rising anger of the spirit with each frosty breath she took, and she braced herself to face it head on.

"Why don't you enlighten me with your newfound knowledge, Miss Montgomery?"

The hard, steely voice sounded directly behind her. Without question, the moment she turned around, there would be no more than a foot between them, and he would be completely visible.

Nevertheless, she refused to budge from her rigid stance. "For starters, you betrayed your country as well as the trust of those who served under your command. In all likelihood, you are directly responsible for the Union defeat at Chickamauga and heaven only knows how many of the deaths that took place there. And last, but certainly not least, you killed your best friend in cold blood. You sir, are none other than Captain Tristan Jordahl!"

Having said her piece, she whipped around ready to face him. She gasped in shock as he leaned down, bringing his face close to hers.

To say he was not at all what she expected

would have been a gross understatement. The sight he presented diffused all further comment and all further thought as she stared up into his mesmerizing, deep blue eyes.

The smile he gave her was at once terrible and frightening. "Ever at your service, Miss Montgomery."

Chapter 9

Shae glanced down on her notepad and found she'd been doodling again. A series of ghostly faces stared back at her from the lined paper. Tristan Jordahl, obviously, but once again she failed to do the incredibly handsome captain justice. In a fit of pique, she scribbled over the not-so-artistic faces of her childish creation before she grabbed hold of the page and ripped it away from the notepad. She wadded it up and tossed it toward the garbage can, along with all other such pages.

She sighed as she pushed away from her desk, walked over to the window, and gazed out past the trees. Again. She shook her head and turned back to her desk with renewed determination. After sitting down, she picked up her pen as well as the first record slated for translation and stared at it. The document may as well be Greek. She tossed her pen across the desk. She followed the projectile's bounce as she leaned back in her chair and began rubbing her temples.

Shae counted just a little over a week since she confronted Tristan with his unsavory past. Well, perhaps she shouldn't use the word "confronted." Accused and condemned would probably be a little more accurate. Yet, for the life of her, she just couldn't shake the look of pain and disappointment that briefly marred his perfect face. Why? Why would her words bother him? More importantly, why did it bother her that it bothered him? Whatever the cause, Shae instantly regretted the harsh words. But before she could utter an apology, Tristan's expression became arrogant. With a mocking bow, he acknowledged his identity and then disappeared. Along with his disappearance, the friendly camaraderie she enjoyed with the other residents of Starling disappeared as well. She found she really missed them.

"Look, I'm sorry! How many times, and in how many ways do you want me to apologize?" she asked as she fixed her gaze toward the ceiling. "But really, it's not as if I am the bad guy in all of this, am I? I just stated the known facts, perhaps a bit brusquely, I'll admit—and again, I'm sorry for that."

Silence. Nothing she said mattered to anyone and it made her feel so alone in this big house.

She glanced at her worktable, studied the stack of documents she willfully neglected, and found no remorse for her lack of attention. Instead of working, she spent all of her time going through each document looking for the affidavit in support of the warrant mentioned in the letter to Colonel Moore. The affidavit would surely give the details pertaining to the case. Where were the letters Goudson mentioned? She thoroughly searched every document in her possession. Yet, besides Goudson's letter and the summary report matching the torn fragment, nothing else emerged from the endless sea of documents.

For the umpteenth time, she picked up the official report reviewing the events that transpired in late October of 1863. Her eyes scanned the page.

Certificate No. 128183
Army of the United States
Summary of Proceedings In The Matter of:
Major Nils Adlundsen and Captain Tristan Jordahl
Be it known that on the 27th day of February, 1864, that before me came the Undersigned, that I certify to be respectable and entitled to credit; who being by me, duly sworn, came personally and

testified to the following event that took place the 23rd day of October 1863:

That, Major Nils Adlundsen was issued a warrant for the arrest of Captain Tristan Jordahl for the cause of Treason, pertaining to his actions in betraying the United States of America to the enemy. That Major Nils Adlundsen personally and willfully disregarded the order as written; That the said Major along with a small support staff, took it upon himself to escort Captain Jordahl to the Adaria First Presbyterian Church, allegedly out of compassion and friendship and was at that place taken by surprise and assaulted by the said Captain Jordahl once they entered the structure. Whereupon, it is stated, that the individuals involved became at once engaged in brutal physical confrontation, a contest that proved fatal to both parties.

It is testified further, that Major Nils Adlundsen, severely wounded and fainting with loss of blood, stumbled out of the church requesting immediate aid before he succumbed to his death. The undersigned testify further that after finding Captain Jordahl still alive inside the Church, they carried him to Starling Plantation, where the alleged traitor died three days later. No further inquiry is deemed necessary in this matter.

Quincy A. Bell, Provost Marshal
Witnesses to wit:
Capt. Casper Berntsen
Forseth Ericksen
Burke Frandsen
Zepheniah Henry
Alfred Johnson

Shae gazed at the list of witnesses and for the first time, one of the names caught her attention. Forseth Ericksen; she had read the unusual name just recently. But where? She shook her head and scoffed inwardly over the absurd question. Where, indeed? In all likelihood, she read the name on one of the never-ending documents she continually waded through in her attempt to find the—

No, wait a minute. Her heart began racing as she took hold of the file containing the pages of the medical ledger and opened it. She needed confirmation. Her fingers flew as she sorted through the stack of papers looking for the one noting the arrival of the captain. The page took less than a minute to find.

Forseth Ericksen, the name recorded just above that of Tristan Jordahl, came to the hospital the day before the captain. The doctors amputated his leg, shortly thereafter. Therefore, he couldn't possibly have witnessed the incident at the church. Once again, Shae read over the medical notes concerning Tristan. She gasped softly, suddenly perplexed. If Tristan "surprised and assaulted" the major, then he surely wouldn't have suffered defensive wounds. What else did she miss on that statement in her haste to judge him?

Taking great care, she reread the summary report, and this time without her former prejudice. At the end of it, something else occurred to her. If the witnesses were already inside the church as the report stated, why would Adlundsen need to "stumble out of the church" asking for their help? Wouldn't they have dispatched Tristan at his first strike, before he had the chance to kill their commander? Surely, all of men carried weapons. The men were battle-hardened soldiers, for heaven's sake! But, if they weren't inside the church as the report indicated, how could they have possibly known just who attacked whom and why? The report cast doubt on everything she thought she understood.

The captain could answer all of her questions if only he would just speak to her. While chewing on her bottom lip, she gazed toward the ceiling. Thus far, she lacked the courage to address him personally. Perhaps if she tried singling him out instead of talking to the group as a whole.

"Captain," she began, her voice wavering with uncertainty. "Could I talk to you for a minute, please? It's really, really important—"

Silence.

"Please?"

She waited for a few minutes, hoping for a response, but none came. Shae tried again, softer and more contrite this time. "I'm so sorry. I shouldn't have said what I did. My actions were inexcusable and I humbly beg your pardon."

Again, no response.

Did she really expect instant forgiveness for her biased outburst? Feeling miserable, she shook her head as she picked up the summary report. Then as her eyes hovered over the list of witnesses, she focused on one other name: Zepheniah Henry. *Henry*! Could this man be Isaac's grandfather? In that instant, she recalled their conversation with absolute clarity.

Isaac said some things that—well really, it wasn't what he said. It was more the *way* he said it. Her mind repeated the phrases exactly as she remembered them. "I suppose that *could* sum it up," "official report *says*" and probably most cryptically "been paid quite handsomely for the betrayal to his country, or *so it would seem*."

Isaac Henry knew something more than what he told her on the day they met. All at once, she had a burning desire to extract every shred of information concerning Tristan Jordahl. She glanced at her watch. Just a little after three. Would he be home? Better yet, would she be able to find his house? She needed to try.

With the summary report still in hand, she

pushed away from the desk and stood up. After dragging the keys off the desk, she hurried to the front door and over to the carriage house. Once inside the jeep, she slammed the key into the ignition. She turned the engine over and backed out. Without bothering to close the doors behind her, she dropped the stick into first gear and tromped on the gas. She sent the vehicle flying toward the church. Once she arrived, she parked in the same spot as before and began following the trail.

As she approached the church, the entire structure loomed toward her with arms wide open as if to snatch her body and soul. The image she conjured caused an involuntary shudder. She eyed the building warily as she passed and continued in the southeasterly direction, which Isaac pointed out.

About ten minutes into her journey, she could see a small turn-of-the-century home up ahead. The name painted on the mailbox, just outside the white picket fence, confirmed she found the right place. She took a deep breath, entered through the gate, and walked up the cobblestone path. Just as she ascended the porch steps, the door opened. She peered past the screen door and into Isaac's smiling face. He looked pleased to see her.

"Well, good afternoon, Shae. I thought I saw you coming up the walk," he said as he stood back allowing her entrance into his cozy little home. "Please come in and sit down."

"Thank you," she said as she sat down in the chair he indicated.

"So, to what do I owe the pleasure of this visit?" he asked.

Shae shifted a little more comfortably in her seat and waited for him to sit down before she spoke. "Actually, there are a couple of things I hope you can help me with. First, it finally occurred to me after our conversation that somehow you are aware the spirit of Captain Jordahl resides at Starling. I just wondered *how* you know that. And the second thing I need to ask you about, well—I suppose I can only explain that one as a really bothersome J.D.L.R., which simply refuses to go away."

"Excuse me?" Isaac looked perplexed. "A J.D.—what?"

She let out a bit of a laugh. "Oh, I'm sorry. I suppose I should tell you my dad is a police officer in the state of Washington. He has served in that capacity for well over thirty years now, and I have maddeningly acquired the tendency to use his expressions. J.D.L.R. is the acronym his department uses, for anything that 'just don't look right.'" She cocked her head to the side and shrugged. "I suppose the analytical part of him that questions everything, has inevitably rubbed off on me, and—well, I found something."

Isaac chuckled as he clasped his hands. "Ah. And you believe I can help you with whatever it is that 'just don't look right' to you?"

"I'm hoping," she answered with an accompanying nod. "So?"

"Your question pertaining to the residence of Captain Jordahl, let's deal with that issue first, shall we?" Isaac's eyes took on a faraway expression and he paused for several seconds as if gathering his thoughts.

"With the deepest gratitude, my mother accepted a housekeeping position at Starling during the Depression. Grateful that is, until Captain Jordahl *invited* her to leave. I can assure you, she quickly obliged."

"Oh." Shae mulled that one over for a moment. She could see the captain doing something like that. After all, he "invited" her to leave shortly after her arrival, as well. "But, how did your mother know the voice came from Jordahl?" she pressed.

"Simply because the man who owned the house at that particular time said so, and it did agree with the facts as we knew them. Of course, there is always room for doubt. I suppose in fairness, I would have to admit the voice she heard could have come from anyone," he said.

"All right, so, on to the J.D.L.R., then." She cleared her throat a bit before she leaned over and handed him the summary report. "This is a copy of one of the documents relating to Tristan Jordahl and Nils Adlundsen. One of the witnesses to the events of this report is a man by the name of Zepheniah Henry. Is he the grandfather you mentioned the first day we met?"

Isaac met her eyes from across the small room and nodded in confirmation. Then pointing toward the document he asked, "May I?"

"Of course, that's why I brought it." Shae handed him the report. She waited as he picked up his reading glasses, put them on, and focused on the page.

After he finished his study of the document, he laid it on his lap and simply said, "How very interesting."

"Yes," she agreed. "But, there are a few things that bother me about the report."

"Such as?" he prodded.

"Well, for one thing, it isn't logical. If the major's men accompanied him inside the church to arrest the captain, how could any kind of scuffle break out between the two men? After all, the men at the church outnumbered the captain. And if Adlundsen's men stayed outside, as the report indicates, then how could those men possibly know what took place inside the church?

"Oh, and there is one other thing as well. I recently obtained a copy of the existing medical journal for Starling during the time it served as a hospital. One of the witnesses to that report, the man by the name of Forseth Ericksen, couldn't possibly have been there when the incident took place. According to the records, he arrived at the hospital the day before the event, and I doubt very seriously, after just having endured a leg amputation, he would have been up to the task."

All of the words came out in a rush. When she finished her summation, she clamped her mouth shut and waited for Isaac's reaction to her reasoning.

His eyes gleamed, and he nodded as a smile tugged at the corners of his mouth. "I can see why this situation has nagged you."

"There is more to your grandfather's story, isn't there." She made the comment more as a statement of fact, than a question.

He closed his eyes as he leaned the back of his head against his chair. "I understand now, why this incident bothered my grandfather. He was just a young boy of seventeen when this event took place and an old man of eighty-nine when he related it to me. I remember his eyes—they were full of regret. At the same time, they begged for my understanding.

"I can tell you right off hand these witnesses here,"—he swept his hand across the names at the bottom of the report—"did not escort Captain Jordahl, anywhere. In fact, they didn't accompany Major Adlundsen to the church, either. During the early part of that fateful week, the major gathered four men—not five, for this mission, just as you suspected. I don't recollect my grandfather ever mentioning the name Ericksen to me in connection with his party, so I believe you're probably right on that point.

"My grandfather said that being hand-selected for this mission filled him with tremendous pride. Especially since Major Adlundsen stated their task could prove a dangerous one *if* Jordahl didn't wish to cooperate. You have to understand the captain's battle skills were legendary. Even though none of the witnesses of this report knew the man personally, they were all very aware of his reputation. Anyway, these men, sworn to secrecy, were briefed as to the captain's supposed traitorous acts as well as the results of those acts at the battle of Chickamauga."

"Why do you say, 'supposed'?" she interrupted.

"Because much later, my grandfather wasn't so sure," Isaac continued. "As I told you, the major stated he didn't want to arrest the captain in front of his men as ordered. He said he didn't want to humiliate him in front of his own men."

"Yes, I actually have a copy of that order too, written by Colonel Moore. I didn't think to bring it with me, though," she said as she swept away a stray lock of hair.

"That's all right, perhaps another time. Well, according to my grandfather, the major said he arranged to meet Jordahl at the Adaria church at noon on October twenty-third, where he would quietly arrest him. He asked the men to arrive shortly thereafter, so they would be waiting outside to escort Jordahl to headquarters after the arrest was official. Their presence would also ensure the impossibility of escape. As I told you when last we spoke, Adlundsen stated his reasons were those of compassion and friendship.

"My grandfather told me they arrived on time, as ordered. Yet, as they approached the church, they could hear all hell breaking loose inside. He said they heard several thundering crashes coming from the interior of the church. They dismounted as quickly as they could in an effort to offer assistance. But halfway to their destination the door burst open, and Major Adlundsen stumbled out of the doorway, with his dress sword in his right hand. According to my grandfather, blood dripped down his shirt as he clutched his chest with his left hand. The major just managed to call for help, before he collapsed where he stood.

"They raced toward him, of course, but nothing could be done. He died before they arrived at his side. He and Captain Casper Berntsen were the first two men to go inside the church. My grandfather could see a great deal of blood on the floor, and the sight troubled him. Jordahl lay sprawled out on the floor amidst the debris, holding onto a knife. They hurried toward his body. Berntsen kicked the weapon out of his hand, sending it across the room. My grandfather knelt down, fully expecting to find the captain dead, but the man briefly opened his eyes. He said his eyes filled with anguish and disbelief. As he gazed at my grandfather, he simply shook his head, and then lost consciousness.

"By that time, the rest of their party also arrived inside the church. My grandfather told them Jordahl still lived, and in their anger, they dragged him out to his horse. One of the men wanted to finish him off right there, but Berntsen said his death shouldn't be that easy. He wanted Jordahl patched up so he could publicly hang for the crimes he committed.

"So, they decided to transport him to Starling. At that point, one of the other men noticed three horses tied to the post outside the church, not just two. Berntsen ordered my grandfather to go back inside the building. He said that Jordahl probably killed someone else, but after a thorough search, he found nothing but the knife Berntsen kicked out of Jordahl's hand.

"My grandfather recognized the distinctive knife immediately. The weapon belonged to the major. He picked it up, took it outside, and gave it to Berntsen. They opened the saddlebags in the hope they'd find something that would give the unknown rider an identity. But they only found a clean Union uniform, much too small to have fit either the major or the captain. Both men, according to my grandfather, were very large in stature."

"How very odd," Shae murmured.

"Odd, indeed. Anyway, several weeks later, the army called upon my grandfather to sign the official report. He did so reluctantly and only by direct order. Another order soon followed. That order swore him to silence for anything pertaining to the incident. By then my grandfather suspected something amiss. The notion always bothered him, he said, that Jordahl did not use the loaded pistol, still snapped and secured within his holster, even though he had plenty of time and the reputed skill to do so."

Chapter 10

Questions swirled around inside Shae's head, and all the while, she kept her gaze fixed on the ground as she followed the path to her jeep. Therefore, it did not surprise her that she could feel the church before she lifted her eyes to see it. Her heart slammed inside her chest, and a flush stained her cheeks, all before she looked up and noted her location. She stopped even though any rational person would keep moving. Nevertheless, a power over which she held no control drew her toward the weathered door, so very familiar to her now. Instinct rather than intellect guided her steps.

As she arrived at the top of the rickety stairs, she extended a hand, and like a puppet on a string, took hold of the rusted latch. A shiver coursed through her body as she turned it downward. Despite its lack of use, the handle moved quite easily in her hand. With a gentle shove, the door opened and she peeked inside. She exhaled short, shallow breaths as she gazed into the dark, musty room that seemed almost too quiet.

Then just as she found the courage to step all the way inside and explore it further, a fury of icy wind crashed against her body, causing her to teeter backward. She raised her arm and ducked her head behind the open palm of her hand. The vicious force thrust her out the door, and then slammed the portal shut inches away from her face. At once, the boughs of the trees began moaning eerily under the weight of the gusts, which pressed and twisted around and through the branches. Scattered debris from off the ground swirled toward her with an alarming velocity. She looked up toward the sky. Dark gray clouds swirled and churned as they marched across the horizon. A wicked-looking storm approached.

She took off running. Self-preservation fueled her flight. She didn't stop until she approached the safety of her jeep, yanked open the door, and crawled breathlessly inside. Shae bowed her head toward the steering wheel as her hands grasped the soft leather that encased it. She remained there until the last vestiges of ragged breathing eased, and her trembling body quieted.

As logic kicked in, she shook away the fear and berated herself for being silly. For the briefest of moments, she allowed herself to believe the evil entity inside the church recognized her and reacted with the rage of her nightmares. The approaching storm, the foreboding church, as well as the newly acquired details of what took place inside those chapel walls, simply threw her imagination into overdrive. With a toss of her head, she started the engine and turned the jeep toward home.

All throughout the drive, she concentrated on the conversation she had with Isaac. He had a valid point. Why didn't Tristan use his pistol that day? Using the gun would have been so much easier, so much cleaner, if he really wanted his best friend dead. Why did he have Adlundsen's knife in his hand? Did he have it all along, or did he take it away from the major, who threatened him with it first? That would explain the defensive wounds if he did, but why use the knife in the first place? If Adlundsen walked into that church with the intent of arresting Tristan and he showed any signs of resistance, wouldn't the major have drawn his own pistol to enforce the issue? Why use the sword or knife at all?

And then according to Isaac, Zepheniah Henry carried one final burden to his grave. Despite the order of silence, whispers abounded. Months after the incident, Isaac's grandfather walked inside a tavern, seeking refreshment. The very sergeant that served under the command of Tristan Jordahl also sought refuge inside the tavern. The sergeant argued with someone at his table. In direct response to a derogatory comment the man made about the captain, the sergeant bellowed, "With my right hand on the Bible, I could solemnly swear before all that's holy, nothing or no one could make Tristan Jordahl betray his country. Do you understand that? And he certainly wouldn't have taken the major's life when he protected it far too often, at the risk of his own."

That statement filled Zepheniah with doubt. He began to wonder over the reason the major wanted to arrest Tristan Jordahl without his men in attendance. Could it be those men would never have believed the charges and therefore, would never have allowed the arrest to take place?

Shae blew out a sigh. Nothing made any sense. If only she could get Tristan to talk to her and help her understand, or even Amy for that matter. Amy could shed a great deal of light on the subject. At least some of her comments certainly hinted at it.

Somewhere amidst the muddle of her thoughts, Shae discovered that she had returned to the carriage house at Starling. Yet, she didn't have any memory of the actual drive home. Shaking out of her reverie, she took the keys out of the ignition, slid them inside her pocket, and exited the vehicle. Since the thick storm clouds now spread from horizon to horizon, it appeared much darker than usual inside the garage. She needed to feel her way out. After closing and latching the doors behind her, she hurried toward the house. About halfway to her destination a sudden rush of heavy raindrops pounded the dirt beneath her feet.

She didn't feel them. Her thoughts, focused on the latest facts Isaac provided as well as her frightening experience at the church, prevented it. From the corner of her eye, she perceived a hulking, shadowy movement. Startled, she whipped her head toward the sight. She could now see the familiar red truck parked off the side of the driveway and underneath the trees. The driver stumbled out of the cab.

"Oh!" she gasped out in surprise. It took her a moment and a flash of lightning to realize that Perry Adler stood by the open door. She forgot about their appointment to exchange the first set of documents for the next. How long did she keep him waiting?

"I'm so sorry, Perry," she said. "I forgot you were coming today. I didn't keep you waiting too long, did I?"

Perry furrowed his brow as if her simple question confused him. Several seconds passed before he nodded and then muttered something she couldn't quite make out. His odd behavior captured her full attention.

"You did. You did keep me waitin' and much longer than I wanted to be here in this hideous place. If you weren't such a pretty lil' thing, I might be upset 'bout that—but, maybe I jus' might—might forgive you, if you'll come on o'er her an' let me have—"

The slurred words caught Shae's immediate attention. He took a stumbling step toward her. The nauseating odor of alcohol rolled from his breath. The way he ogled her from head to toe disgusted her.

"Go home, Perry," Shae commanded. She could only hope the coldness and authority inflected in voice and tone would be enough to make him leave. As drunk as he appeared, she knew the defensive tactics her father taught her would have no impact on someone his size.

Perry chuckled as he advanced toward her. Unsure of her footing, Shae inched backward. Then just as she turned to run, he lurched forward. His big hand extended forward, grabbed hold of her waist, and then yanked her to his chest. Just as a massive lightning bolt lit up the sky, she took a deep breath, opened her mouth wide, and screamed bloody murder at the top of her lungs. Not a soul would hear it. The booming roar of thunder swallowed the sounds of her scream, and he held her so tightly, she couldn't expel another.

Knowing Perry wouldn't expect it, she allowed herself to go limp while raising both her arms high over her head. The maneuver caught him off guard and enabled her to slide through his arms and fall to the ground. She rolled to one side, and catlike, rose to her feet. If only she could make it to the door before he caught her, she'd be safe.

As she ran toward the only haven available, he thundered up behind her. Then, just as she made it to the door, he grabbed hold of her waist and twisted her around to face him. He repeatedly tore at her thin, rain-soaked blouse while crushing his slobbering lips on top of hers, forcing her downward. She pushed against him with all of her might while at the same time, trying to get her legs in a position to kick.

Before she could put the plan into action, Perry let out a horrific scream and abruptly released his hold. She gasped in stunned amazement as he flew backward. Twisting awkwardly against an unseen assailant, the large man landed face down on the ground. As he attempted to get to his feet, he flailed downward once more.

Perry rolled onto his back and looked up as if searching for his attacker. He didn't see one. Blood gushed from his broken nose, but he didn't appear to notice the blood or the pain he surely had to feel. At that point, he drew his hands upward in an awkward attempt to cover both his face and his chest.

All the while, his eyes darted about, looking for his unseen opponent. He babbled incoherent words, and then as he rolled onto his stomach, he began crawling toward his truck. Yet, just as he grabbed hold of the passenger door handle and eased himself into a standing position, the same force whirled him around and slammed him against the vehicle. He flailed about as if trying to free himself.

The captain materialized. Shae caught her breath. Perry's eyes grew wide with terror. Could he see the ghostly presence too? She didn't really know. Perry didn't focus on his face. Perhaps he didn't want to look the captain in the eye. Tristan spoke to him then, but not loud enough for her to hear what he said. Perry nodded and while finally wiping the blood away from his face, he opened the door. He backed all the way into the driver's seat and shut himself inside the vehicle. The motor rumbled to life. Scant seconds later, the truck backed haphazardly down the driveway, moving faster than what she would consider safe. The sounds of his grinding gearshift told her he made it to the main road. The screech of his tires against the wet pavement proved he sped recklessly away. Relief overtook her and she could feel the tension leave her body in that same moment.

Shae rose on unsteady feet as Tristan turned and strode toward her. He looked very solid, just as solid as Aulric always looked, and she studied his form in complete fascination. The glimpse he afforded her the one time she cast her gaze on him, did not give her the detail she could see now.

She stared, but really, how could she help it? The man stood well over six feet tall and looked every inch the legendary Norse warrior. Except, he wore the Civil War uniform of a Union captain. His hair, containing all the colors of a ripened wheat field, fell in feathery waves, just below his collar. As he closed the distance between them, she could see the dark stubble on his face contrasting his deep blue eyes. Eyes the color of the sky, just before day faded into the darkness of night. Wonderful eyes that somehow seemed so very familiar and appeared filled with concern for her. She had the strangest desire to throw herself into his arms, cry her eyes out, and have him give her the comfort she so desperately needed.

He approached her with caution, as if not wanting to frighten her further. Then, in a gentle but quiet voice said, "Shaelynn, are you all right? Did he hurt you?"

The questions filled her mind with all the horror of Perry's attack. Once again, she could feel his vile hands on her body. The mere image of that man's face, his breath, his intentions, sickened her. If not for Tristan, he would surely have—

The thought evaporated as the captain fused his gaze to hers. He winced visibly and stiffened. The moment Tristan believed his presence produced her outward show of loathing, he disappeared.

"No! Tristan, please, wait!" she called in a futile attempt to prevent his departure. Turning quickly toward the door, she grasped the handle. The knob did not budge. She frantically yanked the keys out of her pocket and searched for the one that would unlock the door. Her wet hands shook with the effort, and it took forever to find the right key. When at last she found it, she thrust it into the lock and turned the handle. The door swung open, and she slammed it behind her as she bounded up the stairs.

"Tristan," she panted, as she reached the top floor. "Please, you misunderstood!"

She fell against his door in her hurried attempt to reach it. Then, after grasping the knob, she turned it, knowing it wouldn't open, even before she made the attempt.

"You've got to let me in, you have to let me explain, please," she begged through the barrier that separated them. "I swear on everything dear to me, I'm not moving from this spot until you do. Do you hear me? I'm not leaving!"

"I am not interested in anything you have to say," he growled back.

"I don't care. I'm staying right here until you hear me out!" she shouted.

****

As the minutes ticked by, the captain tried desperately to ignore her presence, but finally, his shoulders slumped in defeat. The chiming of the clock told him over an hour had passed since Shaelynn obstinately decreed her intention to remain in the small hallway until she said what she wanted to say. He hoped her wet clothes and the trauma of her earlier experience, would force the issue otherwise. But true to her word, she still waited outside his door.

Stubborn little hellion.

With a sigh of resignation, he opened the door and met her defiant gaze. She stood against the opposite wall, with one foot resting against the baseboard. Her arms wrapped around her waist as if seeking warmth against her wet, torn clothing. On top of that, she shivered with the cold. She looked so pathetic standing there.

"Shaelynn, you need to get into some dry clothes," he said. The words surprised him. They weren't anywhere near what he planned to say. The soft tone didn't match either.

Shae clenched her teeth and shook her head. "Not until we have talked."

"We're not going to talk until you are more presentable," he said as his eyes deliberately raked across her body, taking in every detail of her disheveled appearance. Once again, he could feel his anger rise as he reminded himself of the reason for that. Tristan's rage exploded the moment that man dared put his hands on her. He had needed every ounce of self-control to allow him to leave in one piece.

He waited as Shaelynn self-consciously looked down at her clothes in an effort to see herself through his eyes. Her tattered blouse left little to the imagination and the image produced a blush. She tossed a large portion of her still damp hair forward, in an attempt to regain some modesty. Her cheeks flamed as she looked up and met his gaze.

"You can come back after you've changed your clothes and you're dry," he reiterated. "Take your time. The door will be open, I promise." She looked as if she wanted to protest, but he simply shut the door.

****

In concession, Shae made her way down the stairs. In all likelihood, she couldn't have kept her mind on what she wanted to say while in her current state. Especially not after Tristan drew her attention to the condition of her tattered blouse. Besides, it would only take a minute to change her clothes, and he promised she could come back. She picked up her pace, suddenly anxious.

As she reached her bedroom, she could hear water running from her shower faucet. Her black cargoes, a clean long-sleeved black T-shirt, and matching shoes lay across her bed. Her brows knit in confusion.

"You are going to catch your death of cold," Amy scolded in disapproval.

Shae gasped as Amy unexpectedly appeared in

front of her. She shook her wet curls and sputtered, "But I—"

"Hurry along, dear," the nurse brusquely cut in. "Get out of those wet things and right into the shower."

"But Amy, I can't, he's—" Shae protested, gesturing toward the ceiling.

"Yes you can, and you will. The captain isn't going anywhere, I daresay, so your conversation can surely wait until you've taken care of yourself, now come along. You're soaked to the skin."

Seeing the futility of argument, Shae peeled off her wet clothes and got into the shower. The hot water felt so good against her cold skin, and she wanted nothing more than to linger. But her solitude allowed the memory of what almost happened to crash into her consciousness. She didn't want to think about that. The vivid memory of Adler's repulsive hands and his foul breath disgusted her. She didn't want to remember. She didn't want to dwell on what might have happened if Tristan failed to come to her rescue.

After scrubbing as much of Perry Adler's memory off her body as she could manage, she turned off the shower. She found a couple of towels already waiting for her. Amy's kindness led her to believe her ghostly friend finally forgave her.

Ignoring the shoes altogether, Shae simply threw on her clothes, and then towel-dried her hair. She raked through the tangles with her fingers as she raced out her bedroom door and up the stairs, taking them two at a time. Her steps slowed as she approached the captain's door, and she gazed at it warily. She needed a clever way to begin their conversation. So many questions begged for an answer. Yet, she didn't want or need to offend him any further than she already had.

Without a doubt, he didn't deserve any of her

former aversion. But still, how does one tactfully ask about one's "involvement" with treason and the subsequent death of one's friend? Perhaps he could offer a reasonable explanation for both. Something not quite as fiendish as history would lead her to believe.

Just as she raised her hand to knock at his door, it creaked and shuddered its way open. The only thing providing light to the room came from intermittent flashes of lightning through the square-paned windows. Nevertheless, she took a deep breath and for the first time, entered his private sanctuary. She stood still for a moment, allowing her eyes to adjust to the darkness.

"Tristan?" she called softly.

"I'm here."

Shae whirled toward the sound of his voice. He stood just inches away, his gaze intense. He remained silent as if waiting for her to say what she wanted to say. She took another deep breath.

"Is there any kind of a light source..." Before she could finish the question, a small lightbulb, hanging center of the ceiling, switched on.

She turned her eyes away from the intensity of his gaze as she sought to compose her thoughts. In an effort to buy a little more time, Shae took in her surroundings. She didn't know what she expected to find inside his private domain, or if she expected anything at all.

The sloping rooflines made the attic room appear much smaller than what the floor space revealed. Large wooden timbers outlined the ceiling. Yet, no dust or cobwebs hung off them. A small bed sat between the dormers, a tattered wool blanket and a small feather pillow covered the mattress. Her gaze took in the old trunk pushed against the wall on the left side of the bed. Situated in the corner across from the bed, sat a worn, dilapidated desk.

She could just discern the silhouette of books, papers, and a small wooden box, which lay on top. Why would there be books and papers up here? Did he actually read them? Curiosity compelled her to approach for a better look.

"You wanted to say something to me," Tristan reminded her.

Shae turned away from the desk to face him. After wrapping her arms about her waist, she nodded, and fused her gaze to his.

"Yes, I do. But first and foremost, I want to thank you, so very, very much…for saving me…from him." She finished the words in a ragged whisper.

"Think nothing of it," he replied. "The man got no less than he deserved."

Shae gazed at him for several seconds. She didn't detect so much as a trace of derision in his voice, nor could she see any malice in his eyes. Admittedly, she expected both, and who could blame him after the way she treated him.

"You misunderstood, you know," she finally managed to say. "You made me feel safe and protected. But I could see in your eyes that you thought my um—my revulsion was attributed to your presence, and that's not the case at all. It was just…when you asked if he hurt me…the memory of what he intended washed over me and I—"

Finding it difficult to continue, to give voice to her feelings, Shae once again turned toward the desk. She needed to make sure he understood and truly believed he had nothing—

Before her mind could think to finish the thought, her eyes locked on the old photo lying atop the wooden box. She could feel the color drain from her face. Without giving a thought to her actions, a trembling hand picked up the photograph, and lifted it closer to her face. Not that she really needed any more assurance as to what, rather, at whom she gazed.

"Please, you must tell me, who is this woman?" Her voice, just a notch above a whisper, wavered.

In every detail of the old carte-de-visite photograph, she gazed upon the woman from her dreams. The woman who's sorrowful eyes begged for her help. The woman who dearly loved *Odin*!

The lengthy silence drew her gaze away from the portrait. She looked into Tristan's eyes, which seemed to probe the depths of her own before he answered the question.

"My mother," he finally said.

Chapter 11

For the first time in her life, Shae wondered if she might pass out. Or maybe she would laugh hysterically and uncontrollably, instead. What was she supposed to make of all this madness? Tristan's *mother* loved Odin. She wanted her, of all people, to help Odin. Why? What could she possibly do for the man? And most unsettling of all, how did the woman even know she and Odin, or rather, she and her son, were destined to meet?

"Shaelynn, are you all right?" Tristan moved a step closer. He extended a hand toward her as if he truly expected he might have to catch her. His eyes filled with concern. "Do you want to sit down?"

She could hear his voice. Yet, it sounded distant and located somewhere in the deepest recesses of her mind. His words seemed more like background noise, and she gave them no heed. She couldn't. A host of other thoughts crashed into her mind and clamored for attention. She needed to make sense of them before she could do anything else.

Finally, and not remembering exactly how she got there, Shae discovered she sat on the edge of Tristan's bed. She still held the photograph of his mother in her hands. And she sat on the bed long enough to come to the stunning conclusion, that just as surely as the church existed, so did the woman in her dreams. Even if she'd lived her life well over a century earlier.

All the known pieces of the bewildering puzzle flooded into her mind. Although she tried to make sense of them, despite the missing pieces, only one thing filled her with certainty. Fenrir *was* the entity residing inside the church because Fenrir *was not* the captain. Fenrir was the *major*. The captain lived at Starling because *he* was Odin and not Fenrir as she supposed. She glanced over at Tristan, who stood at her side during this journey toward understanding. He appeared confused, maybe even concerned over her mental stability. In any other circumstances, she might have laughed.

"You didn't do it," she said in a small, quiet voice, as if almost surprised at her own conclusion.

"Do?" Tristan shook his head, perplexed over her statement. "You are not making any sense, Shaelynn. Are you truly all right? You look a little pale. Perhaps you ought to get some rest. We can talk later if you'd like."

Shae waved his concern aside and said, "I'm fine, really, I am. I'm just telling you I know you didn't do what they accused you of doing. You are not guilty of treason, and I've concluded you killed Adlundsen in self-defense. I just don't know all of the whys and wherefores to this puzzle. At least, not yet. But you can rest assured, I will."

Tristan stared at her in stark amazement. Her unexpected assessment took him completely by surprise. Did he really think her that bull-headed?

"Would you care to explain how you arrived at that particular conclusion?" he finally asked.

"Uh—hmm. Actually, no, I'd rather not," she hedged. What kind of an explanation could she offer without sounding like a complete idiot?

"Come on," he coaxed. He gave her a devilish smile and then added, "You owe me."

The bestowal of that devastating smile stole away her breath and robbed her of what little sense remained. That grin alone fueled the need to give him anything he desired, not the reminder of his timely rescue. However, the reminder probably would've worked just as well.

"You don't play a very fair game, Captain," she accused while miserably failing in the attempt to suppress her own smile.

"Never remember making that particular claim, either." He shrugged and stepped a little closer. "So?"

"I don't even know where to begin." She tossed her head, closed her eyes briefly, and let out a sigh.

"Well, as it appears we are relying on assumptions, let's assume for a moment my mother's likeness has something to do with your conclusion," he said, nodding toward the photograph. "Why don't you begin with that?"

"Ah. You want the tale from the beginning then," she replied. Shae scooted backward until her back rested against the wall, crossed her legs comfortably, and then patted the foot of the bed. "Please, sit down. This may take a while, and it's making me nervous for you to just stand there and stare at me."

"You know, I find that an interesting thing," he said, clearly amused. "Your nervousness doesn't come from speaking to a disembodied spirit. Your discomfiture comes because the spirit is standing, and apparently, staring at you." He shook his head and took the offered seat. "All right then, the spirit is seated. Please go on."

Ignoring his mirth, Shae said, "Before we get started, I think it reasonable, since I intend to answer all of your questions honestly, that in turn, you should answer all of mine in like manner."

"Agreed, and you're stalling," he stated as he locked his gaze with hers.

"Yes, I guess I am. Okay, then—" Shae pulled her hair away from her face and tossed the bulk of it behind her shoulder. "Here we go. How much do you know about the Norse myths?"

"What?"

"Just answer the question, please," she said.

"My mother was a gifted storyteller. I probably know my fair share of them, but what could that possibly have to do with—"

"Fenrir and Odin and their last battle at Ragnarok," she cut in, furrowing her brow. "Do you know the story?"

"Yes," he replied using a tone of impatience. "The hulking wolf hunts down Odin after having escaped from his imprisonment. They fight, Odin dies."

"And Vidar?" she prodded, keeping her gaze fused with his.

Tristan sighed in exasperation and rolled his eyes. "Avenges Odin. Shaelynn, are you deliberately trying to drive me insane?"

"Truly, I'm not," she said as she took hold of her bottom lip. "It's just that the story is important because it is central to my recurring dream or rather, a recurring nightmare that I have. And before we go any further, I need to tell you about that dream, so you will understand the rest of what I have to tell you."

His eyes flickered in sudden comprehension, but Shae didn't give his facial expression any more thought than that.

"I'm listening." He folded his arms against his chest and lifted his chin a notch.

"I had the nightmare for the first time shortly before I left Oslo, and I must say it didn't make any sense to me whatsoever. I thought perhaps it occurred because of my complete immersion in the culture, and that I put in too many hours on all of my projects. And then, of course, I went through my unpleasant experience with Simon." She shrugged, lost in the memory.

"Simon? Who in the bloody blazes is this—this

Simon?" he raised a brow as he blurted out the question.

Shae waved a hand in dismissal and shook her head in disdain. "He is not important to any of this. He's just my ex-fiancé, and at the time, he abruptly ended our engagement. So, I thought perhaps the incident played a part in conjuring the nightmare.

"Anyway," she continued, "in this dream I am walking down a moonlit path that leads to a small country church. I am terrified as I come to the door. I can hear terrible noises and voices coming from inside. Despite my fear, I crack the door open, and that's when I see the two of them fighting."

"Them?" he urged.

"Fenrir and Odin. They are viciously battling each other inside this old country church. Debris from the carnage is flying out in all directions. The battle is lengthy and horrendous. Finally, Odin slams Fenrir down on the floor, but Fenrir takes that small opportunity to lunge at Odin. He swallows his entire body, just as the myth dictates. I am hiding in the shadows, waiting for the arrival of Vidar. But the warrior never comes.

"Once I know Vidar isn't going to come, I notice the woman on the opposite side of the room. Somehow, I know this woman deeply loves Odin. She is looking at me, and her eyes beg for my help. I know then, she wants me to take the place of Vidar and avenge Odin myself.

"I feel compelled to help her. I know that according to the story, I must take hold of Fenrir's jaws and tear the wolf open. This act is the only way to end his life. As I step forward to attempt the impossible, he sees me hidden there in the shadows. He is growling his hatred and scorn as he approaches.

"In the beginning, when I first began having the dream, at this point the wolf would lunge toward me.

He has his enormous jaws open wide to consume me, just as he consumed Odin. However, I always woke up before he completed the deed, thank heaven."

"In the beginning?" he asked.

Shae nodded as she smoothed away a wrinkle on the blanket. "After I arrived at Starling, the dream sort of evolved. The woman began falling to her knees after the death of Odin, sobbing in tremendous agony and pain. Seeing her weep and listening to her mournful cries tore at my heart. I had to do something to help her. I could see no other recourse. But this time as I step forward, Fenrir takes hold of the magic chain that held him bound throughout the ages and seizes me with it. He wraps it so tightly around my body that I can't move or even breathe properly. You know, it's a frightening thing to experience, not being able to breathe, I mean." She looked away, remembering.

Tristan nodded in understanding, but said nothing in response.

"Anyway, I am suddenly enveloped in a thick black, darkness. Each small breath I take is difficult and painful to endure. The wolf is keeping me from doing what I have to do, what I must do. I struggle, but it does no good. I start crying tears of rage and helplessness. I beg him not to do this to me, but he only laughs maniacally in return." Her eyes, brimming with unshed tears, focused on her ghostly companion, gauging his reaction. She needed him to understand how very real the nightmares seemed.

Tristan remained quiet and attentive. Nevertheless, she could see by expression alone that he understood the devastating effect this dream had on her soul. He didn't discount it as an inconsequential dream as she feared.

"Now that you have the background," Shae continued, satisfied with the acceptance in his eyes, "I'll move forward to the day you destroyed my printed documents. I think you must surely remember it."

"Clearly." He tossed her a lopsided grin and said, "You accused me of having a tantrum as I recall, but I have to say when it comes to temper tantrums, you are by far—"

"It's better that you stop right there," Shae said with her hand outstretched and palm forward. "Trust me."

Tristan only chuckled in response to the veiled threat.

"So, that day, after I left the house, I thought a drive might do me some good. You know, calm me down a bit. And don't you dare say it!" His eyes twinkled with merriment as he raised a mocking brow in response to her last comment.

"Anyway, after driving around for a while, I could see this belfry, rising out above some of the trees, and I wanted to get a closer look at it. Norman Lamont provided me a brief history of the place, and so I had this sudden desire to explore the structure. I couldn't find a road leading to it, but I did find a path that looked promising."

She paused as she recalled the memory. Tristan tilted his head to the side as he waited for her to continue. She took a deep breath and slowly released it. She clasped her hands together and lifted them to her chin.

"As I walked the path, it started to look hauntingly familiar. I began to feel—agitated, scared. And then understanding dawned. I walked the same path in my dreams, only this time, I walked it in broad daylight. The trail would lead me to the church. Although I expected to see it once I rounded the turn, I found I really wasn't prepared when the structure loomed into view."

"Your church is here?" The statement surprised him and it showed.

"Down to the very last weather-beaten detail," she replied as she dropped her hands to her lap. "I affirmed that fact again today when I finally mustered the courage to open the door and take a peek inside. An evil presence still emanates from that building. I could feel it."

"What do you mean, 'an evil presence still emanates'?" he asked as apprehension filled his eyes.

"Oh, come on, Captain." Shae leaned a little more toward him, thus gaining his full attention. "Surely, you have figured this out, by now. Evil still emanates because I could feel it as I stood in front of the Adaria First Presbyterian Church. Evil still emanates because the spirit of Major Nils Adlundsen is still inside the building, right where you both fought and right where he died."

"If you really believe that, then why, of all the foolish things you could possibly think to do, would you try to go inside that structure? The very thought of you making such an attempt terrifies me beyond measure. What were you thinking?" he berated her.

She took no offense. "I must go inside the church, because there is something I have to accomplish in there. It's all part of my dream. Don't you get it? He represents Fenrir, just as you represent Odin. And that's why I know you didn't do anything your peers accused you of doing."

"Are you certain your conclusion isn't faulty?" he questioned with a hint of bitterness in his tone. "According to the official reports, you have that backward. Besides, how could you possibly see a correlation between your nightmare and what happened at the church?"

Shae held up the photograph, turned the picture toward him, and pointed at the subject. "Because, Tristan, the woman from my dreams, the woman who loves and mourns Odin, is your mother."

The revelation moved him to his feet, and for

several seconds he stared at her in disbelief. He shook his head, and at once, began pacing. His thoughts became a jumbled mass of confusion. How could she possibly think the woman in her dreams was his mother? He could accept the fact they might bear a strong resemblance to each other, but his mother died several years before he did. Therefore, how could she possibly know the details surrounding his death? Why would she use such a horrendous dream to contact Shaelynn, even if somehow, she did? How would she even know of her existence and find her in Oslo of all places? He whirled around to face her.

"You actually think the woman in your dreams is my mother?" He raised a brow in disbelief.

"I don't think, Captain. I know she is the woman in my dream." Shaelynn tilted her chin in defiance. "Want more proof? The dress she is wearing is a light blue silk. Both the lace trim and the buttons are white. Although her hair is a shade lighter than yours, you both have the exact same shape and color of eyes."

Her accuracy stunned him. "All right, let's say for arguments sake, the woman in your dreams is my mother. Is that what you have based your entire assumptions on?"

"I do have to admit she is the determining factor. But, she isn't the only factor," she replied. "There is more—"

"Such as?" He folded his arms against his chest and waited for her answer.

"Such as the medical journal, detailing the patients treated here at Starling. The notations next to your name state you sustained several defensive wounds," she said. "It seems clear to me that if you attacked Adlundsen first, he would have been the one with the defensive wounds, not you. There is also the fact that one of the witnesses to the 'incident,' a man by the name of Forseth Ericksen, couldn't possibly have been around to witness anything. According to the medical journal, he lay here at Starling the day before you arrived with a recently amputated leg."

Tristan found himself nodding in agreement. "Yes, I know about that. Seth badly injured his leg in a stupid and senseless accident while at the encampment. The kid just happened to come along at the wrong place at the wrong time. I wished a thousand times I could have somehow prevented it, but—"

He suddenly discovered her gaze fixed firmly to his, almost as if she peered inside his very soul. The depth of her probe made him feel a bit uncomfortable. "I'm sorry, you were saying?"

"Yes," she replied. "Another person began to doubt the official account, and it bothered him his whole life. Does the name Zepheniah Henry mean anything to you?"

"His name is listed as one of the witnesses to the report. But other than that..." He let the words trail off as he shrugged indifferently.

"Well, he's the last person you made eye contact with just before you lost consciousness. I know this because I met his grandson, Isaac, in front of the church the first day I discovered its existence. You know, Isaac is really a very nice man. In an interesting sort of way, he reminds me of my grandfather. Anyway, he seemed quite happy to share everything he knew about the incident with me."

She grinned, tossed her head slightly as if he amused her in some way, and said, "You're standing and staring at me again. So, if you want to hear the rest of this, you really are going to have to sit down."

Tristan sat, listened patiently and without interruption as she went on to give him the details of her first meeting with Isaac. She also gave him the reasons behind her second, and it touched him that she cared enough about the discrepancies in the documents to try to find the answers despite his silence.

"Well, there you have it," Shaelynn said as she clasped her hands together. "For whatever it's worth, I've given you all of my reasons for believing in your innocence. And now it's your turn to give me the answers to my questions."

He crossed his arms against his chest and nodded. "All right, Miss Montgomery. What is it you want to know?"

"I want to know why they accused you of treason in the first place."

Chapter 12

Tristan chuckled bitterly. "Now that's the most puzzling question of all, isn't it? And I'm afraid I don't have the answer for you. At least, not all of it. I can only give you the incoherent ramblings of a lunatic."

"A lunatic?" Shaelynn knit her brows in confusion. "I don't understand. Didn't anybody ever tell you or make you aware that, that—" Her hands gestured the words she did not want to say.

"That a warrant for my arrest existed? No. I had no idea any charges were pending against me, least of all, those for treason." He spat the words that filled him with pain and distaste.

"Such a thought would never have entered my mind. I knew, of course, shortly after the battle that Rosecrans received faulty information. One would have to be an imbecile not to know that. I was also aware the general ordered Nils to find out where the misinformation originated, and that he seemed very pleased with the assignment. Other than those two facts, I knew nothing else concerning the investigation. At least, I didn't know anything until the day I met Nils at the church prior to my death."

She cringed when he mentioned his exit from mortality. Although, for the life of him he couldn't figure out why it should bother her. The deed happened well over a century ago.

"I'm sorry," she mumbled as she cast her gaze downward. "You don't have to talk about it, if you don't want to."

"The telling of it doesn't bother me. I've gone

over the memory of that day more times than I care to count. But if you would rather I didn't, then, of course—"

He gazed into her eyes as he spoke, searching for the telltale emotions that would give away her true feelings on the subject.

"No, please, I want you to continue." She swallowed hard a couple of times.

Tristan grinned at her then. The look of horror shining so clearly from her expressive eyes, contradicted her statement. The woman would rather face down a cantankerous black bear defending her young, than hear the circumstances surrounding his death. Nevertheless, he wanted to tell her. He wanted her to know what happened that day, and that fact surprised him.

"Once they gave Nils the assignment to take charge of the investigation, his presence in camp became quite scarce. No one thought anything of it. In fact, I'm not sure how many of us even kept track of his absences. I know I didn't. I didn't try to piece it all together until well after my demise. At that point, I couldn't help wondering where he went, and what he did during the times of his absence.

"Several days before my death, I received a note from Nils. His runner delivered it, a man by the name of Janssen. Nils said he expected to return to camp the following day, and that he discovered some vital information concerning his investigation he wanted to discuss with me. He said this information needed to remain confidential and secret, until he presented it in court. Therefore, he asked if I would meet him at the Adaria church the morning of his arrival, which he anticipated to be no earlier than 11:45. I told Janssen to convey to Nils that I would meet him, as requested. Honestly, I didn't give the meeting any further consideration than that. My own duties precluded me from dwelling on his assignments."

"But didn't it seem odd to you, that Nils wanted to discuss what he found if he needed to keep the information secret?" she asked. "I mean, you weren't part of the investigation, were you?"

"No, I wasn't part of it. But it also wasn't unusual for Nils to seek my opinion on a great variety of things, both in and out of the military. As Isaac Henry already mentioned, Nils and I formed our friendship when we were small children. I would venture to say he sought my advice quite often as the years passed, all part of being his friend, I suppose. I never thought anything of it.

"Anyway, the following morning I got up early and tended to my duties. I finished earlier than I expected and thought I would just go on over to the church and wait. Wanting a bit of solitude, I took my time getting there. Even so, I arrived at about 11:30 and it surprised me somewhat to find Nils's horses already tethered at the post. They looked as if they had been there for a while.

"I dismounted, tied my horse next to his, and went inside. Nils stood toward the front of the chapel with his back facing me. My entrance startled him. He turned toward me. He looked frenzied in a way I can't explain. His eyes appeared glazed, his cheeks flushed, and he gasped as he looked into my face. From his expression alone, one might believe he hadn't expected me to show up at all. I found it disquieting, to say the least. I asked him if he was all right." His voice broke.

At that moment in his narrative, Shaelynn sought the hand he had placed on his thigh. She probably would have tried to take hold of it, if not for the grin he just couldn't suppress. She looked horrified as her eyes looked down at the close proximity of their hands, before her gaze shot up to meet with his.

"Oh. I'm sorry," she stammered as the hand in question flew to her mouth. "I forgot that you—well, it's just that—"

He chuckled in response to the delightful blush spreading across her cheeks, as well as sight of the offered hand dropping onto, and then toying with, her bare toes.

"Believe me, there is no apology necessary. What I wouldn't give, though." He sighed, allowing his gaze to linger over her face. "What I wouldn't give."

"You asked if he was all right," she reminded him as she swept a hand across her face.

The blatant attempt to shift his attention off her plight and back to his story, made him grin anew. Nevertheless, he obliged and allowed the memory to continue.

"Yes, I did. He didn't answer my question, though. He just stared at me for several seconds, and then asked why I showed up so early. His tone was reproachful and at the same time, suspicious. He started walking toward me at a very slow pace. He dropped his gaze, and furrowed his brows. It appeared to me that he made every effort to answer his own question and came up short. Finally, he met my gaze, sneered, and made a bunch of statements that didn't make any sense at all.

"I remember him saying things like, 'You think you are so much better, so much more intelligent than I am. You always have, and I want you to know I despise you for that. But I am not going to let you get away with it. Not now, not again. I know what you've been up to, and I will not allow you to have what is rightfully mine—'"

"What did he mean, rightfully his?" she interrupted.

"I have no idea," Tristan replied as he lifted a hand and then dropped it onto his lap. "I asked him that same question myself, and he only laughed a hideous, hysterical laugh that made my blood run cold. Then, while he still approached me, he began rambling.

"He said, 'I've already taken care of everything. No one will ever be the wiser. You are going to see just how intelligent I really am, or maybe you won't. I am sorry, Tristan, that it has to end this way, but the opportunity is just too perfect to ignore. I find it a shame really, that you are the one who is going to have to die a traitor to his own country. I wonder what people will think about that?'"

Shae gaped at him in astonishment. "He actually said you were—"

"The sacrificial lamb? Yes, indeed," Tristan finished. "Although I must admit, I didn't completely understand the comment when he said it. I didn't fully understand it until I could no longer do anything about it. You see, at that point, Nils made his initial attack. He lunged at me with his knife, which he already held in his hand. I didn't see it earlier because while he faced me, he kept both arms behind his back as if he had his hands clasped. Such was his normal stance. I thought nothing of it, until I could do nothing about it.

"I won't burden you with the gory details. Suffice it to say, I fought for my life, and Nils fought to end it. At the end of the day, both our mortal lives ended and for what? I have never been able to understand the 'why' of it." He ended in a harsh whisper.

Tristan looked up and caught Shaelynn searching his eyes with a pained expression on her lovely face. She leaned forward and shook her head slightly.

"I am so sorry, Tristan, so very sorry for all you suffered," she murmured softly.

"You want to know the worst part?" he asked as he returned her gaze. "My own father believed the lie. I never understood that. How could he believe such a thing of me? You would think for the thirty years we shared as father and son, he would have had just a little more faith in me than that.

"Yet, after they informed him of the accepted circumstances surrounding my death, he told the commanding officers that he didn't want to take possession of my body. He told them they could do with it as they saw fit; burn it, if it pleased them. They offered him my personal effects. He said they could burn them too, that he didn't want any reminders of a son who would betray his own country. Then, before he walked out the door, after completely disavowing my very existence, he turned toward them one last time. He said he felt a semblance of gratitude that my mother didn't live long enough to see what I had become, for surely, I would have broken her heart."

As Tristan grew quiet, Shae closed her eyes in an attempt to hold back the tears. They fell anyway. She bowed her head as she considered the final, painful injustice he endured and continued to endure. The knowledge his own father rejected him. Tristan's face registered surprise as the first of her tears wandered down her cheek. She met his gaze as he lifted a hand to wipe them away, and the action surprised her.

"Here now, we will have none of that, especially when there is no need," he said.

A light, feathery caress swept across her face as he brushed his fingertips against her skin. Interesting. Aulric never touched her. Until this moment, she didn't know one could actually feel the touch of a spirit, but she could feel Tristan's gentle caress as well as she could anything else. Shae remained quiet as she gathered her thoughts. She could hear the rain pouring harder now, along with the rumbling sounds of thunder. The steady rhythm pounding against the roof somehow soothed her soul. She hoped it had the same effect on Tristan.

As she wiped away the remaining tears she said, "Do you think Adlundsen discovered the man responsible for the message given to Rosecrans and covered it up, or do you think he planned to blame you from the beginning? You know, so you 'wouldn't take what rightfully belonged to him.' At the same time, he could be the brilliant leader who routed out the traitor and be counted the hero of the hour."

"I have asked myself those same questions, many times over. I don't have any of the answers."

Shae looked down at the photograph and sighed wistfully. "It's no wonder your mother is pleading for my help."

"You can't tell me you seriously believe that." Tristan raised an incredulous brow.

"Yes, I really do," she shot back.

"But she doesn't know about any of this. The woman preceded me in death by three years. She wasn't even around when the incident happened," he argued.

"What difference does that make?" she asked. "Why is it so difficult for you to believe that within her realm of existence, she is aware of your circumstances? And that maybe, just maybe, in her own way and in her own time, she finally found a way to help you?"

"The whole thing just seems so unlikely to me."

"Just as unlikely as the existence of ghosts, who by popular consensus is nothing more than the figment of childish imagination? However, if you ask the majority of those who do believe ghosts exist, they would simply tell you they are only shadows of their former selves. A harmless, shapeless, sheet like phantom, who can do nothing more than moan and groan a little. Perhaps, make a scary face or two. However, I think we both have to agree Perry Adler would heartily disagree with those assessments, and so would I." She raised a triumphant brow, smiled smugly, and dared him to refute her claim.

Her comment elicited a quiet chuckle, and as he shook his head, he said, "Shaelynn, even if you are right—"

"And I am," she stubbornly insisted.

"What exactly do you think you can do about it?" he asked, clearly amused.

"No, that isn't the question. The real question is, what does your mother think I can do?" she replied, as she pointed to the woman in the photograph.

Ignoring his exasperated sigh, she allowed her mind to consider the possibilities and gave voice to them. "We have to remember, she is the one who used the battle of Ragnarok to gain my attention. In all likelihood, she used the event because she found it the closest thing in Norse mythology to explain the details surrounding your final hours of mortality. She had to know I would relate to and understand it.

"She anticipated my understanding because of my lifelong love affair with the Norse culture and mythology. That love is in my very blood. All throughout my life, I could never get enough knowledge concerning the people or their culture. I have always thirsted for more. I knew most of the myths inside and out before I ever entered college and began to learn the languages connected with them.

"Somehow your mother had knowledge of all that. She had to know I would go to Oslo as part of my education and training. She knew I would meet Professor Todd Andersen, who just happens to be a direct descendent of Hans Christian Heg. Because of that relationship, she could foresee that one day he would have the desire to create an exhibit in Lierbyen, Norway, featuring the famed Wisconsin Fifteenth Regiment his grandfather commanded.

Given that knowledge, it is only logical to assume the exhibit would need copies of the same records and photos housed here in the United States. If the people in the Scandinavian countries were to benefit from those historic records, they would need to read them in their own language.

"I am the only person the professor knows who can do all the various translations he wants done. And somehow, your mother anticipated my breakup with Simon would provide the motive I needed to accept the job offer." The sudden look of irritation on his face took her by surprise. Did she say something wrong?

"I have to say, you've given my mother some exceptional abilities. I think in the old country they might have called someone with that kind of foresight a witch." He stated the comment nonchalantly, though his expression belied the tone.

"Oh, don't be so melodramatic." She rolled her eyes and tsked. "I prefer to think of her as your guardian angel. And such beings have exceptional, extraordinary abilities, especially when it comes to their charges. She must have known everything about me, even before my birth. Such knowledge is the only explanation for all of this."

"My guardian angel? I don't think I've ever considered such a possibility before, and I'm not sure I even deserve one. Besides, the function of guardian angels end once their charges die, do they not?" he asked.

"Perhaps the job doesn't end, until their charges are safely where they belong," she countered.

"Oh, come on, Shaelynn. My mother is a wonderful woman, but an angel?" He looked at her skeptically.

"Yes, I'm sure that's exactly what she is now." She caught her bottom lip with her teeth, as she looked down at the woman in the photograph.

Suddenly, she wanted to think of her as someone other than "the woman in her dreams."

"I don't know, Shaelynn, I think you're grasping at straws."

She ignored his skepticism. "So, tell me, what is this angel's name, anyway?"

"Bryn, or Brynhild Bakken Jordahl, if you want to know her name in full," he replied.

She detected a notable fondness in his tone, and it made her smile. "Ah. Her parents named her after one of the beautiful Valkyrie maidens. That's fitting. Did they do that on purpose or did they just like the name?" she asked.

"I don't know." He shrugged. "My mother never said. All I can tell you is that her grandparents kept one foot this side of Christianity and one foot firmly entrenched in the old ways. I think that's where my mother learned all of her stories. She could keep us entertained for hours on end with tales of valor and heroism. So much so, that we often finished our chores before we realized we had even started them."

"How many brothers and sisters do you have?" she asked, suddenly curious.

"My parents produced seven children; three boys and four girls," he informed her. "I am the oldest of my siblings."

"So, this lovely Valkyrie angel managed to pass along all of the old traditions to her children so they would remember their roots," Shae mused as she lightly touched the area around Bryn's neck. For the first time then, she noticed the omission. "But in this picture, she is not wearing her lovely pendant. I wonder why she chose not to wear it for this photograph. Did she not have it yet?"

"What did you just say?" he asked, clearly stunned by her statement.

"Her necklace," Shae repeated. "She has a beautifully carved pendant of Thor's hammer, set off by a faceted amber jewel that's just—Tristan, what's wrong?"

Tristan stared at her as if she'd suddenly sprouted two heads. He abruptly left his place on the bed, strode over to the trunk and lifted the lid. "Would you be so kind," he said, gesturing toward the contents.

Shae clambored off the bed, knelt by the side of the trunk, and gazed into his eyes. "What do you want me to do?"

"Search inside the pocket of my coat, right here on top," he replied. "You can do it faster and easier than I can."

"This trunk is yours?" she asked.

"Yes, it is. As I already mentioned, my father didn't feel inclined to claim my personal belongings, so Amy just kept my trunk here. For safekeeping, she said. The dear woman actually thought that perhaps one day my father might change his mind. Of course, he never did. But by the time Amy passed from mortality, I'd already claimed this room as my own. No one, living or dead, ever disputed my claim. After all, I did die here and thus, my possessions have remained intact."

The comment surprised her, although it probably shouldn't have. A flood of emotions swirled as she picked up his military coat, which remained in remarkably good condition. As she held it up, she caught just a whiff of the scent that still clung to the collar. The manly scent surely belonged to Tristan while he lived.

She dipped her fingers inside the pocket he indicated. The realization that she held a piece of clothing Tristan actually wore while he lived, overwhelmed her. But even that couldn't compare with the feeling she had once she extracted the delicate silver chain out of the pocket. Down to the last vivid detail provided in her dreams, she now

135

held Bryn's necklace in the palm of her hand.

She gasped in delighted surprise as she examined it three dimensionally. "Oh, Tristan, my dream didn't even begin to do the piece justice. How did you happen to have it with you?"

"As I told you earlier, my mother preceded me in death by three years. She was dying of cholera, and was aware of that fact. The day before she passed, she asked me to get the necklace out of her jewelry box. I thought she just wanted to have it on as it always meant a great deal to her. In truth, she wore it most of the time. Her grandmother gave it to her when she was just a young girl if I recollect the story correctly.

"Anyway, I got it out of her box, went to slip it around her neck, but she stopped me. She said that as her eldest son, she wanted me to have it. That it would be just a little memento by which to remember her. She said one day, at the right time and place, I would pass it along myself to the person of my choosing. Then, that person would do the same and so on. In this way, the pendant would continue to exist. Because the pendant would continue to live on, she said, so would we. I have always suspected she heard those very same words from her grandmother."

"Well, I'm really glad she gave it to you. I wouldn't have wanted to miss this chance to see it for myself. Thank you for sharing it with me." She could see her statement pleased him, although he simply nodded in response. "Do you want me to put it back inside your coat pocket or would you rather have it at your desk where you can admire it a little more often?"

"In the box, on top of the desk, if you don't mind," he said.

"I don't mind at all." Shae rose to her feet, still holding on to Tristan's jacket. The movement caused a folded piece of paper to fall out of the pocket and flutter to the ground. She stooped down and picked it up, using just her fingertips.

"What's this?" she asked as she held it in the palm of her outstretched hand.

Tristan drew his brows together as if trying to recall. "I'm not sure. Why don't you open the note, and see what it says?"

"All right. The paper doesn't feel especially brittle, so, I guess I can give it a try. Let me put this stuff down first."

She placed his coat gently on the bed, walked over to the desk, and opened the box with the intention of placing the necklace inside it. However, a small breath escaped her lips before she completed the task. As the necklace dangled from her fingertips, she looked down at the unexpected portrait of Tristan, dressed in full uniform. The CDV photograph, which captured his image to perfection, lay on top of his personal letters and papers.

The man was extraordinarily handsome, no doubt about that, and here lay black-and-white proof of that fact. She glanced up and found him gazing intently in her direction.

She flashed him a smile, tilted her head toward the picture, and asked, "May I?"

As she awaited his permission, she could see Tristan drop his gaze to her mouth. The length of time he lingered there made her feel a bit self-conscious. At the same time, she could feel her smile fading.

"If it pleases you," he finally said.

Gazing at the photo she cradled in her hand, the notion that it should become part of the exhibits suddenly took hold. The portrait would be a wonderful addition, and after all, she knew that sooner or later she would clear Tristan's name. Bryn already decreed as much.

"Tristan," she began hesitantly, uncertain as to how he would take the request. "Would you mind if I made a digital copy of this photograph as well as the one of your mother? I can do it down in my office, and I can promise you there won't be any damage done to the original pictures. Making the copies would also ensure their preservation for generations to come."

He shrugged as he folded his arms against his chest. "I can't imagine my photograph being of great importance or desired by anyone now living, but if you wish to copy them, you may."

She thanked him with another smile, laid his photograph on top of the one of his mother, placed the necklace inside the box, and closed the lid.

"Now for your note." Shae took a deep breath and turned her attention to the folded piece of paper. Using great care she lifted the edges with just the tips of her fingers. She could feel Tristan's presence behind her. He continued to study her measured progress until the small sheet revealed its entire content.

"Oh. Of course—it's the note from Nils I told you about," he said. "I didn't realize I still had it."

Shae slid her fingers underneath the paper and swept the note into the open palm of her hand. She lifted it closer to the light so she could read the faded writing. Nils's poor penmanship made the task even more difficult. She cleared her throat and read the note aloud.

"Tristan,

Breakthrough. I have to discuss findings surrounding my investigation. Secrecy is vital to security. We need to meet in a safe location. Suggest Adaria Church tomorrow morning; my arrival estimated no earlier than 11:45. Please confirm prompt arrival.

Nils"

She looked up from the paper and said, "I think we should add a copy of this note to our ever growing file."

"What file?" he asked.

"The file I'm going to make with all the compiled documents I'll need to clear your name," she said, surprised he didn't already understand. "Tristan, your mother arranged to bring me here, in order to translate a mountain of records. Surely, all the proof we're going to need to set history aright, is somewhere in that mound of information. You have to remember, I don't even have all the documents in my possession yet."

The sudden, urgent banging on the door downstairs caused momentary panic. She turned instinctively toward the sound, though her eyes, wide with apprehension, never left Tristan's face. Visions of a drunken Perry Adler leaped into her mind. An involuntary shudder coursed through her body. "Who could that—"

"Not to worry," he said, giving her a reassuring wink. "The cavalry just arrived, albeit a little late, to do you any good. I believe you will find Norman Lamont and his company on your porch, and they are very concerned about your welfare."

Chapter 13

Just as Shae and Tristan touched the bottom step, the insistent hammering on her door grew even louder. As she hurried toward the foyer, she hollered out, "I'm coming, just give me a minute."

She slid to a halt in front of the door while turning the handle. Norman, Reuben, Ian, and George huddled together on her doorstep, seeking refuge from the relentless storm.

"Well, hello everyone. I certainly didn't expect to see you out here tonight. Come in, you're all soaking wet and look chilled to the bone."

"Shae," Norman croaked out as they passed over the threshold. "I must apologize for the lateness of the hour, but we were so very worried about you."

"You all worried about me?" Shae looked into each of the rain-soaked faces and could see the concern there. But she didn't know why. "I'm not sure I understand."

"The truck," Norman said. "Perry left the motor still running and the door wide open, just outside Ian's office. We didn't see him anywhere near the vehicle. Why, if not for the fact that Ian and Reuben conducted a late meeting, we wouldn't have noticed the truck until the morning. Ian said that Perry left early this afternoon to bring you the documents, yet the boxes still sat inside the vehicle, untouched. And we found blood all over the steering wheel and the seat. Then when we repeatedly tried to call both the office as well as your cell phone numbers with no answer, I'm afraid we jumped to all kinds of conclusions. None of those conclusions gave us any comfort, so we just had to come out and make sure you were all right."

"Oh. I'm so sorry about that. I didn't have my phone with me. I guess I must have left it in my bedroom." She glanced briefly at Tristan, who at that moment, took hold of the door and slammed it shut. She didn't know if he did it in response to her apology or the mere mention of Perry Adler's name. Either way, it scared the wits out of her visitors.

"Wow, that wind is really wicked out there tonight isn't it?" Shae cleared her throat and then added, "Why don't you all make yourselves comfortable in the drawing room, and I'll go get something to warm you up."

Her suggestion managed to take their focus off the door. Shae waited for them to disappear into the room before she turned toward Tristan.

"Please, Tristan," she whispered. "These men didn't have anything to do with Perry's actions today. You don't need to scare the living daylights out of them just because they sent him out here."

Tristan's lips twitched in response. He folded his arms across his chest and locked his gaze with hers while he considered the request. Shae sought to press her advantage.

"Look, I don't want anyone else to know what happened here today. Not if I can help it," she said. "The whole incident is a humiliating nightmare, and I just want to forget it ever happened."

"You don't think that man should be punished for his actions?" he asked. "You think he should just walk away unscathed after what he did to you?"

Shae blew out a derisive breath. "He didn't get the chance to do anything as you recall, and he didn't just walk away unscathed, either. The blood inside the truck is witness to that fact. So, I think the 'punishment' you dished out is more than sufficient, don't you? Please, Tristan, for my sake, just let it go."

"If those men remain unaware of his vile intentions toward you, they might send him back here again," he said.

"And you'll be waiting, right by my side if they do," she replied. "What better person to watch over me, than you, hmm? Please?"

At that moment, Tristan concluded he could not deny her anything she asked for, not even this. He'd already proven that to himself when they were upstairs in his room, and she asked to copy his likeness.

He shook his head and sighed in defeat. "You win. But I'd better make myself scarce while you entertain your visitors, lest I go back on my word."

Shae smiled, and just before he disappeared she said, "Don't go too far away, I may need you."

Her words had a greater effect on him than he cared to admit. Nonetheless, he found himself grateful for this opportunity to disappear for a while. No, he wouldn't go too far away, nor would he be gone overly long. *She might need me.*

He looked at the evening sky as he journeyed toward his destination. The storm continued its relentless fury. Lightning spilled across the heavens in wild abandon. The thunder quaked and boomed with such intensity, it threatened to shake the very foundations of the Adaria First Presbyterian Church. Nevertheless, Tristan approached the structure with the overpowering need to see the place for himself. During the passage of time in his spiritual state, it never once occurred to him that Nils might also have remained behind, or that he would choose the chapel for his place of refuge.

Yet, as he stood beneath the boughs of the old oak tree, he placed all of his concentration inside the barrier surrounding the chapel walls. Within that constructed barrier, he could see the sinister spirit of

Nils Adlundsen. Right now, the entity stood by the side, center window. From that position, Adlundsen looked out over the storm and fed on its energy. So caught up in his frenzy, Nils remained unaware of Tristan's presence. Of course, it might not occur to the man to look for another spirit this close to his domain. That gave him the advantage he needed.

Tristan folded his arms across his chest as he continued to study the man who so casually ended his life. In retrospect, he should have seen it coming. He recalled the day Nils told him about the assignment. Nils all but burst through his tent to tell him the news. He had a triumphant smile on his face as he read the order aloud.

"Sounds like a daunting task," Tristan remembered saying, as he sat at his makeshift desk.

"Which is probably the very reason they gave this assignment to me," Nils replied. "I've no doubt they have every confidence I can solve this little mystery for them."

"No doubt," Tristan repeated off-handedly, as he signed the final letter requiring his signature. "Have you spoken to Rosecrans yet?"

"I'm not a simpleton, *Captain*," Nils snapped before he hurried to soften his tone. "Of course, I began at the top. Not that he was of any use. He couldn't even offer a description of the man who relayed the message."

A gleam appeared in Adlundsen's eye when he made the comment. Of course, at the time, Tristan paid it no heed. "I'm not surprised, given the chaos of that particular battle. Unfortunately, it will make your task all the more difficult," he said.

"Don't you worry, Tristan." Nils paused then, cocked his head to the side, and looked him over for several seconds.

If someone asked him to describe the expression on Nils's face at that moment, he would have to say it reminded him very much of a predator, stalking his prey. Why didn't he see it then?

Finally, Nils said, "Rest assured that I'll hand the perpetrator over to the proper authorities in due course. And you can also rest assured that I'll have all the necessary evidence to convict him."

Tristan shook his head as he recalled the memory. Shaelynn was right. A powerful evil did emanate from Adaria. He could feel it all the way out here, just as she did. That made this particular place more perilous than she realized. He could not allow her to come anywhere near it. She *must* not come anywhere near it, despite her preconceived duty.

Her nightmares still puzzled him, though. If his mother had a hand in them, like Shaelynn so vehemently insisted, what did she hope to gain by plaguing her with such horrors? What could Shaelynn possibly do to alter the events that took place inside the church? Why would his mother want her in there, knowing Adlundsen had claimed it? Clearing his name held no importance if it meant placing Shaelynn's life in any kind of danger. Surely, his mother would understand this.

At that very moment, an unearthly wail emitted from inside the church. The maniacal shriek chilled his very soul. He had no desire to understand its meaning. He'd left Shaelynn alone far too long, and it was time to return to Starling. Minutes later, he entered the foyer and could hear Shaelynn speaking to her guests.

"Of course, I understand," she said. "However, I am a little concerned over the documents you scheduled Perry to deliver today. You did say they were safe and still inside the truck?"

"Yes, I did," Reuben replied.

"Are you going to bring them out to me soon?" she asked. "I really am going to need them if I am to stay on schedule."

"Yes, I know, and we had the presence of mind to bring them with us. We didn't want to leave them unattended in the truck." Reuben set his empty cup on the table and inclined his head toward George.

"George, why don't you hurry out and get them, so we can allow Shae to have what's left of her evening. I am sure she has better things to do than put up with all of us."

"I'll help you," Ian offered as he rose from his chair.

"All right, while you're doing that, I'll go get the completed set for you," Shaelynn said. "If you'll excuse me for just a minute?"

Tristan popped into her office before she arrived. He sat down on the edge of her desk and folded his arms against his chest. She gave him a smile as she entered.

"See?" she said. "No worries."

"No worries? What do you mean?"

She walked over to the file cabinet, unlocked the drawer, and pulled out the boxes she wanted to return. "Didn't you hear them say they were going to fire Perry for leaving the documents unattended? Well, they're going to fire him if they can find him, that is. He appears to be missing," she said.

"So they should."

"I thought that bit of news would make you happy." She took hold of the boxes and headed for the door. "Let me get these documents exchanged and I'll send them on their way. I'm anxious to see what we can find in this next set. I'll be right back."

Tristan waited inside Shaelynn's office while the men said their goodbyes. He could hear her thanking them for their concern and for coming all the way out to check on her. Yet, she failed to realize that concern should never have been an issue. The fact they worried that something might have happened to her in the first place, said much about the known character of Perry Adler. They should never have sent him out here alone.

Tristan heard the door close and then the sounds of her bare footsteps, making their way back into the drawing room. Now that her guests had vacated the premises, he wasted no time in joining her there.

****

Despite their good intentions and obvious concern, Shae breathed out a sigh of relief as she bid her visitors goodnight. Anxious to get her hands on the new set of documents, she hurried into the drawing room. Just as she took hold of the first box, she found herself surrounded by all of Starlings residents. The huge grin on her face surely matched the ones they gave in return.

Tristan shook his head and looked pointedly at the box she held in her hands. "Not tonight, Shaelynn. It's late and everything inside those boxes can wait until the morning."

Shae glanced down at the container and said, "You're right." She didn't want her ghostly companions to think the documents were more important to her than their offers of renewed friendship. The boxes would have to wait. With a bit of reluctance, she placed it back on the table.

"I thought those people would never leave," Chauncey said, breaking the silence that followed her comment.

"Yes, but you know they needed to make amends after Shaelynn had no choice but to tell them Perry showed up here drunk," Beau pointed out.

"And they didn't even know the half of what happened out here," Amy spat in disgust.

"Well, none of it would have happened, had they been a little more selective as to whom they sent to her door. Don't you agree, Miss Amy?" Tristan turned to face her as he asked Amy the question.

"Absolutely, Captain," she replied. "I think after tonight, they'll be a little more careful. And that's as it should be. We certainly do not want a repeat of what happened here earlier this afternoon."

Everyone agreed with Amy's statement, as did she. Shae wanted to express her gratitude to Tristan in front of the others, so they could hear it for themselves. She also wanted to convey her regret over the erroneous assumption of his guilt. She turned toward the captain and fused her gaze with his. Yet, in so doing, she suddenly realized that tender emotions would get in the way of what she wanted to say. Nonetheless, she made every effort to clear the tightness away in her throat.

"No, we truly don't want a repeat of that experience, not ever. Tristan, I want to thank you again for coming to my rescue the very moment I so desperately needed your help, despite my earlier callousness toward you. You didn't deserve any of my accusations, and I'm so sorry for all of the things I said. I'm sure there are many men out there, when in your position wouldn't have concerned themselves with my plight." Although she tried to contain them, the tears fell anyway.

Tristan once again hastened to her side and brushed the wayward drops away from her face.

"I think you're wrong about that, Miss Montgomery. You should probably know I had to beat Chauncey and Beau off with a stick, so that I could get to you first. Amy too, for that matter.

"I'm of a mind to believe there isn't a man out there who wouldn't move heaven or hell to come to your rescue, living or dead. Nevertheless, you're welcome," he said.

At that moment, she wanted to throw her arms around his neck and hang on just as tight as she could, for as long as she could. She fought off the urge, knowing such an action would land her face down on the floor. Instead, she looked into each of the faces of her companions, smiled, and said, "Thank you—all of you. I want each of you to know that you are very dear to me, and I really missed your company."

As the hour grew later and the conversations waned, Shaelynn finally excused herself. Yet, instead of heading toward her bedroom, she turned and made her way to the staircase. An immediate tug on the back of her T-shirt halted her progress.

"Where do you think you are going?" Tristan whirled her around to face him.

"I'm going to go upstairs, get the photographs you said I could borrow and the note Nils sent you. I would like to get them copied tonight," Shae replied, thinking the answer should be obvious.

"But it's late, Shaelynn. You need to get some rest, especially after the day you've had. You can do all of your copying in the morning," he replied.

"No, you might change your mind about the pictures. Besides, it's only going to take me a few minutes," she argued. "I promise you, after I get the images scanned and saved into my computer, I'll go right to bed. Well, actually, I'll go to bed as soon as I get our file made and put copies of everything I have pertaining to your situation into it. I'll hurry, I promise."

Tristan expelled an exasperated sigh, followed her up the stairs and into his room. All the while, he muttered something indecipherable about the foolish stubbornness of redheads. She merely laughed in return.

Chapter 14

The tender salutation captured Shae's attention. Though she normally did not take time to read letters written in English at this point in her work, curiosity compelled her to continue.

She settled a little more deeply into her office chair.

January 3, 1863

My Dearest Beloved Companion,

We are now set to camping on the banks near Stoney River.

We finally were able to repulse the bedeviled rebels back after they erroneously made not one, but two stands against us. They were both awful battles that took place, and the ground was covered thick with the blood and bodies of my friends, as well as of my enemies.

Countless good and decent men were bloodied, mangled, and killed in reaching this Union Victory. Countless more lay injured and dying in the dust from whence they came. Their screams were horrifying, and just as we have come to expect, against orders, Captain T. Jordahl bravely entered the battlefield time and again to retrieve the suffering men, even though our regiment was still in grave danger from shells and artillery fire. As you can imagine, he is well loved and respected by all.

I shall not attempt to press any more of the awful details of this skirmish upon your delicate and sensitive soul. I merely wanted you to know that I have survived this battle and that I am well at present. Might this letter find you enjoying the same.

I cannot write more as we have been ordered to commence our march. Give the babies my love, and keep the greater portion for yourself.

Yours forever and always,
Christofer

Shae read the letter twice, savoring each word regarding the heroic actions of her captain. She turned her head in an effort to conceal and wipe away her tears before glancing over at the table, where he concentrated on another recently scanned certificate of promotion. After composing herself somewhat, she cleared her throat in an exaggerated manner just to gain his attention.

As he looked over at her in response, she said, "So, I take it that, so far as you've read, there is *nothing* in this current stack of documents to add to our file?"

Tristan shook his head as he shoved the certificate to the side of the table. "Nothing and we've been at this tedious process for weeks now! I really think you need to slow your pace down a bit. You're not eating properly. You spend each waking moment hoping to find something that most likely doesn't exist, and all for my benefit. I know you are wearing yourself out, and I really think it's time you just let go of this obsession. None of this really matters now, anyway. No one is going to care about a dispute that happened well over a century ago."

"Of course it matters, and everyone will care," she shot back as she allowed the precious letter to drop to her desk. Yet, even as she did so, she quickly scooped it up once more.

"Might I remind you that we've been nigh on inseparable since the night that Perr—since the night of the thunderstorm? And it's all because you have put in just as many hours as I have into this quest," she said. "If not for the fact that you read each document as I scan them, we wouldn't have come nearly as far as we have this quickly."

"I don't need to sleep, Shaelynn, and I don't get tired," he countered. "You do. Look, I know you're not keeping to your translation schedule, and all because of your zeal to clear my name. So, I think we should just end this particular pursuit right now. If you happen to come across something while you go about your normal daily routine, then fine, we can go from there. What do you say?"

Shae shook her head ever so slightly as she looked down at the letter she held in her hand. After twirling her chair a little more to the right to meet his gaze head on, she tilted her chin a notch and said, "I'm really glad you feel that way, because you're fired, Tristan."

He knit his brow in consternation. "What are you babbling about?"

"I'm not babbling," she said. "I simply said you're fired. That means you are free to do anything that pleases you, save reading my documents. It sounds like the others are upstairs watching a movie, why don't you join them?"

"Shaelynn, what exactly are you trying to get at?" he asked in exasperation. "You know I won't let you do this alone. You are completely missing the point."

"Whether you help me or not, I intend to continue this particular *pursuit,* and I can't have you working on my task force if you are going to miss important evidence." She held up the letter written by Christofer Berven, to his "beloved companion" and gave it a wave. "Like this one, for instance."

She began reading the letter aloud then, and emphasized the portion that mentioned his valor. He merely shrugged indifferently. She rolled her eyes in return.

"I fail to see where that letter has anything at all to do with the charges of treason against me," he said. "It's a man's personal letter to his wife."

"But it has everything to do with your character. Don't you get it? A man that would face down enemy fire to rescue his troops simply isn't capable of treason." She sighed in frustration. On top of everything else, the captain had to be irritatingly modest.

"Look, I want a copy of anything and everything that mentions your name in any way. I'll be the one to decide what to do with it from there," she emphatically stated. "Do I make myself clear?"

Tristan laughed outright.

"What do you find so funny?" she demanded.

"You," he replied. "I find your feeble attempt to portray yourself as officiously demanding downright hilarious."

"I'm serious, Tristan," she said.

"Yes, ma'am, anything you say, ma'am," he chortled out, while giving her a salute.

Feeling annoyed at best over his amusement, Shae turned away from her desk, stood up, and stepped over to the scanner. All the while, she muttered something about the cockiness of spirits, possessing the luxury of disregarding heavy objects hurled in their direction, in retaliation for that cockiness. Thereby, for lack of fear, they believed they could get away with such boorish behavior toward the living.

The comment delighted him, although he knew she didn't say it for his amusement. "You know, this is most opportune. Since you bring up the subject of fear, or the lack thereof, it brings to mind a question I've been itching to know the answer to."

"Is this a clever ploy to take my mind off the subject at hand, or do you really have a question?" she asked, raising a brow.

"As it so happens, I really do have a question, although I must admit, it is also part of my clever ploy," he confessed.

"And your question is?" she prodded, as she made a second copy of Christofer's letter, and then added it to her growing file.

"Well, it's my experience that mortals fear those who choose to remain behind in their disembodied state. Take Norman Lamont and his cohorts as a prime example of that fact. Yet, from the very beginning, you blithely entered this house, already knowing of our existence ahead of time and didn't feel the least bit put off or concerned about it. In fact, you seemed to feel right at home." Tristan stopped short of reminding her of his initial reaction to her friendly overtures, but he knew she remembered it just as well as he did. "I can't help but wonder why you weren't afraid."

"Because of Aulric," she replied as she placed the next document face down in the scanner. "My Viking chieftain."

Her Viking chieftain? "Would you care to explain that?" he asked.

His tone came out a bit harsher than what he anticipated, but then again, he didn't expect to hear the obvious fondness in her unexpected reply. *First Simon and now Aulric,* he silently seethed. Who in the blazes was this Viking chieftain of hers, anyway, and what annoying name would roll off her tongue next?

"There's not much to explain, really." She glanced over at him and shrugged. "As it so happened, a team of Norwegian archeologists unearthed a Viking ship burial in the Slagen District a couple of years ago. One of many, I might add. The archeological representatives assigned my team to preserve it, and get it ready for display at the museum in Oslo. However, unbeknownst to us, the ship still housed its former occupant."

"Aulric, *your* Viking chieftain, I presume?" he

asked dryly.

"Yep. They found the ship in remarkably good condition. As I recall, it still contained most of its grave goods. It also held two complete skeletons, both of which rested inside the burial chamber. The interesting thing is that even though one of the skeletons belonged to a female, somewhere between the age of twenty-five and thirty, Aulric didn't have a clue as to her identity, or the reason we found her in his bed. He didn't remember leaving her there, he said." She laughed as she gave her head a little toss. "You should have seen his look of bewilderment when he looked at her remains. I found the whole thing pretty funny."

"So how old was this Viking chieftain at the time of his death?" he asked.

"He didn't really know that answer. But, after careful examination of his skeletal remains, we estimated him to be around sixty or so, and he felt that he lived every year of that and then some. He prided himself on surviving countless battles and being the victor time and again when he faced opponents less than half his age." Shaelynn smiled as her voice trailed off.

The man's age made Tristan feel a little bit better. Still. "You became friends with this Viking?" he asked.

"Well, we certainly didn't start off that way." She met Tristan's gaze and grinned. "In the beginning, not only did I have to fight the shock of learning that ghosts do exist, I also needed to learn about their abilities, which no one ever bothered to mention."

"Such as?" he asked.

"Well, let me begin by saying that Aulric was—upset, when the archeologists unearthed his ship. According to what he told me, the vessel, which belonged to him personally, took him on countless voyages. While he lay dying, he instructed his sons to bury him along with his finest possessions, inside his ship. He fully intended to sail away to Valhalla and join Odin's ghostly army. He harbored no doubt the gods would readily accept him. No one could fault him for failing to die in battle, so he could be chosen for the honor by one of the Valkyrie," she said.

"Aulric didn't have a clue eight centuries had passed away while he attempted to gain the necessary skill to sail his ship to the unknown location of Valhalla. He only knew we interfered with his plans to do so. By then, the archeological team transported the ship to the museum and housed it in our work area. We kept all kinds of sharp, heavy tools and implements there, which he promptly took hold of and began throwing haphazardly in my direction." Shae shivered in recollection.

"I hope you were quick enough to take cover." Tristan grinned at the image he conjured at her words.

"I'm not sure anyone could have ducked and rolled as quickly as I did, despite my astonishment," she replied. "And while he threw things, he screamed out curses not fit for a modern day sailor to hear. He damned me to Niflheim where he hoped that Hel would give me my comeuppance. So not only could I hear him quite clearly, I could also see him quite clearly. He looked very solid, appearing to my view as any mortal still living. I always thought if ghosts did exist, they would be—you know, transparent and harmless otherworldly beings. Just as they portray them in the movies.

"Anyway, despite the intensity of his rage, we needed to preserve his ship, or it would quickly fall into ruin. It took me quite a while to convince him of that fact. But once I explained he couldn't take the ship to Valhalla unless we made it seaworthy, he finally let us proceed with our work. Over the course of time, his hatred became grim tolerance, and tolerance finally turned into friendship.

"Because of that friendship, he willingly answered a lot of my questions regarding his spiritual state, as well as those concerning the time and culture in which he lived. Unfortunately, I couldn't put any of that knowledge into academic writing. I don't think any of my professors would have accepted, Aulric, the Viking chieftain, circa A.D. 1200ish as my source." Shaelynn smiled as she made needed adjustments to the scanner and reprinted her current document.

"So in making a very long story short, I guess because of my experience with him, I didn't fear coming to Starling once Norman revealed your presence here." She raised a brow and shrugged. "After all, I didn't think anyone at the plantation could be any worse than Aulric."

"Is this Aulric still in Norway and attempting to sail his ship to Valhalla, then?" he asked.

She shook her head. "No. Aulric finally decided to move on. Although it took eight full centuries, he suddenly realized he didn't need a ship to enter the 'brilliant light of Valhalla' as he referred to it. On that very day, he laughed joyously over his newly acquired knowledge and bid me a fond farewell. He simply bowed, gave me a friendly salute, and then walked off the bow of his ship. Right after he disappeared, I could hear the echo of his laughter for several delightful seconds. The joy in that laughter made me feel that he found the peace and contentment he searched for, and it made me happy."

"Besides Aulric and those of us here at Starling, are there any other spirits you have personally interacted with?"

"No, why do you ask?" The way he phrased the question gave her pause. She stopped working on her current document and thankfully, gave him her full attention. He needed it.

"Because not all of us can be reasoned with, Shaelynn, not all spiritual beings are simply upset or angry. Some entities were truly evil during their mortality, and that evil nature did not end with their death. They are very difficult to deal with, even for other spirits. Trust me on that. We here at Starling, in some of our earlier days, encountered such spirits from time to time. Their presence is not a pleasant thing to deal with or resolve when we do."

Shaelynn knit her brow. He could see her confusion over his explanation. "Yes, I understand that, but why are you telling me all of this?"

"I'm telling you this because it deeply concerned me when you said you wanted to walk into the church all by yourself. Nils is evil, Shaelynn, just as you have already surmised. I didn't see the inherent evil in him myself until it was far too late. You must promise me you will never go inside the church again. In fact, it would please me if you would stay away from it altogether," he finished fervently.

Shaelynn chewed on her bottom lip as she considered his request. Finally, she gave her head a little toss. "I don't know if I can promise you that, Tristan. I think you have to agree that my dreams make it clear, I have to go inside."

"No. No you don't," he countered as he drew close to where she stood. "Your presence inside the church is designed to show you what took place within those walls, to give you understanding and nothing more."

"But what if it is more than that," she argued. "You can't forget your mother begged me to take the place of Vidar. She asked me to deal with the embodiment of Fenrir myself. There must be a reason she needs me to deal with Nils Adlundsen directly."

"No, I don't think she meant for you to deal with him personally. I know my mother, Shaelynn. She wouldn't ask that of you. Don't you see? One can infer that tearing the jaws of the wolf is the same as destroying the lies Nils fabricated. Exposing his deceit would accomplish everything that needs accomplishing. You said yourself you would probably find the evidence to clear my name right here within these documents." He pointed to the large stack of records on the table. "That's why we are feverishly going through them at this pace, isn't that right?"

She glanced over at the documents he indicated before her gaze traveled back to him. "Yes. I am hoping we'll find what we are looking for and that what we find will be enough to accomplish everything that needs accomplishing.

"But if when all is said and done, and it turns out that more needs to be accomplished—I guess what I am trying to say is, if it should become necessary for me to go inside the church and face Adlundsen, then I am going to do it. I *have* to do it. I'm sorry, Tristan. As much as I'd like to, I don't want to make you a promise I can't keep."

Tristan folded his arms against his chest, leaned back against the wall, and released a heavy sigh. Why did this particular woman have to be so tenacious? Nevertheless, he tried another avenue. "Then at least promise me this one thing. Don't go inside that church alone. In fact, don't go inside unless I am the one who accompanies you. Please, Shaelynn, please, you have to give me that much. If you want to go just say so, and I'll take you." He waited for what seemed an eternity for her to speak.

"All right, Tristan, I guess I can give you that much. I promise I won't go inside the church without you." She shrugged in resignation. "I simply don't understand what you are so worried about, though. I'm sure everything is going to be all right."

Tristan's thoughts went immediately to the last part of her nightmares, the part where Fenrir inescapably binds her, leaving her in total darkness and suffering in pain. Nils was quite capable of carrying out such an act. He shuddered inwardly as he recalled her pitiful, agonizing cries during that portion of her dreams. Despite the vivid details provided in her nightmare, she remained oblivious to the fact that Nils could seriously hurt her. In fact, he could take her life. He would not allow such to happen.

Managing a devilish smile, he tossed her a playful wink, hoping that she couldn't read the terror behind his eyes. "Haven't you guessed? I just want to make sure that I'm the one who gets to play the hero."

Chapter 15

Midnight came and went. So did one A.M. Yet, she still stared up at the ceiling with a thousand thoughts swirling around inside her mind. Not that the plastered beams or the ornate medallion were of any help to quiet them down. Shae sat up, pushed away the covers, and got out of bed. She made her way over to the French doors, brushed the curtain aside, and gazed out over the garden. On a sudden whim, she opened the doors and stepped outside.

A cool breeze accompanied her as she strolled along the garden path leading to the pond. So did the recollection of Chauncey's sincere declaration pertaining to Tristan's innocence. Earlier today, she asked him why he felt so sure about that, knowing he must have heard the rumors surrounding the captain's death at the time.

"Oh, I heard them all right," he said, looking quite disgusted. "I didn't believe a word of it, though. But then again, you need to know that I witnessed his actions on the battlefield, myself. He never once cowered behind his men as some of the other captains did. Of course, most officers had orders to stay out of the line of fire, as the enemy targets them first. The generals need the officers to command their men, and once they lose them to enemy fire they are difficult to replace. So, it's an understandable thing, to be sure.

"But despite those orders, I witnessed the captain riding out onto the field atop that great beast of his to direct his men and give them courage, when courage was a hard thing to come by. While still under heavy fire, I watched him take the wounded off the field, and get those men to the wagons where the field surgeons could look after them. He saved many lives by taking no thought for his own. A man who would risk his life for his men and for his country would not have the mind or the heart to disgrace either."

She found it such a shame that she couldn't have Chauncey stand as witness. A sigh escaped as she made her way to the pond. She sat along the ledge, but tonight she failed to see the light of the moon or the stars reflecting in the pool. How ironic that storm clouds pervaded the skies tonight, for it seemed those same clouds cast a blanket over her heart.

The disappointment reflected in Tristan's eyes each time they sifted through a box of documents and found nothing definitive to clear his name cut deep. She drew her bare feet up on the ledge, buried her face in her knees, and let out another wistful sigh.

"What's the matter? Are you having trouble sleeping?"

Her head came up, and she smiled as she awaited Tristan's approach. She welcomed his company tonight. "Yeah, I guess so. I thought that maybe some fresh air might help. But it doesn't look like that's going to happen tonight either. Instead of fresh air, I get to fill my lungs with about ninety percent humidity."

Tristan sat down opposite her and said, "Tennessee can surely dish that out on a regular basis, especially during the summer months."

"You say that as if you had your fill of it somewhere along the way, yourself."

"I suppose at one time I did. Didn't much care for the gnats or mosquitoes either." He turned a little more toward her and gave her a smile. "I don't hear you complaining about it too much, though."

"Oh, I guess I'm more used to it than most." She raked her fingers through her wind-blown hair, pulling it away from her face. "We received our fair share of rain where I lived in Washington as well as in northern England and throughout Scandinavia."

"You're a well traveled woman, I see," Tristan remarked.

"Only because the Norse people were such an adventurous lot," she returned off-handedly. "So tell me, just how long did you have to endure the weather and the bugs out here, anyway?"

"That depends on what you mean by 'out here,'" he said. "Let's see—we faced our first real battle in Kentucky, near Perryville in October of 1862. After that battle, we marched into this state and fought at Stoney River a few months later. Then we fought at Tullahoma before we battled at Chickamauga. So, I guess all total, I've been in Tennessee since a little before December of 1862."

"Not quite a year, then. At least you didn't have to endure two hot, humid summers," she said as she dropped her hand and scooped up a handful of water. She let it drip through her fingers. Tristan chuckled as she dipped her hand a second time.

"What's so funny?"

"Nothing. Just you, playing with the water. You did that the day of your arrival, you know. And you do it every time you come out here," he said. "You must have a thing for water."

Shae's mouth dropped as she stared at him, wide-eyed. "You were the one who followed me around that day?"

"Guilty as charged," he said.

"Why?"

Tristan shrugged as he tossed her a grin. "Curiosity, I suppose. I wondered what you were doing here with Norman. At first I considered the possibility that you might be his assistant or something."

"You should have just asked," she said. "I did invite you to talk to me, you know."

"I know." He nodded, leaned a little closer, and lifted a brow. "But how was I supposed to know you had no fear of ghosts? I didn't want to send you running and screaming into the next state when you discovered a disembodied being instead of a depraved gardener, lurking around in the bushes."

Shae laughed over the comment. "Maybe if you had chanced it, we could have bypassed all the misunderstandings and been so much farther ahead than what we are right now."

"Is that what drove you away from your comfortable bed and outside tonight?" he asked. "My situation again?"

"Partly, I guess. I just feel like we're missing something. Something important, and I'm beginning to wonder if the answer isn't somewhere in my dream," she said. "I've been thinking about that possibility all night."

Tristan said nothing. He simply crossed his arms in front of his chest, cocked his head to the side, and waited for her to elaborate.

She shrugged as she dropped her fingertips to the water and created a series of swirls. "I don't know. I just have the feeling your mother provided me everything I need to clear your name within the dream itself. Especially since the thing keeps repeating. Now that I know Adlundsen represents Fenrir, I started concentrating on the myths surrounding the wolf. Do you know very much about his history?"

"Other than his battle with Odin at Ragnarok, no, not really," he said.

"Well, Loki fathered three children with Angrboda the giantess. Horror and outrage consumed Odin over these not-so-blessed events and so he sent the gods to kidnap these children. However, since Fenrir looked like an ordinary wolf at the time, the gods just let him roam free in the fields of Asgard. They said they would keep an eye him, but the only god brave enough to feed him was Odin's son, Tyr.

"Subsequently, the Norns warned Odin that one day, Fenrir would destroy him. Because of this terrible prophecy, and because the wolf grew larger and more evil as time passed, the gods decided to capture and bind him for all time. First, they made a chain of iron links they called Laeding. They presented it to Fenrir and asked him if he, with his mighty strength, could break the chain. Fenrir, being a cocky wolf, said he would not find such an easy task difficult and would gladly prove it to them."

"That sounds a lot like Nils," Tristan cut in. "The cockiness, I mean. He always did have a right good opinion of himself."

"You know, those were my thoughts too, after learning what he said to you at Adaria. Anyway, to sum it all up, it took three tries to bind Fenrir. The last chain, called Gleipner, made by the magic of the dwarves, had the look and feel of a thin ribbon of silk. Once again, they asked Fenrir if he could break the chain. This time he didn't know if he wanted to chance it, since they created the chain by the use of magic. However, the gods assured him that if he couldn't break it, they would simply let him go. Fenrir told them he could never endure an eternal fetter. However, he didn't want anyone to think him a coward either. So, he compromised," she said.

"Nils was not above making compromises," Tristan replied.

Shae considered that for a moment. Did some sort of compromise figure into Tristan's death? Had the major conspired with someone? If so, with whom and why? How would they ever find out now that so much time had passed?

"You were saying?"

"Yes, Fenrir agreed to try the chain, but only if one of them would place his hand inside his mouth as a token of their goodwill and intention to keep their word. Tyr stepped forward as the only god brave enough to do as Fenrir asked. As luck would have it, the magic chain worked. The gods finally succeeded in binding Fenrir and in the process, Tyr ended up sacrificing his hand," she said, finishing the tale.

"So Fenrir is the embodiment of a cocky wolf who compromises, and then eats the hand of the one person who took care of his needs, when he needed that care." Tristan stroked his chin as he mulled the scenario over in his mind. The profile didn't fit Nils. "I don't know, Shaelynn—"

"At this point, neither do I. Still, I'm trying to find something symbolizing the magic ribbon that held Fenrir bound, and we will need to find someone who represents Tyr." She shrugged as she gave him a half-hearted smile. "This is just something to keep in mind as we assess and accumulate the documents for our file."

"Which right now isn't much," he said.

"No, but it's growing and more will come." Shae extended a hand toward him, and very lightly stroked his face. "Just today we found the letter Amy left for your father. I think destiny played a hand in that, don't you agree?"

"Destiny?" He laughed as his gaze shot heavenward for a brief moment.

"What else would you call it? I mean, just look at the chain of events. You survived your battle with Nils long enough for them to bring you to Starling. In your last few precious hours of life you tell your nurse exactly what transpired at Adaria. And you told it many times over with no deviation to your story.

"In turn, she did not hear of your father's visit or his erroneous position concerning your death, until well after he had returned to Wisconsin. Her conscience would not allow her rest until she picked up a pen and detailed your last hours in a letter. In that simple act, she hoped the truth would bring him a bit of comfort in dealing with your loss," she said.

"What good did it do? He wouldn't even read it," Tristan replied, as he sent a small pebble flying into the pool.

"And I think your mother might have had a hand in that too. Don't you see? He returned the letter unopened. Amy could have just thrown it away but instead, she placed it inside the Bible in your trunk, hoping that one day your father would reconsider. If that day ever came, the letter would be there for him to find. Instead, that letter sat safe inside Starling for well over a century, waiting for *me* to take possession of it."

Tristan shook his head as if he still didn't see the value of it.

"That letter is really important, Tristan, don't discount it. Her correspondence is an easily datable part of your military history. Furthermore, the document comes from a respected nurse who is refuting the circumstances surrounding your death. Her words must be taken into account when all the known facts are presented," she said.

"I think we're going to need more than a few simple letters that offer testament as to my character or records the words of my feverish delirium," he said. "Especially since the summary report, with sworn witnesses, contradicts the letter."

"I am aware of that," she said without hesitation. "To clear your name absolutely and without doubt, we'll need some hard, irrefutable evidence, as well. Even though I feel it is significant, all we have to offer right now, besides the two character letters, is a page from a medical journal, which doesn't coincide with the facts listed on the summary report. There are still a lot of questions that need answering before historians and the military, will come to some sort of consensus."

"And we have to face the fact those answers as well as the proof you seek, may never be found," he replied.

"Oh, for goodness sake! Don't be such a pessimist," she said. "Of course we're going to find our proof. Your mother wouldn't have come to me, if a way to accomplish our goal didn't exist."

"Perhaps," he said as his only concession.

Shaelynn nibbled her bottom lip and gazed into his eyes as if concocting something in that adorable brain of hers.

"What would you think about meeting Isaac Henry?" she finally blurted out.

He met her suggestion with an incredulous stare. "What did you just say?"

"Well, I've been giving this a great deal of thought," she said. "I'm sure he knows more than what he has revealed this far. I just haven't asked him the right questions in order to trigger the memory. I thought if we both went to his house and sat down for a little discussion, perhaps something new would manifest itself. Something that might help."

"I don't think that's a very good idea, Shaelynn," Tristan said. In the first place, they would have to pass by Adaria in order to get there. He could not chance giving his earthbound existence away to Nils. Especially not with Shaelynn standing at his side. Such a thing would put her in very grave danger. "Showing myself and speaking to you, is one thing.

Speaking to Isaac is quite another," he added.

"Why?" she asked. "It's not as if Isaac isn't aware of your existence. The man knows you are here."

"I am aware of that," he said. "But despite what people may think, most mortals are scared spitless the moment they see a spirit, even if they are expecting one. They cannot even string so much as one coherent sentence together upon encountering us, you being the exception. Trust me, I know from my own experiences. If you want answers from Isaac, having me present is not the best way to get them."

Shaelynn blew out a small breath, and nodded. Perhaps he wouldn't have to argue the point.

"You're probably right. You know, right up until the day Aulric left, Simon refused to go anywhere near him. Poor man seemed terrified of the very notion of actually seeing a ghost, even though he knew Aulric existed." She let out a bit of a laugh as she recalled the memories.

"Is that right?" he asked.

"Yep," she replied as she tilted her head to the side. "Well, what about this instead. How about we try to come up with a bunch of questions, invite him over to Starling, and see what he might remember. You can remain in the room with us, but not show yourself, of course. If something he says triggers another question we haven't thought of, you can bring it to my attention, and I'll ask him for you. What do you think of that idea?"

Tristan smiled, placed a gentle hand underneath her chin, and said, "I think I can handle that. Now all you have to do is convince Isaac to pay a call at the creepy old mansion."

Chapter 16

Shae finished stirring the lemonade just as the doorbell sounded. After placing the spoon into the sink, she dried her hands and raced out of the kitchen, heading for the door. She didn't want to keep Isaac waiting after he finally accepted her invitation. Despite his lack of enthusiasm for this visit, she needed him here. The afternoon should prove interesting and she hoped, productive.

"Isaac!" she called out in greeting, "I'm so glad you're here. Please, come in. I thought we'd go into the drawing room for our little visit, if that meets with your approval. Come on, it's this way." She gestured for him to follow her into the roomy hallway.

"Any place is fine," Isaac said as his gaze traveled about the foyer.

"Can I get you anything before we get started? I have a pitcher of ice-cold lemonade if you'd like some, and I made some oatmeal cookies if I can tempt you with those. They are pretty good, if I do say so myself, and unfortunately most of the time I usually have to." She smiled in an effort to put him at ease.

"The cookies do sound delicious, but I'm fine for the moment, thank you," he replied.

"Well, if you don't mind my bringing it to your attention, you don't look fine. In fact, you look a bit pale. Or maybe 'queasy' would be the better word to describe that greenish hue attached to your face," she teased.

"You have to forgive me. I've come not knowing

what to expect. You must remember I know a bit of the history of this house, from not only my mother, but from other hapless victims—I mean visitors as well. They all say the same thing. Mortals are not welcome here, you being the one obvious exception."

Shae only smiled in return. After all, what could she really say to that?

"Such being the case, should I anticipate the angry spirit of Tristan Jordahl to threaten my life inside the drawing room? Or will he merely pop through one of the walls once I sit down and thereby startle me out of my wits? Of course, for that matter I suppose he could plummet through the ceiling just as easily," he said as his eyes twinkled with merriment.

Shae laughed over his various scenarios as they entered the drawing room. "I suppose he is capable of doing any one of those things. Lucky for you, though, today he won't. I promise."

"So this is the place where your *guests* are detained, I mean, entertained." Isaac nudged her with his elbow and winked.

"You got it," she answered in return.

Isaac leaned on his cane and pivoted a bit to the right. As his gaze lit on the photographs, he nodded toward them and asked, "Relatives of yours?"

"Most of them. The color portraits are of my parents, and my twin sisters along with their husbands and children. The solitary female is my baby sister, Nicole." Shae folded her arms and tilted her head as her gaze wandered to the photo of the handsome Union captain. "However, the other two pictures you see there are of Captain Tristan Jordahl and his mother."

The comment elicited his surprise. He switched his gaze from her face, to the photo of Tristan, and then met her gaze once more. Nevertheless, he remained silent and simply nodded.

"Have a seat and just make yourself at home," she said, "and I'll go get my file. I promise you don't have to worry that the captain will plummet through the ceiling and land in your lap while I'm gone."

She walked out of the drawing room and toward her office with the sound of Isaac's gentle laughter echoing behind her. Tristan appeared at the bottom of the steps, just as she placed a hand against her office door. The grin on his face told her he listened in on the light-hearted conversation she and Isaac just shared.

"Are you sure you don't want me to plummet through the ceiling?" he asked as he matched the stride of his steps with hers.

"Well, if I really thought you'd land in his lap, I might be tempted to take you up on that offer. The look on Isaac's face would be priceless, I'm sure." She grinned up at him and raised a mischievous brow. "However, I did promise. He is elderly and probably in delicate health, so—"

Tristan waited as she retrieved her file. Once she had it in her hands, they ambled into the kitchen to fetch her refreshment tray. On the way back to the drawing room she said, "Don't forget. If something else occurs to you during our visit, bring it to my attention."

"Will do." Tristan gave her a little salute as they made their way toward the sofa.

Shae focused her attention on Isaac before she took her seat and gave him a smile. "All kidding aside, Isaac, I want to thank you again for coming today. I know you're not really comfortable, but everything I have pertaining to the captain is here, and as I told you earlier on the phone, Reuben has asked me to keep all of my documents under lock and key, even the copies."

"Think nothing of it. I am happy to do whatever I can to help resolve this issue, and I'm certain my grandfather would expect no less of me either," he replied.

"Are you sure I can't get you something before we get started?" she asked, noting his lingering discomfort.

"Perhaps some of that lemonade wouldn't be such a bad idea, after all," he said. "All of a sudden, I feel a bit dry."

"I'm not surprised. We've enjoyed a rather warm day," Shae replied. She poured Isaac a glass of lemonade, and then offered him the cookies. He grabbed one off the plate, took a bite, and slowly chewed it. He needed a moment of composure and used the cookie to obtain it. She understood and took a bit of time extracting her list of questions from the file. Only then did she take a seat next to Tristan.

After Isaac finished eating, he brushed the crumbs off his hands and said, "You mentioned you had a few questions you hoped I could answer?"

"Yes, I do. I thought we could begin by discussing the men who acted as witnesses to the summary report," she began. "Do you happen to know why Nils chose these particular men for the assignment in the first place?"

"As time passed, my grandfather finally came to believe the major chose them at random," Isaac replied as he dabbed at the corners of his mouth with his napkin. "At first he thought otherwise. He said in the beginning his cockiness led him to believe the major sought men with special skills, and his captain noted him as such. However, much later he concluded that Adlundsen simply walked into their camp and randomly pointed to the four of them without knowing anything about them at all. His pride suffered a bit of a blow after the discovery."

"I don't suppose you know why they might have added the name of Forseth Ericksen as a witness to the incident?" she asked. "As you recall, he was the patient here at Starling who underwent surgery the day before."

"You know, this part is hazy, so you will have to forgive me for my uncertainty." Isaac hesitated as he cupped his hand around his chin and gave it a rub. "I tried to think back after you mentioned his name. I'm certain my grandfather never introduced that name during our conversation. Something occurred to me then. I wondered if Forseth Ericksen and the captain knew each other."

"Yes, we knew each other. He served under my command," Tristan whispered to her ears alone.

"Yes, in fact, Forseth Ericksen served under the captain's command," she repeated. All the while, she remembered to keep her focus solely on Isaac.

"Did he know any of the other men on the list?" asked Isaac.

"No, none of them," the captain answered.

"No, he didn't." Shaelynn cleared her throat. Tristan could see that this was not as easy as she first anticipated, and he grinned.

"Then perhaps that's why they wanted, maybe even needed, his name on the list of witnesses," Isaac suggested.

As Tristan considered the idea, he found merit. Why not use the name of a man who knew him well enough to testify against him, yet was much too ill to refute the statement he supposedly signed, should one question him later.

"You know, he might be right at that," Tristan acknowledged.

"Is there anything else?" asked Isaac.

"Yes," she said, glancing down at her notes. "You told me that Nils briefed your grandfather along with the other three men, regarding the case he compiled against Tristan. Did he share any of his supposed facts with you?"

"As a matter of fact, he did share a few. My

grandfather told me Major Adlundsen called a meeting with the group of men he assembled to assist in his arrest. After swearing them to secrecy, he confided that he only began to suspect Captain Jordahl as the person responsible for the defeat at Chickamauga, when a soldier he did not choose to identify, stepped forward several days after the battle.

"According to the major, this man said after the skirmish ended, he happened to see the captain on the field talking to one of the Confederate captains. After their brief conversation, it appeared to his eyes that Jordahl shook his hand in a most friendly manner, after which they both walked off the field in opposite directions. The informant went on to say, he didn't witness any animosity between the two of them. He said that under those circumstances there should have been some hostility, at least on the captain's part, given the outcome of the battle.

"Shortly thereafter, someone who again remained nameless, intercepted a note addressed to Jordahl by a Confederate commander, and that person gave it to the major. According to Adlundsen, the commander thanked Jordahl for his timely assistance on the battlefield at Chickamauga."

Tristan could see that Isaac related the memory just as he remembered it and without any hesitation or uncertainty.

He glanced over at Shaelynn to gauge her reaction to this newest revelation. She steadily met his gaze, her faith in him unwavering. Although he personally never laid eyes on the referenced note, he could easily explain the matter, which held no great importance.

"We had a lot of casualties on that particular day," Tristan said. "Thousands of bodies littered the field, both Union and Confederate. Neither side felt as if the current battle truly ended. Therefore, neither side moved to claim their wounded or dead. I walked out onto the open field then, and Captain Harris, commander of the Southern army, stepped out to meet me. During the course of our conversation, we agreed upon a short cease-fire, so that each side could tend to their injured and fallen.

"I'm sure the note expressing gratitude from the Confederates arrived because so many of their men fell very close to our line. Dispatching any Confederate soldier brave enough to collect their comrades wouldn't have been at all difficult for us. Nevertheless, both Harris and I felt enough blood spilled into the ground that day. Neither of us wished to see any more good men die for their cause. I can tell you he desired an end to the war, just as much as I did," he finished quietly.

Shaelynn paused for just a moment before she relayed the details to Isaac, just as he gave them to her.

Isaac merely nodded as if satisfied with the explanation.

"Did Nils say anything else?" she asked.

"No, he said those were the only details the major divulged concerning the captain's actions. The major simply added that during the course of his investigation, his collection of evidence grew insomuch that he could no longer deny his guilt. He said that during Captain Jordahl's court martial, he would most regrettably present the rest of his evidence," Isaac replied.

"I see." Shaelynn took a moment to gather the accumulated paperwork from her file and handed the documents off to Isaac. She patiently waited for him to sift through each of the pages. They discussed her findings, and then she shared some of the details relating to Tristan's final day of mortality. Those details included portions of what Nils Adlundsen, in his madness, revealed before he made his attack.

Isaac remained thoughtful as their conversation ended and finally said, "I wonder if you can answer a question for me. The question has nagged me for decades. Perhaps you might now know the answer."

Tristan had to smile over the carefully phrased question. Isaac suspected his presence. The man had stamina. He had to give him that.

"I'll answer it if I can," Shaelynn replied.

"As you recall, my grandfather mentioned that when his company arrived at the church, they found three horses tied at the post. Captain Berntsen sent him back inside the structure, feeling there must be one other person they needed to find. Of course, after a thorough search of the surrounding area, they discovered no one else. Have you discovered who the third horse belonged to?" Isaac took another sip of his lemonade and gazed pointedly in Shaelynn's direction.

"Both horses belonged to Nils. He used the gray to carry his provisions whenever he traveled," Tristan said, feeling he solved the mystery easily enough.

"Both horses belonged to Nils. He used one of them as his pack horse," Shaelynn repeated.

"Why would he need a saddle on it then?" asked Isaac, as he shot a glance at the photograph. "And in case you have forgotten, the company of men removed a clean Union uniform inside the saddlebags. A small uniform, which couldn't possibly have fit either Captain Jordahl or the major."

Tristan stared at Isaac as he struggled to call the scene to memory. He shifted toward Shaelynn and said, "I must admit I never gave Nils's horses a second thought, other than the fact they were getting a bit impatient. Nils left them tied to the post, instead of allowing them to graze. However, now that he brings those horses to my attention, I think he might be right. Both horses did wear saddles, just as his grandfather reported."

Once again, Shaelynn repeated what he said.

"Well then perhaps you can understand my bewilderment. Logic would tell us there should be another rider around somewhere," Isaac said. "Yet, they could find no one else on the premises."

"And you're certain he said the saddlebags contained nothing but the one uniform?" she asked for clarification.

Isaac nodded as he placed his glass on the coaster. "Yes and again, he said the uniform wouldn't fit either of the men."

"That doesn't make any sense. Why would Nils carry a uniform that didn't fit?" Tristan asked the question that Shaelynn in turn, repeated aloud.

"Well, that's the very reason Berntsen sent my grandfather back inside the church. He said someone else surely needed assistance or a body needed recovering," Isaac replied.

Tristan shook his head as he lifted his shoulders in bewilderment. "I didn't see any evidence of anyone inside or outside of the church, other than Nils."

Long after Isaac bade them goodbye, Tristan and Shae continued to discuss the mystery of the saddled horse and the small Union uniform.

"Putting a saddle on the horse just doesn't make any sense, unless Nils intended for someone to ride him. But whom?" Tristan rubbed his fingers across his chin as he mulled over the quandary.

"Tristan," Shaelynn began, with a hint of excitement in her voice. "When Adlundsen said 'it was just too perfect an opportunity to ignore,' could he have been referring to the meeting with Captain Harris and the note from the Confederate commander he intercepted?"

He considered the notion for a moment, and had to agree with the likelihood of such an occurrence.

"You're probably right. That may give us the reason he accused me of treason in the first place, but it still doesn't explain the why of it. And it certainly doesn't explain why he made the decision to forgo his presentation of fabricated evidence at my court martial and chose instead, to end my life at the church."

Shaelynn sat quiet for a time, with her legs crossed on the sofa. She began playing with her bare toes as she shifted her gaze toward the window. The action made him smile.

"You know, I find it interesting you didn't remember seeing saddles on both horses until Isaac brought it to your attention. Therefore, the possibility exists that you might have missed something else as well. A small detail that went unnoticed. A detail that might help us discover the identity of the rider. Maybe he's the key to solving the whole mystery surrounding your death. Given the circumstances, I would say there's at least a chance you might have overlooked something else, don't you think?"

"That is possible."

"I just wished that somehow we could know for sure." She exhaled a sigh and settled a little deeper into the sofa.

Tristan caught and held her gaze as he considered her comment.

She tilted her head to the side as she regarded him. "What are you thinking?" she asked.

"There is a way, actually," he replied.

"A way for what?" She raised a brow in confusion.

"A way to show you, in minute detail, exactly what happened after I arrived at the church, if you've the stomach for it, that is," he added.

"Show me?" She shook her head as if still confused.

"There is a way for you to, 'experience,' shall we say, the events leading up to my death. You would see it, kind of like watching a movie." He waited as his words inched their way toward understanding. At that moment, an involuntary shudder coursed through her body. Perhaps he should toss the idea altogether. He shouldn't have mentioned it.

"I would have to watch you die?" She blanched over the very thought of such a thing.

"Bad idea." He shrugged indifferently as he crossed his arms against his chest. "Sorry, I mentioned it."

Chapter 17

At that moment, a thousand thoughts simultaneously screamed for attention inside her head. Sorting through them proved difficult, at best. Then her nightmares concerning the battle of Ragnarok propelled to the forefront, shoving all other thoughts into the back of her mind. Bryn stepped forward then, to tell her that in a sense she already witnessed Tristan's death, many times over. Perhaps, through the dreams, she prepared her to see it as it happened all along. She prepared her because she *needed* to see the unfolding events. The details of Tristan's death had a purpose.

Shae understood then, without question, she needed to take Tristan up on his offer. Swallowing back her fear, she fused her gaze with his, shook her head, and tried very hard to sound confident. She lifted her chin a notch.

"No, that's where you're wrong. It's a very good idea, Tristan," she declared with sudden certainty. "I *know*, somehow I just know, this is something I have to do. You just can't expect me to like it."

She could see he debated the issue, and that he regretted even mentioning it to her. Shae could not permit him to change his mind. Not now—not after she made the decision to move forward. He must allow her to proceed. The sooner the better, before she changed *her* mind. Without giving her resolve the opportunity to falter, she stood to her feet, and Tristan followed suit.

She gave him a smile meant to reassure, and said as if they both agreed to the plan, "Now that we have that settled, let's get started. Shall we watch your hideous movie in here or would you rather go upstairs where it's dark and spooky?"

Tristan's lips twitched for a moment before the broad smile appeared on his face. He followed the smile with outright laughter.

She failed miserably to appear straightforward and brave when she made her statement. So what. Still, the look on his face irritated her. "Tristan—"

As he regained control, he shook his head and said, "I'm rescinding the offer."

"Oh, I think not." Shae slammed her folded arms against her chest and defiantly met his gaze. "It's too late. I've already accepted your offer, so you can't take it back."

"Really? Do you think you can see the memory without my help?" he shot back.

"Tristan, don't back out on me now." She took a step toward him, placed a very light hand against his chest, and locked her gaze with his. "I'll be the first person to admit there is at least a million other movies I'd rather see right now. Nevertheless, I know that I must see this one, whether I like it or not. This is something I have to do."

"No, you don't have to do anything," he said as he placed a gentle hand against her cheek. "I'm sure there is nothing more to learn than what I have already told you. There is no need to put you through that particular experience."

"No, we can't be sure." Shae inched her way forward, so as not to step through his feet. "Please, Tristan, please? I really want to do this. Don't make me beg."

He dropped his hand, closed his eyes, and sighed in defeat. "All right. But if I find the experience is too much for you, I'll end it," he warned.

"Deal! Let's get to it, then." Before he could change his mind, she added, "Um, just exactly how do we go about doing this anyway?"

Tristan laughed, despite her rising ire. He simply couldn't help himself. Then, when she lifted a brow in indignation, he laughed even harder. She blew out a breath. "Oh for goodness sake!"

"I'm sorry," he managed to say while attempting to rein in his laughter.

"Tristan," she snapped irritably. "This isn't funny!"

"Wait a minute," he said. He placed his hands on her shoulders in an obvious attempt to still her rising temper. So far, it had no effect. She shook her head and tsked.

"Just wait. This isn't something I can do right now this very minute. What I have suggested is a little more involved than what you might think. But I promise that as soon as I can arrange it, we'll get it done. You have to be patient and give me a little bit of time to prepare myself."

She put her hands on her hips and looked him over with blatant suspicion. "You promise? I have your word?"

"You have my word." He crossed his heart and grinned. "I'll come and get you once everything is in place."

Much later that night, as Shaelynn slept, Tristan entered her bedroom. He didn't tell her that she would witness the details relating to his death in a dream, or that he would show them to her this very night. If he revealed either, she probably wouldn't have lapsed into the deep sleep so essential for this particular type of dream to take place.

He sighed inwardly and berated himself over his pathetic selfishness. If someone asked for honesty, then he would need to admit he had an ulterior motive in suggesting the idea in the first place. However, since she insisted they carry through with it he would allow himself to have this moment, for there could never be another.

After he sat down beside her at the edge of her bed, he gently placed his hand on top of hers and whispered, "I'm here, and if you're ready, it's time for us to take a little walk."

****

Shae didn't recognize her current location. As she and Tristan walked along the unfamiliar path, a sudden breeze danced through the boughs of the tall trees that surrounded them. The brightness of the morning sun remained hidden under the density of the woodland, leaving shadows to take its place. Shae shivered from the chill that enveloped her. In response, Tristan drew her close to the warmth of his body. She nestled a little more comfortably into his embrace. He made her feel safe and protected in his arms.

Although they didn't speak of it, they strolled toward the Adaria First Presbyterian Church. She could feel the structure getting closer with each step she took. At that moment, she fervently wished to run away from the coming ordeal. If she could find a plausible way to escape, she would take it. An apprehensive sigh escaped her lips.

"You don't have to do this, Shaelynn," Tristan said. "We can end this right now, if you wish."

"Keep your feet moving, soldier," she quipped, using a playful tone. "And have a little more faith in me than just that."

"I've never questioned your faith, let alone your ability," he said, as at last, he halted their steps near the edge of the forest.

From her vantage point, she could see the church in the distance as well as the horses that belonged to Nils. For a brief moment, she closed her eyes in silent trepidation and swallowed past the lump in her throat.

Tristan placed gentle hands atop her shoulders

and turned her toward him. He searched her eyes and all the while, she made every attempt to mask her uneasiness.

"Are you sure you want to continue?" he asked.

"I'm sure," she said in a calm, steady voice. "What do I do now?"

A smile tugged at the corners of his mouth, and then he cupped her face with his hands. He fused his gaze with hers and absorbed every detail of her face as if he would never get another opportunity to do so. The notion gave her pause.

At last, he said, "Keep walking until you reach the edge of the forest. Wait for me to arrive, and then follow me inside the church. I will not be able to see you or hear you speak, so it's useless for you to try to communicate with me in any way. You must remember this is only a movie. Neither of the actors can feel any pain nor do they suffer. All of this happened over a century ago. The deed is done and over. Do you understand that? You needn't be concerned in any way. Your task is to look for the details you think I might have overlooked," he said.

Shae nodded, she would try to remain focused. Yet, how could she accomplish such a feat when the way he looked at her this very moment, set her heart on fire?

"Then all that's left is this."

Without further warning, Tristan lowered his mouth to hers. The intensity of his first kiss stoked the fire, burning deep inside her soul, and the flames roared into every particle of her being. She found herself returning each subsequent kiss with a blazing passion of her own. At that moment, she felt as if they shared many such kisses somewhere in the distant past, and neither of them ever forgot the feelings they inspired. She never forgot those feelings because she loved this man with her whole heart and soul. There had never been a time she didn't, and a time would never come she wouldn't. He belonged to her, just as she belonged to him.

Finally, with what seemed the deepest regret, Tristan gave her one last light, feathery kiss. He glanced over her shoulder and into the distance as if seeking something. She could now hear the faint sounds of hooves approaching the church. They must proceed or end this here. She gazed at him with uncertainty.

"Are you ready?" he asked, without relinquishing his hold.

"Yes," she whispered.

"Then this is where I must leave you. When you see me riding up, it will be time to follow. You can end this any time you wish. All you have to do is wake up. Should that be the path you need to take, there will be no recrimination. You will never even remember having this dream," he said in a voice gentle and kind.

Shae simply nodded and then after he lightly touched his lips with hers, he disappeared. She didn't realize until this moment, how very much she relied on his strength. Despite her misgivings, she took a deep breath and stepped out of the shadows. She walked to the forest's edge, gazed toward the front of the church, and waited. She could see two horses, both wearing saddles, tugging impatiently at their tethers. They looked as if they wanted to partake of the tall sweet grass just out of their reach. Moments later, she witnessed Tristan's approach.

Chauncey's words concerning Tristan's horse flew into her mind. She swept her gaze over the tall, muscular buckskin bearing him with ease. But then again, the captain would need a mount like that. She did not see anything in Tristan's demeanor that indicated any forewarning of what awaited him inside the structure. Shae wanted to warn him. She wanted to shout out for him to stay away, to turn back.

After a sigh of resignation, she summoned a bit of courage and made her way toward him. She neared his side as he tethered his own horse. He spared nothing more than a brief glance for the other two. Despite the coolness of the day, he wore only a shirt and his trousers. She could see his pistol strapped securely to his side. He left his saber attached to his saddle and without any hesitation, made his way up the rickety steps.

Shae remained a single step behind him as he opened the door and crossed the threshold. Simultaneously, she and Tristan caught sight of Adlundsen, standing at the far end of the church. She understood now why Zepheniah Henry mentioned the fit of the uniform. Nils and Tristan looked like brothers in stature, with Tristan being just a bit taller and broader across the shoulders than Nils. Odin and Fenrir, indeed. However, that's as far as the resemblance went. If she saw Nils without knowing his identity, she would never have guessed his Norwegian heritage. He had black hair, dark brown eyes, and a swarthy complexion, in all likelihood, inherited from his mother. Other than his physique, she found him very ordinary looking.

Shae allowed her gaze to sweep the room. Just as Tristan recalled, she didn't see anyone but the major. And clearly, the arrival of her captain startled him. Nils jumped a bit before he turned around. His glassy eyes widened in surprise as he expelled a gasp.

"Nils, are you all right?" Tristan shut the door behind him then and ambled toward his death. "You're not sick again, are you?"

Shae could see his concern as he made his way down the center aisle of the chapel. Adlundsen narrowed his eyes, which in the instant, filled with mistrust.

"You are much earlier than I anticipated, Tristan. I can't help but wonder why that is. I believe I asked you to be here promptly at 11:45, so that makes you at least fifteen minutes early for our appointment, doesn't it?" He snorted a derisive breath. "Then again, you never could follow even the simplest of orders properly."

Shae repositioned herself so she could keep her eyes on the major. He held his hands behind his back, and she could now see the handle of the large bowie knife he hid in the folds of his coat. The sight of it made her feel queasy.

"Just finished up sooner than I expected, and thought I'd come on over and wait for you," Tristan replied using a casual tone. "I guess it all worked out fine since you're already here."

At that moment, Tristan came to a halt. Shae could see his confusion over the odious expression that suddenly appeared on the major's face. He tried to make sense of it. Nils continued strolling forward at a very slow, leisurely pace. He furrowed his brows in consternation, and he muttered something unintelligible to himself. Her heart beat faster. Time grew short. Once again, she allowed her gaze to search the room. Nothing seemed out of place, and she still didn't see any sign of anyone else. At least, not inside the chapel.

"Ah, Tristan," Nils said as he gazed heavenward while allowing himself a menacing chuckle. "Tristan, my very good friend. You think you're so much better, so much more intelligent than I am. You always have, and I must tell you I really despise you for that. But, I've decided I'm not going to let you get away with it. Not now, not ever again. I know what you've been up to, and I will not allow you to have what is rightfully mine. What I have worked so hard to attain."

"What are you talking about?" Tristan couldn't make sense of his words, and it showed. "I don't have anything that belongs to you."

"Do you not?" Nils raised a dubious brow as he sneered.

Shivers ran up and down Shae's spine as Nils suddenly threw back his head and laughed maniacally. It took all her effort to keep her feet planted right where she stood. Then eerily, the laughter stopped just as abruptly as it began. The major snapped his head forward and thrust out his jaw in a show of defiance. He spared a brief glance toward the window before he shifted his gaze to Tristan. Did he seek the men due to arrive? Better yet, did he want their assistance or their continued absence?

"I've already taken care of everything. There are no more loose ends. Because of my cleverness, no one will ever be the wiser. Finally, Tristan, you are going to see just how intelligent I really am." Nils laughed again as if he alone knew the joke and then added, "Or perhaps you won't get that chance, after all. I am sorry, Tristan, so very sorry it has to end in this way, but it was just too perfect an opportunity to ignore. You all but laid the thing in my lap, so I'm afraid you must take the blame as well as the consequences."

Shae stared in horror. Tristan took a step backward as comprehension dawned. She held her breath and cringed.

"It's a shame really, that you're the one who is going to have to die. And I should probably tell you, you're going to die as a traitor to your own country. I wonder what people will think about that? The perfect, noble, heroic Captain Tristan Jordahl!"

He shrieked the final words as he lunged forward. Simultaneously, he brought his knife forward, and in one fluid motion thrust it toward

Tristan's heart. Tristan never used his pistol because he never expected his friend to attack him in such a vile, cowardly manner.

For the smallest of moments, Shae dropped her head and closed her eyes against the assault. She didn't want to see the blow that led to Tristan's death. No. She must see the details to fulfill her purpose. She forced her eyes to open.

Streaks of blood had already smeared across the floor. She stared at the sight in horror. *Please, please, not Tristan's blood.* She lifted her gaze and found the two men just yards away from where she stood. Tristan repelled the knife each time Nils thrust it toward him. Blood covered his hands from the effort, and blood stained the front of his shirt from the first wound he suffered. Nonetheless, he stood on his feet and fought for his life.

Shae wanted to scream her horror as she watched the two men viciously battling each other. Though impossible, she wanted to shield Tristan with her own body. A movie, he said, she stood here watching a terrible, gut-wrenching, horrible movie, and nothing she could do would change the outcome of it.

The fight sent them smashing into the benches, sending pieces of wood flying chaotically throughout the room. Nils continued to thrust the lethal blade toward Tristan, and each time he deflected it. Finally, Tristan slammed the major into one of the pews and while holding him there, forced the knife out of his hand with a mere twist of his own. Tristan now wielded the weapon.

Nils reached for a jagged piece of wood atop a broken bench and swung it toward Tristan's head. Yet, before it reached him, Tristan ducked and plunged the knife into Adlundsen's chest, then shoved the major's body backward with his foot. All the while, he retained the weapon in his hand.

On adrenaline alone, Nils screamed out every curse he could think of as he lunged for Tristan's throat with his bare hands. Blood oozed down his chest and his arms. Shae choked back a scream as the drama unfolded. Tristan grabbed hold of his opponent with his free hand and slammed him down onto the ground. Nils lay there, without moving. Tristan took a deep breath and stepped back. In that same instant, Nils grasped the sword at his side. He flicked the weapon upward without removing it from the leather frog on his belt. The small, inconsequential movement miraculously found its mark just as Tristan turned to walk away. He drew in a breath, clutched his chest, staggered backward, and fell.

Nils rolled onto his knees. Despite the blood that gushed from his chest, he struggled to his feet. He grasped the back of the nearest bench and leaned against it as he removed his sword. With great effort, he heaved his body away from the pew. He stumbled and weaved toward the door then, using his sword for support.

Shae hurried to Tristan's side. She knelt on the floor next to his body, now soaked with his blood. Her heart shattered into a million tiny pieces. Tears streamed down her face and she wanted so much to cradle him in her arms, but she couldn't. Her hands went through him, instead of around him. Oh, how she needed to hold him.

"Please, Tristan, oh, please don't—" she cried in agony. She tried to brush the tangled hair away from his face so many times and failed each attempt. Somewhere in the deepest recesses of her mind, she could hear the door open and Nils requesting aid. Voices and footsteps responded to his plea. All at once, she could feel arms going around her. Tristan drew her to her feet, and then turned away from the painful vision on the floor.

He gazed down into her eyes and smiled as he brushed her tears away. "You promised not to cry, remember?"

Shae came to the sudden realization they now stood inside the forest. She could no longer see the church. Tristan, whole and uninjured, held her close against his chest. Even though she could hear the beating of his heart and feel the strength of his arms, he didn't feel close enough. She tugged his face downward and brushed her lips against his mouth. At this moment, she needed to feel the warmth of his kisses. Only his kisses could erase the vision of his impending death from her mind. "Please, Tristan—" she begged.

Tristan needed no further encouragement, and at once, he joined his lips with hers. Each kiss bespoke the intensity of love he gave this mortal woman, though she could never be his. What he wouldn't give to have just one day or even one hour with her as a mortal man. What he wouldn't give. He closed his eyes against the sudden pain.

Despite the cost, he would take this moment and hold onto it. Each warm kiss filled him with elation, and each kiss bound them ever closer together. But even in dreams, time does not stand still.

The coming of dawn approached, and therefore, this dream needed to end. If Shaelynn advanced any nearer her conscious level, she would remember far too much. Despite the difficulty of his task, he drew away. He breathed softly against her lips as he brushed his fingers through her hair.

"I'm afraid our time is up."

"I thought spirits never minded the time," she replied in quiet protest, as she too, refused to surrender her hold.

Tristan chuckled. "Only when such is unavoidably necessary. Nevertheless, I want you to know the time I have spent with you here, will be counted among my most treasured memories, and I will hold it ever close to my heart for the rest of my existence. I love you, Shaelynn Montgomery, from the very depths of my soul. Somewhere, deep down inside, I want you to know that and always, always remember it."

A mixture of disbelief and panic shot across her face then. She shook her head as if trying to ward off what he just said. He had the distinct impression she somehow understood this would be their only moment.

"And I love you, Tristan, so very, very much. Don't ever forget that. Please, you mustn't ever forget until such time as we can be together again."

As if he would, or even could, forget such a wondrous thing. Tristan left her dreams after one final, blissful, unhurried kiss.

He gazed down upon her sleeping form then and whispered, "As much as I would will it otherwise, you won't remember everything we shared tonight. The knowledge of our private moments would serve no purpose. I will not allow you to suffer over my selfishness in wanting to have this memory. Therefore, you will only clearly recall the events that led to my death. If you found the detail or details you sought, you will recall them come the morning."

As he tucked her sheets around her shoulders, he shook his head in wonder. As impossible as it seemed, this beautiful woman returned his love. Would the knowledge be worth the price he'd have to pay in the end? For that matter, did he have the strength to leave it with this one memory as he first planned? What would he do if somewhere down the road, she found the frog destined to become her prince? Thrusting the agonizing thoughts aside, his fingers brushed through the length of her hair. Then, he placed a gentle kiss on her lips.

"Sleep well, my love. I'll see you in the morning."

He stood to his feet, and after one more backward glance, he left her room as quietly as he entered it.

Shae stirred, rolled over, and burrowed deeper into the covers. She tried to open her eyes but exhaustion won over the feeble attempt. Her mind grew heavy, and she could feel a thick, swirling cloud sweeping her body heavenward. The rocking motion soothed her. Someone sank into the softness next to her. The mere presence of the unknown person filled her with joy and contentment. Once again, she opened her eyes, needing to see who lay next to her on the cloud. Deep blue eyes gazed back. She shot straight up and smiled her excitement.

"Bryn!" she half whispered, half exclaimed.

"Hello, my darling," crooned Brynhild Bakken Jordahl.

"But, what are you doing here?" she asked as she gazed about her nondescript environment. She didn't quite know where *here* was.

"Though listed as a virtue, one can also count patience as a torment," Bryn said, returning her smile with a mischievous one of her own. "And I just wanted to see you now."

"Am I on the right track?" she had the presence of mind to ask. "Have I left anything undone thus far?"

"No. As usual, you have exceeded all expectations. I find it interesting that Tristan still doesn't remember that you and he fell deeply in love ages ago," she mused aloud. "This is the precise reason you seem so familiar to him now and why it took him no time at all to fall in love with you all over again."

"I remember," Shae said. "*I* remember."

"I know. And he too, will remember all of it soon enough. You are destined to share forever, and you will have all the ages stretching out before you. You will soon come to understand this is compensation enough for the sacrifice you are making now," Bryn replied.

The beautiful angel lifted a hand, smoothed a stray lock of hair away from Shae's face, and lifted a mischievous brow. "Contrary to my son's wishes, my dear, you won't completely forget the extraordinary dream the two of you just shared. You will remember all of your feelings upon waking, and then bits and pieces of your moments in the woodland will begin to fill your mind in the days to come. And then the day will arrive, when you remember it in full. So, let's start with a glimpse of the forest, shall we?" She tossed her an impish, conspiratorial smile—and disappeared.

Chapter 18

Shae took a slow, unhurried journey toward awareness. Images, so vivid a moment ago, faded from her mind during the process. She tried so hard to grasp them, knowing Bryn figured in there somewhere. But it was like holding water in the palm of her hand. For a brief moment, it appeared as if her room shone with an ethereal, almost blinding brightness. She blinked and opened her eyes wide once more. Yet, she could see nothing out of the ordinary. In all likelihood, she experienced an amazing dream of some kind. No, wait a minute.

At once, she sat upright in her bed, coming to full alert despite the early morning hour. The entire memory of her dream crashed into her consciousness. Tristan kept his promise. She experienced the events at Adaria as if she witnessed them firsthand. As she recalled each vivid moment, she found herself sinking back into her pillows. She wanted to relive the dream detail by detail, in order to commit it to memory.

The beginning of the dream seemed a bit hazy, though. She remembered something about trees in a beautiful lush forest, and while she and Tristan walked along—no. That couldn't be right. She remembered walking *toward* Tristan as he rode up to the church. Perhaps the better course would be to write each detail as she remembered them, while they remained fresh in her mind.

She opened the drawer to the nightstand beside her bed, withdrew the notepad and pen, and then rested the pad against her inclined knees. At once, she began recording the dream, exactly as it transpired. The writing of it became more difficult than what she imagined. Before volunteering for this experience, she didn't realize how deeply the vision would distress her, or how intensely she would feel the pain as she witnessed the details leading to Tristan's death.

Tears cascaded down her cheeks, as she lived each moment over again. When at last she finished her task, she let the pen slip out of her hand, curled herself into a ball, and released the torrent of emotions she could no longer suppress. The tears continued to fall as pain washed over and then consumed her. The vision of Tristan's body, bloody and torn, ripped at her very soul. She would give away everything she ever held dear to have prevented that day from ever taking place.

Sometime thereafter, the late morning sun streamed into the windows and woke her from her slumber a second time. Her eyelids fluttered open as her gaze swept over the room. Somewhere along the way, she cried herself to sleep with the notepad still in her hand. Yet, as she considered the depth of her feelings for Tristan, the devastation and pain she experienced inside Adaria shouldn't really surprise her.

Wait just a minute. The depth of her feelings? What did she mean by that? Exactly what did she feel for the captain, anyway? At once, her heart hammered. Her breathing became shallow and uneven as she recalled the varying emotions she experienced in her dream. And most especially, she recalled her agony as she knelt over his fallen body. In her dream, she deeply and completely *loved* him.

Was it just the dream or did she love him now that the last vestiges of sleep escaped her consciousness? She pondered long and hard over the notion because such a thing would be ridiculously impossible. His mortal life ended long ago, and a host of considerations accompanied that fact. Life with a spirit would in no way reflect life with a living, breathing man. Yet, knowing and understanding those things didn't make a bit of difference or alter its truth. No matter how ridiculously impossible, she easily and quite naturally, fell in love with the spirit of Captain Tristan Jordahl. Except, she didn't know quite what to do about it. Should she shout this news on the rooftop or keep her feelings under lock and key? An unexpected knock on her door interrupted her thoughts.

"Yes?" she called out.

"Shaelynn, are you all right?" The voice belonged to Tristan. Her heart fluttered in response.

"Yes, I'm fine." She sought to reassure him. She didn't want him to regret his decision to share this memory. Nevertheless, she could hear the remorse in his voice. She hurried out of bed, raced to her closet, and grabbed the jeans and T-shirt closest to her position. As she slid into them, she said, "I'll be right there."

Minutes later, she found him pacing in the drawing room. She carried with her the pages from the notepad upon which she recorded her dream. While she shared her experience, she hoped she could get through it without blubbering like a baby. She gifted him with a dazzling smile. But how could she help it? She loved him.

"Good morning, Tristan!" she sang out in her quest to appear normal.

Tristan ceased his pacing as he returned her smile with lifted brow. He could see right through her attempt to convince him the night's ordeal left her unaffected. She had to fix that somehow.

"Good morning, Shaelynn. How did you sleep?" He put a hand to his chin and gave it a rub as he captured her gaze.

She gave her head a little toss and said, "Just like a baby. I woke up every couple of hours."

As he opened his mouth to speak, she lifted a hand to stop his words. Self-recrimination consumed him. She could see by his very expression that he berated himself for sharing his final battle with Nils. She couldn't allow him to feel that way.

"Thank you, Tristan." She gulped several times. Her throat tightened. She found it difficult to push the words she wanted to say past the lump in her throat.

Tristan cursed under his breath.

"Please Tristan, don't. In order for us to move toward the next step, we need to know every detail of what transpired inside that church. You must understand that, and I am grateful you shared it with me," she said.

"No, I shouldn't have shown you, and I'm so sorry." He shook his head and turned away. "I feel like such a heel for making you cry."

"Please, don't do this," she whispered brokenly. "You have come to—to mean a great deal to me Tristan. Of course seeing the details of your death is going to affect me. What kind of a person would I be if it didn't? Nevertheless, I needed to see those details. You and I both know that. Now please, come over here and sit down. I would very much like it if we went over my experience together. Perhaps between the two of us, we can discover something new. Please?"

As she wiped at her tears, she patted the space next to her on the sofa, sniffed, and plucked a tissue from the box. She needed him close to her right now. In fact, if she could figure a way to do it, she would climb onto his lap and make him hold her for a little while. From out of the corner of her eye, she caught sight of Amy as she bustled toward her. She welcomed the distraction.

"Shaelynn, dear," Amy said with a tone of motherly disapproval. "You haven't eaten breakfast yet, and it's getting close to lunchtime. Please come and get something to eat before you end up skipping the meal altogether. I'm sure whatever you are discussing with the captain can wait a few more minutes."

"Really, Amy, I'm not hungry," Shae protested as she dabbed at her nose. Arguing the point seemed a useless exercise as Horace entered the room right behind her, carrying a plate full of muffins, a bit of fruit, and a large glass of orange juice.

He placed the tray directly in front of her and then gave it another little shove, bringing it closer still. His actions made her smile despite the lump still ebbing inside her throat. Her ghostly friends took such good care of her, whether she liked it or not.

"Thank you, Horace. You are always so very kind to me."

"You can thank me by eating something, Miss Shaelynn," he replied shrewdly.

Shae could see his small victorious smile as she dutifully picked up a muffin and took a healthy bite. Satisfied they'd accomplished their purpose, he and Amy discreetly left the room. After finishing the last of her juice, she felt composed enough to hold up the notepad. She took a deep breath and smiled. "Shall we begin?"

"By all means," he said as he locked his gaze with hers. "Where do you want to start?"

"At the beginning, of course. And the first thing I remember is walking toward you, after you reached the church on that gorgeous buckskin stallion of yours. I couldn't help but wonder where you found him. I mean, I've never seen such a huge horse in all my life," she said as she shifted her weight a little more comfortably on the sofa, dropped one leg over the edge, and began swinging her foot in circles.

The comment solicited a bit of a smile. "I bought him in Wisconsin, from one our neighbors. I raised him from a colt and trained him myself. We got along very well together, and I have to tell you, he became quite an asset on the field of battle. That horse possessed a noble spirit, courage, and a great deal of intelligence."

"Much like his rider," she said as suddenly she found herself lost in the depths of his blue eyes. She could feel herself blushing over the intensity of his return gaze and hurried on.

"The major's horses paled in comparison, which made it difficult to concentrate on either one of them. Even so, I forced myself to take a good look while I stood next to you. The palomino wore only a saddle and bridle. I didn't see saddlebags, bedrolls, or weapons of any kind. That surprised me because after reading the note he sent you, I thought he'd just returned from a trip of some kind. Anyway, since only the gray carried saddlebags, I assumed that's where the soldiers found the small uniform after—"

"Wait a minute." Tristan drew his brows together and leaned toward her. "You didn't see any bags on the palomino? Are you sure about that? Nils owned some very distinctive saddlebags. They are black in color and have his initials tooled on the leather flap. His father presented them to him the day he received his first promotion," he said.

"I'm very sure, Tristan. Why do you ask? Do you think it's important?"

"Possibly. You see, Nils never saddled his horse without those bags being part of the process. He carried everything important to him inside them. As far as I remember, he never let them get very far from his sight. He even carried them over his shoulders indoors, just so he'd have the contents with him if he found he needed them. But you know, now that you bring it to my attention, I'm not sure if I remember seeing them myself that day." He shook his head and shrugged. "We'll have to give that one some more consideration. Please go on."

"Let's see." Using the tips of her fingers, Shae traveled down each line of the notepad until she found her place. "All right, once we walked inside the church I looked the room over thoroughly and didn't see anyone but the major. Adlundsen seemed startled to see you, just as you said. You asked him if he was sick again. What did you mean by that?"

"After our regiment arrived here in Tennessee, camp fever deviled Nils at least twice that I can remember. His behavior was so strange that day, I thought maybe the sickness returned and he needed my help. I didn't realize the problem lay within his troubled mind." He pointed toward his temple and expelled a sighed.

"I'm so sorry, Tristan." Without thinking, Shae extended her arm and for just a moment, placed a very light hand on top of his thigh. The gesture made him smile.

"You needn't be sorry. You are not to blame for any of this. What else have you written there?" he asked.

She glanced down at her notes as she withdrew her hand. "Let's see, well, most of what I wrote next corresponds with everything you already told me. Oh, except right after he said he couldn't ignore the opportunity, he also said he blamed you for that. He said you needed to take responsibility for laying the whole thing in his lap, and therefore, you must take the consequences for it as well. Do you remember him saying something along those lines?"

Tristan nodded as he leaned forward and clasped his hands. "Now that you mention it, I do remember him saying something like that. As I recall, I didn't have a clue as to what he meant when he said it. I still don't."

"Well, now that I have witnessed his demented rant myself, I'm sure he could mean just about anything. But I also think it strengthens the theory regarding you and Captain Harris at the battle of Chickamauga. I don't think we should dismiss that until we come up with something better." She shook her head ever so slightly as she gazed on the most cryptic statement the major made. "There are no more loose ends."

"Loose ends?" he repeated blankly.

"Nils made the statement right after he said he took care of everything. Do you remember?"

"No, I don't. Nevertheless, those words are probably part of his twisted insanity. I'm sure they only made sense to him. In fact, we need to consider everything he said that day came from the delusions of a very sick mind," he replied.

"Very possible." She flipped the first page over. The second page would be a little more difficult for her to discuss, because *she loved him.*

She read Adlundsen's final words of madness before he lunged toward Tristan with his knife. She shivered as she recalled the blade he kept hidden until the last possible moment. A ragged sigh escaped her lips as she dropped her gaze to the next line and contemplated whether she should just skip it or bite the bullet and disclose it.

"What is it?" he asked when he noticed her hesitation.

"Well, I'd rather not tell you this next part, because it will reveal what a ninny I really am." She breathed out a bit of a laugh.

"Maybe it will simply reveal that you are human," Tristan replied as he placed a gentle hand underneath her chin.

"All right, then. Just as Nils lunged toward you, I closed my eyes for a brief moment. I'm sorry, Tristan, I just didn't want to witness the knife plunging into your body. But then, knowing that I must look, I opened my eyes. That's when the blood, smeared on the floor, grabbed my attention. For a split second, I believed it came from you, and I panicked. However, you were still standing, and even though your hands and shirt were covered—"

"What did you just say?" he interrupted.

"I said you were still standing, but that your hands—"

"No, before that—about the blood smear?" he asked as he refused to release her gaze.

"I said when I opened my eyes, I saw blood on the floor, and I thought it belonged to you," she repeated. Tristan looked puzzled. She needed to know why. "What is it? What's wrong?"

"How big of a smear did you see?" he prodded.

"Oh, I don't know, maybe a foot wide by a foot and a half long or so at the widest points. Why? What difference does it make?" She had a bit of trouble keeping up with his train of thought.

"Shaelynn, you said you closed your eyes briefly, *briefly*, after Nils lunged toward me. Blood couldn't have fallen to the floor that fast, even with a severe wound. Not at the beginning, and certainly not a smear of that size. And even if somehow it did, you would see a *pool* of blood, with prints from our boots leading away from it," he patiently explained.

As comprehension dawned, she knit her brow in consternation. "Then where did the blood come from?"

"Are you certain it was blood? Perhaps the smear originated from something else altogether. I'm asking because the possibility of fresh blood already on the floor just doesn't make sense. Fresh blood would indicate an injured body, male, or less likely, a female. If the body left the church on his or her own accord, then logically, the body would want or need to use the horse to make his or her escape," he said.

Shae hesitated as doubt nagged. Now that he asked, could she really be so sure? She shook her head and tsked. "I don't know, Tristan. I am as sure as I can be. I know I'm not perfect. No one is. All I can tell you with any degree of certainty is that when I first opened my eyes, I believed I was looking at blood."

"Then where did the body go and how far could he get on foot?" Tristan directed the question inward as he left his seat on the sofa and walked his back and forth trail.

Tristan did have a point. Whether dead or alive, there should be another person, somewhere. Perhaps she missed something herself. She also needed to consider the possibility that she didn't actually see blood at all. The importance of this quest compelled her to find the answer to those questions. She could only hope he would indulge the whim.

"Tristan, you are going to have to show the dream to me again," she said.

He whirled around to face her, firmed his jaw, and shook his head. "Absolutely not. Have you taken leave of your senses? I will not put you through that again. We are not even going to discuss it."

"Look, it's the only way to be sure," she argued as she rose to her feet and halted his pacing. "I've already seen all the gory details. I know what to expect. Besides, this time my focus will be on the chapel itself, and not on you and Nils. I have to make sure that red stain is really blood, and if it is, I need to see if I can locate the body that goes with it. Maybe Nils stuffed him in a corner or underneath a pew."

Tristan conjured a deep sigh, shook his head,

and looked heavenward. "Shaelynn—"

At that moment, her cell phone rang. She yanked it out of her pocket and looked down at the screen. Her mother's name flashed across it. Unsure of whether or not to answer the call, she gazed up at Tristan. They needed to get this issue settled right now, before he closed his mind to the idea altogether. She could call her mother later.

"Aren't you going to answer your phone?" he asked, nodding his head toward the device.

"No, it's just my mom, and I can call her back in a little while," she replied. "I'd like to get this issue settled between us first."

"No, what you'd like is to get your own way first." He raised a brow as if challenging her to dispute his comment.

She tried hard, very hard, not to smile over his astute observation, but it didn't work, and she finally gave up on the effort altogether. He met her smile with a roguish grin of his own. While on the verge of laughter, her voice mail alert beeped. She bit down on her lip. "I'd better see what she wants. There might be an emergency."

Tristan laughed outright then and said, "So, you will only use the phone when it suits your purpose?"

"Yep." She placed the phone to her ear and concentrated on her mother's message. She sounded excited.

"Hello, Shae. Your dad just called me from work to tell me that he and his entire squad are flying out to Atlanta in two weeks for some training. On their final day there, they are going to have about a ten-hour window with nothing to do before they catch their flight home. Therefore, your father and his cohorts elected to take the opportunity to see the Chickamauga Memorial Park. He is hoping you can arrange to meet him there and spend the five or six hours they have before they need to dash off to the airport. Call me back as soon as you can to let me know if you're available and we can discuss all the details then."

Tristan smiled as her eyes lit up with excitement over the prospect of visiting with her father. She turned her gaze toward him at the end of the message, and tilted her head to the side.

She cleared her throat and said, "Well, that was my mom, and it seems that my dad—"

"I know, I could hear her," he said. "I'm happy you'll get an opportunity to visit with your father. I know how much you've missed your family."

"But the thing is—I really want you to come with me." She held his gaze as well as her breath while she made her appeal. "I would like to bring along your file, and let my dad look it over while he's here. He knows all about you and the work we're doing to clear your name. With all his experience in law enforcement and most especially the years he spent working homicide, he might be able to see something we might have missed. I know my request is selfish, but I would feel more comfortable if you hear everything we discuss first hand. Perhaps you'll think of questions or can supply the answers that I don't have."

"Why do you think the request is selfish?" he asked as he folded his arms against his chest.

"Well, being at the park will in all likelihood bring back unpleasant memories. I'm sure most, if not all, those memories are better left forgotten," she said as she dropped her gaze.

"Spirits have a different perspective on a lot of the things that happened during their mortality, Shaelynn," he replied. "I'm sure visiting the park with you will have no untoward effect on me."

"Then you will come with me?" she asked.

He could see the hope shining forth from her lovely eyes. She chewed on her lip as she awaited his reply. For just a moment, he allowed himself to enjoy the sight she presented. Yet, at the same time, he didn't make her wait overly long.

"If it pleases you." He winked.

Shae flashed him a dazzling smile then. He found it a wondrous reward for so simple a thing.

"Wow. You made that easy enough," she said, still smiling. "Since you are in such a giving mood, maybe now would be as good a time as any to continue our previous conversation and convince you to repeat the dream. I can handle it, I swear. And I promise you will have no regrets this time. What do you say?"

He lifted a hand to his brow, dropped his gaze, and sighed in exasperation.

Chapter 19

Shae slowed the jeep as she drove through the impressive Point Park entrance to the Chickamauga and Chattanooga National Military Park.

While eyeing the walls made of stone and castle turrets on either side of the road, Tristan raised an eyebrow and said, "I don't remember seeing anything like this before."

"I suppose not. The Army Corp of Engineers built it in 1905. Just a little bit after your time, I think."

"I wonder what possessed them to build something like that in the first place," he murmured.

"I don't know. All I know is they built it to memorialize the Battle Above the Clouds, a phrase the famous quartermaster general, Montgomery Cunningham Meigs coined in reference to the action that took place on Lookout Mountain. Seems that during the fight, a very thick fog rolled in on the battlefield. Neither army could see a thing in front of them. Nevertheless, both sides kept the guns blazing at each other in their quest to win the day. The good news, they say, is that very few men actually lost their lives during the battle." She glanced over at him then as she wondered if he might have fought in that very battle and seen the fog himself.

"But then again, you probably already know all about that first hand." She cleared her throat. "Did you happen to know him?"

"Know who? Meigs?" He shook his head and turned his gaze toward the window. "No, not intimately."

Something in his tone made her search his face. Did Meigs do something to displease him? At once, she sought for an immediate change in subject. "We're a little bit early. My dad is not set to arrive for another half an hour or so. We could wait for him at the visitor's center and look at some of the displays, or if you'd rather, we could walk the grounds for a while. He's supposed to call me when he gets here, so it doesn't matter what we do in the meantime."

"Well then I think maybe I would like to walk the grounds, if you don't mind. Ever since you mentioned this little outing, I've anticipated seeing this place again," he replied as his gaze swept over his surroundings. "If nothing else, just to see the changes."

"We didn't have to wait for my dad's visit to come here, you know. Anytime you want to go somewhere or see something, all you have to do is ask. I'd be happy to take you." She said as she signaled a left hand turn.

Tristan tossed her a lopsided grin. "I suppose if I really wanted to see something that bad, I could just take myself, Shaelynn."

She shot him a glance. "Oh, right. Then how about, I'd be happy to accompany you?" Yet, now that he made the statement, she really wanted to know. "Exactly how do you get from one place to the other—at great distances, I mean."

"Oh, I don't know. For lack of a better explanation, I guess you could say we just sort of think our way there," he replied.

"You think your way there. Hmm. Then, how long does it take you to 'think' yourself, to say, the east coast, and see the ocean if you want to visit it?" she asked.

"Probably not very long. We don't keep track of time in the same manner you do, so it's hard to say.

The last time we visited the coast off North Carolina, it didn't take us very long to get there," he said. "We left well after sunset and returned home about dawn."

Shae drew her brows together as she considered the statement. In all her time at Starling, she'd never seen the spirits leave the premises. Not that they couldn't or didn't while she slept or lost herself in her work. "When did you last see the ocean?"

"Probably decades." He shrugged and then grinned. "Chauncey proposed a visit to England once. He thought it would be a great adventure to see far-off places. Beau put a damper on it, right away. Despite his love for the ocean while he lived, we discovered he's afraid to go near it now that he's without his physical body. For his sake, we stay away from them. He doesn't seem to mind lakes and rivers, though."

"Why is he afraid of the ocean?"

"He said he's just not sure how a spirit and a large body of water might mix, and he's not brave enough to want to find out. Although we told him we could remain above it easily enough, he still worried over the possibility of a giant wave shooting upward to grab hold of his form, and then mercilessly dragging him underneath the water. He said he didn't want to reside down there for an infinite amount of time, with all the drowned pirates and sailors. They scare him, you know." Tristan tapped the side of his head and laughed over his reasoning.

Shae still pondered Beau's fears as she drove into the Chickamauga Visitor's Center parking lot. At the same moment, her father and the members of his squad exited their rented SUV.

Her eyes lit up with excitement as she pointed toward the vehicle. "Well, it looks as if we're going to have to hold off on that walk. That's my dad right there in the white shirt. Apparently, they are early too."

Tristan kept his gaze fastened on her as she bounded out of the jeep, leaving the door wide open. She rushed into the open arms of her father and received a crushing embrace. They looked truly happy to see each other. Their reunion made him smile. Once upon a time, he and his father enjoyed a relationship like that. He forced the painful thought aside, and instead, concentrated on Shaelynn as she greeted each of the men who gathered around her. They seemed happy to see her as well. But then again, she did mention that most of these men watched her grow from child to adult. A few minutes later, she shot a glance his way, excused herself from the group, and returned to the jeep.

"Sorry. I didn't mean to leave you sitting here," she said as she leaned inside and reached for the keys. "I guess I thought you would just follow me over."

"I wanted you to have a private moment with your father," he replied.

She rolled her eyes. "How private could it be with five other men crowding around us? I felt like a four-year-old again as they passed me from lap to lap."

Tristan joined in her laughter. "I guess you have a point there. Are they planning on accompanying you and your father while you tour the grounds?" he asked.

"No, they're going to allow us a private visit and I'm truly happy about that. I need his undivided attention when we show him the file. Anyway, they are arranging for a time and place to regroup, so my dad will wander over here in just a minute. Oh, here he comes now."

"All right, Bret, have fun." The short blond waved as her father started toward them. The man turned his gaze toward Shaelynn then and said,

"Shae, it was good seeing you again."

"You too, Woodrow." She tossed him a smile as she grabbed her bag out of the jeep and slung it over her shoulder. Once she locked and closed the door, she faced her father and said, "All right, Dad, where to first? Do you want to start with the visitor's center or would you rather walk the grounds? Unfortunately, you don't have enough time to see everything inside the park, so we'll need to pick the sites you really want to see, in the order you want to see them."

"We might as well start with the visitor's center since we're already here," Bret said as he took in his surroundings. "Is there a display with all of the records you've been working on yet?"

"No, not yet," Shae said. "Reuben wants everything unveiled at the same time, during the opening ceremony, with the press in attendance. He's been gathering all sorts of artifacts and photos to go along with the documents. I haven't seen everything yet, but I hear it's going to be spectacular. And of course, Professor Andersen will have a similar exhibit in Norway."

"Sounds really interesting," her father replied. "Have they settled on an opening date, then?"

"Yes, their target date is September," she replied. "They would like to have the display coincide with the anniversary of the first battle of Chickamauga."

"That makes good sense." Bret shifted his gaze toward the building and tilted his head toward it. "Well, let's go in, shall we?"

Once inside, they made their way to *The War Comes to Chattanooga* display, the first of many such displays that caught her father's eye. As they walked along, Tristan shared his memories. Shae learned more at the center than she ever learned from him at Starling or from the displays themselves. Too bad Reuben and his team weren't privy to the conversation.

After leaving the center, they toured the grounds. They stopped at each of the monuments, the historical tablets, and scenic vistas as they hiked along the historical trails. However, this time, Tristan said nothing. Shae wondered if he recalled the devastating battles he fought here or if something else bothered him. She would need to wait until after her father left for the airport, to ask.

"I think after all this walking, I'm getting a little hungry," Bret said as he glanced down at his watch. "Is there some place we can get some lunch before I have to leave?"

"Yep, there is a restaurant just a few miles away. One of your favorites actually," Shae said as they crossed the parking lot and headed toward the jeep.

Minutes later they entered the restaurant just as the rest of her father's squad exited the same building. All of the men chatted amiably amongst themselves by the door. After taking note of the time, Victor paused, and asked him if they had taken the opportunity to visit the Cravens house.

"Yes, we did, on our way up the mountain," Bret replied. "Did you guys get a chance to see it yet?"

"Not yet," he said as he held the door open for the last member of his group. "But we are heading in that direction now, and time's a-wasting. So, we'll catch up with you at the Point Park Visitor Center and compare notes in a few hours. Shae, I really enjoyed seeing you again."

"Likewise, Vic," Shae replied as she then turned her attention to the hostess who awaited them with an armful of menus. "There's just the two of us, but if you have one available, we would like a booth near a window."

The pleasant woman nodded and motioned for

them to follow her down the aisle. Tristan slid into the seat first, and she took a seat beside him. Her father sat opposite her, and wasted no time in perusing his menu.

"Let's see what looks good today," he said while taking his reading glasses out of his shirt pocket. "I'm starving and they sure don't give you a whole lot to eat on the plane."

As their lunch meal progressed to the dessert, Shae finally maneuvered the conversation toward her work. Her patience in discussing Tristan's situation with her dad evaporated altogether and right now, she wanted to share her file and get his input.

"Well, I'm very pleased you could take some time off and spend it with me today. I really enjoyed your company. I'm just sorry your mom couldn't be here. You should probably know she pouted for two full days over the slight," he said.

Shae gave her dad a smile. "That sounds like Mom."

"I promised her that I'd get her here for a long visit before you leave. She seemed satisfied enough with that," Bret said. He leaned back a bit so the waitress could set his dessert plate in front of him and he wasted no time picking up his fork. "So, tell me, how is the work coming along anyway?"

"Well, as I said, the scanning of all known documents is finally complete, and as per Reuben's request, I am focusing primarily on translating the Norwegian records into English. Reuben said he wants to have the exhibit at Chickamauga completed first. I think that's mostly because they are still working everything out in Norway."

"Have you found the translations at all difficult?" he asked as he shoved a bite of his strawberry cheesecake into his mouth.

"No, not really. The only problem I have

encountered so far is the faded handwriting on some of the records. I can still read them well enough once I enlarge and sharpen them up a bit. And I think I can safely say that I have over two-thirds of the Norwegian to English documents completed. Unless, of course, they find something else they forgot to give me." Shae moved her elbows off the table so the busboy could clear away the empty dinnerware. "Everyone seems very satisfied with my progress thus far."

"Still, you'd be a lot further ahead if you didn't focus so much of your attention on sorting through endless records, in the hope that one of them might mention my name," Tristan whispered.

She turned her head and rolled her eyes in return.

"That doesn't surprise me in the least," Bret said. "You have always taken your work very seriously. Even as a kid in school, you always got your assignments done well ahead of the due date. I can see that work ethic continues now, despite the quest you and Captain Jordahl have taken on."

As if to say, "so there," Shae stuck out a small portion of her tongue behind her hand and toward Tristan. He chuckled in return.

"Have you found anything new since the last time we spoke?" asked Bret, as he dabbed at his mouth with his napkin.

"No, not yet. There are still a lot of records, mostly written in English, that we haven't read, so we are hopeful there is still more to find." Shae took a sip of her water, set her glass on the table, and took hold of her bag. "Nevertheless, I would like you to read what we have gathered so far, if you don't mind. Perhaps you can see something we might have missed."

"I don't mind at all," Bret said as he tossed his napkin on the empty plate. The moment it landed, their waitress fluttered over and scooped up the remaining dishes. He glanced up, smiled, and said, "Thank you."

As the woman retreated, Shae pulled the file out of the side pocket, and placed it on the table. She sorted through the documents, withdrew the sheets detailing her dream, and laid them off to the side. Once she organized the remainder of the records in order of importance, she handed her father the file.

"The record on top is a copy of the medical journal I told you about several weeks ago. Following that one, you'll see the summary report, and then the letter from Colonel Moore. After you get those read, you'll find his promotional records and papers that detail his command. Everything else that follows testifies as to his character."

She leaned back in her seat and waited for him to read each document. As always, he took his time in assessing the facts. Every now and then, he glanced up and focused his gaze out the window.

"Very impressive," Bret said as he pointed toward the current document. "I see here they promoted Tristan to a captain following his first battle as lieutenant."

"He shouldn't read too much into that. As I told you, they were simply shorthanded at the time," Tristan said.

"Yes, I know," said Shae. "Tristan believes they did it because they were shorthanded."

"Not likely," he said.

"You know, I had those very same thoughts." Shae sniffed. Tristan chuckled.

Once Bret finished with his given task, he closed the file and gazed at Shae with approval. "Seems you've thought everything through on your own. I am proud of what you have accomplished so far. I take it the affidavit in support of the warrant, or the warrant itself, remains missing?"

"Yes, I'm afraid so, and I'm not sure we're ever going to find them," she lamented. "The national archives gave me everything they had in his file, and we've just about gone through all of the documents I'm working on. However, there is one more thing I would like to get your opinion on."

"And what would that be?" He lifted a curious brow.

"Well, Tristan knew a way to show me in minute detail, what took place inside the church." She swept the pages from off the table and held them up for him to see. "In a dream, actually. The minute I woke up, I wrote the experience exactly as I remembered it. I'd like you to hear it."

Her father gave her his full attention as she began reading her notes. Therefore, it came as no surprise that he stopped her progress at the very same place Tristan did. In fact, she found herself waiting for the interruption.

"That can't be right. There shouldn't have been a pool of blood large enough to become a smear that quickly, especially since he never hit the floor. His clothing would have sopped up a great deal of the blood beforehand, anyway." He pinched his brows in consternation. "Are you sure you were looking at blood?"

"Tristan asked me that very same question. I don't know, Dad. I can only tell you the smear looked like blood. I have asked Tristan to show me the dream again so I can make sure. However, I didn't want to repeat it until you gave me your observations as well as your suggestions."

Bret nodded in approval as he propped his elbows on the table and clasped his hands. "Have you considered the possibility that if the suspicious smear is indeed blood, it might have come from another source?"

"Yes, we thought perhaps it might have come

from the rider of the second horse," Shae replied. "However, neither of us saw another body inside the building to corroborate the notion of a second rider, much less an injured one."

"Did you happen to notice whether or not any blood appeared on the blade of the knife *before* Adlundsen attacked the captain?" her father asked.

"I don't know. I don't remember." Shae shook her head and shrugged.

"How about droplets of blood sprinkled on the floor?" he asked. "Did you see a trail of blood you could follow? Perhaps such a trail would lead you to the location of the mystery rider, if there is one and if he is the source of the blood."

Shae drew in a sharp breath. The notion never once occurred to her. "Not that I remember, but believe me, I'm going to look for one when I experience the dream again."

"The pattern of the droplets will tell you if the blood fell from an open knife wound or is the result of a projectile. Do you remember what I taught you about that?" he asked.

"Yes, you said a bullet will cause a splash pattern while blood coming from a knife wound would look more uniform," she replied.

"Very good. You might possibly want to look for one more detail," Bret added. "Check Major Adlundsen over carefully if you can. My experience in the field taught me the mentally impaired are not above self-inflicted wounds. Perhaps the blood comes from the major himself. He might have wanted to make sure no one doubted, but that Tristan attacked him first and wanted his wound as proof."

Tristan and Shae exchanged glances. "That is a possibility," she said. "I don't recall seeing any blood on Nils, but that doesn't mean he didn't have some. The whole event happened very quickly."

"Yes, it usually does," Bret replied.

"Thanks, Dad." She smiled as she gave his hand a little squeeze. "I knew you would be able to come up with something helpful."

"There is one last thing you might want to do, Shae," Bret added as he rose to his feet and tossed some bills down on the table. "I know we are looking at a period of time when the majority of able-bodied men fought a brutal war. Still, if we are theoretically assuming the spot you noted is blood and came from the unknown rider, a record showing him to be missing in action might exist. However, if the man didn't serve in the military, as the uniform inside the saddlebags *might* suggest, perhaps you may find something about a missing person in the local newspapers of the time. Either way, someone would surely have taken note of his absence."

Chapter 20

Tristan remained at a discreet distance from the Point Park parking lot as Shaelynn said goodbye to her father. Once the men disappeared from view, she returned to his side.

"We still have a few hours of daylight left. Do you want to go home, or would you like to visit some of the other sites we didn't get to see with my dad?" she asked.

"Are you tired?" he countered.

"No, I'm not tired at all. In fact, I have rather enjoyed the day, and I really don't want to see it end. At least, not quite yet."

"Then let's stay awhile longer." He didn't want to waste this rare opportunity either. However, he harbored a selfish reason. He wanted to have Shaelynn all to himself without enduring the ever-present audience of his ghostly companions. "I think I'd like to see a bit more, if you don't mind."

"I don't mind. You lead the way, and I'll follow," Shae replied as she made a sweeping motion with her hand and then fell into step beside him.

"The place has changed a great deal since the last time I was here," he observed as he cast his gaze about the area.

"When did you see it last?" she asked.

"Not since the last day of the last battle," he replied.

"Is that what made you so quiet this afternoon?" she asked as she peeked up into his face. "Reflecting on the memories of all the battles, I mean?"

"Partly, I guess. There is also the fact that many

of the men who lost their lives during those battles are still here, and that surprises me more than you realize. There's no way in Hades I would choose to stay here, if this is where I fell."

Shae shot him a wide-eyed glance and then looked over her shoulder as if expecting to see a ghost or two following them. The action made him smile.

"You saw them wandering about the fields?" she asked.

Tristan nodded as his eyes searched the grounds ahead of him. "And even spoke to a few."

"You spoke to them? Today?" Shae knit her brow. "I didn't hear you speaking to anyone."

"A spirit doesn't need to speak audibly to another spirit. At Starling, we speak to you audibly because that's the only way you can hear our words. When we communicate with each other, it is through our minds. Therefore, the languages we spoke during our mortality are not an issue when we happen upon each other. Just like today when I spoke to those who belonged to other times and other cultures. Our former languages didn't matter. We simply shared our thoughts.

"Along the way I discovered some of them are going about their business as if they never died, while others are wandering aimlessly and searching for something that can't be found. At least not here," he said.

"Other cultures?" she repeated. "What do you mean? Are you speaking of the Norwegians who lost their lives during the various battles?"

"They are represented here, as are those born in other countries as well. But I've also seen quite a few Indians in this area, men, women, and children," he replied. Then without giving it any thought, he inclined his head in acknowledgement toward a pair of children playing at the bottom of the hill. The

221

little ones waved as they passed by.

"Children? Here?" She took hold of the necklace she wore and briefly toyed with it before she dropped her hand once more. "Oh, I think that's so sad. You know, according to the historical markers, the Trail of Tears passed through this place, so it's no wonder Native Americans are here. But my question is, why? Why do the spirits of people stay, instead of moving on? Especially in a place like this," she whispered.

"The Indian people called this particular bit of country home, well before the federal government forced them to leave it, and as far as their motive for clinging to the only life they know? Well, everyone has his or her own reasons," Tristan answered.

Shae dropped her gaze as she considered his explanation. Finally, she said, "I know why you stayed, and I know why Amy stays. I think Timothy is waiting for the arrival of his mother so they can say goodbye. But what about Beau and Chauncey? Why do they remain behind, or is it none of my business?"

Tristan lifted his brows and shrugged. "I feel no qualms in telling you their reasons, knowing full well they would tell you themselves if you asked. But it's like this. Chauncey and Beau feel that if they step beyond the light, they will find themselves roasting in the hellfire and damnation, their ministers preached about during their Sunday sermons. Therefore, they'd rather stay put where they feel comfortable, at home, and where they can enjoy the association of a few good friends."

Shaelynn halted her steps and drew in a breath as her mouth dropped open. She stared at him for several seconds.

"Why in heaven's name do they feel that way? They are two of the sweetest, most gentle, kind, and considerate— Well, if anyone deserves to go to heaven, they do," she said.

Tristan chuckled over her long list of favorable qualities. "Perhaps you ought to tell them that yourself. Chauncey believes, as does Beau, that when the Lord said 'thou shalt not kill,' He meant it. They are troubled over all of the lives they are responsible for taking during the war."

"God's talking about cold-blooded murder," Shaelynn huffed. "Not the unfortunate lives taken in a time of war when men are so commanded by their superiors!"

"I agree, but no amount of talking has convinced either one of them of that fact, yet," Tristan responded. "Perhaps you'll fare better."

"Perhaps."

As they strolled along in companionable silence, Shae recalled walking this same path the day she so foolishly and erroneously confronted Tristan about his past. She released a sigh of self-recrimination as she called her words to mind.

"Why the sigh?" asked Tristan as he sidled a bit closer and gave her a gentle nudge.

Shae shook her head, glanced heavenward, and tsked. "The last time I walked this path I drove home and let my temper get the better of me. I think you'll remember that day. After all, I accused you of doing terrible things you didn't do. I'm so sorry about that, Tristan. I just wished I could go back in time and set it right."

"Shh," he whispered. "We've let that one go, remember?"

"I know *you* have, and I know you've forgiven me. Really, I do," she replied. "Nevertheless, you didn't deserve my attitude or what I said. You are the most wonderful man I have ever met and I just wished that I—" *Could scream to high heaven that I love you.* She laughed inwardly as she conjured the expression Tristan would surely carry if he ever got

223

wind of that fact. And then as he caught and held her gaze, she could feel the blush steal across her cheeks. *Great.*

"Look, as I told you, after what Isaac said at Adaria, no one could fault you for your conclusions. Besides, you've made up for your little fit of Irish temper many times over now," he said as he gave her a playful wink.

Despite the multitude of butterflies taking sudden flight, Shae's mouth fell open as she lifted a hand to her chest. She stopped in her tracks and stared in mock indignation. "*My* little fit of Irish temper? My fit? What about *your* Norwegian fit? Might I remind you that you started the whole thing by spewing paper all over my office that night?"

Tristan shrugged as he so obviously fought to control his laughter.

"A fit had nothing to do with my actions. I just wanted to gain your attention so I could tell you my side of the story before you read the report, which you diligently sought to find. I did see the shred of paper you held in your hand, you know."

"No, I didn't know that. But you could've just appeared in front of me and said so," she replied as once again, she fell into step beside him.

"Nah. You weren't in any mood to listen," he teased.

He brushed a wayward lock of hair over her shoulder and his touch made her shiver. Temperature had nothing to do with it, either.

"I might have listened if given the chance," Shae countered, once she could speak.

Tristan burst out laughing then. "Right."

Her lips twitched as she fought to quiet her own laughter. "So, how about that Kentucky Derby."

"What?" Tristan knit his brow and cocked his head to the side. He looked perplexed over the comment that didn't make any sense whatsoever.

She didn't mean it to. "Kentucky—what?" he repeated.

Shae leaned in close and whispered, "It's a clever ploy to change the subject, so just go with it."

He laughed anew and kept walking. "Kentucky Derby, huh?"

Shae nodded as she lifted a brow. "Yes, where one can see a vast array of beautiful horses all in one place. You should plan to see it sometime."

Despite the ploy, she discovered she didn't need a clever change in subject. For at that very moment they entered the quiet of the Chattanooga National Cemetery and began strolling up and down the well-manicured rows. She watched as Tristan paused over some of the names as if calling the men to mind. At times, he related an incident or two, and the memories fascinated her. Aulric shared his past much in the same way. She found it enthralling to speak to someone about a distant time that actually experienced it firsthand.

"Are you buried here, Tristan?" She regretted the question the moment a pained expression settled over his features.

"They don't bury traitors in cemeteries such as these. This type of cemetery is for those who served their country honorably," he replied.

She seethed as he made the comment. At the same time, she curled and uncurled her hands into fists. How could they? Just how could they? After everything Tristan had done for his country, the men he had saved, and the good he accomplished.

At that moment, she caught Tristan's gaze. His mouth twitched as he regarded her rising temper. Then it seemed he couldn't stop the grin that appeared on his face. She blushed in return.

He softened his tone and said, "No, actually, my body is buried in the little church cemetery, just down the road from Starling."

"And let me guess," she hissed as she folded her arms and slammed them hard against her chest. "They dug a hole and unceremoniously dumped your body into it, carelessly covered it over, and let it go at that!"

"Oh, come on, Shaelynn," he replied, with an indifferent shrug. "Do you really think they were that heartless?"

His expression told her she guessed correctly. She felt her temper rise even higher. "Do you really want me to answer that question?" she countered as her eyes continued shooting daggers toward the unseen enemy of his past.

"If it makes you feel any better, some friends of mine said some nice things over my grave, once they found it," he said.

"Well," she muttered under her breath. "We'll just see about that."

Tristan chuckled as they made their way toward the parking lot. Once the Point Park Visitor Center came into view, he said, "Do you want to finish up our day by seeing what they offer inside this visitor center?"

Shae released a breath and nodded. She didn't see the sense in allowing her irritation to ruin this lovely, memorable day with Tristan. They had precious few of them.

As they walked inside the charming structure, Shae focused on keeping her conversation with her unseen companion quiet. Truly, she didn't want anyone inside to think her insane. Yet, as they approached the last of the framed documents, one of the signatures appearing at the bottom made her gasp.

"Jeppe Adlundsen, *Provost Marshal?*" she sputtered aloud as several heads turned in her direction. At once, she lowered her gaze. Behind the hand that now covered her mouth, and in a voice as quiet as she could make it, she asked, "Is that Nils's father?"

"None other," Tristan answered.

She settled on a single nod as they moved through the rest of the displays. They perused everything the center offered its guests and all the while, question after question popped into her mind. She found it difficult not to ask them. After walking out of the door and crossing the parking lot, she unlocked her jeep and climbed inside. A scant second later Tristan appeared in the passenger seat.

"So, how about that Kentucky Derby?" he asked as he gave her a devilish smile.

Shae couldn't refrain from laughing as she inserted the key into the ignition, started the vehicle, and then turned it toward home. "Spill it, Jordahl," she demanded once they reached the highway.

"What is it you want to know?" he asked.

"Everything, of course," she said as she adjusted her mirror, and then added, "to start with, I am under the assumption that both you and Nils joined the army in Wisconsin. Am I right?"

Tristan folded his arms against his chest and nodded. "You are."

"It stands to reason then, that the Adlundsen family also resided in Wisconsin," she said.

"They did," he replied.

Shae breathed out a sigh of exasperation while rolling her eyes. "Enough with the two-word answers, Tristan! If the Adlundsen family resided in Wisconsin, how in the world did Jeppe Adlundsen become a provost marshal here in Tennessee?"

Tristan laughed over her impatience and for his trouble, Shae threw her sunglasses straight through him. They smacked against the door and bounced onto the floor. He leaned down, picked them up, and set them on the dash just out of range. Probably a good thing, too.

"I should start by telling you that Jeppe amassed a great deal of wealth after his arrival to this country," he said. "Over the years, he used that wealth to back several political figures, which aided them in their successful campaigns for public office. Nevertheless, for all his assistance, they never included him within their 'elite' circle. They never invited him to their social parties and such. The slight riled him a bit.

"However, once Nils joined the army, Jeppe began calling in favors from those very people. They owed him that much and they were aware of it. In thinking back, I believe that perhaps Jeppe harbored political aspirations for his son. As provost marshal, he could keep an eye on Nils and ensure the assignments given him kept him out of harm's way. At least, that's the way it appeared to me. I don't remember a single incident of Nils actually going out onto the field of battle, though he sent his troops in often enough. Something always happened to defer him from getting too close to the line. A cryptic message, an unexpected assignment. Something."

"I see," Shae murmured as she mulled over the vast differences between Nils and Tristan. She found it truly a wonder they ever became friends at all.

"Of course, it's all conjecture on my part, but I think Jeppe believed that with his son holding some kind of political office, the so-called upper echelons of society would finally welcome the entire Adlundsen family with open arms," he added. "Personally, I've never had much use for such people or their pretensions. In my book, people are just people. Every man puts his trousers on the same way, regardless of how much money he has in his pockets, what color of blood flows through his veins, or the position he holds."

"I couldn't agree with you more. So, are you

telling me that during the whole of the war, Jeppe ended up wherever they happened to send Nils?" she asked.

"Yes, pretty much," Tristan replied. "At least he did until our deaths. After that, I don't have a clue as to what Jeppe did. I never heard his name mentioned again. In all likelihood, he went back to Wisconsin."

"Do you think his aspirations had anything to do with your death?" she asked.

"I can't see where it would," Tristan replied. "I didn't have anything to do with politics nor did I harbor any desire to go in that direction."

"Well, *something* triggered Nils's madness. When I visit the dream again, I am going to look for all the things I missed the first time. Maybe I should bring a list with me." She gave him a sideways glance as she stepped on the brake at the traffic light. "And speaking of that visit, how about we repeat the dream tonight, while all this stuff is fresh in my mind?"

Tristan placed an arm on the console as he shook his head. "You know I can't repeat it when you are expecting it to happen. We've covered this ground before."

"Maybe you'll need to do something to take my mind off it then," she challenged as she lifted a mischievous brow and smiled. Then, when he didn't reply to her little taunt, she turned her head toward him. She forgot to breathe as she beheld the sheer force of his penetrating gaze. For that one precious moment, time stood still as they regarded each other. What she wouldn't give to know where his thoughts had taken him and know what that expression actually meant.

Chapter 21

"Shaelynn, it's past midnight," Tristan chided. "You need to get some sleep. Come the morning we can pick right up where we leave off tonight. None of this paperwork is going anywhere, I promise."

Somewhere in a remote corner of her mind, Shae could hear Tristan speaking, but she truly didn't know what he said. Instead of listening, she placed all her attention on the letter she now held in her hands. In fact, she couldn't take her eyes off the thing. She ran across it quite by accident as she searched through the Norwegian letters looking for those written by Hans Christian Heg. Reuben asked her to make sure she didn't miss any of them. Since the newest exhibits focused on the famous commander, he requested she finish translating them first. In her quest, she didn't find anything else written in Norwegian, but she did find this one written in English. With her eyes glued to the sheet of paper, she turned her chair toward her companion.

"Tristan, did you know a month or so before you died, Hans Christian Heg recommended you for a promotion to lieutenant colonel?"

"There is probably a mistake on that somewhere. I'm sure if you keep reading, you'll see it," he said as he ambled toward her. "The army doesn't make a practice of skipping ranks. Not unless all of one's commanding officers died on the battlefield, and you're next in line. Even then, it's only a temporary assignment."

"Oh, I beg to differ." She met his gaze, lifted a

brow, and tossed him an impish smile. "If you will give me your undivided attention, sir, then I will be happy to enlighten you." She sat up a little straighter, cleared her throat in an exaggerated manner, and read the amazing letter aloud.

All the while, Tristan peered over her shoulder. She called attention to the passages, which noted his courage, valor, and honor. Shae placed a great deal of emphasis on the paragraph noting his "excellent leadership attendant to the field of battle." Colonel Heg ended his post to the General by recommending "Captain Tristan Jordahl be found satisfactory in filling the demands inherent with the rank of Lieutenant Colonel."

As she finished reading the letter, she looked up at Tristan's astonished face and grinned. "See? Lieutenant colonel."

Tristan shook his head as if mystified. "That is very interesting. No one I know has ever received such a recommendation before. My guess is they promoted everyone holding a higher rank at the time and needed to take captains."

Shae wore a bemused smile as she rose from her chair and headed for the copy machine to make another copy of the letter for their file. "That is so like you to ignore the praise of your commanders and focus on the military order of things."

"I'm just telling you how things are done," he said as he then turned his gaze toward the clock. "I feel the need to remind you, yet again, that it's late, and you need to get some sleep. So put all your documents away, and we'll get back to it in the morning."

"Not yet. I'm really not tired and maybe there is something else I can find that will help us to—" Before she could complete the sentence, all the lights in her office shut themselves off. She blinked several times in a failed attempt to peer through the darkness. Tristan placed a gentle hand on her waist, turned her toward the door, and nudged her toward it. She breathed out a sigh as she rolled her eyes heavenward.

"All right, all right. I'm going, since I have no choice in the matter. But I want you to know I probably won't sleep a wink. I'll toss and turn and wonder if something else is within my grasp that will clear your name."

Tristan shrugged as he escorted her down the hall and toward her bedroom. "I don't care. Toss and turn all you want. However, just so you know, the lights will remain off, and the door will stay locked until morning. You won't be able to find a way to get inside until I say so. I guarantee it."

"You are such a bully," she grumbled.

"You'll have to do better than that. I've been called much worse."

"Well if you give me a minute, I'll see what I can do," she threatened as she entered her bedroom and shut the door against his laughter. Despite all assertions to the contrary, as she slipped into her nightgown, a sudden fatigue carried her off to bed and toward peaceful slumber.

Almost immediately, the first vestiges of dreams overtook her mind. She could feel Tristan's presence within this dream and along with his presence, she could sense his impatience. And for a brief moment, she puzzled over the reason for it. He spoke to her then and the need to understand disappeared altogether as she locked her gaze to his.

"Care to take a walk with me, *min kjærlighet?*" he whispered as he curled his fingers around hers and inclined his head toward their magical woodland.

****

The forest seemed a familiar friend now, if not what awaited at the edge of it. Nevertheless, she prepared herself for this moment days ago, and she would not falter now. She could not falter now, no matter the difficulty of the task ahead. She promised. Tristan gave her hand a gentle squeeze as if aware of her troubled thoughts. She turned her face toward him with every intention of giving him a smile meant to reassure. But as she fused her gazed with his, she could see the same expression reflecting in his eyes that he wore once before inside this woodland. Just before he—just before he what?

The memory of it seemed so hazy, and she wondered at least half a dozen times if she imagined it. Perhaps she simply recalled a dream of her own making. Still, right now it didn't matter. Nothing mattered but the feel of his arms as he halted their footsteps. He placed his hands at her waist, turned her toward him, and gathered her into the warmth of his embrace. In return, she snuggled in all the deeper. She fit perfectly in his arms. They were two halves, which made the perfect whole.

"Tristan." His name came out sounding more like a sigh. Yet, he denied her the opportunity to say anything else, as his lips now brushed against hers. Time ceased to exist, and so did her purpose as her arms traveled upward from his chest and encircled his neck. For now, this instant, she found enchantment in his embrace as he kissed her quite breathless. If someone granted her one wish, then she would forever remain inside this forest with her captain. The church didn't matter and neither did Major Adlundsen. Despite the fervent desire, somewhere off in the distance the sound of hooves intruded on her contentment. As Tristan groaned his displeasure, she drew back. After making time for one more kiss, he caressed her cheek with the back of his hand.

"Are you ready to do this?" he asked.

"Yes, I'm ready," she said. Then just as before,

he escorted her to the edge of the woodland before he disappeared.

Moments later, Tristan approached the church on his magnificent buckskin. She made her way toward him then, just as she had once before. He dismounted and tethered his horse to the hitching post. All the while, Shae studied the major's horses. The plain brown saddlebags on the back of the gray did not have the major's initials. Therefore, she would need to look for Adlundsen's missing saddlebags once she entered the church. Perhaps, as Tristan suggested, he carried them inside.

As he opened the door and stepped inside, she shot past him. Nils stood at the front of the chapel, facing the wall. Shae spared him naught but a glance. Instead, she focused her attention on each individual bench as she made her way down the aisle. Her gaze traveled along the walls and over the floor in search of the missing saddlebags. She didn't find them. Adlundsen had not placed them on any of the pews, nor were they on or behind the pulpit.

She came to an abrupt halt just as the major took notice of Tristan's arrival, and whirled around to face him. Shae seized the opportunity to look him over from head to toe. No visible signs of blood stained his hands or his clothes. She couldn't see the knife to check the blade, for Nils already held it within the folds of his coat. That meant she needed to stand here and witness his first strike. The thought made her shudder.

"Nils, are you all right?" Tristan shut the door and began walking up the aisle. "You're not sick again, are you?"

Shae looked down at the floor then, where she remembered seeing the smear of blood and gasped when she gazed upon it again. The stain existed well before Tristan's arrival. She knelt down to get a closer look. How she wished she could touch it or even smell it. She could do neither of those things. Nonetheless, she could see without any doubt whatsoever that blood created the stain. The smear simply couldn't be anything else. The stain still held a reddish hue and the flies gravitating toward and settling in it confirmed that fact.

"You are much earlier than I anticipated, Tristan. I can't help but wonder why that is."

She could hear Adlundsen's accusatory tone as she searched for any droplets or spatters that would serve as a trail.

"Just finished up sooner than I expected, and thought I'd come on over and wait for you. I guess it all worked out fine since you are already here," Tristan said.

Shae busied herself searching each direction from her kneeling position on the floor. No droplets or splatters appeared on the weathered planks. None. However, all of a sudden, something else caught her attention. The smear traveled toward the pulpit, and then abruptly halted. The formation of the stain told her something had lain across the floor to stop the flow and created a straight edge. What did that mean?

"Ah, Tristan, Tristan, my very good friend. You think you're so much better, so much more intelligent than I am. You always have, and I must tell you I really despise you for that."

Shae willfully shut out the chilling voice of the major as she continued to search the room. Perhaps Nils used a rug to move the body from this spot. If so, then surely she could find other telltale signs. The dust on the floor would be disturbed if he dragged a rug across it.

"What are you talking about? I don't have anything that belongs to you."

"Do you not?"

Shae concentrated all her efforts on looking for

something Nils could use to move a body instead of on the voices. Yet, she didn't find a thing. She didn't see any trails of dust either. In fact, nothing appeared disturbed in any way. How very odd. She chewed on her bottom lip as she sought an answer to her quandary.

"I've already taken care of everything. There are no more loose ends."

Cringing over the impending scene, she peeked up at Nils. From her position, she could see his nervous fingers twitching along the handle of his knife. Nils repositioned his hand to grasp the handle a little tighter as he continued his demented rant. He began inching the weapon away from his back. Instinct commanded her to close her eyes away from the sight but she needed to look. She needed to see the blade. *Just keep watching the blade*, she told herself.

"It's a shame really, that you're the one who is going to have to die. And I should probably tell you, you're going to die as a traitor to your own country. I wonder what people will think about that? The perfect, noble, heroic, Captain Tristan Jordahl!"

Forcing herself to focus solely on the weapon, she held her breath as Nils thrust the knife toward her captain. A gasp escaped her lips. She *could* see blood on the blade. Nils used the knife on someone else before he used it on Tristan! In an effort to concentrate on anything but the ensuing battle, Shae left her place on the floor and began walking the perimeters of the chapel in search of Nils's previous victim. A vital clue still escaped her, and she couldn't seem to find it. A body just couldn't disappear into thin air.

And then she recalled the missing bedroll that one of the horses should have carried. What if Nils used that bedroll to move the body? Where could he take it in such a short amount of time?

A small hallway off to the left of the chapel caught her attention. That hallway led somewhere. Perhaps it led to the preacher's office or the stairway to the belfry. The notion gave her pause. Tristan arrived early. Did Nils have time to drag a body all the way up there? There was only one way to find out. At once, she moved toward it, filled with the need to explore the church in its entirety. Despite the burning desire, some sort of invisible barrier blocked her path. She found that no matter how hard she tried, she could neither enter nor move past it.

Nils expelled a weak, but victorious chuckle as he gazed at Tristan's fallen body. She turned toward the major as he struggled to his feet and headed for the door. His eyes could no longer focus on his path. The outside voices grew ever louder, and any minute now, they would come for Tristan. She couldn't stay here and witness the callous dragging of his body outside and over to his horse. She just couldn't! She squeezed her eyes shut as she sought a solution. Tristan said something once about waking up—

In that same instant, his arms were around her and he drew her close to his chest. "Come now, *min kjærlighet*, everything is all right now," he crooned.

With gentle hands, he wiped the tears from her cheeks. She stood on tiptoes as her arms encircled his neck. Only then did she open her eyes. A relieved sigh escaped her lips as she took in the welcome sight of their lush forest.

"You said you were going to be able to do this without focusing on me, isn't that right?" he asked as he stepped back, tilted her chin upward, and gazed into her eyes.

"I'm sorry, it's just that I love you so much, and it hurts when I have to see what Nils did to—"

Tristan quite easily smothered the rest of her words with the intensity of his kiss. Shae didn't mind. She couldn't remember the rest of her sentence anyway.

Between the kisses, he told her how very much he loved her. She responded in kind. At that moment, Tristan didn't know if he wanted to erase this memory. He didn't know if he possessed the strength. She loved him just as deeply as he loved her and surely, that would be enough, wouldn't it? Didn't she deserve to know what transpired between them, thus allowing her to choose her own path? Couldn't fate smile down upon him just this one time and make him the man, who would someday, become her prince?

He needed to make a choice. If he stayed with her here much longer she would become cognizant enough to remember, and he would not be able to erase this dream from her mind. Yet, how could he make an intelligent decision when her kisses were so sweet, so full of love, and he wanted nothing more than to stay?

Despite his tremendous desire to do otherwise, Tristan finally dug deep and found the strength he needed to break away. He cupped her face and gave her one last kiss. The kiss bespoke the depth, fierceness, and totality of the love he felt for his Valkyrie woman. He gave it in such a way as to last him for the rest of his miserable existence. She deserved so much more than what he could give. Her entire mortal life stretched out before her. He could not doom her to half an existence with a man who could do nothing more than express his love through words and dreams.

"Don't go, Tristan," Shae said, as if she understood what he meant by that kiss. Panic filled her beautiful eyes and she shook her head.

"I need you to stay with me, forever. Please, oh please, you mustn't ever leave me. I couldn't bear it if you did!" she begged.

The sudden terror in her eyes cut deep. Once again, he found that he could deny her nothing. At some future point, should she choose to live her life as intended, he'd retreat and remain in the shadows. The pain of standing by, doing nothing, as she found someone else to love and bear his children would consume him. He understood that truth. Nevertheless, he silently vowed to remain at her side. He could see no other choice in the matter.

He smiled to give her the reassurance she needed. As he caressed her cheek he said, "Didn't you know? There is nothing on this earth that could make me leave you now."

"Promise me, Tristan," she demanded. "Promise me."

He chose to seal the promise with a kiss, and then hurried to leave her subconscious thoughts. As he sat on the edge of her bed, she smiled contentedly before whispering his name. Somehow then, her fingers curled around his without penetrating his spiritual form. He couldn't imagine how she accomplished such a thing, but he made no move to extricate himself from her grasp.

"I desire nothing more than to have you remember this dream in its entirety. But once again, you must only remember your experience after you reach the church," he whispered as he closed his eyes against the sudden onslaught of pain that enveloped his soul.

Truly, he experienced his share of pain both before and after his death. But this pain didn't compare with any he had previously experienced. This pain left him feeling shattered.

He released a deep sigh, born of hurt and resignation. What did either of them ever do to deserve this terrible fate? Why did the heavens decree their mortal lives should never touch? Yet, now as he considered the totality of his mortal life, would he truly have wanted to leave her a young widow? Would he have wanted to leave her with the legacy of his supposed treason, or have the burden of that label placed on any children they may have shared? No, he could never have borne such a thing. Not ever.

"Tristan," she sighed his name and smiled her contentment.

In response, he leaned down, kissed the adorable dimple at the corner of her mouth, and left the room.

Chapter 22

Shae awakened to the distinct memory of Tristan's kiss. Even though she knew the memory occurred in a dream, she could still feel the warmth and pressure of his kiss against her mouth. She lifted a hand and traced her lips as she tried to break though the jumbled recollection, and found the task most difficult. The dream she experienced concerning the events in the chapel were just as vivid and distinct as they were the first time. But this time—

This time something else transpired before the events inside the church took place, she could feel it. She concentrated on bringing the memory to the forefront. Yet, she just could not break through the dense, thick fog that continued to muddle her mind. The forest, she could remember the forest. Again. Did it belong to the part of the dream Tristan shared with her, or did it belong to another dream entirely?

She sighed as she turned onto her side and hugged her pillow to her chest. Perhaps she loved Tristan so much that her subconscious made up the forest, the kiss and the—

No, wait a minute. With a start, she recalled the snippet of memory with vivid clarity. Tristan kissed her inside that forest. She could see the expression on his face *before* he kissed her. The way he looked at her sent delicious shivers up and down her spine. She drew her knees to her chest and buried her face as she relived the precious memory. If Tristan shared that part of the dream with her, then why did it seem so unclear and difficult to remember when the rest of the dream did not? Surely, her own personal desires extended the dream in the direction she wanted it to go. Unless—

All at once, she felt an overwhelming desire to discover if the forest in her dreams existed. The place shouldn't be hard to find if it did. The direction she faced as she walked toward the church would be her guide. And if it did exist, and appeared just as vivid and precise as the church in her dreams, then surely Tristan showed it to her. That would also mean he shared it with her, and in turn—

"Shaelynn, are you awake?" he called out from the other side of her door.

"Yes." She leaped from her bed and as she hurried into her clothes she said, "Sorry. I didn't mean to oversleep."

She opened the door and slipped past him. "Come on, I'll tell you everything I remember, just as I remember it. Also, I have a few questions of my own I want to ask you."

Tristan followed her into the drawing room, yet all the while his eyes probed deeply into hers. She had the distinct impression that her facial expression mystified him in some way, Had he expected to hear her cry again?

"What did you see?" he asked.

"Well, to begin with, that red spot is blood. And it existed well *before* you came through the door," she replied and emphasized her conviction with a very satisfied nod of her head.

"Did you locate any droplets or splatters on the floor this time around?"

"Nope, not a single one. However, the direction of the smear came to an abrupt halt about three and a half, maybe four feet away from the pulpit. I could see a blunt edge and wondered if a rug could have sopped up the blood, thereby creating the boundary. There is also a possibility that the major's missing bedroll is to blame. I thought Nils might have used one or the other to wrap up, conceal, and then move the missing body elsewhere. That could also explain the missing trail of blood if he did. Don't you think?"

"Yes, that's very possible," he agreed.

"Then as I looked for the logical place he could take the body, I noticed a small hallway. I thought it might lead to the church office or the stairs to the belfry. Either place would be perfect to hide a person away temporarily. But when I tried to explore that possibility, I found I couldn't leave the chapel. I could feel some kind of barrier I just couldn't pass. So I need you to explain why I couldn't go into the hallway."

"I am not taking you back in time, Shaelynn. I'm only sharing a memory. You get to experience that same memory through my eyes. See the same things my eyes witnessed and nothing more. Since Nils and I never left the chapel, neither can you."

"Oh." Shae pinched her brows together and blew out a dejected sighed.

"What is it? What's wrong?" He tilted his head to the side as once again, his eyes probed hers. She made a conscious effort to mask her feelings of disappointment over his rational explanation.

"Nothing." She waved a hand in dismissal, briefly dropped her gaze, and toyed with her fingers. "Except, well—that doesn't make sense. If I can only see the same things you did, then why could I search the entire room? Not only did I traverse the room looking for a trail of blood and the missing body, I also looked for the major's missing saddlebags.

"I searched along each of the benches, as well as looked underneath them. I even walked behind the pulpit, which is something you never did. In fact, I walked over and stood behind Nils as he sauntered toward you. I witnessed his every movement. Why would I be able to do those things if I only experienced the dream through your eyes?" she asked.

"The eyes can see more than we give them credit, Shaelynn. Our subconscious level picks up small little things that go unnoticed by our conscious level. We record movements as well as the smallest details of our surroundings. This is why I suggested sharing the memory with you in the first place. You must also understand that you didn't necessarily have to see the event in the same order it transpired. After one creates a memory, everything within that memory becomes a three dimensional panorama. The memory can be viewed from different points and from different times, depending on how one wants to look at it."

She took a few moments to absorb his explanation before she lifted her shoulders and nodded. "I suppose that makes sense," she replied.

"Did you see if Nils carried any self-inflicted wounds?" he asked.

"He didn't. I looked him over quite thoroughly while he stood near the pulpit. As far as I could see, he didn't have any blood on his clothes, nor did I see any blood on his hands."

"What about the knife?"

"Yes. He kept his knife hidden in the folds of his coat as you approached each other. So I had to wait, but as Nils exposed the knife to my view, I could see blood on the blade," she said.

"Then someone else entered the church before I got there," Tristan replied. "I wonder why Zepheniah Henry never located him."

"I think it's safe to assume he searched the ground floor, but do you think he searched the belfry?" she asked.

"I would certainly think so," Tristan replied. "If someone gave me the assignment, I would have checked every nook and cranny possible. You have to remember, another life was at stake. I don't believe the men would have left without a thorough search."

"Well, I'm going to call Isaac and make sure. He might remember if his grandfather mentioned any specifics," she said as she dipped her hand inside her pocket and withdrew her phone. Seconds later, she placed the call. Once he answered she said, "Hey Isaac. It's Shae Montgomery. How are you doing today?"

"I'm very well, thank you," Isaac replied. "How are things progressing at Starling?"

"We're making progress," she answered, knowing he referred to Tristan's situation. "We seem to find a little here and a little there, but nothing conclusive, yet. That's why I'm calling. I need to ask you one more question."

"I don't know if I have anything else to offer. You picked my brain quite thoroughly when last we spoke, but feel free to ask your question, anyway," he said.

"When Captain Berntsen ordered your grandfather to search the premises after discovering the uniform, did he say whether or not he searched the entire building and surrounding grounds? More importantly, did he mention the belfry?" she asked.

"I don't recall any specific mention of the belfry. However, he did mention the extensive search of the grounds, the office, and the private quarters belonging to the minister. They searched each room very methodically from what he said. But you have to remember, Shae, if the major hid a body inside the building, regardless of where, and my grandfather missed it, surely the smell of decaying flesh would manifest itself in the days to come. As I recall, the incident happened on a Friday. Therefore, surely by Sunday when the congregation tried to hold services, they would have smelled the stench, if present."

She glanced up as Tristan nodded in agreement. "Well, that answers that, and you're right, of course. Thanks, Isaac. As usual, you've been very helpful."

"No thanks necessary," he replied. "If I can be of further assistance, just give me a call."

"None of this makes any sense, Tristan," Shae said as she ended the call, and gave the phone a toss on the tea table. "I mean, it's obvious that with fresh blood on the floor and the knife, as well as the presence of the third saddled horse, someone else preceded you into that church. He just couldn't disappear into thin air. And since the major died where he stood, he could not come back to move it elsewhere after the fact."

Or could he? Shae fixed her gaze on Tristan as she considered the unique abilities that spirits possess. Aulric could pick up some very heavy tools and send them flying through the air. Tristan lifted Perry off his feet as if he weighed no more than a loaf of bread and pinned him against his truck.

"Or am I wrong about that fact?" she asked as she raised a brow in question.

Tristan shook his head. "No, you're not wrong. Nils could not have attained those skills in a few short days. It takes quite a while for a spirit to figure such things out. Learning how to move objects, projecting oneself solidly, and speaking audibly are all abilities we acquire with time and patience. They are obtained over a period of time through trial, error, and a whole lot of practice."

"Then how do we explain the missing person?" she asked.

"There is one possibility we've yet to explore," Tristan said. "Perhaps our missing person not only survived his attack, but walked away from the church on his own accord."

"Then why didn't he take one of the horses? We know he suffered a gaping wound. Therefore, a horse would give him the best means to escape Nils and get the help he needed," she said.

"Not if he didn't want Nils to know he survived. Just follow along with me for a moment. What if Nils only thought he killed our missing individual?" Tristan's hand went to his jaw as he paced the floor. "Let's just say for the sake of argument that he attacked the man with his knife, and the man fell unconscious to the floor. We'll theorize that Nils wrapped the body in his bedroll or made use of a rug. Then, he placed our individual somewhere outside the chapel, in the hallway, or even in the minister's quarters. You have to remember I arrived at the church earlier than what Nils expected. Therefore, he needed to divert his attention to me and not bother with the body from that point forward.

"What if during our fight the man somehow extricated himself from his confines and left the building unnoticed by either of us? He wouldn't want to tip his hand by taking the horse. Perhaps he hoped he could get far enough away that Nils wouldn't be able to find him if he proved the victor of our contest. Perhaps he maneuvered his way into the woods behind the church and from there he—"

"Woods?" Shae seized on the word. Tristan whirled around to face her. He cocked his head to the side as his puzzled gaze met hers.

"You say there's a forest close enough to the church for an injured man to reach on foot?" She made every attempt to sound calm and nonchalant even though her heart thudded inside her chest as she awaited his answer.

"Most certainly," Tristan replied. "During that time period, forest surrounded most of the structures in the area."

Tristan's penetrating gaze continued to probe. She didn't know what he sought, nor could she ask the question she wanted to ask. After all, she

247

couldn't come right out and say something like, "So, I've had this dream where you and I are kissing passionately. If I'm not mistaken, we are inside a forest very near the church. You wouldn't be responsible for that amazing memory, would you? Because if you are..."

Before she said something like that, she would need to know if the exact forest in her dreams existed. But what if time and modern development destroyed their forest? She needed to face the fact that she might never find the place, even if Tristan truly took her there. And she still needed to figure out why that part of the dream seemed so hazy when the rest of it did not. The whole thing continued to confuse her.

He crossed his arms against his chest and lifted his chin as if he wanted her to say something.

So, say something, she silently commanded. She cleared her throat. "Do you think he might have died inside the, uh, the forest, or do you think he went for help?"

"I don't know. I think it's reasonable to assume that if he survived, he would tell someone that Nils tried to kill him. That statement alone would have cast dispersions on what happened between the two of us."

"Not unless he involved himself with something illicit that he didn't want anyone else to know about," Shae replied. "Perhaps he had personal knowledge about the major's plans and didn't want to be implicated."

"That is also very possible," Tristan agreed.

"Still, at the very least he needed someone to look after that knife wound. He lost a lot of blood." Shae gasped as a sudden notion occurred. "I wonder if he came here looking for help. This is the closest place, after all." She called for Amy then and just as the name left her mouth, she appeared inside the room.

"You need me, dear?" Amy asked as she tilted her head to the side.

"Yes, I'm hoping you can help us." Shae glanced over at Tristan before giving Amy her full attention. "We just wondered if someone came to Starling, either by himself or with assistance, around the same time Tristan did. This person would have suffered at least one horrific stab wound, maybe more."

Amy pursed her lips and furrowed her brow. Finally, she shook her head. "No, I'm sorry. I don't really recall anyone that fits your description. Of course, you are asking me to remember something that took place over a century ago, and my memory might be faulty."

"Thanks, Amy." Shae gave Tristan her full attention the moment Amy disappeared from the room. "Let's go to the office and see if anything is recorded in the medical journal that can shed some light on this situation."

As she stood to her feet, Tristan turned around to face her. He might just as well tell her about the phone call now. "By the way, while you slept half the morning away you missed a phone call from Todd Andersen," he said, keeping his tone casual.

"Did I really?" she asked as she fell into step beside him. "Did he say what he wanted?"

He shrugged as he lifted a hand to his chin and gave it a rub. "Among other things, he mentioned taking a trip to this part of the world in the near future. Seems that Reuben called a meeting to discuss displays for the museums. Your professor also said that as a special surprise for you, he is bringing someone else along with him." Tristan halted their progress short of the office door as once again, he caught and held her gaze.

"Who?" She raised a brow in question.

"Simon." If he still possessed the ability to breathe, he would be holding it right now. Shaelynn's look of utter disdain gave him the relief he sought.

"Are you kidding me? Why on earth would that man come here? He has nothing to do with this project at all."

She turned on her heels and while muttering something he didn't quite catch, made her way to the answering machine, and activated the message button.

"Good morning, Shae!" the voice on the recorder sang out. "Todd Andersen here. I cannot begin to tell you about all the glowing reports I have received concerning your progress. Everyone is simply delighted. Of course, they couldn't be anything but de—"

Tristan studied her face as the voice droned on. While she listened to her message, he pondered the instant recognition in Shaelynn's eyes when he mentioned the forest. She couldn't possibly know about the place, could she? He took that memory away from her. Yet, not only did she look at him as if she knew exactly to what he referred, but also that she had knowledge of what transpired between them.

Her sudden look of disdain interrupted his silent ponderings. She stared at the phone as if it had become her worst enemy.

"Well, never mind all of that now," said the professor. "Needless to say, Simon is quite looking forward to seeing you again, as am I. So, we'll both see you soon. Have a good day."

Without saying a word, Shae hit the delete button, and then as she continued to glare at the phone, she punched the same button again for good measure. Afterward, she sat down, and took hold of the file containing the medical records. At once, she thumbed through the pages seeking the patients that met her criteria.

Tristan cocked his head to the side and observed her demeanor while she conducted her search. She kept her mind on the task well enough, but she did it with a definite edge. Without doubt, Simon's impending visit caused that edge, he just didn't know why. Simon ended their engagement, and that's all she ever said about the man. Did he really want to know more than just that? Would knowing the circumstances ease his mind?

After reading all of the handwritten notes beside each name, she released a sigh. She shook her head as she closed the file and tucked it back in its proper place.

"I'm sorry, Tristan. If the man survived Nils' attack and sought medical help, he didn't do it here. Even so, we are still waiting for the arrival of the Prisoner of War/Missing In Action reports for the same period from the national archives. Perhaps those records will give us the clue we need to figure this whole thing out. At least, I hope so." She raked her fingers through her hair and tossed it behind her shoulder.

Ignoring the comment altogether, Tristan said, "Shaelynn, would I be treading into places that are none of my concern if I asked you about Simon?"

She met his gaze with directness and he appreciated that fact. "No, not at all. What would you like to know?"

Everything. "You told me once he ended your engagement. Did that upset you?"

"At the time, yes it did," she said, using a tone of nonchalance. "But not for the reasons you might think."

He masked the pain her words inflicted with a quiet chuckle. "I'm not at all certain you would come close to what I think, but I would like to hear your explanation, nonetheless. If you don't mind, that is."

"How shall I put this?" She put a finger to her mouth and gazed out the window for several long moments. He waited without interruption.

"By breaking our engagement, Simon managed to shatter the tranquility I needed in my life," she said as she took on an expression of self-reproach.

"I don't understand what you mean by that," he said.

"Well first of all, I want you to know I never gave any of this much thought during our engagement, and I hope you will take that into consideration as I tell you the rest of the story." She bit down on her lip as her eyes begged his understanding.

"I can do that."

She took a deep breath then, and slowly released it. "Okay, here we go. I should start by telling you that I met Simon Hollander in Oslo, while we both attended college. He and I shared a couple of classes taught by Professor Todd Andersen. The professor could see something in the two of us, I suppose, that excited him. Perhaps he found our love of the Norse culture unique, or maybe our over-abundance of enthusiasm is what thrilled him most. Whatever the motive, he took us under his wing and gave us opportunities and experiences in the field most of our peers never had. Even some of the graduate students didn't get to do all the things we did. Those experiences set us above the rest.

"During this particular time, Simon and I worked very close together. We became good friends, and we arrived at a point where we were comfortable in each other's presence. One evening, we worked late at the museum. Simon paused, cracked this goofy grin, and bounced his eyebrows. He said with the schedule we kept, working so many days in a row and so many late night hours together, it might be wise just to marry each other. That way we would never have to put up with a crabby spouse who just didn't understand our passion for our work. I laughed at his little joke and said he had a valid argument. Then he got all serious on me and said, 'Well, why don't we then.'" Shae shook her head and let out a bit of a laugh.

"Without giving a whole lot of thought to the repercussions, I accepted his very *romantic* marriage proposal once I understood he meant what he said."

"Why would he end it then?" he managed to ask in an even tone. For whatever the reason, he didn't like the idea that she promised herself in marriage to anyone. For that matter, what would possess the man to end an engagement once she agreed to it? If during his lifetime she said "yes" to him, he would have carried her off to the nearest preacher before she could change her mind.

Shaelynn tossed him a half-hearted smile and then hid her face behind her hand. "If I'm brutally honest, then I must confess the blame is mine. Would it surprise you to know that during our twenty-two month engagement, neither one of us ever once said, 'I love you' to the other? That it never once even occurred to me to express such a sentiment? I could never force myself to set a wedding date either, despite his numerous requests that I do so.

"This is going to sound so horrible, but I found that by simply being engaged, all of my friends finally left me in peace. They no longer dragged this guy or that guy over to my apartment in the hopes one of them would turn out to be the love of my life. My distant extended family members quit expressing their pity and concern over my single status. So, in making this long story a bit shorter, I discovered I just didn't want to marry the man, I only wanted to wear his ring." Shaelynn briefly nibbled a nail and shrugged.

"Anyway, when he ended our engagement, which he did in the most cowardly way imaginable, I might add, he ended the tranquil existence I found for myself. However, in my defense, you also have to understand that I truly didn't realize any of this until after he broke off the engagement. I just didn't take the time to sit down, think about, and scrutinize our relationship from every possible angle until then."

"How did he break off the engagement, if you don't mind my asking?"

She gave her head a little toss and rolled her eyes. "Believe it or not, Simon Hollander couldn't muster the nerve to end our engagement in person. In fact, he couldn't even find the courage to tell me on the phone. He left me a recorded message while I worked my shift at the museum."

Tristan shot her an incredulous look. "Not very gallant or courageous, is he?"

"Nope, not at all. He's more of a gutless pansy, and I'm sure I must have suffered from sleep deprivation when I accepted his proposal in the first place. That's the only explanation I can come up with right now. However, if you give me a little more time, I might be able to come up with something that doesn't make me sound quite so hideous or self-centered."

Tristan couldn't help but laugh outright over the declaration. He only hoped she didn't detect the relief in that laughter. Joy filled his heart in knowing she never gave her heart or her love to Simon Hollander. She never once uttered those precious words to him. Yet, she bestowed both upon him.

The tone of his laughter told Shae he understood. Part of her feared he would think badly of her, but the way he looked at her this moment spoke otherwise. In fact, right now he looked at her just as he did during the drive home from Chickamauga. His expression also mirrored the one he wore inside the forest *before* he left her there. The full memory of the dreams crashed into her consciousness now and became clear and distinct. In that same instant, she drew in a breath as she returned his gaze.

The need to find her woodland superseded all else at that moment, even the need to clear his name. Because only there in that very place, could she tell him that she remembered every treasured kiss and every cherished word they shared. She could also tell him, without the cloak of dreams, that she loved him.

Tristan folded his arms against his chest and tilted his head to the side as he regarded her. Did the look in her eye or her facial expression give away her thoughts? She tried so hard to keep both under control as the precious memories flooded into her mind.

He pointed a finger at her then and said, "You know, if I didn't know better, I would say you are up to something."

Unable to string a coherent sentence together, Shae simply lifted a brow and smiled in return.

Chapter 23

"What has you so troubled?" asked Tristan.

"I just didn't think there would be so many names to sort through. When I first ordered this report from the national archives, I truly thought we'd find just a small handful. I assumed we could research each person individually. But look at this." She swept her hand across the bundle of pages. "There's just no way we can delve into the personal history of all these men. At least, not in my lifetime."

She stapled the stack together and then tossed him the packet, thereby giving him access to the complete list. "I feel very much like we are looking for the proverbial needle in a haystack. There are literally thousands of names on those pages, and none of them mean anything to me."

"I know," he replied as he slid the report into position. "If memory serves, we had over four thousand captured or missing from the battle of Chickamauga alone."

"Yes, that's what the original report says, and over two thousand men are listed as missing on the side of the Confederates. Anyway, take a look at them and see if any of those names mean anything to you."

She lapsed into companionable silence then, thus allowing Tristan to concentrate on the list of names while she turned her attention to translating the Norwegian journal. She wanted to keep ahead of schedule so when she found an opportunity to search for her forest, she could take it.

"Hmm," Tristan said several minutes later.

"This one is interesting."

"Which one?" she leaned over and glanced at the name he indicated on the report. Somehow, it looked familiar. "Who is Anders Janssen?"

"Remember Nils's runner?" he reminded her. "The man who delivered the note from Nils?"

"Oh, that's right. I remember now. You did tell me his name was Janssen." Shae furrowed her brow as she met his gaze. "He went missing?"

"That's what the report says. However, the strange thing is they reported him missing right after the second battle at Chickamauga."

"That can't be right. He gave you the note from Nils much later than that."

"Exactly. His name shouldn't be on this list, yet here it is."

"The report doesn't say anything about him being found at a later date, does it?" she asked, as she slid her chair next to his. Her eyes fell on the page.

"Not that I can tell," he replied, turning the document a little more toward her. "See?"

"Well, I think I am going to order his complete file from NARA and see what's in it. Maybe we can find the answers to our questions among his personal records." She jotted the name in her notebook so she wouldn't forget.

"Sounds good to me. Perhaps—" Tristan stopped short when the office phone rang.

Once she picked it up, Shae discovered Simon Hollander on the other end of the line. Her hand went to her brow and at once, her fingers massaged her forehead. The mere sound of his voice grated on her nerves.

Simon said he and Professor Todd Andersen had arrived and asked if she could meet him for lunch at the hotel restaurant. He said he found himself with a lot of spare time on his hands while Andersen attended his meeting with Reuben, and he would very much like to see her. How annoying.

"Oh, I don't know, Simon. I'm just so busy right now. I am on a very tight schedule, and I don't want to break it." Just as she made the statement, a flash of inspiration entered her mind.

She had no desire to see Simon, for truly they didn't have anything left to talk about. Everything she needed to say, she said in the letter she left on his desk in Oslo. Nonetheless, meeting Simon for lunch and enduring his presence for the length of one meal, would give her the perfect opportunity to search for her forest.

Despite the remoteness of the possibility, part of her remained convinced the place existed intact. With a bit of perseverance and luck, she could find it. She would have all afternoon to explore the area surrounding the church, and surely, Tristan wouldn't volunteer to accompany her on this particular outing. As the plan settled into her mind, she turned to face her captain, met his inquisitive gaze, and lifted her shoulders in a helpless shrug.

"Oh, all right, Simon. I suppose I can spare an hour or so if you insist. Where do you want me to meet you?" She scribbled the name of his hotel on her notepad.

One hour later, Shae drove into the parking lot. Leaving Tristan behind proved a little more difficult than what she first anticipated. For reasons he didn't specify, he didn't want her meeting with Simon without him. Despite his misgivings, she convinced him of the need to meet with Simon by herself. She didn't recall the list of reasons she rattled off, but they seemed to work well enough. And once she promised she would call the minute she finished so they could meet up somewhere for the drive home together, he agreed. More than anything, she wanted him to meet her in the woodlands behind the church. They would have a lot to discuss before coming home, but only *if* she could find it.

The sight of Simon waving to her from his table near the back corner put an end to her blissful daydreams. She took a deep breath in preparation for the coming ordeal and made her way through the crowded room.

He leaped to his feet and while helping her into her chair, he said, "You are looking really good, Shae. Tennessee must agree with you."

"Thank you. Tennessee agrees with me very well. I find I really love it here." She sat down and inched her chair forward. "In fact, you could say coming here is one of the best choices I've ever made in my life."

"In all honesty, a part of me hoped you wouldn't look quite so good," he said as he took his seat opposite her. "In fact, I've never seen you look quite this lovely. You have a glow about you that I don't recall seeing before. Surely it isn't because of all those dusty records you're translating for the exhibits?"

Shae puzzled over his odd comments. "Why would you say that? And what difference does it make to you, whether I look 'lovely' or not?"

Simon hesitated for just a moment. "Well, because looking lovely, um, denotes happiness, and we miss you of course. This assignment of yours meant we lost the most valuable member of our team. You should see all of the things we are working on right now, you would be both thrilled and amazed over some of our discoveries."

He launched into the full details of all their latest projects with his enthusiasm at full bore. Shae only half-listened though, and she hoped she inserted enough coherent responses to appear attentive to his aimless babble. Her mind didn't focus anywhere near the conversation, and that surprised her. Once upon a time, not too long ago, she would have hung on his every word. Now she simply wanted this luncheon to end, and the sooner the better. She thrust her napkin on top of her half-eaten plate of food, propped her elbow on the table, and rested her chin on top of her hand.

"Shae?" Simon waved his hand in front of her unblinking eyes. "Are you even listening to me?"

"I'm sorry, what did you say?" she asked as a guilty blush rose to her cheeks.

"I said I wanted to take a drive to the Chickamauga Memorial this afternoon, and I asked if you would come with me. I would really like to see the place while I am here. As you can imagine, the professor talks a great deal about the museum."

"I'm sorry, Simon," Shae said, without feeling the least bit remorseful. "I have something else I need to do. In fact, I should have left a long time ago, and it's getting late."

"What is so important that you can't take a few more hours and spend them with me?" he asked sullenly. "Two hours surely wouldn't make or break your precious little project."

"There is just something I have to do at...at this church, and I need the daylight. My errand has to do with the forest behind it and I can't see if it's dark. Look, I'm very sorry, but this just can't wait." She rose from her chair, grabbed her bag, and tossed it over her shoulder. Simon bounded from his seat and rushed to her side.

"Come on, Shae," he begged. "Just a few more hours of your time, is that really asking too much?"

As a matter of fact, it is, she wanted to scream. Instead, she gave her head a little shake and said, "Why? What is so important? I mean we exhausted just about every subject we could possibly discuss over lunch."

"No we didn't, not everything. You know we didn't leave things resolved between us before you left Oslo. I admit I took the coward's way out when I left you that message on your phone. But I just didn't want to see your response, especially if it became indifferent or if you expressed relief."

At that point, Shae took note of all the people within earshot of their table. They all stared back, looking from her to Simon as if awaiting her response to the unfolding drama. "Let's take this conversation outside, shall we?"

Shae clenched her teeth as she hurried out to the parking lot. She quickened her steps as she spied her jeep and the escape it promised. After unlocking the door, she turned toward him and released a sigh. "Simon—"

"Wait!" he implored her. "Just wait a minute. I know you are angry with me, and I admit you have every right to feel that way."

"I'm not angry with you, Simon," she said, using a tone of indifference. "You're right, and I said so in the letter. Didn't you read it? There is no love or passion in our relationship, just as you pointed out. We have nothing to base a marriage on and therefore, had no business pretending otherwise. I believe it's a very good thing we didn't get married. We are friends and colleagues, nothing more. Marriage would surely have ruined a good working relationship."

"Are you so sure about that, Shae?" He raised a brow and leaned in a little closer. "Haven't you missed me, even a little bit since you've come to Tennessee?"

She chewed on her bottom lip as she considered her reply. If nothing else, she and Simon had always been honest with each other. She wouldn't change that now, not even to spare his feelings.

"Quite frankly, Simon, no. I haven't missed you

at all. I am very happy with my life here. In fact, it's going to break my heart the day I leave this place in ways you can't even begin to understand. The moment I board that plane and return to Oslo, it will be because that is where my work takes me, nothing more."

"I see." Simon cast his gaze at the pavement and released a dejected sigh. "Professor Andersen encouraged me to come along on this trip, you know. He was so sure you wanted to see me as much as I wanted to see you. He said if I tagged along on this trip we could sort everything out. I guess he doesn't know everything, does he? So, I guess that, as they say, is that."

"Come on Simon, don't sulk. You know this is the right decision to make," Shae said as she turned toward her jeep, opened the door, and tossed her bag inside. She glanced at him over her shoulder and smiled.

"You are a wonderful man, really you are. Love will find you one day and probably in the most unexpected place. Trust me on that one. And when it comes, you will be grateful you didn't settle for something far less desirable."

Simon stuffed his hands inside his pockets and stepped away from the vehicle. Shae got into her jeep, gave him a wave, and headed for the church. All thoughts of Simon and their conversation fled her mind as she focused on the woodland. She berated herself for spending far too much time at the restaurant in an effort to be polite. Now she had to fight against the rapidly setting sun.

Shae parked the jeep just off the path and exited the vehicle. She took nothing but her cell phone and keys. With certainty in her steps, she followed the all-too-familiar trail leading to the church. Her heart hammered against her chest in anticipation of what lay ahead. As she approached the steps of Adaria, she turned toward the hitching post where Tristan tethered his horse. She rested her hand atop the small wooden beam, closed her eyes, and called her dreams to mind. Then after turning toward the path she walked in those dreams, her gaze swept across the horizon. Tall, ancient trees and lush vegetation filled the area on all sides. A slight smile tugged at the corners of her mouth as she moved a single step forward.

At that same moment, a blast of icy rage shot through the door of Adaria. Shae gasped over the onslaught. Her breath heaved out in short, frigid gasps that she could see each time she exhaled. She fell back as her wide-eyed gaze wandered over the odious structure. An evil haze seeped out of the cracks and crevices. The mist swirled all around her then, coming not from above, but from the ground below her feet. A wave of nausea swept over and through her. An execrable force beckoned her toward the door. A need to enter the building overwhelmed her desire to do otherwise. For a moment she wavered, and then, with all her strength, fought against it.

"No!" she gasped aloud.

She did not come here to visit the church. She sought this place because of the deep love she had for Tristan and she wanted to share those feelings with him. The sure knowledge of that simple fact banished the enticing force. She took a deep cleansing breath, turned her gaze away from the church, and made her way to the woodland.

Shae picked her way through the density of the trees and foliage. A power she could not see guided each step. And each step confirmed that she traversed the correct path. She followed a curve to the right and with certainty, recalled strolling beside Tristan at this very location. His warm embrace cuddled her close to his chest. His body radiated the warmth she needed to ward off the chill. She snuggled closer, as they continued their journey toward the church.

The full memory flooded into her mind. She closed her eyes and lifted her face heavenward. Chills covered her entire body as she recalled his words.

"You don't have to do this, Shaelynn," he whispered. "We can end this right now, if you wish."

She didn't. He turned her around to face him then and asked one last time if she wanted to continue the quest. She said yes and asked him for directions on how to proceed. Tristan cupped her face with gentle hands, told her to watch for his arrival, and then follow him inside the church. He made sure she understood that she would witness naught but a past event and told her to look for the details he might have missed. He gave her that look then that spewed liquid fire through her veins.

"Then all that's left is this—" he said before he lowered his mouth to hers. Shae could feel her cheeks flaming as she called to mind the intensity and passion of Tristan's powerful kisses. She returned each of them in kind and without shyness, because she loved him, had always loved him, with each miniscule speck of her being.

She remembered feeling so lost in his kisses that she had almost forgotten her purpose. When he stepped away and looked toward the church, she remembered her objective. He left her then and soon thereafter, she could see him riding toward the church. The Union captain looked so handsome, so noble riding atop his stallion.

Shae could feel her knees weaken as the memory of the dreams continued to wash over her. Just off to the side, rested a large flat rock. She made her way to that rock and sat down. As the memories continued to unfold, she hurried passed the painful recollection of the battle between Odin and Fenrir. The dream didn't truly end there, though.

For now, she recalled the agony of kneeling next to his body and her desperate attempts to take him into her arms. A futile effort at best. Nevertheless, the need to hold him overtook all sense of reason. She cried in anguish as she witnessed his mortal life slip away. Then in what seemed a miracle, he knelt beside her. She could feel the strength of his arms as they wrapped around her waist. He lifted her to her feet and whisked her here to this very spot. With a mixture of tenderness and passion, he kissed away her sadness. She wondered if Tristan had any inkling of what his kisses did to her.

Wave after wave of tender emotion filled her as she recalled both dreams in their entirety. Once again, she experienced each kiss, each look, and each word they shared. Tristan loved her, just as she loved him. Nothing else mattered. Nothing else would ever matter.

Right now, she had the overwhelming need to share this moment with him. She wanted to tell him that she remembered everything that passed between them, even though he willed it otherwise. They had so much to talk about, so much to share.

Her hands trembled as she retrieved her cell phone and selected her office number from her list of contacts. He said he would wait for her to call. One ring. How long would it take him to get here? Ring number two. *Oh, come on*, she silently screamed, *please answer the phone!* The third ring ended. How many more did she have to endure before he answered? Just then, she heard the sound of the receiver as it lifted off the cradle.

"Tristan?" She let go of her phone as an outraged, guttural wail shattered the silence.

Terror consumed her. Her hands flew to her

mouth as she stifled a scream. She whirled toward the bone-chilling sound. Yet, she couldn't discern the location. Did she hear the odious howl inside her mind? In answer to her silent question, Nils Adlundsen appeared before her. His fiery eyes became angry slits, and his face twisted with hatred and contempt. Time ceased as he glared at her, and she found she could not look away from the intensity of his terrifying, wrathful gaze. Nothing Hollywood ever offered could match the terrifying spectacle presented by this wolf son of Loki. Then just as suddenly as he appeared, he disappeared from sight. He muttered something about Tristan as he vanished. But how could he know of their connection?

The reason dawned on her then. She said Tristan's name aloud the minute he picked up the receiver. Her legs trembled as she rose from the rock. Indecision consumed her. What should she do? Would Nils try to follow her home in an effort to locate Tristan? What would happen if he did?

Her own observations told her that spirits could touch each other. The spirits at Starling demonstrated this ability on a daily basis. She witnessed their interaction as they wrestled, swatted, hugged, and even kissed each other. Did this mean Nils could also harm Tristan as her nightmare suggested? *Odin and Fenrir and their last battle at Ragnarok.* No! Her mind screamed the word. She couldn't allow that to happen. Not again and not now.

Heaven help her. She didn't know what to do from here, which course to take. *Heaven help her.* The phrase repeated in her head. *Heaven help her?* Bryn! Bryn foresaw this moment, and prepared her to face it. She showed her each step to take. Shae just needed to follow the steps. Therefore, she would follow the same path she walked in her nightmare.

Nils wouldn't expect her to come from that direction. Not if he had already retreated to the church. If he followed her at this moment, then taking a different path wouldn't make any difference, anyway.

By the time she reached her jeep, darkness filled the skies. The only light to guide her steps came from the full moon, directly overhead. Taking a brief moment, she looked up into the night sky. She may as well have been dreaming. Everything looked just as it did in her nightmares. After a deep breath, she gazed at the path ahead, and stepped toward her destiny. She didn't exactly know what to do once she reached the church, but surely, Bryn would guide her. At least she could draw comfort in knowing the battle between Fenrir and Odin ended over a century ago. She did not need to witness the death of Odin again just as long as she could keep Tristan away from the church. The thought gave her the strength she so desperately needed.

The beat of her heart accelerated as she walked up the porch toward the weathered door. She could feel herself gasping for breath the moment she lifted the latch. Hesitating for the briefest of moments, she called to mind her promise to Tristan. She promised him she would not enter this building without him. But then she also remembered him saying that evil spirits could pose a difficult problem, even for other spirits. She closed her eyes in an effort to stay the tears. *Fenrir and Odin.*

"I'm so sorry, Tristan," she whispered as her heart begged for his forgiveness. "But this is something I need to do by myself."

Her hand trembled as she inched the door ajar, and then stepped through the crack. Darkness enveloped her, and it took a few minutes for her eyes to adjust to a room devoid of light. She cast a cautious gaze about the boundaries of the chapel. Nils wouldn't show himself if he didn't choose to, and even if he did, she didn't know how to respond. She prayed the knowledge would come. Perhaps Bryn might appear as she did in her dreams.

"Welcome," the disembodied voice hissed in the darkness. "Come in. There is no need for such fear."

"I'm not afraid of you, Major Adlundsen," Shae shot back with a boldness she didn't feel.

"Are you not?" the evil apparition mocked. "Then why are you trembling?"

"Because it's cold in here," she snapped. A true enough statement. She could quite literally see the mist of breath in front of her.

"Well, there's not much we can do about that now, is there," Nils crooned.

The dark spirit of Major Nils Adlundsen ambled toward her as if time meant nothing, and the slow pace filled her with trepidation. She inched her way back toward the door and the escape it promised should she find it necessary.

"So tell me, where has our dearly departed captain been hiding all of this time?"

The smugness she detected in Nils's tone infuriated her.

"Oh, yes, I know all about that now. Shouldn't the heroic captain come rushing in to rescue the damsel in distress? You needn't deny it, for you spoke his vile name in the forest, did you not?"

"Tristan has no need to hide from you. He's not the coward you are!" Shae's temper soared, and now she met his gaze without a shred of apprehension. The act irritated him. In fact, her presence aggravated him no end, and that surprised her. Just then, a pitch-black, smothering darkness filled the area surrounding her body. Her eyes fought to adjust to the deepening gloom. She found it difficult to breathe.

"Whatever it is you and Tristan have planned behind my back, it will not work, you know," Nils spat.

Shae whirled around toward the sound of his voice, which had now changed locations. The major stood in front of the door, barring her exit. She inched backward down the aisle. Stale, putrid air surrounded his being, and the smell made her gag. She took another step backward.

"Tristan isn't planning anything. As far as I know, he doesn't even know you are here," she lied. "I, on the other hand, am planning to expose you for the murderer and liar you are. Soon the entire world will know your name. They will know exactly what you did, step by devious step."

Nils continued to amble toward her, and she continued to retreat.

"How do you plan to accomplish such a miraculous feat?" he crooned.

His constant shift of mood unnerved her. A cornered animal couldn't feel any more frightened than she did at this moment, and somewhere in the back of her mind, she sensed that Nils herded her in the direction he wished her to go. Yet, she would not allow him to see her fear.

"I have all the pieces to the puzzle, Adlundsen. You left an amazing trail of loose ends. I didn't find it all that difficult to follow them. Piece by despicable piece your plot has unraveled. If you have the guts and want to hang around long enough, you can watch me set history aright," Shae stated, using the most defiant tone she could muster.

Adlundsen's enraged shriek caught her off-guard. She gasped as she took an involuntary step backward. Her foot came down on a thick piece of shattered wood. She stumbled over it. The movement caused her to lose her balance, and she could feel herself falling. Her hands flailed outward, in search of something that would stop the fall. A small yelp escaped her lips.

The menacing, shapeless black mass that had become Nils Adlundsen's soul thundered toward her at that very moment. With a dizzying sickness, she could feel her body lift off the ground. An unseen force carried her toward the highest point of the vaulted ceiling. The sensation terrified her. She opened her mouth and drew in a ragged breath. She wanted to scream as loud and as long as she could, but only a whimper passed through her lips. Her lungs tightened and it became even more difficult and painful to breathe. Then, something horrible and unimaginably strong gripped her body in several places at once. She struggled to free herself from its iron grasp. Yet, no matter how hard she struggled, she couldn't move. Tears coursed down her cheeks, just as they did in her dreams. *Bryn,* she silently screamed, *help me!* Bryn did not come.

"You can't do this," she rasped. "Please, you can not do this."

Nils laughed, and the ominous sound terrified her beyond measure.

"You mortals are so predictable," he sneered. "Such an easy task, welcoming you into my domain."

He circled her body. She shut her eyes to ward off the repulsive vision. He laughed again in return.

"No need to cower," he hissed. "Your little ordeal will be over soon enough. Your life will end, and I will claim your soul for all time. I find the thought of a new playmate so very delicious."

Far below, a portion of the floor gave way, and she could see naught but blackness looming upward from the hole. Seconds later, Nils thrust her body down into the gaping jaws of Fenrir. The journey downward seemed endless, with no way to stop the descent.

Chapter 24

Tristan stared at the telephone receiver, now off the cradle and discarded atop the desk. Shaelynn called out to him seconds earlier. Before he could answer, she let out a frightened little yelp and nothing more. The chilling sound filled his soul with dread.

From the moment she walked out of the door, he restlessly paced inside her office. He didn't have the heart or the mind to read any of the scanned documents piled on the table or continue his search through the MIA reports as she suggested before her departure. His troubled thoughts rested solely on her odd behavior. He did not want her to leave without him. Yet, for the first time since Perry's attack, she insisted on going alone.

All sorts of disturbing notions plagued him because of that resolve. He tortured himself over the possibility that she desired to see Simon more than she admitted. Or perhaps once in his company, she discovered she harbored feelings for the man after all and wished to remain in his company. Then when she didn't call him within a reasonable amount of time as promised, his doubts and worries escalated.

Logically, he knew other circumstances could detain her as well. She still needed to meet with Todd Andersen. Perhaps the professor's meeting with Reuben ended early, and he simply joined Shaelynn and Simon for lunch. In all likelihood, they would have much to talk about, and it would take time for them to catch up. Then just as he accepted this explanation, for nothing more than the peace of mind it gave him, the telephone rang. In his haste to answer, he fumbled the thing, and it took him much longer to lift the receiver.

"Where do you think she is, Captain?" asked Chauncey.

One by one, the other spirits joined Tristan inside the office. They were all privy to the frightening phone call as well.

"I don't know, Chauncey." Tristan activated the play-message button and listened once again to the incoming call from Shaelynn. He listened for any background noise that would aid his search, playing the message repeatedly. Yet, they could hear nothing discernible, but what sounded like small pebbles moving underneath her feet. A sound like that could come from almost anywhere.

"She sounded scared, Captain, right after she said your name," Timothy whispered. "You have to find her."

Tristan turned toward him and managed a smile as he ruffled his hair. "Don't worry, I will." He gazed into each apprehensive face of his companions. "In fact, you all needn't worry. I promise you, I will find her."

"Chauncey and I will thoroughly search this entire community and its surroundings," Beau said. "Maybe even pay a visit to Reuben, if we can find him."

"After that, we'll try the Chickamauga battlefield," Chauncey added. "Perhaps with all the fuss surrounding the exhibits, Simon asked to see the place for himself."

"What about me, Captain?" asked Timothy. "I could search, too."

"Tim, I need you to stay here in case she comes home or calls again. She might find the opportunity to tell us where she is or at the very least, let us know what's happening." Tristan replaced the receiver and took hold of Timothy's shoulder. "If she does either, I need you to find me as quickly as you can."

"I'll find you faster than lightnin'," he promised.

"I believe between the two of us, we can gather you all in a hurry if the need arises," Horace added.

"Very well." Tristan glanced down at the name of the hotel, written on the notepad. He remembered passing that place on the way to the Chickamauga battlefield. Yet, before he could leave, Amy took hold of his arm. She locked her gaze on his.

"Bring her home, Captain. Just—bring her safely home and soon," she said.

"You know I won't come home without her, Amy." He gave her a gentle kiss on the cheek and then disappeared.

Scant minutes later, Tristan stood in front of the hotel. He found the restaurant inside the building easily enough, but he did not see Shaelynn nor could he detect any visible remains of her perfume. That meant she left the premises quite a while ago. He didn't know what Simon Hollander looked like, nor did he know what room the man occupied, but he would find that information nonetheless.

After making his way to the front desk and over to the clerk, he leaned close to his ear and whispered, "You need to know what room you assigned Simon Hollander, and you need to know that information, right now. Nothing else is more important."

The clerk stared straight ahead. He furrowed his brow for just a moment and then turned toward his computer. Tristan peered over his shoulder as the man brought Hollander's name up on the computer screen. Room 506. A scant second later, he stood in front of the door. He could hear the sound of water as it turned off and a shower door sliding open. That meant two comforting things. Simon and

Shaelynn were no longer together, and Simon just ended his shower. Perfect.

From his position in the hallway, he waited as Simon tied the belt of his robe around his waist and quit the bathroom. Tristan made sure he didn't make it all the way to his suitcase before he stretched his hand over the elegant door and caused the wood to bend inward. The action captured Simon's immediate attention, and he stared at the thing with his mouth agape. Then while he pondered the cause of the phenomenon, Tristan burst through the door.

Simon screamed like a frightened little girl and dashed for the bathroom. Tristan shook his head in disgust as he blocked his path. Hollander screamed again, pivoted, and turned in the opposite direction. He took several unstable steps toward the closet, then after thinking better of it, turned and faced him with wide-eyed terror. Standing with his feet apart, Tristan folded his arms against his chest and waited for him to choose a course of action.

"You are um...a Civil War...Ah...wha-what do you want from me? Why are...why are you here?" he stammered. His hands covered his face and his bulging gaze filled with tears born of terror. "Please—j-just go away."

Tristan eyed him from head to toe and back again. He disliked this man the moment Shaelynn mentioned his name. Now that he stood so *fearlessly* before him, his opinion wouldn't change anytime soon. The man was every bit the gutless pansy Shaelynn accused him of being. He leaned toward his victim and raised a disdainful brow.

"Where's Shaelynn?" he asked, getting right to the point.

"Why, I, I d-don't know..." the pansy stammered. He knit his brow in confusion. "How—how do you, know Shae? What d-do you w-want with her?"

Tristan could hear Simon's heart thumping wildly in his chest. The man also had a bit of difficulty meeting his gaze, and for a moment, he feared Simon Hollander would pass out before he extracted the information he sought.

"When did she leave the hotel?" he asked as he moved toward him. The very act caused Simon to shrink back and retreat even further.

"I'm, I'm really n-not sure," he stuttered as he continued to gulp the air around him.

Tristan shook his head in disgust, gazed heavenward, and released a sigh. "Why don't you tell me what you do know?"

Simon raised his brows as understanding dawned. "Why? Has s-something h-happened to her?"

"We don't have time for this pointless conversation," Tristan snarled. "Just tell me what you know. Now!"

"Oh!" Simon twisted the knot on his belt. "Well, I w-walked her out to the parking lot. I, um, hoped she would, um go with me to the—ah, to the, ah, Chickamauga Memorial. She wouldn't come though. Because, let's s-see, she said she needed to go somewhere else—"

"Where?" he demanded. "Where did she say she needed to go?"

"Um...yes, she uh, she said something about a church. Yes, I'm sure of it now. She mentioned a church and n-n-needing daylight to see the wooded area behind it. I know that sounds crazy, but...I swear that's what she said. That's all she told me."

Simon's answer stunned him. In the instant, he recalled the expression on Shaelynn's face as they discussed the second dream, and he made mention of the forest as a possible place for their mystery rider to hide. At first, he wondered if she remembered that portion of the dream, but later dismissed it as impossible. He shouldn't have. She attained a higher level of consciousness than what he first believed. Without giving Simon and his irritating cowardice further consideration, he left the hotel.

Moments later, he entered the forest in search of his woman. Despite the remote possibility, he needed to consider wild animals, and venomous snakes. If she suffered a snakebite, she could be unconscious and in desperate need of help.

He traced the path he believed she would follow, if in fact, she remembered the dream in its entirety. If she did, she would want to know for herself if the place truly existed, and she would want to do it alone. In all likelihood, this is the reason she wanted to go without him. Simon didn't have anything to do with it. The man had merely been her tool.

He called out to her numerous times. She did not respond, even as he searched the area thoroughly. Then finally, he arrived at the place where they shared their private moments. He closed his eyes as he relived each precious memory. Did Shaelynn do the same? He detected excitement in her voice the instant she called his name. But then the excitement faded and fear took its place.

Tristan opened his eyes and swept the area, looking for telltale signs that she'd occupied this area. He found nothing indicative on any of the surrounding branches. Not a strand from her hair or a thread from her clothes adorned any of the bushes. But then, just as he convinced himself she hadn't come this far after all, he spied her cell phone lying abandoned on a nearby rock. So, she did find her way here. This is where she made her call, and dropped her phone. But, what made her drop it? What terror did she encounter at that moment?

Once again, he called out her name. As before, he received no answer. A host of scenarios crashed into his mind. Something caused her to stifle that scream. If she happened upon a wild animal, surely he would see the evidence. Then, an awful possibility crashed into his mind and erased all others. The idea took root and grew of its own accord.

If Shaelynn remembered her dreams, she would need to take this path backward. Not from the direction he had just conducted his search. She would need to start her journey at the church because that's the only way she could find this place. He began the dreams in the middle of the forest. Therefore, she would need to take such a step in order to find it.

Did Nils see her as she approached Adaria? If so, then surely he recognized her as the same woman who opened his door and stepped inside the chapel months earlier. He would know her as the same woman who spoke to Isaac outside his domain. The curiosity of his twisted mind would compel him to follow her, even if nothing else did. Subsequently, he would hear her say Tristan's name when she made her call. But would he leave his sanctuary and follow her all the way out here? More important, did Adlundsen manifest himself to her if he had?

He did not need to ask those questions, for with absolute certainty, he already had the answers. Nils did see Shaelynn as she approached Adaria and he did follow her. The moment she uttered his name, Adlundsen's rage compelled him to materialize. Fear seized him as those very conclusions led him to—

No! She wouldn't have gone that far. She promised she wouldn't go inside that church without him. She promised.

But she did go inside, the voice inside his head whispered. Right now, at this minute, her nightmare unfolded before her eyes. Detail by detail, the horrendous dream played out in its entirety. Right now, Nils held her captive inside his domain. Fear, anger, and his love for Shaelynn propelled him toward Adaria. Heaven help that man if he harmed her in any way.

A mighty roar of crashing thunder announced Tristan's arrival inside the church. With his anger unleashed, he looked for retribution and found Nils Adlundsen waiting to receive it. He used that brief moment of surprise to grasp him tightly around the throat and slam his adversary against the wall of his self-made haven. A thing which stunned his old friend, and he noted it with satisfaction.

Strength and sheer power of will factored into accomplishing this difficult but not impossible task, and right now, he would not let Nils have Shaelynn. He possessed the stronger will as well as the greater need. A fact he just proved by bursting through the major's domain, uninvited. Yet, in that same instant, he ascertained the walls of Nils's sanctuary did not hold Shaelynn inside.

"Where is she, Nils?" asked Tristan as he tightened his grip.

"Why, Tristan! How...how very good of you to stop by," Nils sputtered. "How did you... Ah, but of course, I expected you to come into my lair so you could retrieve that hideous woman. This is surely the reason you—"

"Where. Is. She?" He ground out between clenched teeth as he whirled him around and slammed him against the opposite wall.

"If you want to see her again, I suggest you let me go," the major replied using a scathing tone. "At least, long enough for us to have a civil conversation. After our discussion, I will be quite happy to take you to her if that is your wish."

Tristan loosened his hold, but kept his eyes fixed solidly on his opponent. At least for the moment, he would allow Nils to believe he held the upper hand.

"That's much better," crooned Nils. "Now, what

shall we talk about first? There is just so much to cover!"

"I don't see where we have anything to talk about, except of course, the whereabouts of the woman."

"That's cold, Tristan. That's really cold. After all, how many decades have passed since we last laid eyes on each other?"

"Not nearly enough of them," Tristan growled.

"You could at least tell me what has kept you so busy all this time," Nils said, shifting to a more pleasant tone. "I mean you haven't come by to acknowledge my presence or even see how I'm doing since we left our dusty old bodies behind. In fact, I didn't even know you remained among the living until just recently. I find that puzzling. One would think heaven would throw open the doors and welcome the noble Captain Tristan Jordahl for all his heroic deeds, heralded by a concourse of angels singing your praises. I simply can't understand why you are still here."

"Can you not?" Tristan raised a mocking brow.

"Oh, surely our last squabble hasn't kept you earthbound, has it?" he asked, feigning innocence. "After all this time, I should think you'd put that nasty piece of business behind you."

"You know, I might be able to put 'that nasty piece of business' behind me, if I but understood it," Tristan replied. "Why don't you enlighten me as to the reason for it?"

"Well, why not then." Nils smiled as if pleased with the question. He clasped his hands behind his back and shrugged. "I've always hated you, Tristan. Even when we were very small children, did you know that? You were too stupid to see it. In fact, you were too stupid to see many things. Still, I endured your loathsome company because it was advantageous for me. For whatever their reasons,

279

you always had the right people clamoring for your attention. I wanted them to know me, as well."

While Nils began his idiotic ramblings, Tristan found himself concentrating more on what he could hear in the background than on the incoherent, nonsensical things he said. He hoped to hear the sound of Shaelynn's breathing. Hints of a sigh, moan, or even a tiny cough, would help pinpoint her location. Nils had to have confined her somewhere in the near vicinity.

"The whole situation became intolerable. Especially when you plotted to take what rightfully belonged to me, something I worked so hard to achieve. You might find it interesting to know that I considered giving you a glorious battle death, just to make sure you didn't get one. Did you know that? They might have called you a hero, you know. Though difficult to stomach I must admit, I still planned to carry out that plan to the smallest detail. I even chose my assassin and I can assure you, with a man of your size, Tristan, he wouldn't have missed his target no matter how nimbly you moved on the field."

Nils began laughing then. Softly at first but his guffaws increased in volume and pitch. "And then we had the breach at Chickamauga. Would it surprise you to learn I designed, planned, and executed that breach? I set the whole thing in motion by sending the message to Rosecrans. Oh, not personally, of course. That wouldn't have done, at all. My plan worked flawlessly, wouldn't you agree? The Union lost the battle as prearranged and as customary, the Confederacy paid me very well for my talents—all in gold. I would only accept payment in that manner from them.

"Of course, you and I both know what happened next, don't we? They assigned me to find the origination of the missive. How ironic, don't you agree? Although a dilemma at the time, you laid the solution in my lap by having your little chat with the Confederate captain. The ever noble, self-righteous Captain Jordahl! At least you were finally good for something, and it gave me the option of making you anything but a hero."

His gaze hardened then, and his eyes filled with suspicion. Tristan shrugged as if nothing he said concerned him in the least, a thing that enraged his adversary and pushed him over the edge.

"But why am I telling you all of this?" he ranted. "Surely you know the rest. You and that interfering woman. She pretended ignorance. But I could see through her lies. The two of you are working against me. Somehow, you found it. And now you think to expose my secrets to the world. Well, I won't allow it! You will give it back, and after you have obeyed that command, you will tell me how you attained it in the first place. I will know your source!"

Tristan tossed him an arrogant grin, crossed his arms against his chest, and shook his head. "Nope, I'm afraid not. You will get nothing from me until you release the woman."

"I am the one who will do the bargaining, Tristan," Nils shrieked. "Not you. You will not tell me again, what you will or will not do. Right now, I crave a little more information before I enlighten you as to your eternal—"

Tristan choked off the rest of his sentence as he grabbed Nils by the shoulders and slammed him onto the floor. He pressed his knee hard against his chest to keep him there. "Where is Shaelynn, Nils? I will not ask you again."

Comprehension dawned. Tristan could see it as it flashed across his twisted features. This newfound knowledge made the major chuckle gleefully, despite his precarious position on the floor.

"Ah, Tristan, you have fallen in love with your

mortal pet. How perfect. How wonderfully perf—"

Tristan's hands circled his throat. "Tell me where she is."

The major's chuckles now resonated with madness. "You are much too late, Tristan. Haven't you guessed? She's already dead."

Chapter 25

Awareness seemed slow in coming. Shae shivered with the cold, and her body ached from head to foot. She lifted a hand and rested it against her throbbing forehead while trying to make sense of her surroundings. Her eyelids fluttered open. Yet, she could see nothing but dense blackness all around her. She dropped her hand to her side, and instantly made contact with the moist, rocky dirt beneath it. Shae remembered then. Her recurring nightmare became a reality the moment she stepped onto the path leading to the church. And just as it happened in her nightmares, Fenrir bound her body and soul.

A violent shiver coursed through her body as she recalled the memory of all that happened earlier. How much earlier, she didn't know. She didn't have a clue as to the length of her stay inside this pit. A few seconds, a few minutes, or maybe even hours for all she knew.

After rolling to her side, she pushed against the ground, sat up, and brushed the dirt away from her arms. She could smell and feel the dampness of the earth beneath her legs. The mustiness of the air made breathing difficult, and the cold chilled her to the bone.

She could see nothing in front of her and, surely, she'd waited long enough for her eyes to adjust to the darkness. After standing to her feet, she patted her pockets in search of her cell phone. Perhaps she could use the light from her screen to see her present location, and then she could call Tristan. Somehow, he would find her.

Her heart sank as she dipped her hands inside empty pockets. She no longer had her phone. Somewhere along the way, she had lost it and with it, all hope to contact Tristan or anybody else. She needed to find a way out of here herself. After a deep breath, she stepped forward with arms extended. In no time at all, she connected with and explored a solid wall of rock, dirt, and roots. She encountered the same thing after turning in the opposite direction. No more than six feet separated the two walls. Five feet to her right, the same type of wall blocked her path. Panic beset her. Where did Nils toss her body? She remembered the fall. She did not know if she could climb such a distance without rope.

She stooped down, rummaged through the dirt, and grasped several rocks from off the ground. One at a time, she hurled them upward. Despite her efforts, she couldn't gauge the distance to the top. She couldn't climb up the walls, either. As near as she could tell, they stood very nearly vertical, with nothing to assist the climb. A sigh escaped as she turned to her left and began a forward journey. She needed to know the boundaries of her prison. Keeping her left hand against the rocky wall for guidance and support, she advanced along the path. Relief flooded her as her pathway extended far beyond her previous limits. She didn't have any idea where the corridor might lead. Nevertheless, she held on to the hope that she could find an exit and some fresh air.

Approximately five minutes into her journey, the wall abruptly ended. Shae traced its edges with her fingers and discovered it veered to the left. However, the path also continued straight ahead. That meant Nils tossed her down some kind of tunnel and now she needed to make a decision. She could get lost down here in the darkness, where nothing marked her path.

If the tunnel continued to twist and turn in different directions, could she remember how to find her way back to this junction, if such became necessary? She didn't know what to do. As she stood in indecision, the sounds of something scurrying past her feet made her vault from her spot. A small yelp escaped her, before she clamped down hard on her lips. She had no more desire to run into Nils down here than she did the rats, and she did not want to give away her location.

Just then, a dim ball of light off the left passageway curbed her troubled thoughts. She stood still, and focused on the light. To her utter amazement, the ball grew in both dimension and luminosity. The orb moved toward her, and then paused, about ten paces away. Her heart thudded against her chest as the ball took shape. In a matter of seconds, the orb evolved into a man that glowed.

She blinked several times as a young Confederate soldier emerged solidly in front of her. His light brown hair, blue eyes, mustache with short, scraggly-looking beard, and round silver eyeglasses shot into focus. He gazed at her for a few minutes as if allowing her to come to terms with his presence. Her earlier panic evaporated. This man did not intend to harm her. She took a deep breath and gave it slow release.

He nodded once and then with just a wave of his hand, requested that she follow him into the darkness. The spirit did not attempt to move his legs. He glided down the pathway. She followed him without hesitation. Every now and then the entity would turn, as if to make certain she still trailed him. Each time, he gestured for her to follow. Then, without warning, he disappeared from view and again, total darkness consumed her. Anxiety set in, and just as she opened her mouth to call out, another type of light appeared to guide her path. This light didn't come from the spirit. The flickering light derived from a conventional source. Finally, the walls of the tunnel opened to her gaze, and she could see another turn just up ahead.

Just as she made that turn, she stopped and stared. The soldier had escorted her to a small cavity within the tunnel. Several wooden crates placed haphazardly inside, sat against the end wall. An old rusty oil lantern sat atop a crate. This lantern provided the light that directed her final steps. Her otherworldly companion stood next to the box, awaiting her arrival.

"Thank you for your help, but can you tell me where I am?" she asked as her gaze swept over the chamber.

Without saying a word, the soldier turned his head to the right and dipped his head toward the crudely built table. Black saddlebags, an assortment of papers, ink well, and quill pen, rested atop the rough-sawn surface. She moved closer to get a better look. The dusty, leather pouches, intricately tooled with the initials *N.A.*, told her the ghostly confederate, led her to Nils Adlundsen's missing saddlebags. A flush rose to her cheeks and her heart pounded in excitement.

Shae glanced up at the soldier, who had yet to take his eyes off her. Thus far, he made no effort to speak. Perhaps he wouldn't or couldn't.

"Do you know Major Nils Adlundsen?" she asked as she traced the worn initials with the tip of her fingers.

The soldier gave her a slight nod. Shae had the distinct impression that she faced the unknown rider. But she needed confirmation.

"The day Nils Adlundsen died, the day he lured Captain Tristan Jordahl to the church with the intention of murdering him, you were also here with him, weren't you," she said the words as if stating fact.

He answered with one solemn nod.

"But you didn't see Tristan, because Nils killed you before he arrived. The blood on the floor of the church belonged to you. I could see *your* blood on the blade of his knife. After he murdered you, he needed to hide the evidence. So, he threw your body down here in this tunnel, and that simple act explains the abrupt stop of the flow of blood." The ghost never changed his facial expression as she spoke. Nevertheless, she could feel his encouragement in the one single nod of his head.

"That would also mean the Union uniform inside the saddlebags, carried by the gray horse, belonged to you." Another nod of confirmation.

Impressions flooded into her mind at a rapid pace. Each piece of the puzzle twisted and turned into their proper order, place, and sequence. She could see the entire picture now, with no missing pieces.

"You are Anders Janssen, aren't you?" she asked, though she didn't really need him to answer. Nevertheless, he gave her a nod.

"You served as Major Nils Adlundsen's runner. You are the one he assigned to carry all his messages to the Confederates, which is why you needed both uniforms. You would need safe passage crossing enemy lines, because Nils actively sold information to the Confederate army. Major Adlundsen sent the false information to Rosecrans himself, thereby betraying his country at the battle of Chickamauga." She gazed at Janssen who now stood with his arms folded across his chest. A smile tugged at the corners of her mouth and with a slight shake of her head, she whispered the word, "Tyr."

This ghostly soldier assisted Nils until the major cast him aside. Whatever his earthly deeds, he paid for them, many times over. He too, became a victim of Nils Adlundsen's desire to tie up all of his loose ends. Still, she had a few questions that needed answering.

"Can you tell me why he chose Tristan to take the fall? What thing, real or imagined, did Tristan ever do to deserve being branded a traitor to his own country?" she asked him.

Janssen pointed to the saddlebags, indicating the answer lay within them. At least, she hoped that's what he meant.

Shae tested the rickety-looking stool in front of the table before she eased herself down. She gazed at the pile of dusty papers laying on top of the crude table. The top page looked as if someone or something interrupted the writer in the middle of his letter. She would take time to read it later. Nevertheless, she pointed to the sheets of paper, looked up at Anders and said, "Nils?"

The spirit lifted a brow and nodded.

Shae blew off the dust and took great care in moving the fragile stack of pages to the top corner of the desk. The quill pen and ink well followed. She slid the saddlebags toward her, untied the leather strap, and opened the flap of the left pouch. The bag contained the major's personal belongings. He kept his wallet, a grooming kit, and an assortment of miscellaneous items inside it. Pushing the left bag aside, she turned the right bag toward her and used small careful movements to open it. This pouch contained various sized documents and his Bible.

Gazing up at her companion, she lifted the Bible out of the bag first. "Did he ever bother reading anything out of this book?" she asked.

Anders merely shrugged.

"Perhaps he should have," she said. Shae used caution as she retrieved the fragile documents. She placed the large stack on the table, and began reading.

The first few records did not note anything of great importance. They dealt with Nils and his various duties as major. The next document in line was an official certificate issued by the military. Tristan's name, boldly scrawled in the appropriate line, caught her immediate attention. With the greatest care, she scooped it up into her hands, and turned toward the light. Time had faded the handwriting on the certificate, but she could still read it easily enough.

The Commanding Officer of
the Fifteenth Wisconsin Regiment
of the Wisconsin Volunteers
To all who shall these presents greeting:

Know ye: That we reposing especial Truth and Confidence in your Patriotism, Valor, Conduct, and Fidelity; in the name and by our authority; Do hereby constitute and appoint Tristan Jordahl as Lieutenant Colonel under the Third Brigade of the First Division, Twentieth Army Corps, Army of the Cumberland, Wisconsin Fifteenth Regiment Volunteers; to rank as such from the Tenth day of October 1863. He is therefore carefully and diligently to discharge the duties of such office by doing and performing all things thereunto belonging.

And do Strictly charge and Require all Officers and Soldiers under his command to be obedient to his orders. He is to observe and follow such orders and directions from time to time as he shall receive from the President of the United States or General or Superior Officers set over him, according to the rules and description of War. This commission to continue in force until further action by higher Command.

In Testimony Whereof; I have caused these letters to be made patent and the great seal of the Military for the United States of America, to be hereunto affixed.

Given under my hand this tenth day of October, in the Year of Our Lord, One Thousand, Eight Hundred and Sixty-Three.

> A.L.Martinsen
> *HDQRS. FIFTEENTH REGT.*
> *WISCONSIN VOLS.*
> *Chattanooga, Tennessee,*
> *October 10, 1863*

Shae lowered her trembling hand to the table. She gave her head a little shake and smiled wistfully. Not only did Colonel Heg recommend Tristan for promotion to Lieutenant Colonel, he actually attained the rank before his death. She sighed as she considered the terrible cost of that single sheet of paper.

"Nils deliberately kept this certificate away from Tristan, didn't he?"

Janssen, his eyes full of sorrow, simply nodded.

"Why?" As she asked the question, their gazes locked and held. At that moment, she could see Nils Adlundsen as she did in her dreams. She could see him walking toward Tristan. His flushed face and the madness in his eyes spoke louder than his words.

"I have decided I am not going to let you get away with it. Not now, not ever again. I know what you have been up to, and I will not allow you to have what is rightfully mine. What I have worked so hard to attain—"

She finally understood what he meant. "Nils wanted this promotion for himself," she said. "And wanted it badly enough to kill for it. He probably convinced himself that Tristan sought for and campaigned for this position behind his back. He thought with Tristan out of the way, the promotion would surely come to him. Am I right so far?"

Again, the spectral figure nodded.

"I'm sure it galled him to see Tristan given a promotion in which he skipped a rank. A rank which

290

'rightfully' belonged to him and which he worked so hard to attain," she mocked. She placed the certificate off to the side. "The promotion, of course, would set Tristan above Nils in both authority and command. I'm sure he didn't possess the ability to deal with that situation either."

Janssen smirked over her astute observation.

"So, what else do we have here?" she wondered aloud, as piece by tedious piece, she read each scrap of paper, each letter, and each official document. Although her companion remained silent while she read, she was grateful for his presence. Somehow, just having him here provided comfort and a little dose of needed courage. The spirit of Nils Adlundsen lurked somewhere nearby and she didn't know how much time she had until he sought her out.

She smothered a yawn as she placed yet another letter from Adlundsen's father, into its appropriate pile. She wanted to separate the major's personal correspondence from the official documents he carried. Also, just as Tristan suggested, she discovered proof that Nils's father fueled his son's ostentatious ambitions. The stack of letters introducing his son to various people, considered influential or important at the time, grew ever larger on the table. She wondered if Nils used any of them to further his cause.

She paused in her quest long enough to wipe the moisture from her eyes. After taking a deep breath of stagnant air, she picked up a torn fragment of paper. Weariness fled as shock took its place. She read the damning note three different times to ensure accuracy before she gazed at her companion. Her lips curved into a triumphant smile. Shae held all the proof she needed to clear Tristan's name, in her trembling hands.

"Finally," she whispered as for a brief moment, she closed her eyes and held the shred of paper close to her heart.

Captain Jordahl,

We regret to ~~tell you~~ inform you that your contact, ~~Jesse Kendig~~, Charles Kent has unfortunately, been killed in action, one week past. This necessitates an immediate change in plans and transfer assignment of new operative. ~~If you want to receive payment~~ Scheduled payment, for services ~~provided~~ rendered to be delayed exactly one week from agreed date and time. Location will remain the same at which time new ~~agent~~ contact will be assigned.

~~General George E. Pickett CSA~~
Lt. Harmon Massey
Confederate States of America

The practice letter made her laugh. Anders Janssen gained her attention by pointing toward the documents on the table. He made her understand that more such letters or documents awaited discovery. With renewed energy, she sorted through each of the remaining records. She found several practice letters, as well as forged copies of official documents, including Tristan's note of gratitude written by the confederates. Nils practiced writing the signature on that note many times over. In these practice letters, she could see he mainly targeted Tristan, but other names appeared as well in his pursuit to tie up all of his loose ends.

"You somehow managed to keep these documents safe all these years?" she asked.

Anders nodded, bounced his brows, and grinned.

"And are they protected? I mean they are safe from Nils, he can't get them, or destroy them, can he?" she asked.

Anders shook his head, his expression confident.

The young soldier gave her the impression that Nils attempted to collect his property many times over without success. Anders kept them safe enough and he could continue to do so. She smiled as she placed everything needed to clear Tristan's name on top. Everything else went to the bottom of the stack. Then using the skills of her craft, she eased the delicate pages back inside the pouch of the saddlebag. Once she completed the task, she gazed at Anders who patiently waited. "Is there a way out of here?"

He lifted his hand with palm facing outward.

"There is something else?" she asked.

He moved to the other side of the chamber and dropped his gaze.

One of the wooden crates rested apart from the others. She could see the major's rifle and the tattered remains of his bedroll propped beside it. A coffee pot along with a small assortment of cooking and eating utensils lay on top. The very things she expected to see on the major's horse, but didn't. The evidence inside this chamber proclaimed that Nils never went anywhere but here during his so-called investigations. He simply whiled away the time, practicing his forged documents and rambling letters, in the hope of sealing Tristan's fate.

"His home away from home, I presume?"

Anders shook his head.

"No? What are you trying to tell me then?"

He pointed at the crate itself.

"Is there something inside the crate you want me to see?"

Relief etched his features as she asked the question, and he nodded.

Shae stepped over to the box and removed the items on top. She hefted the splintered lid away from its resting place and set it on the ground. A neatly folded wool blanket sat on top. She removed it. The blanket concealed a small but sturdy trunk about half the size of Tristan's. She grabbed hold of the handles. A small grunt escaped her lips as she heaved it out of the crate, and placed it on the ground along side the lid. She struggled under the weight of the trunk, so the lock went unnoticed until she stepped back.

She glanced up at Anders and released a sigh of despair. "The chest needs a key. I suppose I could use a rock to bash it open, but I really don't want to do that if I don't have to," the historian inside her said.

Anders gave her a wink and pointed at the saddlebags.

"Oh, of course. Tristan said that Nils kept everything of importance inside his saddlebags, which is why he kept them very close to his person." After searching through his personal things, she found the key hidden inside his wallet. She took it out and then placed it inside the lock. Turning the key within the rusted mechanism became a battle of sorts, but after several attempts, she finally heard a click, and the shackle popped out of the case. The lid creaked and groaned as she opened it.

The contents caused a gasp of amazement. A huge stash of gold coins and paper currency made by both the Confederacy and the United States filled most of the chest. The horde also contained an assortment of gold and silver pocket watches as well as other personal items of value. She assumed Nils pilfered many, if not all of these items from the dead.

Everything she needed to prove his reprehensible schemes sat inside this chamber awaiting discovery. These things would restore Tristan's good name, and the world would remember him for his courage and nobility. However, she couldn't accomplish her goal unless she could get out of this tunnel and bring this stuff up with her.

"Please, Anders," she said once again, "I need to get out of here. Can you help me?"

He lifted his hand, with his index finger

extended. That finger begged a moment of her time.

"You need to show me something else, first?"

He nodded and swept a hand toward the lantern.

"I guess this means we are going somewhere else," she murmured. Once Shae grasped the tarnished handle, Anders beckoned her to follow. As they left the chamber, she counted her measured paces and memorized the direction of each turn. She wanted to remember her way back to the chamber if for some reason Anders vanished and failed to return. Yet, they simply retraced their original steps. If he wanted her to see something along the path they already traversed, why didn't he show her on the way to the chamber?

Finally, she could see the rounded end of the tunnel. Without doubt, he returned her to the beginning of her journey. Uncertainty set in. Surely, she could not make her escape from here. She gazed at him intently as he turned to face her. A look of deep sorrow and regret filled his eyes.

"Is something wrong?" she asked.

After his customary nod, Anders dropped his gaze.

Shae followed his path and at once, drew in a sharp breath. The remains of her ghostly companion rested at his feet. She counted it a miracle she didn't step on them when she stumbled around in the darkness, trying to find her way out.

At that moment, Anders showed her the final moments of his life. The vision appeared very much like the dreams Tristan shared with her. Only this time, she could see everything with her conscious mind. She could see Anders as he walked into the church, dressed in his Confederate uniform. He wore that particular uniform because Nils ordered him to do so.

The major stood waiting for him about halfway

down the center aisle. As Anders approached him, Nils placed a friendly hand on his shoulder while the other remained behind his back. He turned him toward the pulpit, and the two of them strolled toward the front of the chapel.

Nils nodded and as he spoke, he used a jovial tone. "We're almost finished with this nasty business, Janssen. There is but one more duty I must require of you. I have taken care of everything else. Finally, you'll be free of this whole business."

Anders sighed with relief. He pinched a piece of fabric from his uniform shirt, tugged on it, and said, "I take it you are sending me back to Georgia?"

Nils chuckled softly, and while keeping a firm hand on his shoulder, whirled around and stepped in front of the private. They now stood mere inches apart. The major leaned toward his ear and whispered, "No, my friend, I'm sending you to hell."

In that same instant, the knife loomed upward from its hiding place. Without a shred of remorse, Nils rammed the weapon into the chest of his runner, and twisted it. Anders sucked in his breath, his knees buckled, and he fell where he stood. Blood poured from the gaping wound. Nils used the trapdoor to discard his body, just as he used it to rid himself of her. Although, not part of the vision, Anders made her aware of the hidden trapdoor in front of the pulpit.

"I'm so sorry, Anders," she said as stooped next to his skeletal frame. "I wish none of this had ever happened to you. You must have had family who never knew what became of you and suffered because of it."

Again, he gave her a sorrowful nod.

"I would very much like to bring you out of here and give your remains a proper burial, if that meets with your approval."

He met her request with a joyous grin and then

suddenly, he looked upward as if something very unusual, something out of the ordinary, caught his attention.

"Is something wrong?" she asked as her eyes followed his startled gaze.

Anders shook his head and winked. He gave her a reassuring smile, and drew an imaginary line connecting their hearts. After a playful salute, he vanished. Despite the lantern, a feeling of abandonment beset her as Anders left her to wander the tunnel maze alone. She turned a slow circle and heaved out a sigh, not knowing quite what to do.

Chapter 26

Tristan became aware of Anders Janssen's unexpected presence just as he picked Nils up off the floor and slammed him against the wall. He had no time to consider the reason for his attendance while dealing with Nils. In frustrated outrage over Tristan's surprising ability, the major shrieked out a string of vile curses and struggled for release beneath his hands.

"How can you come and go within my domain and do as you please?" he shrilly demanded.

Tristan flashed a frightful smile, but said nothing in return.

The major looked past his shoulder then, and could see the results of the breach. His eyes bugged in disbelief as his gaze settled on the portion of wall that now lay shattered. He could see the misty, wraithlike pieces strewn haphazardly across the floor. In that single moment, Nils struggled even harder to gain his freedom.

Tristan released him then, backed away from the wall and awaited the major's vengeful attack. He didn't have to wait long. Just as Nils shot toward him, the captain turned to the side and seized his adversary by the shoulders. He hurled him onto the floor and into the wailing pieces of shadowy debris. Recognizing their creator, the broken shards fused themselves in an instant, coming together as bony, vaporous fingers. Those elongated appendages wrapped around, and tightened their grip around the major's body, despite his every effort to evade them. Sheer determination bade them carry out the security and fortification for which Adlundsen created them.

Tristan found a measure of satisfaction as Nils's face registered shock and disbelief over the occurrence. The major struggled against his cage, to no avail, as he gnashed his teeth, spitting his hatred and contempt.

"Impossible!" he shrieked. "You cannot be responsible for this imprisonment. Not you!"

The ear-splitting wail emitting from the depths of his soul shook the very foundations of the church and extended into the surrounding community. Right then, Chauncey and Beau burst through the walls of Adaria. Their instant communication told Tristan that after an unsuccessful search for Shaelynn at Chickamauga and the surrounding area, they thought to check the church. As they came upon her jeep, they heard the sounds of the raging battle in the distance.

They rushed inside the chapel intent on entering the fray, just as the last wraithlike vestige of Major Adlundsen's chains locked into place. Unless heaven itself would show him mercy, these chains would forever hold him bound. Tristan did not hold out much hope for clemency, since Nils never bestowed it on anyone else.

"You have this one last chance to tell me where Shaelynn is, Nils," Tristan threatened. "I can promise this is the last time I will ask."

Nils's face distorted with rage and anger. "I would rather enter the depths of hell before I tell you where I hurled her lifeless body, Jordahl! Do you hear me? She is dead. I killed her myself. You will never see her again."

"Hell is where you'll find yourself if you've harmed her in any way," Tristan shot back. "Chauncey, Beau? Would you take care of this repulsive vermin for me? Nils is looking for a new home, and I need to find Shaelynn."

"Gladly, Captain. You've wasted enough time on the likes of him already," Chauncey replied as he and Beau stepped forward to finish the task.

"Just a moment, if you please, Captain," Anders Janssen petitioned. "If it's all the same to you, I would like to escort the major to his final destination myself, and at the time of my own choosing, sir."

Knowledge of everything Anders endured under the hands of Adlundsen flooded into his mind. Tristan granted his request without reservation.

"I think you've earned that right. As far as I am concerned, he's all yours. Do with him as you will," he answered.

"Thank you, sir, and if you will come with me, I can take you to your woman." With one wave of the private's hand, the spirit of Nils Adlundsen vanished from the chapel. Yet, they could still hear the echo of his futile screams.

"You know where she is? Is she all right?" Tristan placed a hand on the private's shoulder.

"Yes to both of your questions. She is below, sir," Anders replied. "And Captain, I would like to express my sincerest regret for the part I played in your untimely demise. I truly did not know the major planned to kill either of us."

"No need to apologize," Tristan said. "I've known the man almost all my life. I didn't think he possessed the nature to do any of the things he did. While I lived, I would have defended him with my last breath against anyone who claimed otherwise."

Anders nodded as he led them through the tunnel. "By way of explanation, the first of the correspondences I took across enemy lines and gave to the Confederates occurred because the major ordered me to do so. He led me to believe the messages I carried would thwart the plans of our enemies. When they accomplished the direct opposite, and I discovered the major betrayed his country for profit, I told him I would no longer do his bidding. He threatened me with court martial if I refused to obey his orders, and he threatened my family. He reminded me of his ability to produce enough evidence to have me shot. I'm sorry, Captain, but I could see no way out of my dilemma. I continued to do as ordered, until the major no longer required my services."

"I am sorry for your suffering, Private Janssen. I know it is no easy thing to exist in a private hell, forced upon you by someone else," he replied.

Tristan said no more. For just up ahead his gaze fell upon Shaelynn. She looked lost and forlorn as she wandered along the corridor. He quickened his pace, anxious to claim her attention.

Shae turned the moment she sensed Tristan's presence. In that moment of joy, she dropped the lantern. The lamp miraculously landed upright, and without thinking of the impossibility of her actions, she stood on tiptoes as her arms encircled his neck. At the same time, he gathered her close to his chest. Instinct alone drew their lips together. The ability to hold each other in such a manner, to share such a wondrous kiss should be impossible. Yet, the miracle didn't occur to either of them at first. Once it did, neither of them questioned their good fortune.

Fearful it would not last, neither of them wanted to break contact with the other. So the lengthy kiss continued, despite their audience. Not until Chauncey protested the display with a disgruntled snort, followed by Beau's quiet laughter, did they finally relinquish their hold.

"Are you all right, *min kjærlighet*?" her captain asked as his fingers brushed gently against her cheek.

"I am, now that you are here," Shae replied. She glanced over at her ghostly companions before

Tristan reclaimed her gaze. She could feel herself blushing over her behavior.

"How did you come to find me down here?" she asked, feeling the need to shift the focus of attention elsewhere. "I had no way of letting you know what happened and even if I did, I didn't know how to tell you where to start looking, except to tell you that Nils—"

"We'll discuss all of that later. First, we need to get you out of here," Tristan cut in. "I find it obvious that you have endured the frigid temperatures inside this tunnel far too long." He turned toward Anders. "Is there a manageable way to get her out of here?"

"No, wait! We can't leave. Not yet." Shae touched his arm lightly, suddenly anxious. "Tristan, I have to show you first. We have everything we need to clear your name down here. Anders showed me a chamber where Nils kept all of this incriminating evidence. He kept everything inside his saddlebags. I found letters and documents, including your certificate of promotion. Anders protected it all of this time so that Nils couldn't touch it. Anyway, you are just not going to believe everything we have. Come on! It's this way," she said as she leaned down and swooped up the lantern.

"Slow down, Shaelynn. What are you talking about?" he asked as his fingers curled around her hand and gave it a gentle squeeze.

"Nils used this tunnel as his base of operations. All those times he said he traveled in search of the traitor he actually stayed here, planning and plotting. Just follow me, and you'll see it all for yourself."

She hastened her pace in the desire to share the magnificent discovery with Tristan. Then, just as she made the turn into the chamber, she stopped short. Fear and panic set in as her gaze settled on the major. Sensing her terror, Tristan drew her into a protective embrace once she caught sight of Nils Adlundsen's distorted face, and shuddered her apprehension.

The major's spiritual form rested in some type of deformed and hideous looking confinement from which he struggled to extricate himself. Nonetheless, the ominous restraints held him bound. The moment their eyes met, he began shrieking and spewing his hatred and contempt. The sound of his voice filled her with dread and made her blood run cold. She tucked her face against Tristan's chest.

Tristan drew her even closer, ran his fingers gently though her hair and said, "Don't worry, he can't hurt you anymore. He is only here because Anders wants him to share the pleasure of this moment with us. To observe, as all his insidious schemes unravel before his eyes."

"But how is it that he..." she began hesitantly as she turned her gaze toward the major and pointed. "I don't understand how he..."

"The captain attained the ability to defeat his sort," Chauncey cut in as he gazed upon Adlundsen with disdain. "I find it a shame you missed the battle up above. It's always exhilarating to watch this kind of vermin getting what they so richly deserve."

A battle? Did Chauncey just say that another battle had taken place between Tristan and Nils? Is that why Anders left her alone? Memories of her nightmare, and the dream Tristan shared with her, flooded into her mind. At once, she fastened her eyes on him looking for any telltale signs that he suffered under the hands of the major. He steadily met her gaze. His very expression assured her Adlundsen did not harm him in any way.

Still wary, she approached the desk and untied the laces on the saddlebags. Even though she felt safe enough with Tristan standing beside her, she found it difficult to ignore the major's foul retorts, threats, and unholy screams that echoed throughout the tunnel as she did so. Nonetheless, she proceeded to show Tristan everything contained within this chamber. She picked up the promotional certificate first.

"Do you see this? Not only did Colonel Heg recommend you for the promotion, you actually received it. Nils kept it hidden from you because this is what he felt rightfully belonged to him and what he worked so hard to attain," Shae mocked as she tilted her head toward him.

"That promotion belonged to me, and you know it," Nils screeched through clenched teeth. "They would have given it to me if not for you and your unscrupulous scheming behind my back. You held the position of captain. You did not even deserve consideration for this promotion. I hate you, Tristan and I will hate you for all time! I hate all of you! Do you hear me? I will not allow you to do this, I—"

"Shut up, Nils," Tristan commanded.

To her surprise, the major obeyed as if compelled to do so. Once again, Shae gave her full attention to Tristan.

"There are many practice letters here detailing your supposed treason. Although Adlundsen signed them using the names of various Confederate officers, you will notice most of them are in the major's own handwriting without any attempts of forgery at all," she pointed out. "And with the note he sent to lure you here we have proof of that fact."

After he finished reading everything she handed him, she drew his attention to the chest on the floor. She showed him the contents, and he shook his head in disgust.

"These are personal items from some of the soldiers who heroically lost their lives during battle. I find it difficult to believe that Nils did not have a problem stealing from the dead." Tristan turned his gaze to Nils. "You are vile, do you know that?"

Nils hissed in return.

"There's enough evidence in this room to fill a book," Shae said as she tried her best to ignore Adlundsen's presence. "We have more than enough proof to clear your name and set history aright."

"Well before you can do that we need to get you out of here. Is there some way Shaelynn can escape this tunnel, Anders, or do we need to get some outside help?" asked Tristan.

Though she knew he spoke to Tristan, Shae once again received vivid impressions from the private.

The tunnel once served as part of the Underground Railroad. Adlundsen discovered it quite by accident. He walked into the church and found the minister assisting a family of slaves as they climbed up the rope ladder that once hung underneath the flooring near the trap door. The vicar bought the major's silence by allowing him use of the tunnel.

Tristan turned toward Shae and said, "Anders will show us the way out. He tells me there are several exits besides that of the trap door from which you fell."

"Speaking of that trap door," Shae said as she turned to face her ghostly friend. "With the use of your lantern, I discovered it's quite a drop from the floor of the church to ground level. I am amazed I didn't break my neck or something during my fall. Especially since Nils held me so high above it before he thrust me downward. Do I have you to thank for that, Anders?"

The private smiled modestly, dipped his head, and shrugged.

Tristan tossed her a grin. "Anders didn't find it difficult to provide you with a much softer landing then you might have had otherwise. He didn't want you meeting the same fate he suffered under the hands of Adlundsen."

Shae gazed into the private's eyes and smiled her gratitude. "Thank you for taking such good care of me, Anders, and for allowing me the access to everything inside here. I won't forget the promise I made you, either."

Anders winked and once again connected their hearts with an imaginary path drawn by his hand.

"You have my thanks as well," Tristan added as he grasped hold of the private's hand and shook it. "I'm forever in your debt."

Shortly thereafter, Anders escorted them out of the tunnel through a root cellar dug by the slaves who once lived on the plantation property surrounding it. As she rose up out of the ground, she could see Isaac's house in the distance and wondered if the cellar stood on his property. The answer to that question would have to wait for the morning. For the hour grew ever later, and Tristan insisted they go home. She didn't put up much of a fuss.

Once they arrived at Starling, Amy hustled her off to the shower, fearful she would catch her death of cold if she didn't warm herself up that very instant. The solitude gave her the time she needed to sort through a host of differing thoughts. She still needed to talk to Tristan. She needed to explain why he found her at the church in the first place, and what compelled her to go inside, despite her promise to do otherwise.

More important than that, she wanted to tell him that she loved him with her whole heart and soul. She had yet to say it, though her actions inside the tunnel might have given him an indication. The memory not only made her blush, it gave her pause. The physical interaction between them remained a mystery. Though Tristan's body did not feel truly mortal, it held enough substance to allow them to touch as if he were. And right now, she would not question their good fortune.

She hurried through her shower, wanting nothing more than to reclaim her captain. Yet, she couldn't find him anywhere. No one else in the house seemed to know his whereabouts, either. She wondered if perhaps he returned to the church. Janssen spent a great deal of time with Nils prior to his death. Perhaps Tristan sought answers to those questions from the private, or maybe he wanted to get the answers from Nils, himself.

Shae tried going to bed, knowing she really needed to get some sleep. She wanted to feel refreshed and alert come the morning. A great deal of work needed doing inside the tunnel, and she personally wanted to oversee it. Despite the desire, she did naught but toss and turn, as sleep continued to elude her. The jumble of events, those utterly terrifying as well as those amazingly wonderful, occupied every corner of her mind. So much happened in such a short amount of time that she found it difficult to take it all in.

She drew in a deep breath and released the sigh as she shoved her covers to the side and got out of bed. Perhaps taking in some fresh air might help settle her down. Shae opened the French doors and followed the stone path leading to the garden. Pausing for just a moment, she looked up at the full moon, now surrounded by bright, shimmering stars. Not a single cloud shielded their beauty or hid their brilliance. She didn't see a single thing in the sky to cause panic or fear. Odin, in the place of Vidar came to her rescue. A vanquished Fenrir could no longer plague her or anyone else for that matter. She closed her eyes, lifted her face toward the night sky, and took a deep, cleansing breath.

"I believe you left this on a rock inside the forest," Tristan said as he approached her. "Perhaps now might be as good a time as any, to tell me why I found you at Adaria in the first place. And truly, I can't wait to hear all of your reasons for going inside that church without me."

Startled by the unexpected sound of his voice, Shae whirled around to face him as he spoke. He held her cell phone out toward her while giving her that devilish grin she loved so much. Just as each time before, that single smile managed to steal away her breath and rob her of her senses.

Chapter 27

"Oh come on, Tristan. The reasons shouldn't matter anymore, should they? You got there in time to play the hero, just like you wanted," Shae said as she flashed a contrite smile. Her attempt to tease did not mask her guilt. Nor did it seem to dissuade him from his quest to hear her feeble explanations. She shrugged in defeat as he waited with lifted brow during the lengthy silence.

"I'm so sorry, Tristan. Really I am," she began as she took hold of the offered phone. Then, as their hands met, she could feel an electrifying current pass between them. That remarkable current bound and connected them together in a way they'd never connected before. He drew her into his embrace, as his lips sought hers. Just as in the tunnel, she could feel the warmth and depth of his kiss. Rational thought fled her mind as she gave herself over to the consuming fire that raged within. After many such kisses, he drew away and rested his forehead against hers.

"Sorry. I just wanted to see if the spell from your fairy godmother still retained its magic," Tristan whispered into her ear. "And I am grateful that according to her time table, it's not yet midnight."

He backed away from her slightly, grinned, and shook his head as if to clear it. "You were saying?"

Did she say something? Better yet, did she say something so important it couldn't wait for a day or two? A month or two might even be better. Oh yes, that's right. He wanted an explanation. She tucked her cell phone into the pocket of her robe. Totally bemused, she turned around and led him toward the gazebo. The short walk gave her time to collect her thoughts.

As they sat down on the soft cushions of the comfortable bench, she turned toward him and met his penetrating gaze. She didn't know where to begin. Then again, Tristan preferred his explanations from the beginning.

"Those dreams you shared with me? I remember them in their entirety you know." She dropped her gaze for but a moment as she chewed at her bottom lip. "Not just the part from when you arrived at the church, but everything that transpired between us in the woodlands, before and after your battle with Nils."

Tristan nodded, took her hand, and twined his fingers around hers. "I thought perhaps you did. I didn't intend for that to happen. I have no explanation as to how such a thing might have occurred, and I'm truly sorry for it. I know it's selfish, but I created those memories for me and for me, alone."

"Why?" she asked, suddenly perplexed. "Why would you want to keep something so incredible away from me? Didn't you think I would want to share those precious moments with you? That I too, would want to have and keep those memories with me forever? I love you, Tristan. I *love* you. Don't you understand that?"

"Yes, and I love you, more than you know," he said the words with both intensity and feeling. "But I am a spirit, Shaelynn. What kind of future could you really have with someone like me hanging around all the time? Don't you see? I would be damning you to live only half a life while you lived out your mortality. You deserve so much more than that. You deserve to live life the way it's intended. You should have a husband and raise a houseful of children with all of the joy and laughter that comes with having a family of your own."

"But that's what you don't understand, Tristan. Since I met you, I've come to understand I *am* living life to the fullest, and more so than I ever have before. I don't need a husband in the normal sense of the word or children for that matter. My nephews and nieces fill that slot very nicely. They always have. I have given this a great deal of thought. From the moment I perceived just how much I do love you, I've thought of little else. I need only *you*. And to have the man I love with my whole heart and soul as my constant companion throughout the entirety of my life is the greatest blessing I could ever hope to have," she fervently replied.

"This single desire fueled my motivation in having lunch with Simon today. I didn't mean to hurt you when I asked you to remain behind, and I am so sorry if I did. But I needed such an opportunity. You see, I wanted to make sure I didn't create the dreams out of my own subconscious desires, which I then attached to the dreams you shared. I could only prove that to myself by finding our forest and I did find it. I did!"

"I know you found it. That much became obvious the moment I located your phone. When I discovered it abandoned there on that rock a terrible dread overcame me," he said. "What happened after you called me, Shaelynn? What frightened you so much? Why did you go inside the church without me, when you promised that you wouldn't?"

"Because I had to go inside alone, don't you see that?" She placed her free hand against his chest as she begged for his understanding.

"Nils heard me when I made my call. He stood there, glaring at me, not ten feet away from where I sat. He heard me say your name. The look on his face and the blood-curdling, horrific sounds he emitted afterward terrified me beyond measure. Knowing our connection, I believed he might try to follow me home. And I had no idea what he might do to you if he found you at Starling. The possibility that he could hurt you in some way petrified me. I thought he might do something that would take you away from me and that is something that I could never have—"

"Nils doesn't have the power to hurt me, Shaelynn," he cut in. "Surely you know this by now."

"No, I don't know that. I mean, how do you explain the condition Nils is in right now? He is pinned inside a cage and screaming in agony, Tristan. How do you explain the battle you both engaged in this very evening?" she countered. "Those were Chauncey's choice of words, not mine."

"That's a very different thing, altogether. The type of pain and suffering Adlundsen feels right now is what he brought on himself. I only helped it along a little," he replied. "Still, the fact remains, Nils could have seriously hurt *you*. And he would have hurt you if not for Janssen. That is something I would never have been able to endure."

"But don't you see? Your mother meant for me to go in there, and she meant for me to go in there alone. She prepared me for this experience over the course of several months. If you accompanied me inside the church tonight, then I would never have ended up in the tunnel, and you know it. You would have shielded me from Adlundsen. You would not have allowed him to touch me! This being the case, I would never have found his saddlebags or been given the means to clear your name. Everything I experienced tonight, I consider well worth the cost, just to have this evidence in my hands." Shae lifted a hand, caressed his cheek, then weaved her fingers through his hair. "Please, Tristan, no harm, no foul?"

Tristan did not feel the need to argue the point.

He didn't feel the need to point out that Anders would have appeared to them regardless. Or, that Janssen would have shown them the tunnel without her having to endure the terror Nils inflicted upon her. For he could no longer resist the need to take her into his arms or to feel the softness of her lips. He did not want to waste a moment of this impossible gift.

In all likelihood, Shaelynn would believe the gift came from her fairy godmother or his mother and perhaps it did. Yet, it did not matter where this magical moment came from. He just wanted to take advantage of it while it lasted, and take advantage he did.

The miraculous spell lasted until she could no longer ward off the need to sleep. Finally then and with great reluctance, he insisted she return to the house and go to bed. She asked him to stay with her and hold her until she fell asleep. He did not hesitate to comply with her request. Nevertheless, at least to his reckoning, not long after she fell into a deep, peaceful slumber, the ability to hold her waned, and then disappeared altogether.

At that moment, he recalled his fervent wish for the ability to have even one hour with her as a mortal man. Tonight he received much more than that and an overwhelming sense of gratitude consumed him. His eyes looked heavenward and he whispered to anyone who cared to listen, "Thank you, it is enough. I will ask for no more than that."

Before he left her bedroom, he tucked the blankets around her shoulders and gave her one last kiss.

****

Several hours later, the light filtering through the window roused Shae from her sleep. As her hand rested across her eyes, she took a few minutes to gather her thoughts and recall the events of last

313

night. Yet as everything flooded into her mind, she threw her covers off to the side, slid out of bed, and retrieved her phone from the pocket of her robe. She glanced over at the clock and sighed in exasperation as she could see she'd slept half the morning away. She did not mean to sleep so late. So much needed doing, and she wanted it all done today.

While struggling into her clothes, she rested her phone against her cheek as she called Reuben. She asked him to get in touch with Norman as well as Professor Andersen and have everyone in the team meet her at the Adaria church as soon as possible. Very briefly, she explained her discovery. Then as she left her bedroom, she tucked her phone inside her pocket and called out for Tristan. He met her there in the hallway. Yet, before she could fling herself into his arms, he took a step backward, held up his hand, and shook his head. She could see absolute regret fill his eyes.

"I'm afraid we've reached our midnight, princess. Our magical spell expired a little before dawn," he said and then shrugged as he tilted his head to the side. "Everything is back to normal, whatever normal is."

Shae took a step back and searched his eyes. Despite her disappointment, she managed a bit of a smile. "Well, magical spells don't last forever, do they? Still, I found it amazing while it lasted."

"As did I." He brushed against her cheek with his fingers and grinned. "As did I, *min kjærlighet*."

After a few moments of consideration, she said, "Tristan, would you kiss me, please?"

"What?" he asked, clearly amused by her unexpected request.

"Well it's just that from the day we first met, whenever you have touched me, I have actually felt it," she said. "Now I would like to know if I also possess the ability to feel your kiss without benefit of dreams or magical spells from fairy godmothers."

Tristan grinned as he cupped her face with his hands and lowered his lips to hers. The ghostly kiss, though completely different from the ones in her dreams or the kisses shared last evening, held an incredible power of their own. In fact, this kiss set a raging fire deep within her soul, and the blaze consumed her, in the nicest way possible. She flashed him a dazzling smile as she sought to catch her breath.

"And so?" he asked, obviously pleased with her response.

With a smile still plastered to her face, she stepped away, lifted a mischievous brow, and said, "Oh, I don't know. I think we're going to have to work on your technique a little bit. Still, with a little practice, or rather with a whole lot of *daily* practice, maybe one day you'll attain the ability to knock my socks clean off my feet."

She entered the kitchen to the sound of his chuckles. Actually, if she'd been wearing socks they'd already be on the floor somewhere between the kiss and the kitchen, she silently mused. Wow. She could definitely make do with that!

Tristan crossed his arms against his chest as she poured herself a small bowl of cereal and began eating it, even as she carried the bowl to the table. Well, perhaps "shoveling" her food would be the better description.

He furrowed his brow and shook his head. "Shaelynn, you don't need to eat so fast."

She nodded in response as she swallowed down a mouthful of food. "Oh, yes I do. I want to get to the church well ahead of Reuben," she said as she dabbed at the milk on her lips with her fingertips. "After all, I need to stake my claim to those saddlebags before he gets there. He can have them after I retrieve all the documents I want to keep."

Within the hour, she and Tristan arrived at the church with her backpack full of the tools she needed. After entering the chapel, she walked straight over to the trap door. She knelt down and could now discern the finger-sized notch used to open it. Once she lifted the small weathered piece of wood, she dropped a glow stick in an effort to gauge the distance from the door to the ground. She approximated the drop to be at least twelve feet or more, and she silently thanked Anders again for catching her fall. Tristan was right. Falling from the height of the vaulted ceiling, she might have broken her neck if not for her ghostly friend.

"I don't know Tristan, perhaps we ought to use the root cellar if we can get the permission. When we climbed out of the door last night, I could see Isaac's house in the distance. I wondered then if we came out on part of his property," she said.

"Why don't you give him a call and find out?" he replied.

"I think I'd rather show him," she said. "If the root cellar isn't on his property, he will surely know to whom it belongs and can give us directions. Come on, he doesn't live far from here."

Isaac seemed genuinely pleased when she arrived at his doorstep and even more so when he listened to her explanation as to the reason for the visit. He appeared delighted to learn the root cellar, which he owned, would play a part in absolving the captain. Of course, he said, she could use it as long as she wished.

The excavation team took several hours removing the majority of artifacts from within the tunnel. The tunnel's history as part of the Underground Railroad thrilled Norman to no end. Nevertheless, on this trip they focused most of their attention on the artifacts from inside Nils's chamber. Once gathered, they began taking all of the collected artifacts to the museum at Chickamauga for preservation and eventual display. All the while, an eerie, distant wailing accompanied their activities. Most of the team members convinced themselves they simply heard the wind echoing through the tunnels. Their comments and theories almost made her laugh aloud.

"Nils?" She mouthed the question to Tristan as she rubbed her arms against the sudden icy chill that blasted into the chamber.

Tristan grinned and nodded. "Anders is allowing him to observe while the members of Reuben's team do their work. As you can guess, he isn't very happy, especially with the removal of his personal and most incriminating secrets."

"What about the saddlebags, sir? Are they good to go?"

Shae whirled toward the sound of the voice. A man by the name of Carl pointed at her precious saddlebags. Anders glowered in their direction. At once, he stepped in front of the table creating some kind of barrier in his continuing quest to keep them safe. She had to wonder what would happen if they attempted to pass through the barrier only she could see.

"Oh! You needn't worry about those, Carl," Reuben said. "Shae is going to take charge over them for now. When she is finished with the documents they contain, she'll donate them to the museum."

Carl looked from Reuben to Shae and then shrugged. "All right then, I'll just take the rest of this stuff out to the van and be on my way."

Shae thanked her friend for his continued support and devotion with a smile. Anders responded by bowing slightly. In turn, she placed a hand atop her heart and swept it toward him, for she had a promise to keep.

"There is one last thing I need to show all of you

at the other end of the tunnel." She picked up her flashlight and turned toward the entrance. "So, if you will follow me, please?"

Shae led them out of the chamber, making her way through the portion of the tunnel that took them below the church. The open trap door gave additional light to the area. She knelt beside the skeletal remains of her ghostly friend.

"These remains belong to Private Anders Janssen of the Wisconsin Fifteenth Regiment. I would like them to receive a proper burial. If not for him, we would never have made this discovery and attained the proof of what took place at the battle of Chickamauga."

Shae related the entire story. All the while, the howling wind blowing throughout the tunnel grew ever louder. She began her tale with the battle of Chickamauga. She explained how the Union defeat became the catalyst. That defeat set off a series of events that ended in the church above them first, and then finally, down inside this tunnel. She told them of her meetings with Isaac and her subsequent investigation concerning Captain Tristan Jordahl.

She did not divulge the details of her personal interactions with the ghosts or the dreams she shared with Tristan. Even though those dreams gave personal insight as to what took place inside the chapel, she held the memories private and refused to share them publicly. The documented evidence could stand on its own.

After laying out all of her gathered evidence, each of the men remained quiet. Yet, she could see from the expressions on their faces they concurred with all of her findings and subsequent conclusions.

Reuben spoke first. "Given the man's noble character and his selfless actions on and off the battlefield, I think it only fitting to give Captain Jordahl a place of honor within the museum. Shae, I would appreciate it, if you would select some of the best letters and documents for the exhibit. And I believe I speak for all of us present, when I say there shouldn't be a problem in burying the remains of Private Janssen. We can also exhume the remains of Captain Tristan Jordahl and rebury them at the National Cemetery in Chattanooga if you wish. Are we all agreed?"

Shae glanced at Anders. He beamed with joy over the announcement. She returned his smile in kind. Then, she turned her gaze toward Tristan. He tossed her a grin and gave her a wink of approval. Anders Janssen could finally go home.

Three days later, a front-page article appeared in the local newspaper detailing the discovery. Reuben mentioned Tristan in the story as well. He gave just enough information concerning the captain and the Wisconsin Fifteenth Regiment to pique the curiosity of the public. They would unveil the rest of the incredible story, he said, at the museum in Chickamauga in due course. Reuben and Ian's forthcoming project could not have asked for greater publicity.

Shae put the newspaper on the desk after she finished reading the story to her ghostly companions and leaned back in her chair. She laughed as they all erupted into cheers and applause. Even Horace managed an exuberant "Hoorah," with one fist flying chaotically in the air.

The restoration of the captain's good name thrilled each of them to no end. They heaped an embarrassing amount of praise upon her for all of her efforts in making that a reality. Tristan received his fair share of the praise as well, despite his protests.

"We could not have accomplished any of this without Shaelynn's tireless efforts. I didn't have very much to do with any of it," he said. "She is the one who deserves all of the credit and all of my gratitude."

The comment made her blush even though everyone took their obvious shift in relationship in stride. But really, just how many mortals in the history of this earth fell in love with a ghost? The notion gave her pause. For surely, she and Tristan were not the only such couple on this earth. Were they?

"Well, I think there is going to be a renewed interest in the Chickamauga Memorial Park after this," she said in an effort to place their focus of attention elsewhere.

"I believe you have that right," Chauncey said. "And now that the public knows about the tunnels, Norman Lamont and his associates are going to have to do something about the Adaria church as well. Perhaps that means they will leave Starling alone."

"Yep, I think they are going to find out they have their hands full with all the pesky sightseers wanting a glimpse of what's down there. Maybe we ought to sign up as tour guides and help them out," Beau added as his eyes twinkled with mirth. "That ought to stir things up a bit. I noticed some things down there that looked down right interesting."

"At least they won't have to deal with the likes of Nils Adlundsen any longer." Amy sniffed as she lifted her chin a notch and turned her gaze toward the window. "As boorish as the two of you can be, you are still far more acceptable than the major."

"That reminds me." Shae turned and focused her gaze on Tristan. "I've been meaning to ask you about that. Exactly how did you *subdue* the major, anyway? I don't quite understand what happened."

Tristan shrugged as he brought a hand to his chin. "Nils thought he created an impenetrable haven."

"A haven?" she asked. "What do you mean by a

haven?"

"Havens are wall-like barriers, placed around a specific area. They keep other spirits out or in, as the case warrants. The creation of this internal space becomes an entity's own private domain and within this barrier, they reign supreme," he said. "Each spirit that creates one can allow or forbid entrance to any other spirit. At the same time, they can also allow or forbid any spirit to leave, once inside."

Shae shuddered as the thought of Nils Adlundsen eternally holding her captive, took hold.

"Most of the time, only spirits of Adlundsen's ilk create such areas," he continued. "These evil spirits take pleasure in causing havoc, pain, suffering, and maliciousness both within and without their boundaries. Within their own personal boundaries, they cannot be touched. Prayers do not dispel them. Displaying religious tokens, relics, or exorcisms don't seem to do any good, either. Nothing can penetrate this barrier, or so most spirits believe."

"But the captain learned to shatter these walls," Chauncey cut in. "He discovered the secret when one of our former inhabitants, a dour man by the name of Thaxton, created such an area for himself inside the game room here at Starling."

"Yes, but at the time, the area served as the bedroom of a young mortal girl," Amy added. "Poor little thing always looked so frail and sickly. Toward the end, the doctors confined her to bed. Eventually, consumption claimed her life, while the evil entity inside the room, claimed her soul. He didn't allow her to leave or go into the light, as she so desperately desired. Thaxton kept her there, imprisoned and terrified."

"Oh that's terrible." Shae's eyes widened as her mind conjured the vision.

"Indeed," Tristan shook his head in disgust as

he recalled the memory. "Her terror brought him the greatest joy as well as the greatest satisfaction, and he fed on it."

"Tristan finally figured out how to set her free, though," Beau said. "And more such spirits followed. All with the same results."

The fascinating explanation intrigued Shae. Yet, before she could get the details as to how Tristan accomplished the feat, the ringing of her office phone interrupted the conversation. As she picked up the receiver, everyone made a discreet exit. Not that she cared if they wanted to stay. Nonetheless, Timothy took the opportunity to drag Tristan upstairs for a promised game of chess.

"Hello?" She picked up her pencil, and turned the notepad toward her.

"Good morning, Shae, it's Todd Andersen here. Did you see the newspaper article this morning?"

"Yes, I finished reading it just a few minutes ago," she said.

"We are all so very pleased with the coverage. The article gave just enough hints to fuel the public interest. However, that's not the reason I'm calling. You see, I believe I have some very good news for you."

Chapter 28

Shae glanced at the clock on her nightstand, and wished she hadn't. The traitorous timepiece, just one of many found inside this house, continued to taunt her. The clock told her she could sleep another two hours if she wished, but experience said sleep would continue to elude her. Her heart was heavy, her thoughts troubled, and the situation only worsened as each minute ticked off the clock. She rested her hand against her forehead and stared at the ceiling.

In just two days, a little over forty-eight precious hours, she would board a plane headed for Oslo. For well over a month she'd kept this secret hidden away from her ghostly companions. She did not even tell Tristan about Professor Andersen's call the day of the published newspaper article. Todd informed her then of their decision to return her to Oslo far earlier than what they first anticipated. He believed he gave her such good news. If only he truly understood what that statement did to her heart and soul.

They gave her a full month to finish translating all of the Norwegian to English documents, knowing of the generosity of their timetable. She could finish the translations in less than half that time. Todd said she could do the rest of her work just as easily in Oslo. They wanted her to take all of the unfinished copies with her and split her time between translating and field work.

In all honesty, the delay in informing her companions as to her company's decision rested in the hope that something would happen to prevent her departure. She hoped they would discover a reason or a need to keep her here in Tennessee. But no such luck. Her plane tickets arrived yesterday, and she couldn't put off packing her things any longer.

She used the time given as wisely as possible. Shae made sure she and her companions spent as much of it together as possible. She filled that time with laughter and meaningful conversation. They attended the burial of Anders Janssen and Tristan's reburial at the National Cemetery in Chattanooga amid much public fanfare. At that hallowed place, all of the ghosts of Starling met with the private. Before he stepped into the light, each bid him a fond farewell. Afterward, they visited the peaceful and serene battlefields at Chickamauga and then toured the museum just as she and Tristan did not so very long ago. All of these memories needed to last, just in case some future event occurred to keep them from coming together again. At least, in this lifetime.

Also, she found an opportunity to speak to each of her friends privately, in a quest to discover if any of them wanted to leave Starling and go elsewhere. None of them did, even though she desired to take all of them with her to Oslo. For them, Starling was home. She understood and respected their wishes.

The one rainbow in her stormy sky came in knowing she did not have to say goodbye to Tristan. Just yesterday, he reaffirmed his promise that nothing could make him leave her, regardless of where she needed to go.

Still, taking Tristan away from Starling made her feel very much like some callous home wrecker. The spirits of this plantation home counted on Tristan's wisdom and his strength. They loved him and respected him. What about little Timothy? How would Tristan's absence affect him? Since the day of his death, Tristan had taken the place of his father.

She just didn't know what to do about Timothy. Would he grieve? She couldn't bear it if he did.

After releasing a ragged sigh, she shifted her body and faced the other side of her bedroom. Just then, the room filled with an exquisite, ethereal light. The brilliance of that light grew brighter by degrees. As she leaned upward on her elbow, Shae's mouth dropped open in astonishment. Brynhild Bakken Jordahl then emerged from the center and stepped gracefully toward her bed. The white dress she wore looked very much as if she had walked through a field of diamond dust just before she entered her bedroom.

Shae sat all the way up as Tristan's mother sidled up next to the bed and sat down beside her. She did not experience any fear as she witnessed this unexpected vision.

"Hello, my darling," Bryn said. She gave her a loving smile, and used a gentle hand to smooth a stray lock of tousled hair from off Shae's face.

"Bryn," she whispered, with reverence in her tone.

"I wanted to come and personally thank you for keeping your promise," she said.

"My promise?" Shae knit her brow in confusion and gave her head a little toss. "What promise?"

"The promise you made in another time and place, to help Tristan resolve the anger and sorrow he would feel at the time of his death. You promised to bring him peace by restoring his good name. This quest is the reason you chose to be here now, in this time," she explained.

"I don't understand," Shae replied.

"I know, but you will in time." She smiled and then placed a gentle kiss on top of her head. "Until that time comes, I want you to know I am genuinely grateful for your steadfastness and your courage. You did everything required of you and then went beyond those requirements. Your selfless actions meant far more to me than you know."

Bryn took hold of her hand and gave it a gentle squeeze. The troubled look that suddenly appeared in her eyes caused Shae immediate concern.

"That notwithstanding, there is one more difficult thing I must ask you to do on Tristan's behalf. In fact, you will find this task the most difficult thing you will ever have to do in this life. And I am truly sorry for that. I wish I could find another way to accomplish this same goal," she said.

Shae's heart lurched over the statement. She could feel a sudden sense of foreboding. She closed her eyes, and took a deep breath before she said, "What is it you would have me do?"

"You must convince Tristan to leave his ghostly existence, and you must do it before you leave for Oslo," she replied. "He is needed now."

"But I can't!" Shae's eyes popped open, and then widened with horror as she shook her head. "No, I can't do it! I can't live without him, Bryn. Please, you must understand and not ask this of me. Not this, not now."

Bryn's gaze softened in that instant, yet her tone brooked no refusal. "You must, because his presence is required right now."

"To do what?" she demanded petulantly. "Strum a harp for a choir of angels?"

Bryn's laughter was a melody in itself. "Be reasonable, Shae. Do you truly believe there is nothing more important to do in my sphere than strum harps? There is so much more than what you could possibly understand, even should I explain it to you. Everything has its order as well as its purpose. You'll have to trust me on that. Everyone has their given tasks, and we all find joy and happiness in the fulfilling of those tasks. Tristan is needed now to fulfill his."

"But he's been here this long," Shae argued as desperation took hold. "Why can't someone else fill in for him until it's my time to go? Surely, someone else is just as capable in doing the duty to which you refer. In fact, someone must be doing it right now if everything is as orderly as you say."

Tristan's beautiful mother picked up both her hands and gazed deeply into her eyes. "This task is absolutely necessary, and there is no other way to accomplish this particular goal. Once he understands, he will quite happily agree and he will thank you for the sacrifice you are making right now. Trust me."

"Are you sure about that?" she asked as tears filled her eyes.

"I'm positive." Bryn shook her head and gave her a gentle smile. "My darling Shae Lynn, do you truly think I would ask this of you after all you have suffered and endured to help him, if I didn't have to ask? Do you think I would really want to destroy the happiness you have found in each other's presence? The joy you have together is *my* joy."

Shae bowed her head. She wept bitter tears as Bryn gathered her into her arms and allowed her to cry. When at last she gained enough control over her emotions to speak, she took hold of a tissue and dabbed at her eyes.

"Everything is going to fall into place, you'll see," Bryn said as she gave her back a gentle rub.

"Everything is going to fall into place? What do you mean by that?" she asked, puzzled by the statement.

"I know you are worried about Timothy. There is no need. His parents are coming for him shortly," she informed her. "Just imagine the joyful reunion they will have!"

"What about the others?" she asked as she held the tissue underneath her nose.

"They'll each have their own opportunities to choose what's best for them," Bryn replied. "I'm sure their choices will please you. You needn't worry about any of your companions. Trust me. Tristan is the only one who needs your concern right now."

"But I don't know what to say to him. There isn't anything I can think of that he will believe." She sniffed and wiped at a wayward tear. "He knows how much he means to me, and he knows I want him to stay with me always. We promised each other forever, Bryn, and we meant it. We *meant* it."

"I know, and you will have forever, I promise." She gave Shae a gentle kiss on the cheek and rose to her feet. "Don't worry, you will find the right words."

Then as she returned to the middle of the room and stepped into the center of the light, she said, "Oh, and, Shae? Please don't think too unkindly of Tristan's father. He loves his son very much. I know he is anxiously awaiting the opportunity to make amends. Grief isn't an easy thing to endure when you are mortal. You must understand, sometimes people say and do things they later deeply regret." Bryn showered her with an affectionate smile, blew her a kiss, and disappeared.

Somehow, Bryn prevented Tristan from knowing about her visit. Even though he didn't hear a thing that transpired between them, she found herself wishing otherwise. She did not want this responsibility. More importantly, she did not want Tristan to leave her. Ever. But if she needed to do this for his sake, then she wanted to do it quickly. If she delayed at all, she would find a way to talk herself out of it. She got out of bed and slipped into her robe. All the while, her thoughts centered on what convincing thing she could possibly say to make him leave her.

As she approached his room, she still didn't have the right words. In fact, she didn't have any words.

Nothing sounded even remotely plausible. Nevertheless, she tapped on his door, hoping that as promised, the right words would leap into her mind.

"Tristan, I need to talk to you."

At once, the door swung open and the mere sight of him standing there filled her with the desire to rush into his arms and remain there forever. She didn't know if she possessed the ability to do this. Heaven help her. She squeezed her eyes shut as her hand covered her mouth.

"Shaelynn, are you all right?" he asked, as his eyes filled with sudden alarm.

Shae shook her head. She struggled to speak past the lump in her throat and found the task most difficult.

"No, I'm not," she whispered brokenly.

"Is something wrong?" he asked.

"Yes." She wrapped her arms around her waist as she entered his room. She tried so hard not to cry in front of him. But she had already lost the battle.

"What is it? Tell me, please." He placed his arm around her shoulder and led her toward the head of his bed.

After she sat down, he took his usual place at the foot of the cot. They held countless conversations here in this room, on this bed, but never once had she felt so horribly distressed. Not even after the incident with Perry.

"I—they are sending me back to Oslo and I—" She lifted a hand and wiped away the tear cascading down her cheek.

"When?" he quietly asked.

"Day after tomorrow," she mumbled into the hand now resting against the corner of her mouth. "I didn't want to tell anyone. I kept hoping a miracle would present itself and that the plans would somehow change, but they didn't."

"Don't worry, Shaelynn, everything is all right.

We'll just have to prepare the others for our imminent departure, that's all," he said. "I'm sure they'll understand, and it's not like we can't come back from time to time and visit them."

Shae squeezed her eyes shut in an effort to stay the avalanche of tears. What could she say to that? How could she tell him he needed to leave her, that he needed to break his promise? Bryn said the right words would come.

And then as she recalled Bryn's visit, her final words crashed into her mind. She found those last comments bewildering because during the past several months, she didn't give Tristan's father a second thought. If memory served, they never once even mentioned the man since the night they found Amy's letter. She understood then what Bryn meant. In her own way, Tristan's mother provided the means to help her with this final, devastating task.

"Tristan, do you think you could find me in Oslo, if I traveled on ahead?" The question sounded ridiculous, even to her.

"What did you just say?" He raised a brow in confusion.

"I don't know how else to say this, except to just come out and say it." Once again, she wiped away the tears falling down her cheeks. Several times over, she attempted to push past the lump in her throat, to no avail. "In order for you to be truly happy, you need to—cross over and make peace with your father. You need to be whole again—"

"You have made me whole, Shaelynn. I don't need anything or anybody but you," he cut in.

"Yes, yes you do. Your family is very important to you. I know this. There is such joy when you speak of them. I feel as if I have come to know all of your brothers and your sisters personally and...and your mother, even your grandparents. But I don't know anything at all about your father. I don't even know his given name." She sniffed as she twisted the ragged tissue in her hands.

"Frederik," Tristan whispered with eyes downcast. "His name is Frederik."

"I want you to go and make peace with him, before you join me in Oslo." Shae could feel her heart ripping out of her chest, and shredding into a million tiny pieces, as she made the absurd request. She couldn't bear the look on Tristan's face as she asked it. The desolation that filled his eyes said he didn't know if she wanted him around anymore. That look she could not endure. That look she would not endure. She did not agree to break Tristan's heart as part of this assignment. She placed her trembling hands lightly against his cheeks as she fused her gaze with his.

"And please keep in mind that I desperately need you to come back to me, or *I* will never be whole again," she said with all the fervor of her heart.

"What if I can't?" Tristan recalled several spirits who left this earthly sphere, intent on coming back for one reason or another. And yet, he never ran into any of them again. Perhaps one couldn't return to this realm. "What if I can't come back?"

Fresh tears filled her eyes as he asked the question. Yet again, they cascaded down her cheeks. He gently wiped them away as he awaited her answer. She closed her eyes as a little moan escaped her lips. That pathetic sound tore at his heart.

"You must, Tristan. Please, you must find a way because my heart is going to remain forever broken if you don't. I love you so much, and I know I can't live without you."

Her tortured words pierced the very core of his being. If he could find a way to come back once he met with his father, then she wanted him to take it. That knowledge gave him the comfort he needed right now.

"Are you sure you want me to do this?" he asked one more time. "Making peace with my father could wait until the end of your lifetime. I see no reason to do this now."

Shaelynn shook her head pitifully, drew in a deep ragged breath, and closed her eyes. He could quite literally feel her pain.

"No, it can't wait, because the need will still exist. Don't you see? You always exclude your father from all of the memories you share with me about your mortal life. And yet, I know those memories exist. That part of your being remains tattered, and it will continue to remain tattered until you find a way to heal it. Yes, I'm sure. All I ask is that you hurry. Please hurry for my sake and please don't be gone overly long. Remember just how much I love you and just how much I need you. Promise me that you'll do that."

Just as Shaelynn perceived, a long time ago he chose to forget his father existed, just as his father chose to forget about him. Admittedly, his father destroyed part of his soul because of that decision. Nevertheless, he would attempt to reconcile with his father because she requested it. He had yet to deny her anything he had the ability to give.

Tristan rose from the bed, walked over to his box, and retrieved his mother's pendant. He fully intended on giving it to her, but at the time and place of his choosing. This particular circumstance in which he found himself, never once entered his mind. However, he may never have another opportunity. When he turned around, he found Shaelynn standing behind him. She looked so heartbroken and pitiful. Because of that, he found it difficult to understand why she made this request. She hid something from him. That much he could see with his eyes and feel with his heart, but he didn't have a clue as to what.

"I want you to have this." He slipped the necklace around her neck and pulled her hair up and over the chain. "I also want you to take my chest and all of my other worldly possessions with you when you leave, so I will have them in Oslo when I return. And if by chance, I don't find a way back, I want you to have—"

Shae instantly stilled his words as she placed a trembling hand against his lips. "Don't. Please, don't say it. I need to believe you are coming back. Looking forward to your return is the only way I can survive this separation. Don't take that away from me. Please, please, don't take that away," she woefully repeated.

Shaelynn's hand grew warm against his lips. In response, he cupped her face with his hands and then weaved his fingers through her hair. Miraculous warmth radiated between them, and she gazed at him with silent wonder because of it. He knew then. She could feel his body just as he could feel hers.

"I love you, Shaelynn Montgomery, with every fiber of my being. Don't ever forget it," he said before he lowered his lips to hers and kissed her with unhurried thoroughness.

She wrapped her arms around his shoulders and drew him closer still. He could feel the tears cascading down her cheeks as they kissed. His arms tightened around her waist, and he held her just as close as he possibly could. He could feel her heart breaking beneath his touch and it shattered his own. Somewhere then, he found the strength to end the kiss. His hand brushed away the tears. If he didn't leave now, he probably never would.

His mouth grazed lightly against her lips as he whispered, "I'll be seeing you, *min kjærlighet.*"

And with that, he disappeared.

Chapter 29

The ocean looked so beautiful here by the shores of Rathlin Island. The waves gently lapped against the rocks, and the slight breeze provided an enjoyable evening. The sun dipped just below the horizon, and the reflections of the colored clouds made the water look as if it danced to some ancient mariner's tune.

Norman sent Shae here to Ireland a little over a month ago to oversee a newly discovered Norse cemetery near the ruins of an ancient monastery. Her team had worked very hard on the excavation these past few weeks. In fact, she probably drove them far too hard. But no matter how hard she worked, no matter how bone tired she became, she just couldn't banish Tristan from her waking thoughts. She didn't even try while she slept.

Overall, she counted exactly two hundred and eighty-three days since the last time she gazed into his deep blue eyes, the last time they touched, and the last time they shared a kiss, save those in her dreams. The pain of their separation did not diminish as the days, weeks, and months passed. If anything, she missed him a little more each day.

Today's pain escalated a couple of notches above her normal levels. Shae supposed she could lay the blame at the feet of her publisher. She learned early this morning that a copy of the book she wrote detailing Tristan's life, the false accusations of treason and the subsequent documentation clearing his name, waited for her at her cozy little cottage. The volume came fresh off the printing press.

Thousands of copies now traveled to museums, libraries, and bookshelves in various parts of the world. Amazing to some, she completed the book in just a few short months. Of course, they didn't realize she sat at her computer night after night, typing into the wee hours of the morning when sleep evaded. For in many ways the book had become her lifeline and the one connection she still shared with Tristan. While she wrote, she pretended he sat beside her.

She left work earlier than usual, anxious to see the finished product. Then once she held the book in her hands, an overwhelming desire to escape her small cottage beset her. She wanted to go out to the beach and pore over each of the pages while she sat on the sand. But she needed to take a part of Tristan with her as she did so. She crossed the small living room, knelt beside his chest, and opened the lid. After removing his coat, she put it on over her white T-shirt and denim shorts. The sleeves hung way past her fingertips, and if she wanted, she could wrap them around her at least twice. Yet, the size of the coat didn't matter. The fit never mattered when she wore it. She didn't care how ridiculous she might look in it or who else might share her sandy shore this evening. Shae wanted to wear it anyway. She lifted the collar close to her face and took in a deep breath of the scent that persisted in clinging to the fabric. She took comfort knowing that once upon a time, that scent belonged to Tristan.

After taking the keys from off her desk, she left the cottage and then drove the short distance to the now deserted beach. She parked in her usual spot, abandoned her shoes to the floorboard, and strolled toward the sea. Moments later, she found a place to sit near the rolling waves and stuck her bare toes into the sand. All the while, she held on to Tristan's book with his coat wrapped around her body. For a small moment, she closed her eyes and imagined that it was his arms that wrapped around her. She permitted herself to believe he shared this moment with her.

She took a deep breath as she glanced down at the cover of her book. A wistful smile stole across her face. The boldly written words, *Tristan Jordahl, Valhalla's Elect, by Dr. Shae Lynn Montgomery,* streamed across the dust jacket. His picture, the one she kept close to her at all times, gazed back. How she loved that photograph.

She flipped through each of the pages then. The editors did an excellent job. They used all of the copies of the official documents, letters, and journal entries she provided them. They didn't shy away from using the copies of Nils Adlundsen's forged documents or practice letters, either. The one surprise came in a photograph of Lieutenant Colonel Tristan Jordahl's personal exhibit at the museum in Chickamauga. Todd Andersen and Reuben Wallace supplied her with that delightful surprise. The recognition they and the army gave her captain, filled her with pleasure.

"We did it, Tristan," she whispered heavenward. "The book is finished, and now the whole world will come to know the noble man you truly are. Still, I'm sure if you could see this book, you would tell me I went a little overboard on the title. Too bad you weren't here to stop me from using it." A small, quiet laugh escaped her lips.

The tumultuous tears came unbidden then, just as they always did. She shed them so frequently that many times she didn't even notice them streaming down her cheeks unless someone made mention of them. People like Simon Hollander, Professor Andersen, and some of her closest friends. She had become a mystery to all of them.

The professor believed she wanted to return to

Oslo and expressed bewilderment over her lack of enthusiasm once she arrived. Simon hoped that once she left Tennessee, she would find it in her heart to give him another chance. She didn't. He also wanted to know about the relationship she shared with the Civil War captain who appeared inside his hotel room frantically looking for her. She left him without answers. Her friends, so anxious to renew their efforts to attach her to someone new, backed off the effort altogether. It didn't take long once they understood she held no interest in their endeavors. She didn't pretend otherwise.

In an effort to bring her out of her "melancholy," as Professor Andersen called it, he sent her to Lierbyen, Norway to help set up the museum there. And then, after earning her doctorate degree, he gave her the opportunity to go to Sweden. Once they finished the project there, he sent her here to Ireland. The places didn't really matter. Nothing mattered without Tristan. Of their own accord, her fingers began tracing the outline of her captain on the cover of her book.

"I had a dream about us last night, Tristan," she whispered to the picture. Although she couldn't say why, it helped to talk to Tristan as if he sat next to her.

"We nestled together in this amazing place. It was a place we created just for us," she continued. "I could see beautiful trees everywhere. They surrounded us, giving us privacy and shelter. And then, I could see this little river, meandering off to the side. I know this is going to sound strange, but the river sang to us, and its beautiful song took away my breath. A multitude of flowers in every shape and color filled a single bush, and there were many such bushes around us. And the sky! I wished you could see the sky I beheld in my dreams. Colorful stars and planets filled the immensity of space, some

337

appearing as big as the moon. They seemed so close. If we but extended our hands, we could surely touch them. The light they gave glittered and sparkled across the sky for as far as I could see.

"You and I sat underneath the most beautiful tree in the garden. You held me, ever so tightly in your arms. You made me feel loved and cherished. We talked about our mortality, and the fact that our paths would never cross. The knowledge made us sad, but our separation served a far greater purpose with a much happier ending.

"We shared the most wondrous kiss then and afterward, I told you it didn't matter how many years separated our earthly sojourn. I promised you I would never love anyone but you. That such a thing did not even need consideration, for you had already claimed every portion of my soul and every chamber of my heart—"

"And then I said, 'Just as you have laid claim to every portion of mine. I love you, Shaelynn, I have loved you from the dawn of time, and I will continue to love you throughout all the ages ahead.'"

Shae buried her face in her hands as the tears flowed in copious amounts. *Oh, this is just great,* she thought. Now she could hear his voice! What else could possibly happen today to make her pain feel any worse?

"Shaelynn—"

Her head came up as the sound of his voice penetrated her thoughts. His voice did not originate inside her mind as it so often did. This time, she could swear that he stood right behind her. In fact, she could *feel* him standing right behind her. Her heart began hammering inside her chest as she contemplated the possibility that somehow he found a way to return, even though in truth, such a thing could not happen.

Even though she accepted that, she found

herself hoping for the impossible. She wanted so much to look. But if she didn't see him when she turned around, the pain would surely cause a devastation from which she could not recover.

Nevertheless, she had to know. Shae swallowed past the lump in her throat and rose to her feet. She wiped away the tears while gathering her courage. After a deep breath, she turned around. Tears began flowing anew, and her hands trembled as she sought to wipe them away with the back of her hand. Tristan stood less than four feet away from her, and he gave her that devilish grin she so deeply loved. She blinked several times, waiting for him to disappear. Yet the vision remained intact.

"Tristan?" she cautiously whispered as she took a halting half-step closer. Oh, how she wanted to rush into his arms, but something compelled her to refrain from touching him just yet. She held her breath as she waited for him to speak.

"I am really here, *min kjærlighet,*" he said and then as he nodded his head, he grinned. "And you're right. You did go a little overboard on the title of the book."

"But how? How is it possible you are here?" she asked, completely ignoring his comment concerning the book. At this particular moment, the tightly clutched book just didn't seem that important.

"Because just as my mother requested, you selflessly sent me home," he replied. "Yes, I now know about her visit that last night in Tennessee, and your actions made all of the difference, I think."

"I don't quite understand," she said as she knit her brows together.

"Why don't you sit down? You looked so comfortable here on the beach. We might just as well stay here while you ask your questions and I give you my answers." He waited for her to choose the place before he sat opposite her. The way she dressed almost made him laugh aloud. Yet, at the same time, her attire pleased him. He gave his coat a little tug.

"I believe it might need a bit of tailoring," he teased.

Shae gazed down at the coat as a faint smile touched the corners of her mouth. "Oh, I forgot for a moment that I had it on. I'm sorry. I always wear your coat when I need to feel close to you."

"I know you do, and there is no need for an apology. I gave it to you, remember?" Right then, he wanted to take her into his arms and kiss away all the sadness in her eyes.

No one could know any better than he, how much she suffered, and all of the pain she endured after he left her inside his attic room in Tennessee. However, before he touched her, he needed to answer the questions now forming inside her mind. If he should touch her now, all conversation between them would cease, at least for a while. And if he had his way, a very long while.

"I want you to know that you were right. The rift between me and my father needed repairing," he said. "Just as you perceived, I needed to resolve it."

"And did the two of you resolve it then?" she asked.

"Yes, it's the first thing I accomplished after my arrival. He waited for me there at the portal's entrance, and that meeting gave us the opportunity to have a long talk and sort everything out. My father told me he deeply regretted his actions in Tennessee. He regretted his hasty decision to return Amy's letter without having read it first. But by the time he concluded that I couldn't possibly have done what they said, the time had passed to do anything about it. He lived with the pain of regret for the rest of his life.

"He begged for my forgiveness, Shaelynn, and

the moment he asked for it, I had already given it. I could feel a wondrous healing taking place at that moment. The extraordinary experience left me feeling complete once again."

"I'm so glad to hear that." Shae fused her gaze with his and said, "Really, I am."

"You have another question?" he asked.

"Probably too many questions to count, or to put in any particular order, for that matter," she said as she swept away the hair blowing across her face. "But I do have one that's near the top of the list. How did you know about my dream? You said the words as if you knew exactly what you said to me."

"Because you didn't experience an ordinary dream, conjured from your own subconscious desires. Somehow, you unlocked one of the many memories we have shared throughout the eons of time. If I had to hazard a guess, I would say that one might have come courtesy of my mother. She is the interfering sort, as you can well attest."

Shae returned his smile with a wistful one of her own. "I love your mother. She is a wonderful, caring woman. And if she is responsible for returning that amazing memory, then I am grateful. I will cherish it my whole life."

"As will I," Tristan replied. Shaelynn's joyous smile faded away and the deep sadness returned to her eyes. "What is it, *min kjærlighet*? What's wrong?"

She gulped several times before she answered. "How much time do we have, Tristan?"

"Time? I don't understand what you mean," he said.

"When do you have to go back?" She drew in a breath and held it as she awaited his answer.

He understood then. She believed he had come merely to visit. He shook his head, managed a bit of a frown, and said, "I'm sorry. I'm not at liberty to give you the date and details of your death, even if I actually knew them with exactness." He winked.

Shae widened her eyes and gasped in surprise. "You get to stay here with me?"

"If I recall correctly, and someone with my recent experiences should have the gift of recollection, I believe we promised each other forever, did we not?" In return, she gifted him with one of her dazzling, soul-stirring smiles. At that moment, he found it even more difficult not to take her into his arms. Yet, for her sake, he restrained the need. Barely.

"I am certain this is the very reason they assigned your well-being to me. They like us to keep our promises when we make them," he added.

She gasped anew. "You are my guardian angel?"

"Well, after that death defying stunt you pulled in Sweden, it seemed quite obvious that you needed someone to stand watch over you every single minute. What in the world would possess you to back your truck to the edge of a dangerous precipice, tie a thin, inadequate rope around the hitch, and shimmy down the side of the cliff? You would easily have scared me to death if death hadn't already claimed me. And let us not forget the fact that you didn't give a second thought as to walking into that church in Tennessee, knowing full well Adlundsen waited for you inside it. The list could go on, Shaelynn."

He dropped the stern persona then and said, "However, the term 'angel' is—stretching things well beyond the realm of possible consideration. Let's just call me your guardian, your protector, the man who loves you more than life itself, and leave it at that."

The amazement reflecting from her eyes gave way to love. Specifically, he could see the love she gave to him. And he found it a most wondrous thing to behold, to feel and to possess. He took a moment to savor it. She leaned forward then, and while her fingers brushed very lightly through his hair, her lips drew close to his mouth, and she whispered, "I love you, Captain Tristan Jordahl, so very, very much."

"Does that mean you will marry me then, and without delay?" he asked, keeping just enough distance between them, to gaze into her eyes.

"Marry you?" She drew back a little bit more and all the while those beautiful green eyes filled with wonder and delight. "We can get married?"

He flashed a devilish grin, lifted a mischievous brow, and said, "We certainly can't live together without benefit of vows. I think the entire realm of heaven might frown on something like that and take back everything they've given thus far. And frankly, I don't know how much longer I can wait to make you mine. Therefore, in light of this truth, I have some very special witnesses you'll be very pleased to see, and an extremely bewildered minister waiting for us at your cottage. All you have to do is say yes, make quick work of the official ceremony, and kick everyone out."

"Oh, Tristan! Of course, I'll marry you!" In her exuberance, she threw herself into his waiting arms.

Once again, her eyes grew wide with astonishment, for she could feel the warmth of his body and the strength of his crushing embrace, as she had never experienced either of them before. As he brushed his lips lightly against hers, he could see all kinds of questions leaping into her mind. Of course, the explanation as to his mortal form superseded all others. At a more convenient time, he would tell her that fragments of truth exist in every myth and legend. He would remind her of Yggdrasil, the Norse tree of life. How after the final battle of Ragnarok, two humans would emerge from that tree to replenish mankind. Surely then, it should not surprise her to learn that every now and then, when the situation warrants the rare gift, a spirit could return to his or her mortal state, after receiving sufficient nourishment from that tree. But for now, all of her answers would have to wait.

For nothing in heaven or Earth could stop the massive tide of emotion flowing between them, emotion that continued growing stronger with each breath she took. And nothing in heaven or Earth could stop the soul-stirring, earth-shattering kiss, about to take place between them. For right now, he planned to give her the kiss that would absolutely knock the socks clean off her feet. And that was just for starters.

A word about the author...

When she's not busily engaged in writing her stories, Debbie Peterson spends time with her beloved husband, children, and large extended family, endures the heat in southern Nevada, and pursues her interests in all things ancient and historic.